The Trilogy

Book I
Damaged Goods

Veronica O'Leary

Order this book online at www.trafford.com
or email orders@trafford.com

Most Trafford titles are also available at major online book retailers.

Printed in the United States of America.

ISBN: 978-1-4669-8040-2 (sc)
ISBN: 978-1-4669-8041-9 (e)

Trafford rev. 06/05/2013

www.trafford.com

North America & international
toll-free: 1 888 232 4444 (USA & Canada)
fax: 812 355 4082

To the memory of my mother Dolly and my husband Billy

Mom, thank you for your courageous, humble spirit. You equipped me with a shield of resiliency and compassion. Most importantly, thank you for giving me the gift of faith. My love for you is immeasurable.

Billy, only through your final days of pain did I come to truly embrace the realization of life's joy and frailty. Things look so different exiting our lives as compared to entering our existence.

Until we are all together again . . .

IN GRATITUDE TO MY CIRCLE

My Constant Source of Inspiration

My Lord God, my Savior, with you all things are possible. You have never forsaken me. You are my shield, my hope, my constant reminder that your life was given for my forgiveness.

My granddaughter Piper, you are my true source of joy and happiness. Every day with you is a blessing. Love you pass the moon.

My grandson Princeton, you are too new to understand the extent of my love for you.

My daughter Alexis, you are and will always be the driving force of my life. I am overwhelmed with respect and admiration for the woman that you are. You are my greatest accomplishment. Always remember . . . one pepper, a quart of milk, and a pack of cigarettes.

My sister Claudia, you are the true fighter. The depth of our bond goes beyond the human eye's understanding.

My brother-in-law Steve, you are the rock. Our journey confirms your strength and consistency.

My nephew James, the quiet observer of life. Feel secure knowing; it's good to hear a different drummer.

My niece Julia, never give up on your dreams. I will be there for you when your full creativity emerges.

ACKNOWLEDGMENTS

Dr. Robert F. Carroll, MD, FACEP, MBA
Chair and Medical Director
Department of Emergency Medicine
Eastern Ct. Health Network

Thank you for your time and effort. Your gracious attitude enabled me to feel comfortable asking difficult questions. Your knowledge has been the backbone for many hours of pen to paper. You brought true meaning to the depth of Princeton and Tallulah's struggle.

A special thank you to all the artists, who are responsible for being so wonderful at their craft. The songs connected to this book were my inspiration for the development of so many powerful moments that would otherwise be empty without the beautiful lyrics.

Mariah Carey - "Vision of Love"
Joe Cocker - "You Can Leave Your Hat On"
Aerosmith - "Dream On"
Leona Lewis - "Bleeding Love"
Andrea Bocelli - "Con Te Partiro"
Chris Daughtry - "Home"
Michael Buble - "Just the Way You Look Tonight"
The Cure - "Love Song"
Pocket Full of Rocks - "Falling"
The Fray - "How to Save a Life"
Michael Buble - "Lost"

CONTENTS

Circle: "a series or process that finishes at its starting point."

BLOODLINE

Princeton and Tallulah were the "it" couple according to current standards: contemporary, artistic, successful, spiritual, and beautiful to look at. It was almost unsettling that two people could be so perfect for one another. Both creative . . . Princeton (a photographer) would produce fabulous black-and-whites that had depth and simplicity. It was the rage with the who's who when needing to decorate their spaces. Tallulah, an interior designer that touched the markets of real estate, both residential and commercial, was a growing frenzy. The mix of traditional and modern, with a touch of vintage period pieces was her "stamp." The buzz in the industry indicated great things to come.

They inspired one another professionally with their unique ability to understand color, texture, surroundings, and their vision of the "moment." They could capture this and translate it into their work, one feeding off the other. Their home was a bold reflection of their eclectic style and impeccable taste. It showcased their talents of design and art far beyond the imagination of the average eye. It was a portfolio of their substance. Everything that lived inside their walls had a purpose to be meaningful. Fabulous decorating aside, the little statements of food, wine, books, and music set the tone for the expectations of a day in the life of Princeton and Tallulah. Their music was a collaborative collection of the most unusual mix. Andrea Bocelli playing at the highest volume set the tone for their love of red wine and their passion to prepare meals together. It was always more than cooking; it was a place they would go to. Their imagination would transport them to their Tuscany villa. According to the situation, Daughtry, the Fray, and Michael Buble fit nicely into their lives. Contemporary worship found its place when they needed to be renewed and inspired. However, when Aerosmith and Mariah Carey made an appearance, it was their need to reminisce or drift into the story that brought to mind that exact time. It was partly the moment and partly their private cocoon of knowing this was "theirs," this was their separation from everyone else.

Tallulah's strong belief and conviction in her faith were the foundation for her life's application. She believed in God, relied on prayer, and focused her feelings into gratitude. It was always a surprise and slightly uncomfortable when her peers or business associates found out about her deep-seeded devotion to God. She just didn't fit the mold of what people envisioned as "religious." She was sexy, contemporary, and extremely fashionable. Most people referred to her as striking. Even in earlier years when she did a short mission in Congo, Africa, people were puzzled, not quite understanding how this woman and the Congo (at it most destitute time) had anything in common.

Princeton's faith had lay deep inside his heart and soul. It was as if the seed was planted long ago, rooted securely, waiting to show its magnificence. It wasn't until he was with Tallulah that the seed burst open, being nourished by their conversations, and eventually fully blossomed within his inner self. He came to understand and was in tune with his deep feeling of gratitude. They both believed their creative gifts came directly from God (with a lot of help from Victoria, Tallulah's mother).

Tallulah could trace her bloodline of eccentric creativity three generations passed. Her mother Victoria had an artistic hand, which later came to surface in exceptional forms of design. Victoria had a great love for the arts. She was passionate about both music and theater. In her early years, she depended on modeling to bring in the income needed to support her mother and sister. She was gifted with beautiful skin, and of course five feet nine, size 2 proved to be successful. She grabbed whatever came her way, Fashion Avenue showroom previews, bridal shows, and hair salon events at the convention centers. She could always count on Clairol and Vidal Sassoon to use her in the season's premiers.

Later, when she married Luke, she stopped modeling. However, she thrilled knowing she had the best of both worlds: the traditional Italian family core, cooking, family gatherings, dinner at 6:00 p.m., and then her connection to mainstream New York. It was her natural dance ability that supplied her with work in her "other world." She assisted with choreography at nightclubs for the dance reviews, which at the time were a staple in all the hot spots. Chippendales, Hot Rod's, and Hard Rock Café were only a few of the many that she worked at. She was on hand, to find her way into small parts in VH1 videos and USA network commercials, all the time Tallulah at her side. At most rehearsals, the little one wasn't sitting on the side lines; she was right in the mix, up front and center, at ease in front of lights and cameras showing her uncanny ability to dance with the best of them. Victoria knew her daughter had something special. She introduced her to her first concert at age four and traveled her around the city to art galleries, museums, and on and off Broadway productions. Tallulah landed a small part on a soap opera and did some printwork for children's fashions, representing department stores in the Sunday newspapers. Victoria adored her husband for allowing her to be exactly the woman she was. He always supported her and Tallulah in all their endeavors.

Victoria's mother found her niche in photography. She hand-colored black-and-white portraits in the earliest stages of the markets new approach to this process. It was short lived because technology was racing quicker than her hand. However, family portraits were always admired and questioned, particularly when she would change the color of bridal photos. Stating that the color she chose suited the look better than the original. Her mother (Tallulah's great-grandmother) was a seamstress originating in Europe. Her impeccable sense of design with beads and ornaments were found on the most elaborate wedding dresses, every bead hand sewn on yards and yards of fabric. Italy and France appreciated her tedious, beautiful work. The top designers at the time would seek her out to transform their visions to reality. It was once said that she worked on one dress, eight hours a day for six months, which ultimately was worn by royalty.

There was no question that Tallulah was her mother's daughter. Every thread of Tallulah's life was woven into the fabric of their relationship. Victoria adored her daughter and was committed to developing her full potential. When kids were getting Nintendos for special occasions, Tallulah would get *Emily Post's Etiquette.* As a child when she pursued softball, Victoria wasn't the parent sitting on the bleachers cheering her on; she was the coach. When it was Girl Scouts, she was the director of the entire district. When Tallulah was in church, it was her mother standing on the altar as the eucharistic minister. Later, she was the teacher for the preparation of confirmation for the class of fifty teenagers. So it was no surprise that most of Tallulah's friends wanted to be in their circle. After all, she had the coolest mom. Their home was the place to listen to current music, eat great meals, and have lengthy conversations about the meaning of life. If you had a problem, needed guidance, or just wanted to know which shoes looked best with what skirt or slacks, that was the place to be. Even though Tallulah was an only child, there was always a friend that became a family member. A permanent place set at the dinner table, clothes washed and eventually put into "their" chest of drawers, and shopping and packing to go on the family trip.

Tallulah blossomed into a beautiful young woman. The metamorphosis seemed to happen overnight. One day, she sported braces, bad haircuts, and trial-and-error fashion finds . . . and the next, she was a knockout. Her perfect white teeth appeared brighter contrasted against her tanned skin color. Large hazel almond eyes with heavy lashes dominated her face. Her nose was small and perfect. Her lips were full and naturally turned up at the corners. She had amazing long thick hair, which when it found its original brunette color would reflect shades of auburn. Her body boasted the flattest muscular abdomen with beautifully shaped legs on her tiny size 1 frame. Putting that together with her eclectic fashion sense, she would be the object of obvious stares and flirtatious advances. Whether she was in her baseball cap and sweats or stilettos paired with a jersey wrap dress, the pursuit of her number became routine. Although she was use to the attention, she hardly ever responded, seeming uninterested. Instead, her magnetic personality led her to have more male friends than female.

There were times in her early years that Tallulah made some bad choices and wrong decisions. However, even in her mother's darkest moments of disappointment, she stood by her daughter's side, supported her choices, and always believed she would grow into the woman that lay beneath the surface. In many ways, their love for one another was a result of being so much alike, which proved at times to be stormy. One thing was for certain, and that was that Tallulah absolutely loved her mother. She looked to her for guidance, approval, and friendship. So it was no wonder that now, their lives were still intertwined, and the mutual respect as adults found its place, each one being their own person yet sharing every episode of their days. Each morning, Victoria's phone would ring, as if it were the bell at the starting gate for the commencing of the day. Tallulah would touch base for what was on the daily agenda. So, to all that knew them, their relationship was understood. It would seem unnatural for it to be any other way. However, the big surprise was the relationship that Princeton and Victoria shared.

Princeton respected, admired, and loved his mother-in-law. She was his constant source for business direction, creative ideas, and spiritual nourishment. He depended on her to put him on track, when he was confused or indecisive. She had a way of getting to the core of the situation. Victoria understood people. She would make you feel comfortable without being condescending. She could work a room of powerful people, discussing art, literature, and politics; always charming and gracious with a tremendous air of confidence. She was a true classic beauty. At the same time, she could be in your grandmother's kitchen in an apron, and it seemed as if she belonged there. Princeton appreciated her direct approach. Even at times when it could be harsh, he trusted that she had his best interests at heart because she loved him. He was in awe of the connection between Tallulah and Victoria, sometimes a slight bit envious of that thick bloodline. He took pride in knowing that he was "the one" for Victoria's daughter and thrived on having his place in that circle.

His creative bloodline wasn't as crystal clear as Tallulah's; actually it wasn't clear at all. His parents were wonderful, and their love for him was undeniable, but "middle America, wonder bread" was an accurate description. They both worked in the medical field, his father a physical therapist and his mother a nurse. They met at their second year at Princeton, married a year later, and their carefully planned life took form. They were content in the safety of following the rule book for gauging success according to their house, car, and community involvement. Princeton proved to be the risk taker in that circle. He heard the beat of a different drummer, and his strong will to follow his heart always led to people finding him mysterious, deep, and very attractive.

Rachel (his mother) didn't always "get" him. His obvious characteristics were easy enough to understand. His intelligence and his compassion set him apart from others. His friends wanted to be like him, imitating his cutting edge taste in music and fashion. Girls were sucked in by his gentlemanly mannerism. His attitude was a contradiction to the usual behaviors of great-looking guys. Although he had every right to be full of himself, he contained his humble demeanor inside the beautiful sculptured physique he worked so hard at. At first, he used the weights to release his unsatisfied energy, and eventually it became part of his being. He loved the process of pushing himself to the point of pain, squeezing every ounce of strength to reach exhaustion. The results were just a bonus. If there was such a thing as a twelve pack, he had it. He was ripped, and his defined biceps and large pecks hinted a view in most of his shirts. So like him, he never flaunted his package, quite the contrary, keeping it sacred for the chosen few. Some say he was the creator of the perfectly messy do, tapered short, with just the right amount of spiked hairs going this way and that. It framed his beautiful face, which had slight dimples and a sharp jawline. He could easily be a billboard on Times Square for Abercrombie. Although he was a little more rugged and mature, he still had that look.

There wasn't a party or family gathering where eventually the game would begin. Women both young and old would compete for his attention. He seemed unaffected by it, which in turn fueled the game even more. He was holding out for the "awakening of his soul" as he would put it. He was too complicated for such a young person; as if an old soul lived beneath the layers of his existence. Rachel loved that about her son, yet at the same time, she felt inadequate to reach that place deep inside him. She knew the moment he met Tallulah that she was the one. Tallulah got him instantly, unlocking all that he was saving for that missing piece to his soul. He never hesitated for a minute to express his adoring love for her; he was absolutely crazy about her. She remembered feeling a little threatened at first. Not by Tallulah, but by her mother Victoria. It seemed that her son gravitated toward that woman for acceptance and guidance. He described her as a fountain of knowledge, with the gift of wisdom to apply it to life. But only as Victoria could do, she diminished that threatening feeling. She would compliment Rachel about her great accomplishment, producing such a wonderful man. She included her in every family decision and always spoke highly of her with friends and relatives. Ironically, eventually Rachel would go to Victoria for advice or just when she needed a friend to talk to. So for Rachel it was bittersweet. She was so happy for her son's life because *he* was so happy . . . and she was so sad that it wasn't her unlocking his gifts.

Princeton's father Derek would tell her not to look so deeply into everything their son did or said. He was so content to know that he and his son loved each other, and after hearing about his friends' problems with their own children, he was grateful for the man his son had become. He was proud of Princeton's accomplishments. After all, he was successful and had the relationship that most people only dreamed of. There were times when he found himself daydreaming, comparing his life with his son's. The passion that Princeton had in his life was an element missing from his own. He would justify his loss by knowing that anything that appeared to be that extreme, borderline obsessive, could be dangerous. You had to know how to control and balance such powerful feelings. It was a trade-off for the results. He knew in his heart, he couldn't master such intensity . . . not like his son.

A CHARMED LIFE

As Princeton pulled up to the huge metal sliding door, he threw the Jeep Wrangler into park. He always took a minute to take it all in, which resulted in a satisfied smile. This warehouse that they called home was still captivating to his eye. The reddish color brick structure had floor-to-ceiling windows. Not the common perfect windows you see in new construction. These windows were paned and slightly irregular due to the years of wear. Some were clear, and some were cloudy. They were fully exposed as you looked from the outside. Inside, yards of silk fabric framed the sides as they cascaded to the floors, resting on the wood in soft pools of iridescent color. The shimmer of lights bouncing off the windows were obvious that the many chandeliers were in full use. You could see a glimpse of some walls that were deep in color. There was cayenne pepper, deep brown, and a tease of chartreuse. If you looked hard enough, your mind registered that all those square shadows were the frames for the multitude of black-and-white photos. The building itself was large, approximately 5,000 square feet. So it was appropriate that the driveway was actually a parking lot, which could house twelve to fifteen cars if positioned properly. The front porch was a loading dock, which ran the full scope of the exterior. Tallulah had carefully placed large urns of topiaries at the distinctive points and smaller ones on the four steps against the ornate metal railing. The metal door measured ten feet wide by twelve feet high. That proved to be a blessing with bringing anything in or out of the house. The only time it was fully opened was when weather permitted and a party dictated the easy flow of entry. It was so heavy that most days Princeton slid it only enough to accommodate himself. To see this now, it was almost impossible to believe this was the same building years ago before Victoria "happened" upon it.

*   *   *   *   *

The abandoned yarn mill sat unused for years. It was one of those things that was familiar to your eye passing it regularly, yet not really seeing it. Then one day, Victoria noticed a sign that read: For Sale Commercial. Her curiosity sparked an interest to turn her car around and pull into the parking lot. She sat there taking in every detail as her eyes canvassed the building. Her mind went into full throttle imagining the possibilities. She dialed the number as she sat there and scheduled an appointment for the next day. That entire evening was dedicated to the thoughts of her visualizing the interior and transforming it into her home. The next morning, she was filled with anticipation as she drove to her scheduled appointment. Upon entering the mill, the overwhelming size stopped her in her tracks. She stood there trying to take it all in. The heights of the windows were overbearing yet spectacular. There was no designated space, just a huge first floor filled with that lifetime's memories. There were boxes everywhere filled with yarn and debris. Huge cartons holding aged drywall and insulation rested against the walls. The small spots of sun traveling through the windows left a trail of dusty light similar to smoke lying in midair. The lighting was poor and limited, so wherever the fluorescents shined, the layers of dust were apparent. The staircase was prominent and solid. Three people could stand side by side and never touch each other. The second floor mirrored the first, with the exception of some wooden desks and file cabinets strategically placed.

She counted two bathrooms both missing necessary fixtures and one area that might have been used as the employee's kitchen. She walked the building four maybe five times, taking in what she called the "breath" of the house. That was what she did; she reinvented spaces. She had the ability to see a finished product in its earliest stages. Her work was admired, and her reputation to transform hideous to magnificent was untarnished to date. So as she took in the last glimpse, she sighed with disappointment. She saw that the bones once transformed, dictated modern with splashes of traditional. She already saw the finished product, and it wasn't conducive to her European/ French flavor. As always, her belief that everything is for a reason and God puts us where we need to be led her mind and heart to know why she was here. At that moment, standing on the staircase, she dialed Tallulah. After a few minutes of explaining the situation, Tallulah became excited to see this great find. She was so like her mother in that respect; her mind was racing with possibilities. Princeton agreed to change his schedule, to accommodate the next day's appointment. He trusted Victoria's insight and was full of anticipation, wondering if this would be the new project. There was always a project in Victoria's life. Whether it was work or personal, one was just beginning as the prior was ending. This confirmed her philosophy of "the journey, not the destination." Once a project neared completion, the wonderful feelings of creativity, planning, and accomplishment slowly subsided. That journey had ceased, and it was time to embark on a new one.

The three of them stood there as the agent slid the metal door. They entered, one behind the other, a small parade of wandering eyes. The immediate impact was a mixed bag of emotions. As they walked the space, there were expressions of happiness, confusion, wonder, and fear. It was overwhelming and frightening. As Victoria presented her ideas, the decrepit shell started to take form. Life was breathing into the walls—a pulse, a heartbeat, a resurrection. The nagging question in Princeton's mind was the Commercial sign. This was not meant to be a residential building; maybe in Soho, but certainly not in Connecticut. Tallulah was already in a whirlwind, questioning the cost, zoning ordinances, and town rights.

From that moment on, Victoria took the reins of the biggest project she ever orchestrated. This wasn't for a client, this was for her children, and that fueled her to overcome every obstacle in her way. She called in every marker she had with town officials, mortgage brokers, banks, and community leaders. The property was a steal, but the amount of money needed to renovate was huge. Her connections with builders, contractors, electricians, and plumbers made it all seem possible. One thing was for certain, when she was on a mission, particularly accompanied with Tallulah, the odds were they were taking home the prize. Their diligent, persuasive attitude demanded attention. Their prayers that all is possible with God kept them focused and strong. They were a force to be reckoned with.

It took months, but it all came to pass. Victoria used all her collateral and most of her dollars to secure a low mortgage, with enough for renovations. She was setting the groundwork, securing the future of her children and those yet to come. Her reward was the harvest of the seeds sown for so many years. The purpose of her life was to build her family's legacy. The moment God put that realization in her heart so many years ago, was the moment it became the foundation for all and everything she did. She lived for leaving her family a legacy of good things. Not just the material or tangible, but the value of integrity, persistence, and victory. She was heard to say many times, "It's not what you take with you, it is what you leave behind." All that she had become was a direct result of the challenging circumstances of her childhood.

*   *   *   *   *

Princeton removed the keys from the ignition and grabbed two cameras off the backseat. The cameras dangled off his shoulder by their straps, so that he had both hands free to slide the door. As he stepped inside, his body seemed to automatically relax. It was as if an invisible force pulled the tension out of him from top to bottom. He forced himself to stand for a moment, breathing in the familiar smell of burning candles. The fragrance was always the same, not sweet and floral, more clean and woodsy. The three chandeliers were dimly lit, and crystal-like reflections were prominent on the concrete counter and the large slab of the teak wood dining table. If Tallulah were home before him, she would purposely set the lighting and candles accordingly because she knew how much he loved walking into this feeling. This was his sanctuary, his safety, and she knew it. His eyes rested on a piece of furniture a few feet in front of him. It was odd looking, in a romantic way—three drawers at the height of thigh level. A sort of green color that was dull and distressed. What appeared to be hand-painted scroll designs along the borders glistened in a metallic gold finish. The jewelry (hardware) was rosette-shaped crystals, and hanging from each rosette was a tassel of heavy silk threads matching the colors of the piece. He put his cameras on the counter and called out to Tallulah, "Hey, baby!"

A faint response from upstairs said, "Hi! I'll be right down."

"Is this piece going to live here, or is it just waiting to get to its home?"

He heard her laugh as the voice got closer.

"Why, do you like it?" she asked. He turned to see her feet traveling down the last few steps—barefoot, sweats hanging off her hips rolled to the calf, flat washboard stomach exposed, short Yankee tee, hair bouncing past her tiny waist—and when her eyes met his, a smile so broad that every perfect white tooth was exposed. He felt his heart swell and believed it skipped a beat. As she moved closer, her mouth found his, and his hands grasped her back and pulled her in so that she fit perfectly against his chest. Seconds into the kiss, he was already losing control, his body warm and throbbing. He lifted her up with both hands on her waist and sat her on the piece of furniture. He parted her thighs and moved in to stand closer, so that they were eye to eye. Both her hands moved under his shirt to his upper back where she found her grip and put pressure bringing him in tighter. Their mouths were responding to each other's needs. Deep, wet kisses, slow . . . fast . . . resting. The rhythm of their mouths opening and closing again and again. Her pulse was quickening, and he was enveloped in the smell and taste of her flesh, each exploring the other's movement and each desiring to be in perfect timing within this wild dance. The urgency to be one in the same left clothing scattered on the floor at Princeton's feet. He embraced the familiar shot of energy and adrenaline traveling through his body. This was the moment when Princeton would lose himself to a somewhat semiconscious state. He would have thoughts racing through his mind, all different, intermingled fragments of thought. "God, how is this possible? After all these years, this woman can still do this to me? She can bring me places I never imagined. The physical is fed by her amazing mind, her ability to know my heart and soul, her commitment to only want *me* . . . only me to touch her, to taste her, to go so deep that our veins pump the same blood." He was wet with sweat, breathing deep, moaning. His thoughts were in frenzy now, a whirlwind of words . . .

"It's because of the way she wants me, over and over again, knowing every inch of my existence, that puts me in this place. Giving me all of herself, her body, mind, spirit, touching me in a way that makes my mind and body crazy."

They were moving hard and fast, and her moaning forced him back to take charge of where he was. He realized all his strength was being used in his left hand that supported her back. His right hand palm down was gripping the edge of wood. He caught a glimpse of his veins, raised and protruding, branches of bluish color running through his arm. He was pushing harder and harder, feeling as if his chest would crack; his heart beating so fast, he missed breaths. The more she moaned, digging her nails into his back, the deeper he went. Warm, pulsating movement that locked them into a fury of give and take. His body glistened, so wet, so powerful, her sweat dripping on to him; sounds of pleasure mounting, tighter together they pressed, so that every muscle was expanding, working feverishly to squeeze the last ounce of themselves into one another.

He heard himself scream, "Oh, baby!"

As her head reared, her back arched with tremendous pressure as he continued to support it. Her head came down to his neck, her mouth touching his skin and her hair covering his face. The pounding of their hearts seemed loud as they gasped. Each breath hurt as the flow of air hit their lungs, deeply taking in air, exhaling, still holding each other with pressure and strength, pasted to one another. Afraid to let go, they knew the separation would leave their wet bodies cold. Slowly, slowly, releasing pressure as the heavy breathing subsided. Her mouth found his ear. In a hoarse low voice, she said, "Do you know how much I need you? Without you"—she paused—"all this would be nothing, *I* would be nothing."

The words sent a chill directly up his spine. He picked her up while still connected and lowered his knees, to reach the floor. He protected her back by resting his elbows on the floor and gently placed her, without ever leaving her. He looked down at her beautiful face as he rested his lower body against hers. He could feel that his eyes were watering and his nose was getting wet. She immediately kissed the tiny tear running down the side of his eye, and it disappeared before it reached his jawline. She used her index finger to trace his face, all the while gently kissing each eye, feeling the hairs of his eyelashes, each eyebrow, traveling to the chin, and ending at his mouth. His mouth opened to welcome her. He wanted her again as his leg muscles tightened. Her body signaled she was ready to be taken as she positioned herself tightening her grasp, to begin the next episode of Princeton and Tallulah.

When she awakened, she didn't want to move. That sleep, whether it was minutes or hours, she couldn't judge, was always the best sleep. She felt primitive, truly naked. Not just physically, but in a sense of being stripped of all that was her connection with the world.

The moment she readjusted herself, Princeton's hands found her hip and turned her to face him.

"Hey, baby," he said, his tone low and deliberately slow.

"Have I told you that I love when you sleep in my arms?" He paused, hoping to be able to convey what was in his heart.

"This thing we have . . . this tremendous love . . . how is it possible?"

Her eyes were locked into his, and she smiled.

"How do we come to deserve this?" he asked.

Not sure if it was rhetorical, she answered anyway.

"God knows our hearts. He knew exactly what we needed to be complete and purposeful. He gave us each other so that in our everyday lives, we could validate our existence. He nourished us. So our faith always kept us wanting, believing that one day we would be here at this moment, having this exact conversation, realizing the depth of our love, as an example of our gratitude. Every day I thank God for you. Never taking for granted the incredible man that I have in you. You're mine, all mine! Not as my possession, but as my safe place, my protector, my love, my inspiration. We never could have earned this, it's through God's grace and mercy that we're here."

He listened and thought, "Who thinks like this? And what's more amazing, who thinks it and actually lives it?" When she spoke to him, describing their love, he would lock those words into his mind, almost memorized; and later in his private moment of prayer, it would be *those* words that would bring him to his knees. Those words that would help him continue his journey in faith. He would remind himself that its faith, family, and friends. God first, and all that is meant to be will follow. God had given him his muse. Not until Tallulah's and their life intertwined did he reach his full creative potential. The heights of his capability went far beyond anything his eye and lens knew before her. All those years, waiting, believing that there was something coming that would change his life. Something so vast and immense that he couldn't ever explain it, not in words, only in his heartfelt thoughts. It was what kept him going, what made him stand firm, in his desire to try to make good choices, treat people with respect, and not be judgmental. He had been so careful, not to let women tempt him, because he felt like he would be "cheating" on his love yet to come. The price he paid was high. He spent many times alone and feeling lonely, sort of disconnected from the mainstream of people his age. He had so many opportunities to be front and center. So many people wanted to be in his world, but he was keeping his treasures sealed; he was waiting for Tallulah.

He threw his legs into his jeans, not zippering them, because he liked the feel of what was left of her on him. Her tee was on inside out, and her sweats sat below the line of the lace on her thong. She leaned up against the counter, arms and legs crossed, looking at Princeton's bare back. His shoulders looked huge compared to his small waist. From shoulder to shoulder, there it was—dark, bold, each letter four inches high, written across at least twenty-seven inches of skin—**TALLULAH**.

Every time she looked at it, there was a feeling she got that she couldn't explain. Seeing her name on his back made her swell with pride. It was so obvious and so sexy. She almost laughed out loud, now thinking about the story she heard about his tattoo.

*   *   *   *   *

His friend and apprentice, Zach, told it like this. One time, during the summer, Princeton had a tank on, exposing the beginning and ending letters, with the middle ones covered. A girl had come to the studio to see some of his work. It was obvious she was attracted to him and was awkwardly flirting. Zach described her as pretty and ditzy.

Trying to make conversation, she said, "Wow! That's beautiful work on your back. Where did you have it done?"

Princeton told her about his favorite ink spot, where the guy Max (Piper's boyfriend) had the best hand in the business. He was networking his best friend, always trying to get him new clients. Zach said all the while Princeton was talking, he was kneeling down, pulling out photos for the perspective purchase, still with his back to her.

She asked, "What is it? A name of a band? How about you show me the rest of it?" She giggled.

Princeton grabbed his tank with both hands, slipped it over his head still not turning. She walked up behind him, real close, and said, "Talleula," pronouncing it incorrectly.

He turned and stood up. They were almost close enough to touch. He smiled a beautiful smile and corrected her.

"Tallulah, that's my amazing wife."

"Oh . . . er . . . lucky girl," she said. She was gone in minutes.

Zach then lectured him on sometimes having to play the game to bring in the dollars. Princeton smiled.

"Yeah, yeah, I've heard it all before, but that is *never* going to happen. You know that right?"

Zach absolutely knew that.

He was one of the best salesmen around. His job started out to be just that—selling; Networking, websites, brochures, anything that showcased the work. His follow-up was meticulous. Regardless of all his hard work, once clients were face-to-face with Princeton, Zach believed they wanted his photos, as if they were buying a piece of *him*, especially the ladies. Eventually, Zach caught the camera bug and became Princeton's apprentice learning about the subject, lighting, and inspiration. He worked hard and loved being in Princeton's circle. As much as he razzed him, he was in awe of Princeton's life. He wanted the same for himself and hoped it would rub off on him.

His goals were to find the love of his life and mirror his friend's success with home and business. The best days of his life were when he was connected with Princeton and Tallulah's world. He lived for the road trips in the Wrangler, dinner parties with Tallulah and the crew, deep conversations about life and its purpose, great meals, music, dancing, and occasionally too much wine on his part. He hadn't mastered the wine thing yet. Before Princeton, he drank beer and whatever vodka was being circulated as trendy. Princeton instructed him not to drink it as a beverage but instead as a feeling. By the time he appreciated the feeling, he already had too much. When that happened, it left Tallulah tucking him in at his spot of their house because she was firm on no driving and drinking. She was the sister he never had, and she looked out for him.

That was part of her persona. If she took you into their circle, she gave you 100 percent. She learned that from her mother. Zach was in Victoria's good graces, and that made it all the more important. When he listened or watched Princeton and Victoria interact, he was floored. Talk about a charmed life, it didn't get any better than that. She and Tallulah catapulted Princeton's work to its present level. Tallulah using his pieces in almost every project she did. After all, no one understood his work better than she did. His client base had become affluent people, competing for the status quo for their homes. As for Victoria, she networked his pieces at major fundraisers and project makeovers.

Zach's original job became overshadowed by their results. He still had plenty of work coordinating purchases and preview pickups, but it now left enough time to pursue his interest for the camera. He spent time at the studio and was fortunate enough to accompany the artist on some of his photo shoots. Princeton was always patient to explain the mechanics of the camera—angles, buttons, change out of lenses. However, his best work always happened when he was alone, off somewhere by himself being inspired and in the moment. It was what he had grown accustom to. He would never wait until the next day for developing. He had to see the product while it was still fresh, hoping it would reflect what he was seeing.

The studio had its own dark room, which was a must when deciding on a spot for his work. Everything nowadays was digital. Princeton couldn't snap a photo and then look at it on the screen; it felt confusing to him. Capturing the moment was a dance between his heart and eye. The entire beauty behind it was to secure that moment in his mind and let his eye and camera do the work. The exhilaration of waiting to see the product afterward was the true art that fed his passion. So he went to great lengths to only use roll film. He would never submit to having that moment taken away from him. Watching the photo come to life in his hands was the pivotal point of the work. So a dark room was a necessity for his inspiration.

The studio was located in an area of town, which had boutiques, pubs, and upscale eateries, the closest imitation of Tribeca available. It was a little too pretentious for him, but Tallulah convinced him of the importance of visibility, conducive to the market that was interested in his work. The upside was that she decorated it exactly to his vision. It had a modern feel with a European flair, predominately black-and-white interior with pops of bold orange and red. Every piece was framed identical. Black-and-white photo, tiny black border surrounding the photo, larger white border, and black wood frame. The wood was flat color, not glossy. In the lower right-hand corner, his signature was bold, done with a black laundry marker. He only used his first name. His name was powerful enough, so that people came to refer to his work as a Princeton or the Princeton collection. Each photo hung on white walls with four by four inch framed black courtesy line cards. The cards read the title and the price. There were individuals and series. There was one large brown traditional leather sofa, and above it hung the piece titled "Life and Death." It was the largest piece in the studio and the only one not for sale. There were two upholstered chairs, each different. One had a modern flair, white circles on orange silk fabric. The other was white stripes on brown cotton. The furniture rested on an ornate brocade rug. The white tree branches appeared three dimensional against the blood red background. Pieces of red glass accessories sat on the three small Sheraton tables. His favorite spot was the artistic beverage area. Evians and Pellegrinos chilled in the cooler, with an espresso/cappuccino machine. Cups and saucers that were replicas of the Metropolitan

Museum of Art Picasso collection sat on beautiful ceramic trays. Two vases with bird of paradise were prominent on the coffee bar's white mosaic counter. That in itself was a piece of art. Tiny glass mosaic pieces in bold colors of orange, cobalt, and brown hand placed in the white glass background to create on extraordinary design. In the design world, it was referred to as Cosmati. The four stools were distressed brown leather, with nail head trim. They weren't mass produced to have the look of being weathered. They actually were that way due to years of wear of the untreated leather. They were imported from Columbia. Butt up against the side of the bar was the work station. An L-shaped desk, two banker's chairs, one desktop, and two laptops. Tallulah was adamant about not having any photos of herself for sale in the studio. However, the corkboard wall, which separated the desk and the cabinets above, were covered in her, layers and layers of photos with push pins, going every which way. The remaining space was a holding unit for empty frames and photo paraphernalia. To the left was a small bathroom. To the right was the door to the darkroom. Once inside the darkroom, the familiar smell of chemicals reminded Princeton that that was his second favorite place.

*　　*　　*　　*　　*

Princeton turned to face her, arms, and legs crossed, mirroring her stand and leaning against the opposite counter. She appeared lost in thought. He pointed to the credenza and asked, "So is this sexy dresser ours?"

Her eyes came out of the lost stare, and she looked at him, and then the credenza, and then back at him.

"Originally, it was for the Richards project. One of my mother's finds, on her estate hunts . . . but now"—she started to giggle—"I think we should keep it. Maybe in the dressing room?" she asked.

"I'm in," he said. "It could probably hold at least another twenty pairs of shoes."

She retaliated with "*that* or another forty cameras!"

He laughed, and he walked to her, saying, "Whatever you want, baby, is fine with me!"

He lifted her tee just a little so that his skin below his waist, not zippered yet, rested on hers. He wrapped his arms around her, and as he pulled her in tightly, he slowly started to move to find the exact pressure he needed. As he moved, his mouth covered her neck. Her body was so accommodating; she knew exactly how to take him there. He was throbbing. That perfect mix of warmth and steady pulsating fullness covered him. Just as he was entering his euphoric whirlwind, he repeated his words, one at a time in syncopation with his movement. "Whatever. You. Want. Baby."

She watched his body moving, head thrust back, eyes closed, as his beautiful face projected ecstasy. His hands covered her, and the words kept repeating.

"Whatever. You. Want. Baby. Whatever. You . . ."

Each word attached to his precise pressure. She let go, and her release of pressure interrupted his movement. He desperately needed her back. When she did that, it was slightly frustrating and, at the same time, very arousing. He opened his eyes and saw Tallulah's sexy expression. Her face was a mirror of her body's reaction. She changed her position purposely, holding him at arm's length, while he concentrated on not giving in to the explosion he was feeling.

"C'mon, baby, I need you."

She watched him fighting his enormous resistance not to give in as he tried to control his movement.

"Baby . . . please . . . I need you!"

Just as his hands were ready to finish his surrender, she pulled him in and quickly gave him his request.

"Oh my god . . . oh my god!"

His loud voice drifted into their deep exchange.

THE GREAT AMERICAN
LOVE STORY

Victoria had been awake about an hour or so. She was on her third cup of coffee and finished her Bible reading, two chapters of Joel Osteen, and her number 9 CD of Tony Robbins. That was the morning ritual. She had fallen prey to becoming a creature of habit during the first few hours of each day. She wasn't like that years ago, but a lot of things had changed with age. So many things that were very important before were now insignificant these days. She had succumbed to realizing that her life's journey had molded and transformed her to who she was now. Her journey was a challenging one, filled with struggle. Each episode of pain, and fear moved her closer to be better equipped to be the victor, not the victim. She reminded herself constantly through internal dialogue that she had championed her adversities. The abundance of her life now had been well earned.

She rarely sought advice or an opinion concerning situations. Mostly, because she was harder on herself than anyone else could ever be. Her role as caregiver was created for her decades ago. She was so young when she became the go-to person in her family circle. Everyone relied on her to make any and all decisions regarding their lives. She would try to balance not only her own life, but everyone else's. She had become so accustomed to the role, that her greatest joys were when she was fixing something—medical issues, relationships, financial worries. She was so absorbed in her family's needs that without realizing it, she became the last person of importance. She believed sacrifice equaled love. The more you sacrificed for the people you love, the more it revealed your love in action. Subconscientiously, she justified it by believing this was God's plan, and he was preparing her for tremendous blessings. In some ways, she was right, but the road had been a long one.

To people watching, she was an anomaly. To their eyes, she was beautiful, classy, and strong. She gave the impression of a hard, controlling person. However, the core of Victoria was quite the opposite. She had such a tender open heart, that it made her struggle with her reactions to the world around her. In her early days living in the city, she was saddened by the injustice of people's lives. She would be walking and come upon a person sleeping on a sidewalk, and she just couldn't walk by. She would be kneeling in her expensive suit, designer bag on the ground, trying to comfort the person, so saddened by her awareness of all the people walking past them. She would give him a few dollars, wipe her eyes, and carry that vision around for days. Her heart would hurt for that oppressed life. It would make her remember her dark days. Maybe not as extreme as that homeless person, but there were times long ago when she didn't have enough money to buy a quart of milk. She lived with the feeling of responsibility to have to give back because her own life had proved to be victorious, overcoming tremendous obstacles. Her faith carried her through the lowest points in her life. She believed God was in control, and he was preparing her for great things to come. She would tell herself, "You can't know the joy without experiencing pain. The way we react to problems is God's test to build our character. Doors will open, and doors will close. I just don't have the ability to turn the knob; it's according to *his* timetable."

She would volunteer as a counselor for drug-addicted families, pass out blanket to the homeless living under the bridges, and deliver meals to the shut-ins. Her other passion was helping with our veterans. She found time to consistently help at the DAV hospitals. Victoria had tremendous respect for the men and women that secured the safety of our country. Regardless of opinions debating if war was right or wrong, the bottom line was she was thankful that our freedom was due to the lives that were so drastically changed or lost. She wanted to give back believing that "our society didn't give proper homage to our heroes. Instead they were forgotten and lost." Tallulah had displayed similar desires through the years, especially when taking on her Congo mission. She had to listen to hundreds of sermons regarding doing the right thing, gratitude, and giving back. Victoria felt confident that her daughter would develop her own insight and understand the depth of life's meaning. Victoria would sum it up as "the meaning of life is to be of service and be purposeful." Those words were a lot for a little girl to take in. However, lead by example was always Victoria's stance. She wanted her daughter to see the lives of less-fortunate people, hoping she would not take all she had for granted. Victoria made sure her daughter had every opportunity available to her. She was committed to making sure Tallulah wouldn't have to carry heavy burdens as a child and a young adult. Remembering her own life, she didn't want that cycle repeated. However, she walked a tight rope every day, trying to balance the blessing without creating a spoiled, shallow person.

She wanted her daughter to feel confident and equipped to be able to pursue all her dreams. She also wanted her to be a fighter. Her hope was that she would never settle for less.

Victoria would tell her that "settling will leave you accepting mediocrity. There's nothing worse that living a life that's less than what your spirit believes you want or are capable of."

She was very specific when it came to explaining commitment and love. "Commitment is the backbone of who we are. It sends a message that we will not give up on what we believe in. We will see it through at all costs. Where we end is far more important than where we begin."

The conversations about love were Victoria's favorites. She wholeheartedly believed in love. Love for God, love for our country, love for our families. When explaining love in relation to romance, she would feel her heart quicken and would lose herself in the vision of love.

"When you find someone you love, you give 110 percent, or you give nothing at all. Otherwise, how can you differentiate what makes it special? What dictates if he's "the one"? You become selfless and motivated to feel *his* joys, *his* accomplishments, as if they were your own. You give yourself freely every day, building trust and safety within yourselves. You feed off each other to learn, explore, and inspire your heart's desires. You take each other's pain, insecurities, and secrets, and you protect them, never taking advantage of the weaknesses and vulnerabilities that you each have. You commit to each other totally—mind, body, and spirit. You take your journey together, knowing that you chose each other because all this was understood. God opened your eyes and your hearts to know that you are each other's soul mate. That is love! That is the great American love story!"

As her cell phone rang, she looked down to see the name. It was just a force of habit because she knew it would read "Tallulah." It was the first call of every day.

"Hi, sweetheart."

"Hi, Mom, are you working today?"

"I have a three o'clock appointment, why?"

"I thought we could have lunch, I'm free until two o'clock, and then I'm meeting with the Richards. Oh, by the way, you know the credenza you picked up for them? Do you think you can get another one?"

Puzzled, Victoria answered, "Well, first of all, I didn't *just* pick it up. I looked for that piece for a month! And it didn't come cheap. Why? They don't like it?"

Tallulah started laughing. "They didn't see it, your son and I decided to keep it."

"Oh really, well then, you're picking up the check today, put him on the phone."

"Princeton . . . ," Tallulah called out, her voice reaching the upstairs, "come to the phone, it's Mom."

He ran down the stairs, hair still wet from the shower, shirtless, hoodie in hand. He came up to Tallulah, wrapped his arm around her, and rested his hand on her hip. He put the phone to his ear. She took in the wonderful fragrance of his fresh clean skin.

"Hey, Mom," he said, his mouth gently kissing the back of Tallulah's neck.

"Hello, my son, how are you?"

Princeton would always get a thrill hearing Victoria's reference to "my son." She told him so many times that she loved him as if he were her own.

"I'm great, I miss you," he answered as Tallulah turned and kissed his chest.

"I miss you too," Victoria repeated. "I'll see you this week at the fund-raiser. You better make a nice donation, seeing how I'm out the money for the credenza."

"Oh yeah, great piece of furniture!" he exclaimed as his face had a huge smile, remembering him and Tallulah's connection to the piece. "Only you could find such a sexy piece."

He couldn't concentrate on the conversation; he was visualizing last night.

"Flattery will get you everywhere," she replied.

"OK, Mom, see you soon. Love you. I'll put Tallulah on."

He put the phone to her ear as both her hands were caressing his chest.

"OK, Mom, gotta go. I'll meet you at twelve, is Michael's OK?"

Victoria sighed, "It doesn't matter, all you eat is lettuce!"

"Funny, see you at twelve, love you."

Before Victoria could respond, the phone clicked.

"Baby, I think I am going to put you in my pocket and take you with me today. I can't stand being away from you!"

Tallulah laughed, still feeling the effects of their marathon, and said, "Last night was perfect, thank you."

*   *   *   *   *

They would designate a night to get take-out, catch up on movies or TV favorites, and include a massage. They had cult movies, which they would watch over and over again. It ran the gamut of *Serendipity*, *Family Man*, *Life as a House*, *One True Thing*, and their all-time favorite, *A Walk to Remember*. Their common thread was they always rooted for the underdog, the character with depth but a bit of a misfit, usually the one less likely to succeed. They understood those characters and found joy in their perseverance. They were big on romance—romance in all forms. Romance that left them sighing, thinking, "Good for them." Their favorite TV shows were *American Idol*, *Hell's Kitchen*, and *So You Think You Can Dance*. However, baseball season superseded all. They were die-hard Yankee fans. If they weren't at the game, they were fixed to the TV. Last night was more special than usual because Princeton did his rendition of Mariah Carey's "Vision of Love." Whenever that happened, it took her breath away. It became a strong piece of their love. It started when they were in the early stages of dating. Although they were together a short time, both knew they were head over heels for one another.

*   *   *   *   *

Tallulah wasn't sure where they were going that night, but she felt the urge to trade in her casual for sexy. She was trying on different looks listening to Dave, and it resulted in a large pile of clothing on the floor. She felt this desire to wear something reflecting how she was feeling and knew once it was right, she would know it. An hour later, she looked into the mirror and smiled. "That's it"! It was a short empire dress. In her mind, she said, "Umpeer," remembering her mother correcting the pronunciation years ago when she tried one on.

Victoria said, "No, Tallulah, it's not umpire like the guy at the game, it's umpeer."

The colors were bold, in a geometric design of purple and orange. It showed just the right amount of cleavage above the satin sash. It was the kind of dress that was so fashion forward, it could be mistaken for outdated. She worked it, with a fabulous pair of Jimmy Choo she got at the designer consignment shop. They were at least five inches of shoe, which was always OK, because she only stood at five feet three. They were a leather purple peep toe, simple yet deadly sexy. Her legs looked sculptured and beautiful. Either he was going to love it or think "what was she thinking?"

When she opened the door, Princeton froze. He looked at her and immediately felt physical warmth run though his body; she was stunning! She smiled, recognizing his approval; and still standing there, he said, "Baby, you are gorgeous . . . just gorgeous."

He didn't question why she was so decked out, compared to his casual attire, because that was one of the things he loved about her. Her confidence to wear what she was feeling always intrigued him. As a matter-of-fact, Tallulah liked being a little "off" as compared to everyone else.

As they were driving, he couldn't concentrate on the road. He kept looking at this beautiful creature next to him—sleek bronze legs, beautiful natural hair, not coiffed, gorgeous . . . just gorgeous. She wasn't sitting there posing; she was soft and natural, nestling close to him, her left hand resting on the back on his neck, gently stroking his hair. He was taken . . . totally taken. He had a moment when he thought he was going to cry. It was out of control, this love he felt. It was bigger than he was able to comprehend. He remembered Victoria telling him, "True feelings of love create emotions that overpower reason."

At dinner, it was difficult to determine if the stares were for him, for her, or for the pair. There was no question about it, Princeton was incredibly handsome. When he entered a room, all eyes were on him. So between the two of them, it would cause a quiet stir wherever they went. Neither one of them could tell you if there was one or a hundred people in the restaurant that night because they were in their private world. The conversation was always multifaceted: sports, design, music, theater. She challenged him with healthy views and convictions. She was soft and hard, serious, funny, flirtatious, and honest. He had a realization that night that was so profound, similar to an epiphany. It still held true to this day. He realized that the more attention Tallulah got, particularly when guys were secretly flirting with her on her way to the ladies' room or when his head was turned, the more she purposely made it clear she was with *him*. She would do something physical or send a message with her eyes that clearly stated "I'm with him; don't be rude because I can't be swayed." She sent out her message loud and clear. That left him feeling secure and powerful. He was her knight, he held the key; and the love in his heart walked its way to his sleeve that night, and he never looked back. He knew at that moment he was going to spend the rest of his life with his woman.

Neither one of them was a big drinker, but on occasion, they liked to listen to music, grab a drink, and sometimes dance. Both of them were hot on the dance floor. So after dinner, they went in to a local spot to have a drink. It was amateur karaoke night, and the bar was packed. They were both up for the lighthearted laughter that they enjoyed so much on these nights. This night, however, was different. Neither one of them knew that there would be a moment that night that would be repeated in their lives as a monumental statement.

Tallulah loved karaoke. When she was with Piper, they would get up onstage and instantly become the duo that was years in the making. They sang in their hairbrushes on Tallulah's bed, in the car, in the showers, and at amateur night at Mohegan Sun. She was thrilled to learn that Princeton enjoyed it too. When they doubled with Piper and Max, she found out Princeton had a good voice and wasn't embarrassed to get up on stage with Max and belt out Aerosmith's "Dream On." Apparently, they had a history with that song. They exchanged verses, whaled out on air guitars, and knew each other's moves. They couldn't hit Tyler's high note, but they were great! It reminded her of herself and Piper. Tallulah envisioned them rocking out in their room, just as she and Piper used to do.

They found a spot at the bar and ordered drinks. Even though they preferred Cabernet to alcohol, they wouldn't order wine at a bar. Tallulah believed wine was a "feeling." Wine also had to be quality, not some dollar-a-bottle headache inducer. Tonight it was beer. To watch Tallulah drink beer from a bottle, no glass . . . was confirmation of the lady she was. Anyone else might look rough, not her. The beauty she emulated overpowered the bottle in hand, and again her confidence came through.

Princeton always had his hand on her body. She loved the way he introduced her into a room, always guiding her with his hand firmly on her back. Whether it was her hip, shoulder, or thigh, there was a constant contact.

They toasted their bottles, started sipping; and at that moment, Tallulah looked deep into Princeton's eyes. She was having an inner conversation, thanking God for this wonderful man. She was running her hand along his arm, never losing eye contact, feeling as if she was touching his soul. It was spiritual and very physical. Her heart started pounding, and her face was slowly moving toward his. The feeling was confusing to her senses. She was warm, and at the same time, every hair on her arm was standing at attention. She felt slightly unsteady on her feet. It was almost surreal, as if she were standing alongside of them watching herself and Princeton. She leaned in and, for the first time, declared her love for him.

"Princeton, I love you with every breath of my life."

As she heard her own words, she felt completely lost in the magic of that moment. Princeton was in a whirlwind. His eyes hadn't left hers and hearing those words sent him into a frenzy of emotion. He pulled her in and started kissing her with a hunger. His mouth was searching and pressing harder. He was out of control moving against her because he wanted her right here, right now. His body was throbbing as he was trying to resist. "Oh god," he thought, "not in my wildest dreams did I dream that hearing those words would put me into such a state. Oh my god, I love this woman."

He went from not wanting anyone to not being able to control himself at all. This was the way he always envisioned it. He pulled himself apart from her, hearing the bartender say, "Get a room." He looked dazed.

"Hey, baby, I'll be right back."

Tallulah stood there, trying to get her thoughts together while wiping her mouth with a napkin. It seemed as if Princeton was gone a long time. "Maybe he left out the back door? Maybe that was too much for him?" she thought. At that moment, everyone was applauding for the next karaoke round to begin. She looked up, and there he was onstage, with microphone in hand. She moved to the center of the table area and felt her heart melt when she made eye contact with him.

The music started, and what followed was a lifetime memory. She recognized the song immediately. Princeton's voice was on point.

Treated me kind, sweet destiny
Carried me through desperation, to the one that was waiting for me
It took so long, still I believed
Somehow the one that I needed, would find me eventually

He pointed to her, and everyone turned to see Tallulah. She was frozen. He was moving to the music, and it seemed like he was transformed. He could have been at the garden doing a concert, with the amount of emotion and showmanship he was displaying. Princeton was locked into her eyes, and belting out every note, she held on to the table, as the entire bar got super quiet. She was mesmerized, seeing him up there, so strong, so beautiful with his heart on his sleeve. Her eyes started to fill up. Apparently, this must have been one of his favorite tunes because he never looked at the words, not once.

Tallulah' tears were running down her face. Everyone was either locked into her standing there or him singing. When he started the last verse, his heart was pounding. Never leaving her eyes, he started to feel his own eyes watering, and the crowd was going crazy, cheering him on. He was at the edge of the stage, lost in the emotion of his tribute. His right arm was extended in front of him, fist clenched. His face and body were pulling every ounce of energy from his audience. They were all up on their feet, applauding, screaming. Once the last word of the song left his lips, he paused, and then clicked an imaginary shot of her face. "I love you, baby" came over the microphone loud and clear.

As he came off the stage, people were patting his back. "Great job, man." Girls were rooting him on; some of them were actually crying. He made his way to Tallulah. She was still standing in the exact spot, unable to move. She never experienced anything like that. No one ever moved her that way. When he got close enough, she threw her arms around him and was crying uncontrollably. Every eye was on them, guys wishing they felt that way about someone, girls wishing he had sung that to them. His entire body covered hers in love and admiration. He looked at her and said, "I'm going to spend the rest of my life with you."

*   *   *   *   *

Through the years, there were times when Princeton would reawaken that night and sing "Vision of Love" to Tallulah. Last night was one of them. Princeton was feeling completely content and exhausted with Chinese, *Family Man*, and an incredible massage that Tallulah had mastered. She enjoyed giving it as much as he enjoyed getting it. She was still amazed at the sight of his body. Every muscle so pronounced, so defined. She knew how to relax every inch of him and later arouse every muscle she relaxed. Ironically, it did the same for her. When she aroused him, it transferred to her. They went through hours of playing. Eating, resting, movie watching, lovemaking, massages, more eating. On the bed, the floor, and the shower.

Tallulah was lying there on her stomach, naked except for her boy shorts. Her head was at the foot of the bed propped up on two pillows, watching the credits of the movie. Princeton was at the opposite end caressing her legs. He caught a glimpse of her one and only tattoo.

Perfectly placed. Leave it to her to have a tattoo that no one could see except for him. Well, maybe Piper or someone at a fitting room, but not the public eye.

*   *   *   *   *

When she went to Max to get inked, she explained that she wanted it across the lowest part of her back, right above her butt. She didn't want one that was visible when you bent down. Max explained that it would be more painful because of the tailbone. She didn't care. That's where it had to be.

He was right; it was painful but worth every burn. There wasn't anything she kept from Princeton. Unless it was an occasion or a surprise. They shared everything. Her tattoo fell into the surprise category. Aside from Max and Piper (who was with her that day), no one knew. Max not only was one of the best in the business, he also knew what the tattoo meant to her, so patience and precision was key. He felt a little uncomfortable at first due to the area of ink. When he worked on someone, they were just a canvas. However, this was Tallulah, his best friend's girlfriend, with his own new girlfriend looking on. Tallulah assured him, this was the same canvas as any other, with the exception that it had to be perfect.

"No pressure," she laughed.

It took hours due to the font that Tallulah requested. The tailbone area was just as painful as Max explained. Piper thought it was absolutely beautiful, and Max beamed with pride at his finished product. Tallulah flipped when she saw it. It was perfect!

She was determined not to let Princeton see it until it was done scabbing and looked clean. She had Max and Piper swear to secrecy. It took a little longer than a week. The challenge was not to be intimate and not to scratch so as not to draw attention to her secret. She planned her unveiling to include dinner, music, and a soft striptease. All the while she was hoping he would love it. After all, he already proclaimed his dedication with his tattoo. He was so sure of their future; he got inked two days after his karaoke debut. When he took off his shirt and turned his back to her, she nearly hit the floor. The piece itself was beautiful, but to make such a permanent statement was a huge show of his certainty of his love. She remembered her mother telling her, "Stick to your mother's and children's names when getting inked because that never changes." She thought, "Well, Mom, this is one time when you're wrong because this is never going to change."

They had dinner at Tallulah's, which was actually Victoria's at the time. Princeton liked the idea that Tallulah still lived with her mom. It said something about tradition. After seeing them interact, there would be no reason for her to be anywhere else. Victoria was out of town for a few days, so the timing was perfect. The kitchen was huge, so preparing a meal was a cook's dream. Princeton was intrigued with their approach to meals. Victoria and Tallulah always used linen napkins, chargers, candles, stemware, and a bottle of Chilean red wine. It didn't matter if it were dinner for two or twenty; that was the standard. This old world heritage transitioned into today's life was so appealing to Princeton. Tallulah would give the impression that it had to be that way because of her mother, but you could see it was part of her being. She enjoyed it, and it was second nature to her. Whether she realized it or not, it was all she knew.

That's how they eventually came to preparing meals together—Tallulah with all her experience, and Princeton with the desire to be a part of that. It was another area that contributed to the whole package.

Princeton would think, "Wow, what a remarkable job Victoria did with her daughter." This was life as they knew it, yet any other woman Tallulah's age wouldn't have a clue.

He didn't know that tonight was a planned unveiling. He was just soaking up the ambiance that the house secreted. He basked in the feeling of being a part of this. Victoria's house was a paradox of old and new. The old had a story, and the new mixed in gently to serve a purpose. It was odd, eclectic, and extremely fashionable. The moment he stepped foot in their world, he knew he was home. Dinner was fantastic. Asparagus, sundried tomatoes, fresh basil, and shrimp sautéed with angel hair pasta, warm French bread, salad, and wine. The music of choice was Andrea Bocelli, and the candles set off this aroma that was then new to him and very pleasing to his senses. Tallulah was so at ease in this role. She seemed seasoned for someone only twenty-three years old. Princeton marveled at her natural innocence. She wasn't "on"; she was being who she was. He would watch her commanding this space with a charm that was all her own. He helped her cleanup, which proved to be lengthy because he would stop what he was doing to observe her every move. The description that stuck in his mind was "art in motion." She had on a man's tuxedo shirt, long and loose, with fitted black slacks. There was a moment when he caught a glimpse of her elaborate lacy undergarment. He felt himself stir. Never . . . never had a woman had this effect over him. He was intoxicated. She grabbed their glasses and motioned to him to follow her with an exaggerated wink. She sat him on the sectional, gave him his glass, and stood in front of him. She slid off her slacks, grabbed her stilettos that she placed on the side of the couch, along with a black derby. She slipped into them, walked over and hit Play on the stereo. Joe Cocker's "You Can Leave Your Hat On" started, and so did she.

Baby take off your coat real slow, And take off your shoes
I'll take your shoes, baby take off your dress
Yes yes yes
You can leave your hat on

The music immediately resonated in Princeton. "Wow!" he thought. It was very sexy. Gritty, "bluesy," and a little sleaze. The underlining beat was steady and pronounced. Her back was to him, legs apart, which looked sooo . . . long in her stilettos. Her shirt hung to mid thigh. She was rocking her hips from side to side, as she exaggerated her fingers snapping, with her arms following her hips. All she needed were some footlights, and it was as if she were performing at a cabaret.

Princeton was drawn into the lyrics. It actually *was* a striptease. He thought he might have heard it before, he wasn't sure. All he knew was that it was an incredible piece of music! He was somewhere between perplexed and thrilled. If he had to put a fantasy together, this was hitting home. Could she be doing this? Her movements were super sexy, as if she were doing a choreographed piece!

Princeton had never witnessed anything like this. Yeah, maybe in a movie, definitely not in his everyday life. His body and mind were restless. The idea of her doing this for *him* aroused every inch of his body. She was transformed into this beautiful aphrodisiac that was giving him so much pleasure. He tried not to succumb to his body's desperate need to have contact. He was caught in a fantastic wave of arousal and pain.

She turned her head to him, derby half mast, found his eyes, and gave him a sly smile. Her hands were tracing the outline of her thighs as her body continued to translate the music. She slowly started to unbutton her shirt, letting it fall off her shoulders, holding it before it fell too far, exposing the back of her white-beaded Vickie. Then she turned and faced him. He took a deep breath. The silhouette of her hard abs, breasts sitting in a beautiful, sparkling demi, with tiny panties made it difficult for him to sit there. He moved deeper into the sofa, legs apart, running his fingers through his hair. "Oh my god, baby, come here, please."

Although it was obvious that she was performing for him, there was an "air" about her production. She was captured in her memories of her New York days, using all her skill and talent to dance "inside" the music. Princeton realized she was totally taken in, an absolute perfect portrayal of what the music wanted you to feel.

She smiled and continued to move . . . teasing . . . coming closer, and then pulling away. She let her shirt fall to her feet. She placed both index fingers to the sides of her panties and slid them down a tiny bit. Then she turned. With her back to him, she turned her head to see his reaction. His mouth fell open! His heart started beating faster, and although he wanted to speak, he wasn't able to do anything but sit there with an astonished look on his face. Right above that perfect, tight butt, across her lower back was *Vision of Love*.

She just stood there for the few moments of the song's completion. She threw her hat and heels off and laughed. Thrilled with his reaction, she came to him and straddled his body. He held on to her hipbones and was pressing her down, applying pressure to keep her perfectly still as she stretched her upper body, arching her back. His face was even with her cleavage, and he buried his mouth in that space. His mind was full of questions, "When?" "Where?" "Did Max do this?" He said, "I love you, baby, I absolutely love you." He looked up, at the base of her neck, seeing the silhouette of her face. She looked down and locked her eyes into his. He was speaking to her without saying a word. She understood as her hands explored his skin, gently pressing on his pecs and tracing his abs. He was afraid to move, for fear he would explode. Instead, he applied more pressure pushing her down into him, deeper and deeper . . . yet perfectly still. They were completely caught in the surprise of the effect they were creating. Their heavy breathing had a rhythm that echoed in the air. Their moans became synchronized, and somewhere in their heat, they experimented with this game of reaching each other's destination without the usual movement. It was as if their body contact were inside their minds, allowing their imagination and sounds to do the work. That was the first time in Princeton's life that he experienced release through the rhythm created in his mind!

*   *   *   *   *

Catching the glimpse of her tattoo and remembering the unveiling as he caressed her legs triggered his need to get up, go to the foot of the bed, kneel down, take her face in his hands, and sing "Vision of Love" to her. Each time was different. This time it was low, soft, and deliberate. Her heart swelled, watching his beautiful mouth half singing, half talking his tribute to her. God truly did answer their prayers.

*   *   *   *   *

"If you take me with you in your pocket, I'll miss lunch with Mom!" she exclaimed.

Princeton sighed, "OK, I concede . . . only because it's Mom."

Tallulah was still inhaling his postshower scent. Breathing in, she said, "You smell delicious," as she ran her hand down his arm and locked her fingers in his.

"Keep talking like that, and nobody's going to work today."

"Oh work . . . yeah. I'll be home late tonight. This project will probably wrap up this week. I suggested your birth series, they have three kids, what do you think?"

"That's great, baby, call Zach, and he'll package them."

"What's Zach been doing? I haven't seen him in forever."

"Oh! He has a new lady, Makenzie."

She looked surprised. "Makenzie? How long has this been going on?" she asked.

He thought for a moment, "Not too long."

"Let's have them over for dinner. I need to know who Zach is spending time with, have you met her?"

"Only via conversation, he talks about her a lot."

"I'm hurt, he hasn't called me. Usually, he grills me about what restaurant? What wine? Something's up."

She let go of his hand. "I'm going to let go of you, only long enough for you to get your phone, so we can align our schedule."

Princeton hesitated, then grabbed an apple, and said, "Don't move."

He ran upstairs got his phone and came back down. Tallulah handed him a cup of coffee, took his hand, and walked him over to the sectional. The two of them sat there cross-referencing dates and times.

"I spoke to your mom and dad yesterday; they're coming to the fund-raiser Saturday."

"Yeah, I spoke to them too. It's seven o'clock, right?"

"Yeah, black tie."

"Mom lets me get away without the tie, as long as I wear her favorite suit."

"That's because my mother adores you. Anyone else would be on the chopping block. Wait till you see the little number I'm wearing! I picked you up a little something too."

"Baby, you could wear your sweats and still be the most beautiful, sexy woman in the room."

He was playing with her hair, sipping his coffee, and wishing he could stay home.

"That's why I keep you around, my ego loves you," she teased.

"It better be more than your ego that loves me."

She laughed, "OK, this week is too packed; let's have them over next Thursday?"

"Thursday works. What about Piper and Max?" Princeton asked.

"Oh, the poor girl, having to debut for the breakfast club?"

Princeton laughed, "Actually her debut is at the fund-raiser. Zach is bringing her."

"Really? This could be serious."

"Let's see if Thursday works for everyone."

She placed her head on his shoulder, running her finger along the rim of her cup. The light was coming through the windows in lines of patterns. Some of the rays rested on Princeton's photos. "What beautiful work," she thought. She took in the scene, relaxed, grateful, and wishing she could stay in this moment forever.

THE AUTHOR OF LIFE

Victoria took a last look in the mirror. She was so disappointed in herself, examining her face. She always believed she wanted to age gracefully. She envisioned herself being this wise old woman who was proud of every line on her face because it would tell a story, a character map. Now as she saw the reflection, she was ashamed of her desire to want to stop the clock. It made her feel shallow and vain. Her mind said thirty, and her face said fifty. Sure, at a quick glance, people would comment that she was beautiful. She retained her size 2 body through the years. Her stomach was flat and tight, and her triceps and biceps were as defined as they were twenty-five years ago. Her ability to choose perfect clothing to accentuate her assets stayed with her since her modeling days. She could look at a fabric and immediately know how it would hang. She always opted for quality versus quantity. She loved classic and vintage well-fitted clothing. Jackie O Sheath dresses, at least twenty-five pairs of black slacks, beautiful blazers, and dozens of fitted tanks. Beaded, patterned, and intricate designs—everything had to be lined. Her look was timeless. Her signature was an over-the-top designer bag and drop-dead sunglasses. It was the area that had some shock value. If she was wearing basic black and white, the bag would be zebra, marigold, or red. She didn't care for jewelry. Diamond studs were perfect with everything. She never took off her Passion of Christ silver nail on her neck, and the only ring was the yellow-and-white-gold crucifix, aside from her wedding band. Her passion was watches and bracelets. Usually vintage, one-of-a-kind pieces. They were elaborate estate finds and contemporary collectables. She also loved active wear. It included hoodies, sneakers, and lots of Lulu Lemon. So at her age, she was still a head turner.

She thought about getting work done. After all, nowadays everyone was doing it. She would investigate possibilities and then stop herself, thinking, "People don't have enough food to eat, and you want to remove lines from our face?" It made her feel guilty.

She was caught in a strange place in her life. Her work and family always occupied her time and made her feel purposeful. That hadn't changed, but losing her husband five years ago changed everything. That was before Princeton. She always wished Luke could see the life that Tallulah and Princeton made for themselves.

She missed the piece of her life that Luke had given her for twenty-four years. She wanted to move on, yet she was still stuck in her imaginary world with him, and now she truly liked being alone. Still, there were moments when she wished she had the romance and the intimacy that she knew she was so good at. Her families' mission was to get her out there, circulating herself with the living. Family conversations would always find a place to include everyone's opinion concerning her dating. They would try to convince her that she had so much to offer, and going out and having fun was part of life. Victoria agreed, however, she felt that . . .

A. It was too much work, the whole dating thing.
B. No one was interesting to her.
C. God would bring her someone if it was meant to be.

There were times when she and Princeton were out and about, and he would lean over to her ear and say, "Mom, that guy's checking you out, he wants you."

"Oh really, which one?"

He would motion to the guy across the way, saying, "That one."

"My son," she would say, "he could be my son!"

"See what I mean? You still have it, men half your age want you."

She laughed and put her arm in his. Princeton thoroughly enjoyed the attention Victoria got. He was proud when men admired her, and he liked the acknowledgment that he was possibly her son. Deep down he wished for her happiness with someone but knew in his heart it would take an incredible man to turn her head. Looking in the mirror, she concluded that today was not the day she would go under the knife. So she smiled, applied her lipstick, and left to meet Tallulah.

She pulled into the parking lot and looked for Tallulah's Cayenne. It was a force of habit to look for the license plate rather than the car. A short time after they were together, Princeton took Tallulah to the DMV. He had her fill out the papers but didn't let her see what he had printed on the request for the new plate. She was thrilled when he gave it to her. Again, such a bold statement for the new relationship. He made sure that HISVISN was transferred to the Cayenne when they bought it last year. No sign of it, so Victoria assumed she was early because her daughter was one of the most punctual people she knew. She checked her watch, 11:45.

"Enough time to settle in and start my coffee", she thought.

The hostess sat her, and the server placed two menus.

"Can I get you something to drink?" she asked.

"I'll have a cup of coffee with a glass of ice on the side."

Victoria looked at her and asked, "What's your name?" She always asked her server's name.

"Lilly," she said.

"Lilly, that's a nice name."

"Thank you, I'll be right back with your coffee."

Victoria was anxious to see her daughter. Even though they got together two or three times a week, she still missed her and enjoyed hearing about her life.

She looked up, and walking toward her was her beautiful daughter. She had a big smile, and right behind her was Piper.

"Hi, Mom, look what I found on the side of the road!"

She leaned in and kissed her, and Piper leaned over to kiss her too.

"Piper! Hi, sweetie."

"Hi, Ma." (Piper had been calling her Ma since she became a part of their lives fifteen years ago.)

"The two of you look fabulous," Victoria exclaimed.

Tallulah and Piper sat across from Victoria at the round table. She looked at them and couldn't believe these were the same two kids planning their prom together.

"Ma," Piper smiled, "you look great, how's life?"

"Life is good, but I want to catch up on your escapades."

The waitress brought the coffee and an additional menu. They ordered their drinks and started to examine the menu. Piper glanced over and said, "Tallulah, don't bother. Just order your salad and put the menu down."

"Exactly," said Victoria.

"Oh funny, are you insinuating that I'm predictable?" she asked as she looked at Piper.

Piper laughed and said, "Well, that's about all you ever eat when we're out."

Tallulah looked over to Piper and couldn't help but smile. She loved her as a sister and a best friend. There wasn't anyone closer to Tallulah aside from her family. She relied on Piper to know what she was feeling, thinking, and why. Piper always came through. She had a great sense of wit and humor. She was supersonic intelligent with a caring, giving soul. However, Piper's strongest quality was her loyalty. She never judged Tallulah and always had her back. To outsiders, Tallulah appeared to be the mentor, the footsteps that Piper tried to follow. There were many areas that Tallulah did, in fact, guide and inspire her best friend. What the outsiders didn't know was that Piper was one of Tallulah's greatest resource for heartfelt happiness.

All their years together, experiencing milestones of their lives, gave Tallulah some of her best memories. She could go into her box of memories in her mind and randomly pick a time when she and Piper were doing something, and it would fill her heart. The laughter, the tears, the mishaps, the vacations, agonizing over the meaning of life, and how to be the best they could be were pages that could never be erased.

*   *   *   *   *

To Tallulah's eye, Piper was beautiful. Not the obvious beautiful, more a quirky beautiful. Her skin was flawless. She wore fabulous specs (not for fashion, she had poor eyesight), and she had a "china doll" cut. French bangs and long straight medium brown hair. There was a European flair about her. Beauty mixed with an intelligent feel. Maybe it was the specs or her one of a kind fashion sense that sent out this "French flavor," which was not easily understood in Connecticut. They both acquired their look early on, constantly flipping the pages in *W* and *Vogue*. They would sit on the bed discussing their need to be different, to make a statement, about who they were. They weren't comfortable with the trends and attire that everyone in school was wearing. Maybe it was Victoria's design influence, or maybe they just knew they were different. It became natural for them to create unusual head-turning outfits. Tallulah had more of an ease about it, while Piper was fixated and driven not to look like every other girl they knew. Piper thought they were all boring and referred to them as Stepford wannabes.

Victoria's closet was their playground. She, Tallulah, and Piper were about the same size, but slacks were way too long, as Victoria's legs went on forever. So hats, bags, and tops were open season. They would change up the look to suit their much younger taste, but a great bag or hat needed no alteration. They came to be known as the fashion icons. They were the trendsetters to follow. That wasn't their intention; they were just satisfying their own desire to be who they were.

Victoria would tell them. "Everyone has a look, but you shouldn't be locked into looking the same all the time. What you wear should reflect how you feel and be appropriate for the occasion. Your closet should look like it belongs to seven different people. Sportswear, casual, formal, sexy, soft, heels, flats—not just one look. Never wear something because it's in style; wear what looks good on you. A size 9 should be a beautiful size 9, not trying to be a size 3, looking hideous because stomachs protruding over waists of pants three sizes too tight is not attractive. Minis are for women with drop-dead legs, and cropped tops are for the perfect abs. If I had a dollar for every time I wanted to stop a woman and ask her if she lost her mirror, I'd be a millionaire."

She tried desperately to explain "sexy," seeing how young girls were totally confused. "Sexy is a feeling, an essence, not a piece of clothing. If a girl is showing a lot of cleavage, in skin-tight clothes, with too much makeup, all she is saying is that she needs attention because what she has to offer without it is not enough. Sexy is the way you move your hands, your posture, your gait. There is nothing more sexy than a lady, a thoroughbred. She leaves a mark on men with her persona. Sexy is beautiful, elaborate undergarments worn under jeans and tee shirts. This way, only you can feel it, and that transitions into how you feel. No matter what you're wearing, you take care to always have beautiful lingerie on. Knowing what's underneath your jeans will do a lot more than exposed cleavage."

Her conclusion would be about profanity. Victoria was appalled by people using profanity. Tallulah would be more frightened of the effects of a nasty mouth than she was of failing a subject. Victoria would say it was unbecoming. It gave the impression of being ill-educated. She explained it as a weakness.

"When people use foul words to describe their feelings, it's because they won't take the time to search for a better way to find the right words. A woman could look beautiful and sexy, and if she opens her mouth and a trail of filth comes out, then she no longer is beautiful."

It was somewhere around that time that Tallulah knew design was her passion. Her mother's words describing a thoroughbred seemed to coincide with the ability to create beauty, depth, and a visual statement through the core of her existence. She would accompany Victoria on endless excursions, learning and understanding textiles, patterns, fabrics, the mix of bold and monochromatic. Victoria could hold a piece of fabric and explain the depth of the stitch. She knew if it were heated or transferred, mass produced, and the origin it came from. When she held it, her intensity and joy was evident. She would bring it up to her face, close her eyes, and breathe in the aroma.

As Tallulah became more interested, Victoria would share ideas, floor plans, and space functionality. Ornaments on bags became design patterns for wallpaper. At a restaurant, she would question the color on the wall with the mix of the drapes they saw the night before. Patterns on clothing were visualized as upholstery. They would spend hours at fabric stores as Victoria would test her ability to find foundation colors and accent patterns. They would frequent furniture stores and lighting centers and have endless trips up and down the bowery, seeking out antiques and accessories. Eventually, Tallulah became absorbed with everything she saw in relation to design. Her eyes were constantly at work. She would create rooms in her mind, then transfer her ideas to paper. Her inspiration was ignited from a glance of something that caught her attention. Clothes, architectural construction, stationery, even landscaping found their place in her mind to be a part of her next project. Her mother's claim to fame was her ability to find a piece that was trash worthy. Somehow she saw past that, and if the "bones" were good, she would spend hours, days, even months, hand finishing, painting, stenciling, changing out jewelry (hardware) until that same piece looked magnificent! It was true art. Tallulah's design savvy was due to her mother, not her degree.

Piper could have been an aeronautical engineer. Her 4.0 was a breeze. Somehow the creative bug was in her veins, so advertising served her well. She got to fry her brain with the complexity of the business and also create great campaigns. They were computer friendly. She didn't have the hand that Victoria transferred to her daughter. What she did have was great perception. She could take an object whether it be a car or a food product and deliver a message though music, props, and slogans. It would capture the essence of what the general public wanted, needed, or wished for. Her years in training with Victoria taught her to see past the obvious and search for the dreams and desires that people were searching for. The finished product was always a surprise because it would be so abstract from what was expected. Her boss referred to her as the Dream Maker.

*   *   *   *   *

"Are you ladies ready to order?" Lilly asked.

They ordered their salads, no big surprise. Piper and Tallulah ordered ice teas, and Victoria requested lots of rolls. They placed their napkins on their laps, said grace, and turned their phones off. If there was one thing that sent Victoria over the edge, it would be texting or talking on the phone in the middle of a conversation. She thought it to be rude, and long ago everyone survived quite nicely without them. Even now, dinner at her house included no calls received or taken until after dessert.

Piper looked at Victoria and asked, "Do you remember when you took us to Ptown, and Tallulah and I did the *Bye Bye Birdie* rendition in the streets?"

"Oh my gosh, that was ages ago, what made you think of that?"

"Yeah, Piper, what made you think of that?" Tallulah asked.

Piper continued, "What an incredible night. Remember when everyone was looking and applauding? We thought we were Broadway bound!"

The three of them were laughing as their minds searched for that memory.

"Well", Piper said, "Max and I were looking at the theater productions coming up, and *Bye Bye Birdie* is being resurrected. I told him the whole story of that fantastic week and how it sincerely had an impact on my life. Ma, you were responsible for so many revelations, I can't tell you. Max was so into the story we talked all night."

"Speaking of Max, any wedding bells?" Victoria asked.

Piper readjusted herself in her seat and said, "No, Ma, no bells here."

"You and Max have been together since Princeton and Tallulah, my god, he *introduced* you to Max, what are you waiting for?"

"Mom," Tallulah said coming to Piper's rescue, "she's not ready, that's all."

"No," Piper said, "we're not ready, but that's not it." She looked at Tallulah and said, "It's because of you and Princeton, that we're not married."

Tallulah and Victoria both looked at her confused.

She continued as she looked at Tallulah, "You see, you have ruined it for all of us. Me, Max, Zach, and wait till Makenzie gets a whiff."

"Who's Makenzie?" Victoria asked.

Piper ignored the question and continued, "You two have set a standard that rocks our worlds. Anything and everything is pale in comparison. The love the two of you share is unnatural. It's pure and right, and it's obsessive. You know that, right? You're like the poster people for true love."

Tallulah was taking in her words as she gave Piper her full attention.

"First of all, we're not sure who is more beautiful to look at, you or Princeton; that in itself is scary. It's like every day is a celebration of love. As if you two met a month ago. You know, when everything's new and perfect? He lives for you and you for him. Your work is phenomenal. The last three or four projects you did were in Greenwich, right? Soon, you'll be showcased in some magazine. Max said he and Princeton were having beers at El Fresco last week, and a couple approached Princeton going on and on about his work. Max said it was surreal when they asked him to autograph their menus. You live in the most amazing, ridiculous house that this side of the earth has seen. He drives a custom Jeep Wrangler limited edition black-and-white domino, isn't it? With that heavy black trim, which just happens to have beautiful white hand-painted Oriental symbols, which only the two of you know exactly what they mean. For God sakes, even his car is hot! If that weren't enough, you two eat and drink each other 24/7. Not in a nauseating way, in a hot, I-want-you-always way. You two constantly have brain sex. Everyone in this world is just a prop for your great screenplay. So we all watch, we're stunned, envious, wishing *we* had that. Wishing we could have that for a day, a week, never mind the possibility of years. What makes it worse is the two of you are the best people we know. If any of us has a problem, or a crisis, who do you think gets the first call? We're so damn happy for you, even if we're miserable for ourselves. Then of course, there's Ma," Piper said as she pointed to Victoria. Victoria moved in closer, trying to anticipate what was coming next.

"The beyond-wonderful mother-in-law. Zach and Max are blown away by that whole thing. They actually have conversations about it, so now we have a mother-in-law standard. I think they typed up a questionnaire for prospective mother-in-laws! Do you realize that we all agree, the highlight of our social life are your parties and fund-raisers, Ma? Max spent more time getting ready for one of your parties than he did for his brother's wedding. Princeton loves you right below Tallulah, poor Rachel. To top it off, they don't even know about your early years, Ma! If they knew what I know, they would erect a statue in the center of town. So we have Queen Victoria, the

Prince, get it? And the Princess in waiting to the throne. So every day I think, should I marry this man? And then you, Ma, creep into my ear, and I hear you saying, 'Never settle for less than you deserve.' That's brings me right back to nowhere because then I think, am I settling? If Tallulah and Princeton are in love, then I have no right to marry this man. It's been years, you're right, Ma. They got married five months after they met. We all know the reason why, well with that re-virginizing, if they didn't get married, they would be in a hospital! Imagine wanting each other so much and not consummating their relationship because of the God thing and cleansing themselves, or whatever they called it. Don't forget I know about the striptease"—she shot Tallulah a look—"and how Princeton held out is amazing! Because I've seen you naked. Imagine loving someone that much! So . . . when I put that all together, I think I deserve that, don't I? We all deserve that, don't we? So there! I said what everyone in our circle thinks. You have ruined it for all of us. The only bells here are dinner bells and the blue bells my mother has in her garden."

Tallulah looked at Piper, and most of what she said made her feel happy and proud; and yet she felt so sad for Piper, so at that moment, she dug deep to comfort her friend.

"Piper, I love you, and fortunately that's all true, but you forgot the part about the Prince and Princess not being able to have a child, the heir to the throne."

"Oh crap," Piper thought, "I've crossed the line, my big mouth got ahead of my little brain."

"Tallulah," she said as she tried to find words to redeem herself.

"No, let me finish. Princeton and I know we would make good parents. Don't you think I want to give what my mother gave me to a son or daughter? We know she would be the most incredible grandmother, and she's always going on about the legacy thing."

Victoria was about to interrupt, but Tallulah wasn't having it. She held up her hand to motion for her to stop, and Victoria did as she was told.

"So, Piper, you *can* have children. Well, I think you can have children, and that's one thing that you have up on me, so be happy for yourself."

She took her ice tea and started drinking. Piper's heart was heavy. She loved Tallulah so much, and what she thought would be a great rendition turned out to be hurtful. She leaned over and placed her hand on Tallulah's hand and said, "Tallulah, look, there are ways to have children. You could adopt, or there are like one hundred different procedures. Wait a year, and I'm sure you will be able to conceive via email, there are lots of possibilities for you. I'm so sorry that I did that to you right now. You know me, I was just trying to compliment your life and be my usually witty self."

"I know, and I still love you lots," Tallulah said.

"Princeton and I have stopped talking about it and decided to just wait and see what's in store for us. If the author of life doesn't want us to have a baby, there must be a reason, right? Maybe we're not capable of changing our life because of the way we love each other, who knows? But I do know that he created this entire planet—everything, birds, trees, oceans, skies, night, and day. He knows what he is doing, and he doesn't make mistakes. And we'll both know what to do because he'll put it in our hearts. Until then . . . we're just Princeton and Tallulah."

"*Just* Princeton and Tallulah is more than anyone can handle, it's a trade-off, right, Ma?" Piper asked.

Victoria wasn't sure if she could speak. What just transpired at the table was a lot for her to take in. Reminiscing, Piper's soapbox, her daughter's pain. It was a lot. So instead of feeding it, she chose a different path. "Who is Mackenzie, and what should I know about a striptease?" she asked.

Piper and Tallulah started to laugh, and Piper said, "Let me fill you in on the Makenzie thing, and Tallulah can give you all the details about her naughty behavior."

As they ate there salads, Makenzie was discussed, but there wasn't much info there. So the meat of the conversation was Tallulah's unveiling.

"You did this in my living room, on my sectional?" Victoria asked.

"Yes! Yes! It was right up there with karaoke night, and Max's ink of my name on Princeton, it was amazing."

As Victoria listened, she remembered knowing the second she met Princeton that he was "the one." The minute he stepped foot in her house, she knew he was home.

"OK," Piper said, "enough sex talk, who's going to be at the fund-raiser? Just point out the money people, and I'll work my charm on them."

Victoria was committed to many children's causes. She sat on the board of the nonprofit organization for low-income day care centers. She had her hands in dysfunctional families with the cause-and-effect syndrome on their children through the Department of Social Services. She was part of Toys for Tots and always ready to orchestrate the big bash. She had the resources; she knew the right people. People who had more than enough money and needed a reason to feel good about themselves. Now throw in the opportunity to hear good music, eat great food, and rub shoulders with the up and coming, and you have a successful fund-raiser. After all, who says no to children? She truly believed that every child deserved equal opportunities. Beautiful, innocent children caught in the cycle of their sad existence, due to circumstances beyond their control. God was doing a work in her, but deep down, she knew it was a magnified payback to all the children, like herself, that weren't given the opportunities, that were destined to fail. It was a payback for the ones that didn't make it. To this day, she still thanked her mother for her humble, courageous constitution that inspired the will in herself to be such a fighter.

"Mom will point out the money people, and you can discreetly pick their pockets," Tallulah said.

Piper asked, "Why discreetly?"

Victoria laughed as she said, "I'm looking forward to this one. The country club is going to look fabulous, we're doing the white lights on everything, I mean, everything!"

"That's my favorite," Tallulah said.

"Yeah, I know," Victoria replied.

"Now, Ma," Piper said, "when an attractive man that seems to be interested in you starts moving in your direction, don't instantly feel the need to use the ladies' room." Tallulah shook her head and said, "Remember that guy with the LoJack on her at the Christmas party?"

"The one that the prince was getting real uneasy about and stepped in doing the 'knight' thing?" Piper replied.

"Yeah, that's the one. I think Mom smoked a pack on her way home."

"Ma, when are you going to quit?" Piper asked.

"Let's not go around that again, OK?" Victoria rolled her eyes.

She finished her second cup of coffee, and Lilly brought the check. Victoria took it, and Tallulah grabbed it out of her hands. Victoria always picked up the check; Princeton was the only one that had this thing worked out with her when it came to cashing out. They just knew who was in charge that day.

"That's for the credenza," Tallulah said.

"Maybe one knob!" Victoria exclaimed.

"What credenza?" Piper asked.

"The one that was absolutely perfect for the Richards project, the one that aged me ten years. The one that now lives at their home." Victoria's sarcasm came through.

Tallulah got up, put her arms around her mother's neck from behind, gave her a big kiss on the cheek, and said, "Mom, I adore you."

Kisses, hugs, more kisses, and they left into their separate cars.

Tallulah turned the key, looked in the mirror, applied her lipstick, and put her purple CD into the deck. She adjusted the volume and sat there listening to Mariah belting it out. She never tired of it and used it many times to be close to him. Once the song finished, she hit the button on her cell.

"Hey, baby." His voice was better than the music.

"Have I told you that without you, I wouldn't be standing here right now in my studio? There would be no reason . . . because there wouldn't be these photos . . . because without you I'd probably be a personal trainer hating my life or maybe a priest."

"Great, so I'm somewhere between muscle and God?"

He laughed, "How was lunch?"

She hesitated, "Interesting."

"Interesting good or interesting bad?"

"Both," she said.

"Why what's wrong, is Mom OK?"

"She's great, Piper was with us, and she decided to share her aspect of the world according to us."

"Explain," he said.

"Forget it, everything is great now that I hear your voice."

"Baby, I love you sooooo much, you know that, right?"

As she listened, she thought about the word "baby." The sound of that word melted her heart. It was the way he said it. Hard to describe, yet very sexy. He hardly ever used her name. Not when it was conversation between them. The only times were at introductions or as a reference about her when talking to someone. "Baby," a simple little word that could change her whole attitude. "Amazing," she thought.

"I know you love me, but never ever stop saying it. Never stop loving me. If that ever happened, I wouldn't be able to go on, OK? Promise."

Princeton felt a slight panic, he moved to the back of the studio sat down and concentrated on the sound of her voice.

"Baby, what's wrong? Talk to me. Let me take the weight, I'm here for you, because you're the most important thing in my life—no, you *are* my life. I could *never* stop loving you! It's not possible. Nothing and no one could ever make me stop loving you! You rescued me. All those years, I was waiting for you. Everyone thought I was crazy. There was something so deep. I even thought at times there was something wrong with me. But the minute we connected, there was surrender in me. You became my sanity, my confirmation. My heart was so restless. Now I see you in my mind constantly, wherever I am, whatever I am doing, you're there. I get physical pains sometimes, real physical pain because I want you. My body throbs for you to the point where I have to take deep breaths. You're it for me, baby! You're the only thing I want to be in and around, understand?"

"I understand. I love you with every breath of my life."

He smiled as her voice sounded calm and familiar again. If he allowed himself, he could go into a full daydream fantasy, right here and now. He resisted because he knew he'd be ruined for the day.

"Zach is going to drop off the series for you at the Richards, OK?" he asked.

"That's perfect; give him a big kiss for me."

"What kind of kiss? A peck? A cheek kiss? A wet one?"

She was laughing. "I'll see you tonight, have a great day."

"Hey, baby, throw in the purple CD, see you tonight."

She put the phone down, threw the Cayenne into drive, took a deep breath, and hit Play. Princeton hit the button on his cell.

"Hi, my son," Victoria said.

"Hi, Mom, can I swing by tonight? I need to talk."

"Sure," she said. "Dinner or just a talk?"

"No dinner, I want to be home when Tallulah gets there, around seven, OK?"

"See you then."

LIFE AND DEATH

Princeton grabbed his stuff and walked over to Zach.

"I'm going to shoot. You'll have to close up to drop off the Richards stuff. Thanks, buddy."

"No problem," Zack said.

He got accustomed to Princeton's sense of urgency when this occurred. There was a driving force that made him sometimes drop what he was doing to go shoot. It wasn't like he had a choice. Whenever this happened, the photos were perfection. Zach knew that every time it happened, it was connected to Tallulah. He wasn't exactly sure how, but he felt it.

Princeton left, and Zach dialed his cell. Tallulah saw the name come across and thought, "It's about time."

"Hey, you," she said.

"Hi, long time no speak," Zack said.

"What is going on? I feel totally out of the loop. What happened to you needing me for all your dating dilemmas? And who may I ask is Makenzie?"

"Well, first off, I still need you. I just wanted this time to be different. I wanted to walk in blind, you know, without all the prep."

"That's great news. Are you guys coming Thursday? Did Princeton get around to asking you?"

"Yep, your man asked, and we'll be there. What time do you want me to drop off the series? He had to leave to go shoot."

Tallulah thought a minute, looked at her watch, and said, "You know what? I'm going to swing by and pick them up. I have enough time, and I haven't been there since forever."

"Ok, lovely lady, see you in a few. She checked her watch again and jumped on the highway. The ride seemed like seconds because her mind kept hitting the Rewind button on the conversation at lunch. She concluded that she and Piper needed some quality time; they were overdue. As she walked into the studio, she realized that she had forgotten how beautiful it was. Zach was at the coffee bar with a client. He excused himself, walked over, and gave her a big hug.

"You look great, give me a minute to wrap it up here, and I'll get you the photos."

"Take your time, finish your business," Tallulah replied.

As Zach reapproached his client, he saw that he didn't have his attention. His eyes were staring at Tallulah.

"Who is *that*?" he asked.

Zach stepped in front of him to intercede the imaginary line of his eyes to her body. As his view was obstructed, he looked back to Zach.

"That's the proprietor, the artist's *wife*," Zach responded as he made sure to emphasize the word "wife."

"Wow! Lucky guy!"

Zach felt annoyed that his client was checking her out.

He thought, "If I feel this way, I can only *imagine* what Princeton goes through."

"So let's get your piece down OK?"

"OK" was the response as he continued to stare at Tallulah.

Even though the studio theoretically belonged to her too, she never appeared to be anything but a client. This was his space, his sanctuary, and she never wanted to invade his domain.

Her eyes traveled the walls and stopped at "Life and Death." She stood before it and took in every detail. "That seemed so long ago," she thought. "Imagine, that God brought us together through that."

*   *   *   *   *

She was working feverishly to complete a project. She was still new at this, so every detail seemed to take forever. This was a project that could make or break her. The clients had connections to a whole network of people that were waiting to see their finished room, deciding if they would use her services. So far, so good. The foundation was done, and now the icing (as Victoria put it) needed to be placed. Icing included art and accessories. Tallulah was learning that this part was where functionality ended and emotion began.

She had certain boutiques she would frequent because they had tremendous collections of specialties—one of a kinds. She took care to develop a nice rapport with them, so the transactions were always pleasant and not a hard sell. She walked into Yesterday's Yearnings, coffee in hand, hoping she would find what she was looking for.

"Hello, beautiful lady."

She looked over. "Hi, Jack, what's going to take my breath away today?" she asked.

Jack really liked Tallulah. He felt she was well poised and sincere, the contradiction to his usual clients.

"Take a look, you never know," he said.

She examined lamps, throws, music boxes, letter openers; nothing was feeling right. She looked into a showcase of estate jewelry. "Beautiful pieces," she thought. Nothing there that she needed. There was a row of Zippos lined up like little soldiers. Beautiful, ornate series pieces. She examined each one. She never wanted to contribute to her mother's addiction, hoping she would quit. However, through the years, she would go against her grain because it made her mother so happy when she got a new one to add to her collection. It was a connection to her life with Luke, a simple thing that meant a lot to her. She decided on the dragonfly that had aqua and green stones.

As she looked up she saw this incredible large framed photo. It was black-and-white, but she saw color in her mind. It was a tree that was barren. Lots of branches bending this way and that. Beautiful shapes and textures. The sun was evident in the difference of the shading. She thought for a moment that it was dismal, and then she thought it was uplifting. She imagined the tree in bloom, beautiful, and healthy. Somehow now it was old and tired. Much like life and death. She glanced at the signature Princeton. She saw there were a few others. She took her time to evaluate each one. They were beautiful, but her tree kept calling her back. She looked at it again and again, each time she felt this stir inside her. It was speaking to her. She thought, "I don't know why I feel this way, but I have to have that."

"Jack," she called.

He came over. "Ah, you found something."

"Who's the artist?" she asked as she pointed to the collection.

"A local, he drops off every now and then."

"I'll take the tree," she said.

"Not knowing how much?" he asked.

"Expensive?"

"Not at all," he said.

"Also," she said, pointing to the showcase, "the dragonfly Zippo."

They walked over to the desk, he wrapped the photo, and she charged it.

"Your client will be very happy. See you soon," Jack said as he smiled.

She drove home with the photo on the passenger seat. At a stoplight, she took off the wrapping and kept glancing at it each time she stopped the car. "Well, Life and Death, you are staying with me," she thought. She was so thrilled with her find, she didn't seem to care that nothing was purchased for her project.

Jack was putting a bulb into a lamp when Princeton walked in.

"Hi, Jack," Princeton said.

"Ah, the artist, how are you?"

"I'm good, listen, I think I may have given you a photo by mistake. It must have gotten mixed in with the other ones. It's a tree, and I need it back, it's not for sale.

"Well, this is a busy day here because your photo walked out the door about an hour ago."

"No way, you're kidding, right?"

"I kid you not, my friend."

"Well, who bought it?" Princeton asked.

"A beautiful lady, she a designer."

"Listen, Jack, I have to have that back, it's complicated. I need it back. It was never meant to be sold. Do you have a number?"

"Well, I can't give you her personal number, but I do have some of her business cards."

He handed Princeton a card. He put it in his pocket and said, "Thanks, Jack, I really appreciate it."

*   *   *   *   *

Princeton was drenched in sweat as he pressed the barbell up and down. He needed to get his time in because any minute Max would want his weight time before he went to work.

Princeton and Max went back seven years. They definitely had a strong bond, and Max was the only one that sometimes got Princeton. They both struggled in college, not because of the academics, but because they both had this creative side that made them feel like they were wasting their time with books. Paier Art Institution seemed to be the best choice. When they met, Princeton was twenty-one, and Max a year younger. They were an edgy pair, and Max would tell Princeton, "The only reason I hang out with you is because you get all the girls, who always have friends."

Max in his own right really didn't need help getting girls. He had a bad boy package that girls seem to love. He was trendy, masculine, and a little rough. Physically, he was buff, and his tattoos were intentionally visible on his biceps and pecs. He kept his head nearly shaved and always experimented with different facial shaves of his sideburns. His ice blue eyes were the deal breaker. He and Princeton hung out a lot. Their friendship was strong and consistent. Max was the only one that Princeton could stand for long periods of time because he wasn't always trying to pick his brain. Max was also the one that Princeton shared some of his thoughts about life with.

One time, they were going to a movie, and Max asked him about the girl he was with the night before.

Max said, "Man, she was hot, did you get lucky?"

Princeton got real serious, and the conversation that followed stayed with Max a long time.

"First off, she wasn't hot. I came to find out she had body piercings, and you know how that turns me off. At one point, she asked if she could watch me wax my chest! And what does lucky mean? I can't keep doing this."

"What?" Max asked.

"I can't keep sleeping with women and feeling nothing. I mean nothing. Sex without love is cheap. It feel's dirty. You know what's the first thing on my mind afterward?"

"You want more?" Max asked.

"No, I can't wait to get in the shower—alone. When you're with someone, you should feel this enormous pleasure, this supersonic heart beating, like your chest is going to crack feeling."

"Oh, don't start on the soul mate girl that God is going to bring you thing because I'm going to take you to a doctor. You make it sound like you slept with dozens of girls. Now actually, you could if you wanted to. There isn't a girl that doesn't want to be with you. So in that respect, you're almost a virgin. This thing that you're looking for doesn't exist."

"How do you know?" Princeton asked.

"I don't know, it just sounds crazy."

"Well, maybe I'm crazy! But do you know what's *more* crazy? Sleeping with someone and feeling like I could do a better job if I took care of myself. I want the physical, there's no question about it, but I want it to be fed by the way I feel about her mind, her humor, her beauty. I want it to be deep and spiritual. I want her to take me places I can't even dream of. I want it to be the vision I imagined."

"Maybe you're gay."

"Yeah, that's it, I'm gay, and this will probably be the best date I've had all year, and take that stupid earring out of your ear."

Max laughed, turned up the stereo, and pretended that the conversation was over. However, in his mind, he thought about what Princeton said all night.

*   *   *   *   *

So it made sense that seven years later, Max and Princeton were roommates now. Max needed help with finances because his ink shop needed to get off the ground, and Princeton was on the brink of success trying to set up a studio. So he decided to end his lease, save his dollars, and move in with Max.

Max walked in and saw Princeton soaking wet, pressing, pushing every muscle. His abs were ridiculous. They looked as if they were painted on. He wasn't bulky; he was ripped and defined. Sculptured would be the best description.

"Why are you always so angry?" he asked.

In between breaths, Princeton replied, "Empty, not angry."

"You, look angry to me, if you keep going this way, you won't fit through doors."

"Empty, not angry," Princeton repeated.

"It's because you haven't had a sex in a hundred years, that why! It's not natural. Either give up on this "I'm saving myself for my true love" thing or become a priest. Because the rate you're going, you're gonna be big and dead."

Princeton put the barbell on the stand, sat up, and wiped his face.

"Thanks, friend, your encouragement is overwhelming. I hope you're more gracious to your clients."

"Yeah well, you wouldn't know, would you? My best friend, and you don't have one tattoo. That's really flattering to me and my business. At least not a real one, just that tiny cross on your pec that no one sees."

"It's not on my pec," Princeton replied. "It's on the skin that's closest to my heart, and it's not meant for anyone but me."

Max continued, "Well, it's time you got a piece."

"I don't have one because I can't figure out what I want to wear for the rest of my life! And by the way, you're getting carried away with yourself. Don't get another one until you think it through."

Max took off his shirt, laid it on the bench, and took the barbell into his hands. He looked at his arms and thought, "Maybe he's right."

"What do you do with my cologne, drink it?" Princeton called out.

"Nag, nag, I want a divorce," Max said and started his reps.

Princeton went into his pocket and pulled out the creased card. It was black with white lettering. Big letters read Tallulah, beneath it small letters read Interior Designer. "Tallulah," he thought, "awesome name."

Tallulah was sitting at the kitchen table admiring her tree. The phone rang, and she realized it was the business line. She picked it up and walked back to her tree.

"Hi," she said.

"Hi, can I please speak to Tallulah?"

"This is she."

"Oh hi, this is Princeton." As soon as he said his name, she looked at the signature and made the connection. After all, there weren't too many Princetons out there.

"Princeton? As in Princeton the artist of Life and Death?"

He couldn't talk, his mind was scrambling, thinking, "Did I put that on the back? No, I know I didn't."

"Hello?" she asked.

"Why did you say that? Why did you say 'Life and Death'?"

"Oh well, that's what I see when I look at it. It's so obvious, isn't it?"

"No one knows that, no one! I titled that 'Life and Death' in my mind the moment I developed it," he said.

His heart was pounding. "Much like the way I see my life," he thought. He closed the door and sat on the bed.

"Well then, Princeton, your work is in good hands."

They talked for hours. They hit every topic from food, design, photography, movies, and most importantly, God—everything. She thought to herself, "The last six guys I dated combined couldn't keep me this interested." Princeton was three beats away from a heart attack. She was intelligent, witty, and humorous, and she understood him better in this conversation than anyone else had his whole life. He was physically feeling butterflies or maybe anxiety, he wasn't sure.

"Considering this piece means so much to you, I should probably return it, even though I feel like it belongs with me." She paused.

"I'll tell you what," she said, "let's get together. I'll bring the photo, and we'll see if you can strike a deal."

"Dear God," he thought as he looked up at the ceiling, "thank you."

"When and where?" he asked.

"How's Friday? Do you know the Casting Room?"

"One of my favorites. Is seven OK?" he asked.

"Perfect," she said, "see you then."

"How will I know it's you?" he asked.

"I'll be the one carrying the beautiful piece of art. Bye."

He jumped off the bed, ran to the fridge, got a bottle of water, and dreamed about his mystery lady all night. Literally, all night. He woke, slept, woke, slept. He kept repeating "Tallulah" in his mind.

Tallulah told her mom about what happened with the mystery artist. Victoria listened and told her daughter there were quite a few clear signs and messages.

"God brings us signs all the time. We just need to be open to see them and understand them."

Tallulah was preoccupied with thoughts of Princeton all week. "There must be a time change," she thought, "because Friday apparently is never going to come." They never once discussed what each other looked like. The conversation was so nourishing that it never came up.

Now as she looked in the mirror, she was nervous. She wished it were summer and not the dead of winter. She liked the feel of summer clothes and couldn't stand wearing coats. Her only saving grace was the coat she was wearing tonight was off the charts. Victoria passed by and said, "You look fabulous!"

"You think?" she asked.

"Absolutely. Wait, let me get you something."

She looked in the mirror again. She honestly was nervous. Maybe because she never did the blind date thing, or maybe because she was wrapped up in the anticipation of this night. She had on a fitted mid-thigh black wool dress. It had a belt with a heavy silver clasp. At the end of the sleeves, there were silver zippers, with round charms that moved across her hands. She wore no jewelry, and her manicure was French. Black tights and an incredible pair of brown and black boots that went above her knees finished it. No worry about the height of the heels unless he was really short. Her figure looked beautiful, almost as if it were a couture she was wearing. Her hair hung to her waist, heavy and sleek. Her makeup was minimal—lots of bronzer to complement her dark skin, heavy mascara, and muted red lips. She put on her coat, which was the same length as her dress. Very fitted black wool with heavy silver toggles that clasped like the ones on meat freezers. Victoria walked in and handed her the tangelo orange bag.

"Thanks, Mom," she said as she kissed her. "Well, here goes nothing."

She transferred the stuff in her purse to the big bag, grabbed the photo, and left.

Princeton looked in the mirror and felt nervous. He never was nervous about getting ready to go out. He would usually put himself together without a lot of thought. It never seemed to be that important. Sleek chest, shaved face, and cologne were where he put his efforts. His jeans were perfect as always. Not tight, not loose, worn in exactly right. Slightly frayed at the breaking backs at the bottom of his Diesels. Not messy just right. He had at least twenty pairs of jeans, and every one of them fit perfectly. His brown silk wool Hurley sweater was slightly bulky. His hair was perfectly spiked and messy. He sprayed one more shot of Hugo on his neck and ran his fingers along his face to be sure it was super smooth. He grabbed his keys and Burton jacket and left.

The hostess was directing him to a table. As he canvassed the bar looking to see if Tallulah was there, every girl's eye that he caught responded with an invitation to come over. He ordered a beer and kept his eyes on the door. He felt the stares. He heard the flirtatious giggling. He thought, "God, please give these women something to do." He saw two guys to his right stop their conversation and stare at the door. One was elbowing the other, and then another guy next to them turned to the door. He followed their lead, and when he saw what they were looking at, he took in a deep breath. He couldn't see if she was carrying the photo, but by far, she was the most beautiful woman he ever laid eyes on. "She could be on a magazine cover," he thought. He ran his eyes over her, from her feet to the top of her head. Just the way she was dressed was something he had never seen before.

Then it clicked. "Designer? Please be a designer." He was totally in awe of what he was looking at. She caught his eye, he smiled, and she started walking over. It was then that he saw the photo in her left hand. His heart was beating faster. As she came closer, the guys actually turned to follow her with their eyes. He stood up.

"Tallulah?"

"Hi, Princeton."

She placed the photo on the side of table as he helped her with her coat. She ordered a beer, and that was it. He never felt so relaxed . . . so sure of himself. Their nonstop talk and laughter made them the couple to be constantly stared at. She was truly amazing! She looked directly into his eyes when she spoke, and on the occasion when she touched his hand, he felt this deep warmth inside of him. She had this strong sex appeal. Not in an obvious way. It was her movement, the fierce use of her eyes and hands that was captivating. He wanted her. He wanted her in every way. She concluded ten minutes into their date that she never saw such a beautiful specimen of a man. She loved his gentlemanly quality, yet there was a raw animal essence. "Masculine" was what came to mind. His depth was by far, the strongest part of his sex appeal. She was falling and falling hard. The photo went home with Tallulah that night. What followed was the most obvious, incredible display of love between two people that anyone had ever seen. They were part of each other's thoughts, actions, and desires. Their blood ran through the same veins. It was easy, exhilarating, and permanent. There was no need to discuss the development of their relationship with anyone, and they didn't seek approval from family and friends. Their circle knew what was happening immediately. Each one shocked, amazed, and envious of the pair.

Tallulah's only regret was that she wasn't a virgin for Princeton. She hadn't been with many men. There were only two before him, and they proved to be disastrous. She would try to convince herself that technically it was really only one. Her first time, she didn't completely follow through. She wasn't sure if it was fear or just her intuition to know it wasn't right. Her second attempt was disappointing. The afterward guilt she felt overshadowed any tiny thoughts of romance. She couldn't understand what people went on and on about. She wanted her fantasies fulfilled, and that hadn't happened for her.

Princeton was way ahead of her on that one. His celibacy was a spoken vow he took between himself and God, and he knew why. Their actual conversation took place after her striptease. She was soo wanting him. Her body ached for him, and he was constantly in physical pain. They came close many times, yet each resisted consummating their love.

Tallulah explained her feelings to Princeton. Even though he felt he couldn't take much more of this, hearing her words only impacted his love for her that much more. She spoke to him about Song of Songs, one of her favorite chapters of the Bible. She went on to explain that it was a wedding song honoring marriage. She was firm in her belief that God created intimacy and sex to be shared between a husband and wife. "God is honored when we love and enjoy our submission to one another." She declared her desire to want to please God and thought it fitting, due to her feelings of gratitude for bringing this wonderful man to her.

They committed to re-virginizing themselves until they were husband and wife. Five months later on March 28, 2004, with Victoria, Rachel, and Derek present, they married. Dinner with their circle followed. You would think that Tallulah would want the storybook wedding. What with all of Victoria's traditions, it would be the obvious choice. However, Tallulah and Victoria's ideas about that were quite the opposite. Tallulah kept hearing her mother's words spoken to her through the years, "A wedding doesn't make a marriage. Once that day is over, it's over. The marriage hopefully goes on forever. That vow between two people and God is sacred. When the doors shut to the outside world, it's just the two of you. The show of the wedding is usually for everyone else, and couples sometimes lose themselves in the preparation. It's as if the momentum of the love somehow stops. If you have that momentum, keep it, hold on tight with both feet in, and never look to feel the need to display your love through a wedding. Do whatever your heart tells you to do."

Princeton couldn't be more pleased with Tallulah's desire. Again, she had the same ideas as he. The only challenge was finding a place to live. They wanted so much to be together that Tallulah said, "Whatever we find, it's not going to be our permanent home. We won't put our signature on it. We'll wait until we find our dream house."

*　　*　　*　　*　　*

Zach came up behind her and said, "Miss, that one's not for sale."
Startled, she turned away from the photo and smiled.
"Let's have a cappuccino before I go."
"Deal," he said.

CONSUMED FROM THE INSIDE OUT

Victoria pulled into the driveway seeing the Jeep there, she looked at the clock. "Six thirty, he's early," she thought.

She pulled into the garage, and Princeton came to the car door to meet her.

"Why didn't you go in?" she said.

Victoria never locked her doors.

He leaned over and kissed her and handed her a bottle of wine.

"Apalta '05? You must be selling a lot of work!"

"You should know," he replied with a wink.

He helped her with the packages as she dumped everything on the bench in the kitchen and handed him the bottle opener. She was examining his face, hoping to see the reason for the visit. She knew his expressions and was able to read his body language really well.

"What a beautiful face," she thought.

"The blue or painted ones?" he asked.

"Your choice."

He went to the dining room and retrieved the heavy blue crystal glasses. Victoria took pleasure in watching this contemporary sculptured Adonis pouring wine with such ease and grace. He would have fit in perfectly with her Italian lineage in the streets of Little

Italy. He handed her the glass and sat at the table. "To you," he said as he gently tapped her glass. He took a sip and looked pensive as he rolled the wine around the rim of the glass. Victoria waited patiently for his words to begin.

"Mom, you know Tallulah and I wouldn't be where we are today, if it weren't for you. I could never thank you enough. Not just for the last four years, but for what you did with her your whole life. Aside from your daughter, you're the most amazing woman I know. I love you so much. I'm so in awe of your devotion to us. When I grow up, I want to be just like you."

She laughed. "You came here to tell me this?"

"No, I need to know what happened at lunch today. I need to know what I'm walking into."

"Why?" Victoria asked.

"Because I get this feeling when something is off . . . not quite right with Tallulah. My job is to make her happy. You know some people think that's being whipped or losing your stand as a man. I think it's all macho garbage. I guarantee you, none of them have what I have. If she needs to be right, she could be right 24/7. If she needs more shoes, I'll buy her one hundred pairs because in the big scheme of life, it's nothing. What she gives me isn't worth losing over all the trivial things people get caught up in. That's why we don't argue. People say that's not possible. It's definitely possible if you choose to concentrate on the power you have over each other. That power allows you to hurt that person, and each time you do that, you become less of a man or a woman. Years ago, Tallulah started this game that we play if we're frustrated, irritated, or in disagreement. We shut ourselves down—immediately. We don't speak. We go into deep thought, following the compass of our souls. We force ourselves to stay passionate, keeping our eye on the prize. We force ourselves to not let words roll off our tongues that we can't take back. She saved me. She saved me from myself! You know that better than anyone. Ever since I could remember, I knew she was out there. I didn't know her name or what she looked like, but I knew she was there. It was as if there were two separate lives, being groomed and prepped for one another. How did *you* know I was the one?"

"First of all, you're an amazing man, sitting here professing your love. Do you know how that makes me feel as her mother? In regards to your question, I knew instantly! It was a feeling deep inside. You remind me of myself and Luke, only better . . . much better."

"How is it that you me and Tallulah each had the same feeling?"

Victoria placed her hand over his and looked deep into his eyes and said, "The complexity of our souls all match. You see, we need God to transform us from the inside out. With love, we want to be consumed from the inside out. It's just who we are."

He needed to lock those words in his mind as he repeated them. "The complexity of our souls all match . . . transform, consume, inside out."

"You know that you're my sage, right?"

"Your sage?" Victoria asked.

"Absolutely!" he said.

"Mom, tell me about lunch. Not all the details, just the part that affected Tallulah."

"Well, it was interesting to say the least. Piper went on a tangent about you and Tallulah. She didn't mean any harm; you know how much those two love each other. So let's see. There was the Queen . . . me, the Prince . . . you, and the progression to the throne."

He looked puzzled.

"Reasons why she's not married, your Jeep, and some words about you and Tallulah not having children."

"She said that? Piper brought up the children conversation?"

"No, Tallulah did."

"Why do you think it was made that we can't have kids?" he asked.

"I really don't know, but if I had to guess? I think it would be difficult for the two of you. Your lives are different from others.

Sharing your kind of love . . . changing the design of your life? I think God knows best."

Princeton thought about it and put his glass down.

"You're the best," he said.

He got up to hug her.

"That's it? You're leaving?"

"Yeah, I've got to develop a roll and get home before she does."

She hugged him and walked him to the door.

As he was developing the roll, his mind repeated, "The complexity of our souls match, transform, consume inside out."

He rarely called or texted Tallulah when she was working; he felt it was an intrusion. He thought about it and then said no. On the drive home, he was sifting through the murky contradiction of his emotions. How could he be feeling happiness, panic, peace, and discovery all at the same time? He pulled into their parking lot.

"No Cayenne, great," he thought.

He tossed the salad and left the steaks very rare, so he could flame them later. He grabbed the silverware, glasses, and bottle. He ran upstairs and placed them on the glass table. He grabbed two bottles of lotion and threw them on the bed. He checked the temperature of the running water, threw in the petals, and hit thirty on the timer for the jets. Just as he was lighting the candles, he heard the door slide.

*   *   *   *   *

Max just finished doing the piece he had been working on for hours. It was from one of his custom collections. The attraction to the collection was that once a client got one, it was off the market. The catalogue would have checks next to the ones no longer available. It was truly a one of a kind; he never duplicated it. The guy was checking the finished piece in the mirror, totally thrilled with the work.

"Man, this is beautiful . . . it's exactly like the photo!"

His friend was looking on, thinking, "That's the best piece I've ever seen . . . I'm getting one."

"Max," he said, "I need an appointment . . . I'm next."

Max checked his schedule and set an appointment. He ran the credit card and asked for the signature right below the line that read six hundred dollars. He thought to himself, "Everyone uses plastic, no more money circulating nowadays."

His hand and back ached. Every time he did one of those pieces, it exhausted him. They were so intricate, and the precision required made his hand heavy. He opened and closed his fingers, recirculating the blood, popped two aspirins, and guzzled a bottle of water.

He sat down and flipped through the pages of the catalogue. "My god," he thought. So many pieces were checked. "Have I really done *that* many?" Fortunately, there were still dozens left. Ever since he started the customs, tribal bands became yesterday's news. Longitude and latitude were still popular, but nothing came close to the desires for the customs.

If it weren't for Victoria, he would still be struggling alongside with all the other artists. He was in a class all his own now, and he owed it all to her.

*   *   *   *   *

Piper and Max pulled up to Victoria's. The Cayenne and Jeep sat in one driveway. Zach's BMW was in the other, with Julia's mustang behind it. So he parked behind the Jeep. Piper grabbed her bag and the two bottles of wine. She looked over to him excited and said, "Hail, hail, the gang's all here."

Max laughed.

"Yeah, let the games begin."

They walked into the collage of movement, voices, laughter, and music. Victoria looked up, walked over to them, and gave kisses.

"Here, Ma, something to get you through the day," Piper said as she handed over the bottles.

She looked at the labels, approved of the choice, smiled, and said, "Only two?"

Max laughed as he made his way into the glorious existence of the house. All eyes turned to see the next arrival.

Tallulah announced, "Hey, it's the ink man."

Princeton was sitting at the huge counter, with Tallulah standing behind him, her arms draped on his shoulders. There was an assortment of food and beverages displayed beautifully throughout the kitchen and dining room. Within seconds, Victoria handed each of them a glass of wine, with their usual one ice cube floating on top.

"These are beautiful, Ma," Piper said as she looked at her glass.

"New?" she asked.

"New to this house, but very old. I found them at an estate sale," she replied.

Zach was standing looking out the window, with Julia alongside of him.

"Hey, buddy. Hi, Piper," he said as he and Julia walked toward them.

Julia wasn't sure if she should give them a kiss; after all, she was still new to this. Piper relieved her uncertainty by coming over, giving her a peck, and clinging her glass to her bottle of beer.

"Victoria," Zach said.

"The back looks great, Julia loves the rock garden."

"You think? I wish I had done more wild grass, it's too structured."

"Speaking of structure" Max said, "Where's your mom and dad?" he asked as he looked at Princeton.

Princeton laughed.

"My dad's working, so they're not coming."

Tallulah's mouth came close his ear, saying, "Let's have them over this week, OK?"

"Sure, baby, I'll call them tomorrow."

The conversations were endless, all of them catching up, exchanging stories, and reminiscing. Julia tried to keep up, but there was too much history there. At times, she just listened, so not to have to ask who, where, when.

There was a moment when Princeton looked at Victoria and thought, "All this, for us. Her desire to want us to keep our connection." He felt sad, wishing she had a partner to share this day with.

Victoria orchestrated the gathering with pure joy. She always felt fulfilled when she witnessed the collection of their lives, which were so intermingled. Piper came down the steps after choosing one of the bathrooms upstairs.

"Ma, what are all those sketches on your bed for?" she asked.

"You're in Mom's room again?" Tallulah exclaimed.

"What sketches?" Princeton asked.

"Oh, those are some design patterns I've been working on. You know, in the lonely hours of my existence"—she shot a look to Princeton—"I become inspired."

Tallulah got off the sectional and went upstairs to satisfy her curiosity. "Holy smoke," she thought. There were sooo . . . many. They were scattered on the perfectly made bed, some on the dresser, some on the chaise, all over. She collected them and brought them down to the group. They were passed around and around. Each set of eyes scanning the designs. They were black on white, no color. Beautiful scrolls, emblems, and medallions. Each different, yet they had a common thread. There was a hidden crucifix in each one. Zach announced the find, and the group worked at playing the game of finding the hidden piece. Max was floored. His eyes traveled the pieces carefully, taking time to examine each line.

"Victoria, these are phenomenal! Do you know how many inkers would die to do this kind of work?"

Victoria looked at him, and the light went off.

"Perfect, just perfect," she announced.

"That's what you should do, you should offer these at your shop!"

"No, no, Victoria, I was just making a statement, I didn't mean—" Princeton interrupted.

"Could you do these?"

"I'm not sure," Max replied as he ran his fingers over the work of art. Victoria looked at him. He was so deep in emotion over what he was looking at. She realized at that moment what they were supposed to be used for. Up until now, she wasn't quite sure why she was sketching them. "Thank you, God," she thought.

"OK," she commanded.

"My son," she said, looking at Princeton.

"I'm sure you have a camera in the car. Take shots of all of these. I'm not giving the originals. You, Max, take the photos and start offering them at your shop. Put a high price tag because there was a lot of blood, sweat, and tears that went into each one. Go ahead, Princeton, start snapping."

Piper looked over to Max and swore she saw a tear in his eye. Piper caught Victoria's eye, and her mouth formed a thank-you.

Max said, "Victoria, the only way I can do this is if I give you a percentage."

Tallulah looked at Max and said, "You're joking, right? As if Mom would do that."

There was lots of excitement as the group laid out the sketches; Princeton was snapping each one, using different angles, pausing in between to snap random shots of the moment. Tallulah looked into the lens and blew him a kiss. "Perfect," he thought. As they were carrying on in the family room, Victoria was loading the dishwasher. She was in an inner dialogue of prayer. She was giving thanks for her life and all that were a part of it.

As time went on, Victoria would occasionally go to the shop and drop off photos of new sketches. Max never asked when the next batch was coming. He felt so indebted to her. She never took a penny for her work. She changed his life that day and did it with complete confidence that it was the way it was meant to be.

He put the catalogue down, dialed Charles, read off his credit card numbers, and gave him Victoria's address. Victoria looked at the name coming in on her cell.

"Hi, Victoria, it's Max. I'd like to take you to dinner tomorrow, are you available?"

"Hi, Max." (Every time she thought of Max, his eyes came to mind.)

"How sweet, thank you. I can do five o'clock, does that work?"

Max looked down at his schedule. He had appointments booked, back-to-back. All of them were customs. He crossed out the last name, circled the phone number, so he could call and reschedule and said, "Five is great, your choice."

"Let's do Luna, OK?" she asked.

"Luna it is. See you then."

*   *   *   *   *

Tallulah looked down at the wet withered petals stuck to the tub. "Unbelievable" she thought. Her mind and body were exhausted. Good thing she didn't have anything going on today because her eyes were burning, and she knew she needed to go back to bed. It was amazing to her that Princeton needed so little sleep. She put her head on the pillow and wrapped the blankets around her. The sheets felt so good against her skin. She closed her eyes and tried to sleep. Her mind was working overtime, capturing the memory of last night. Her body was restless. She turned and repositioned her pillow. She was feeling warm and wanted Princeton's hands on her flesh. He had only walked out the door a little while ago, and she wanted him back.

There were a few times on occasion when Tallulah needed Princeton in a different way. Each and every time, he seemed to know exactly what to do. She tried to analyze it every time it happened. It wasn't insecurity . . . more like vulnerability. In some way, it always stemmed from the child conversation. Maybe feelings of inadequacies? She wasn't sure. When she got like this, she needed Princeton to comfort her, somewhat like she needed validation that she was "whole." Not in a soft, gentle way; instead she needed a "raw" connection to his flesh. Last night, as always, he gave her exactly what she needed. His masculinity was on point.

*   *   *   *   *

"Hey, baby," he called down.

"Come upstairs."

She slid the door closed, taking in the aroma of steaks. She placed her bag and the stack of fabrics on the counter and answered his request. When she walked into the bedroom, she immediately smiled seeing the array of lit candles. She started to speak, and he raised his index finger to his mouth with a low "shush." He led her into the bathroom and removed each piece of clothing, deliberately being slow as he kissed each area that the garment had occupied. He lifted her and placed her in the tub. She laid back and closed her eyes. He returned with their glasses, and as he sat on the large perimeter behind her, she sipped her wine. The jets felt wonderful circulating around her body. She opened her eyes to focus on a petal dancing around the jet. They really served no purpose other than creating an ambiance that she loved. He moved her heavy mane to one side and placed his mouth to her neck. The touch of his mouth made her body respond immediately. He traveled his mouth to her chin and caught a glimpse of her tears. His heart immediately ached. He dug both arms into the water as her hands held on to his neck. He lifted her out and carried her dripping wet body to the bed. He placed her on her back and placed himself on top of her and lifted her upper body with his hands. His mouth was exploring her wet skin. His jeans were soaking up the water, and the feel of them against her skin was a blanket, keeping her warm. Her voice was strong.

"Baby, I need you . . . only you."

When she was like this, it ignited a response that Princeton became familiar with. It was this tremendous sense of being in charge. She wanted him to take her as her protector, as her safety. It made him crazy, feeling this surge of command. The more she spoke, the more he became full of a passion that ripped his body in different directions. The two of them desperate for one another . . . she begging, and he using every muscle to satisfy their hunger. They had each other over and over again. Her voice of pleasure in his ears, driving him to lift her, turn her, please her. His strong body was orchestrating every move as she allowed herself to succumb to each request. He would get her to a pivotal point, where her moaning was echoed with her body arched, and he found the strength to force himself to hold back. Each time he stopped, he would slowly begin the journey again . . . until he drained her of every ounce of strength and insecurity. Each time her body and her eyes begged for him, it served to give him the power needed, to make certain that his beautiful woman knew he understood her. All that lay beneath the surface was being understood and loved. His sole desire was to give her what she needed. When there was nothing left to give because he fed her body and soul, he turned to filling her mind and heart. They ate in bed with one dish, each feeding the other. He pulled every thought, every insecurity out of her. He spoke to her of his complete devotion and admiration for her being the woman she was. They exchanged thoughts and desires and proclaimed their love for one another through descriptions of tracing their life together thus far. He made her laugh, cry, and exercise her memory remembering all she had done for him through the years. Then he would begin the journey again . . .

In a light moment, she jumped off the bed, put on his tee shirt, and said, "Oh! I have something for you!"

She ran downstairs, searched her bag for the CD, and ripped the wrapper off. She bolted upstairs. Princeton was lying on the bed. She propped up two pillows, and he sat up. She reached past him as she put the CD into the massive stereo unit. That was his baby. She remembered when he and the electrician worked on it for days. The entire house was wired for sound, but Princeton was very specific about how he wanted the bedroom done. The unit was wired into the wall behind the headboard. The speakers were under the California king bed— literally under the bed. They were encased in the floor surrounding the perimeter. The electrician said he never saw anything like it.

As she laughed, she declared, "OK, baby, here's talent in the making!"

He loved when she was playful like this; it touched his heart. He felt satisfied that he accomplished changing her mood and mind-set. She grabbed the hairbrush, stood at the foot of the bed, and tapped it as to test the microphone. He laughed.

She commanded, "Hit Play, it's the first song."

He was so excited to see what this was about.

He looked at her with his beautiful smile and said, "Baby, take it easy on me because I'm still recovering here," and then he hit Play.

The song started immediately.

Tallulah began to sing . . .

Closed off from love, I didn't need the pain
Once or twice was enough, And it was all in vain
Time starts to pass, Before you know it you're frozen . . .

She started to two-step, her hips moving. She pointed to him, signifying the connection of the message of the song. She was gesturing each lyric, keeping to the beat, and moving her body seductively.

She dramatically pounded her heart, expressing her bleeding love. He was elated, mesmerized, and blushing. He had heard the song the first time only a few days ago and loved parts of the lyrics that he was able to understand. Now his beautiful lady was putting her heart out there for him to hold in his memory and hand.

As she repeated the chorus, still moving seductively, she came toward him and sat on his stomach, straddling his body. She continued to sing and move in close, touching his face, chest, still keeping the beat. She horizontal danced him as she was lost in the words.

As the chorus repeated two more times, she completed the song, while stripping him with her eyes. She was so intense; every word was directed to him and his heart. As she hit the Stop button, he grabbed her, rolled her around the bed, and said, "Baby, you're killing me. My heart is hurting because of how much I love you."

Her last thought before she closed her eyes, resting on his chest was, "I wouldn't want to live without this man."

*   *   *   *   *

She forced her eyes open to focus on the empty pillow next to her. It was still dark, and she thought, "I'm so tired, how am I going to do this?" She threw the covers off and searched the bed and the floor. Finding his tee shirt and her panties, she put them on and walked to Princeton's weight room. It was her idea to designate two large spaces to accommodate a dressing room and a weight room. There was so much square footage, and to use it for additional bedrooms seemed such a waste. She stopped in the doorway and watched his body come down, hands clenched behind his neck. As he lifted himself back up, completing the Roman sit-up, his abs expanded. The familiar lyrics from the stereo and the empty water bottles on top of the compact fridge made her conclude that he was in here for a while.

She grabbed two towels from the stack of dozens on the table and started to roll one. She knew the drill. As his body came back down again, his head brushed along her stomach as she stood behind him. He completed the sit-up, released his heels from the pads, and sat up. He turned to her and said, "Hey, baby," as he ran his fingers through his hair.

She handed him the folded towel, and he dried his face.

"Couldn't sleep?" she asked.

Before he could answer, she put the rolled towel on the large thick rug and waited for him to lay on his stomach spread-eagle. The routine was second nature to both. He rested the side of his face on the roll, and she sat on his back straddling him with her knees resting on the rug. She reached up, grabbed a lotion, and slowly poured it on his back. It was only minutes ago that he was wishing for this. He had hoped she would come and relieve all his fears. Her hands worked at distributing the lotion, massaging his muscles. She was afraid to speak, not wanting to hear the explanation that she already knew. Princeton's mind and body were relaxing. It felt so good, so satisfying. Every time she worked a muscle, he heard himself whisper, "Oh, baby, right there . . . that feels sooo good."

Tallulah started to speak, careful not to sound alarmed, because she was truly concerned. As her hands continued to move, she asked, "Bad dream? Or are you hoping for Mr. Universe?"

"Dream . . . same one," he said.

The dream jolted him up, feelings of anxiety and nervousness covered him. He got his bearings, looked over to see Tallulah sleeping, kissed her forehead, and made his way to the weight room. As he walked, he recited to himself, "God takes away all doubt, fear, and loneliness."

"It's only a dream, baby, it's not real," she whispered.

Real or not, the effects left him panicked. The pit in his stomach, with his heart racing, only subsided when he concentrated on his workout. Tallulah heard his breathing, deep and steady. She looked down at him to confirm he was asleep. She got up, grabbed the folded comforter, and lay next to him on the floor, covering him first, then herself.

*   *   *   *   *

Now as she lay in bed trying to sleep, restless, she thought, "How can he not be exhausted after last night? He couldn't have slept more than two hours!" It was either feelings of guilt that Princeton was off at work or that she had too much on her mind, but she wasn't able to sleep. "Tomorrow's the fund-raiser," she thought. "Let me put that together." She put on her sweats, went downstairs, and checked the coffee filter. Full, all set to go. She hit the button and thought, "He never ceases to amaze me." She looked at the beautiful space before her, eyes canvassing each object. She and Princeton were at the "museum state" right now. That's how she referred to the times when the house wasn't being lived in because of their schedule or the need to be alone with one another. They would have peaks and valleys. Sometimes there were lots of gatherings with their circle and family, and sometimes it was stagnant. At that moment, she was glad she forced herself out of bed; she needed to reconnect with her home.

She sat at the table with her coffee, going over the list she pulled out of her bag. "Boy, Mom and I kill a lot of trees," she thought to herself. She and Victoria had lists for everything. Victoria once said, "Putting a check next to an item on her list actually made her smile." She hit the button on her cell and sipped her coffee.

"Slept in?" Victoria asked.

"Yeah . . . hi, Mom! Is there anything you need help with for tomorrow?" she asked.

"No, we're all set. This was an easy one. Since last month, I really haven't done anything, except confirm the arrangements. Are you looking forward to it?" Victoria asked.

"Absolutely, we're due for some dancing."

"Where's my son?" she asked.

"At work. I used two of his series this month. He needs to replenish."

"Fabulous! Finished with the Richards project?" she asked.

"Finally . . . yes. They referred me to Tom White."

"*The* Tom White?" Victoria exclaimed.

"The one and only. I'm not big on working with politicians, they're so boring," she said.

"Well, boring or not, that's great news."

"Mom, do you want to help me with this one?"

"Maybe . . . we'll see. Right now, I have things to do, and I'm having dinner with Max tonight," she said.

"He's too young for you," Tallulah teased.

Victoria laughed. "Why? It seems to work for Ashton and Demi."

"OK, I'll let Piper know he's off the market."

"Have you seen her?" Victoria asked.

"No, I'm calling her, right after I hang up."

"OK, talk to you later, love you."

"Love you too."

She continued to drink her coffee as she looked over to the large stack of mail in the basket. She sighed and thought, "There needs to be at least ten more hours to each day." She knew Sophie was coming tomorrow and summarized, "Not much here, but upstairs is enough to keep her busy." That's the way it always was. The first floor was basic. Large but basic: kitchen, bathroom, office, and the living space. The second floor had the master suite, two guest rooms, two bathrooms, the dressing room, and the weight room. There was major laundry, stacks of CDs everywhere, and the fridge always needed restocking. Sophie knew exactly where everything went. Tallulah remembered her resistance when Princeton announced his decision.

"Baby, I want you to find someone to come in once a week to take care of the house."

"I can do it, it's not necessary," she said.

"I know you *can* do it, I just don't want you to. I don't want you spending an entire day cleaning our house. That time can be used for work, friends, family, or most importantly, us. It's not like we can't afford it, and it would be the best money we ever spent. Trust me."

She trusted him, and now walking upstairs, she was so glad she did. The laundry alone would be half a day's work. Her laundry was minimal, usually active wear and lingerie. Everything else went directly to the cleaners. She took care of that. Her habit was to drop them off the next day, so that if anything came up suddenly, it was ready. She called the dry cleaning bill her second mortgage. Now Princeton, that was a different story. He had a zillion pairs of jeans, shirts, and hoodies. If the laundry wasn't done for a month, he'd still be safe.

She remembered walking Sophie through the house, explaining and directing what she wanted done. Some things were more important than others. The dressing room was the biggest challenge. It was huge and well used. When you walked in through the beautiful French doors, you were transported into a reproduction of an upscale boutique. The walls and ceiling were flat black, with a pattern of large scrolls and leaves. It took Victoria a week to hand paint that design in the stunning chartreuse-and-white effect. The results were bold and very elaborate. It not only covered all the walls, but it continued on the encased pocket doors of the twenty-two feet of closet space. Your eyes couldn't help but to rest on the magnificent lighting. The antique chandelier was ornate and massive in size. There were layers of opulent crystals connected with burnished black metal. The crowning medallion, from which it hung, was in itself a work of art. The deep grooves of the white plaster floriated design pocketed specs of black paint to give the impression of delicate aging. On each side of the glorious statement sat two Roman columns that floated dead center of the room. It was very palatial. In between the columns, there was a white damask chaise and two green pindot slipper chairs. They were arranged in a semicircle on the round brocade rug. The ebony hardwood floors were repeated throughout the house as were the style of the window treatments. (Tallulah insisted on having the continued flow in all rooms of not only her house, but also her clients. That included repeat of flooring and all hardware on doors.) Floor-to-ceiling windows mirrored the one's downstairs. Soft, iridescent silk panels bordered the sides, falling into pools of chartreuse color against the dark floor. They were strictly used for design appeal as not to obstruct the natural light of the beautiful paned glass. It was fortunate that there were not neighboring buildings, so the drapes were never drawn.

One entire wall was dedicated to mirrors, the same as the weight room. The opposite wall was an enormous built-in. Half of it housed a multitude of folded tees and hoodies. The other half was home to a ridiculous amount of shoes. Even though it held dozens, there was only enough space for seasonal. The remaining boxes were stored in the closet, waiting for their turn to sit on the shelves. Two large white lacquer dressers accommodated undergarments and socks. The black pulls had green tassels hanging from each one. The shock value came in the form of broken pieces of white granite adhered to the walls. Each piece held an antique hook, which was used for dozens of hats and caps. The only vacant hooks were the T hook and the P hook. The letters were painted in black on the granite and were used for the ensemble to be worn on a particular day. A small door opened to shelves, with bags lined up like soldiers according to color. Evening gloves and silk scarves were now transferred into the newest addition—the credenza. To sum it all up, it was breathtaking.

When Sophie first walked into the room, all she could muster was "My! My!" Piper often said she could live in that one room, if Tallulah would add a kitchen. She glanced at the room on her way back downstairs and smiled with satisfaction. She grabbed the mail, started to open it, and hit the button on her cell.

DREAM ON

Princeton couldn't concentrate on driving as he switched lanes. He had visions of Tallulah running through his mind. Lots of little snapshots of their glorious night. Fragments of each episode of emotion made his heart beat faster. The vision of her face, eyes, and body, as they reached heights of passion, made his body warm. The laughter, conversations, and her version of "Bleeding Love" kept echoing in his ears. It was always like that. He could recapture their moments and relive them over and over again.

Now as he threw the Jeep into park, he forced himself to hit the Stop button in his mind. He let out a deep sigh and walked into the studio.

Zack looked up smiled and said, "Hey, buddy," as he poured Princeton a cup of coffee. Princeton looked at him and thought that Zach really had become such an important part of his career. He was dedicated and dependable. Always there on time, making sure fresh flowers were placed perfectly, keeping the steady stream of cappuccinos, separating mail, and most importantly working the clients relentlessly. He knew not only their names, but also their spouses' and children's names. He kept in constant contact with each client, sending out announcements of new pieces, birthday cards, and handwritten thank-you's. Clients enjoyed his persona. He once told Princeton that he believed that every person that walked in the studio was hoping they could catch a moment with the artist. He said it was easy keeping them around because secretly they were waiting for him.

At that moment, Princeton was so glad that he had picked up a gift for Zach. There was no question that Princeton paid him generously. As a matter-of-fact, Zach would openly declare, "My BMW was paid for by the Prince." However now, as he looked around, he wanted to show his appreciation.

As Zach stirred the coffee, Princeton walked out. Zach called after him, "Something I said?" Within minutes, he was back with a box in his hand. He walked over, sat on the stool, took his coffee, and slid the box over to Zach.

"I picked you up something because I thought you would really like it."

Zach looked at Princeton with an expression of excitement and surprise. Princeton canvassed his face and thought, "He really is good looking, sort of a Mario Lopez." Zach caught a glimpse of some of the words on the box and was hoping it was what he thought it was. He opened it, and when his eyes saw the incredible camera, he was speechless. He kept looking at it, running his fingers along the border of the lens. His first thought was, "Wow, super expensive!" Even if he wanted to buy one himself, he wouldn't know what to look for. Princeton had all the knowledge and all the right connections.

He was truly touched. Not only because of the purchase, but because it came with the message that Princeton thought he had potential. He was connected to Princeton's world in a very personal way. He immediately envisioned himself working with his new gift—learning and taking direction. He had a surge of anticipation that made him feel like he couldn't wait to get started.

"Wow . . . wow! Princeton, thanks so much . . . I don't know what to say."

"Your face says it . . . you deserve it. I'll get you started on it next week. Check our appointments, and maybe we can shoot Monday afternoon, maybe close early? Tomorrow is the fund-raiser . . . and Thursday's at our house. We'll figure it out. Ready for tomorrow?"

"Are you kidding me? I can't wait. Makenzie is a wreck, she's really nervous about meeting everyone for the first time."

"Well, I'm looking forward to meeting her, especially when I hear you on the phone. Seems like you've been hit hard, my friend."

Zach laughed. "We'll see."

Princeton looked down at the name on his cell.

"Hey . . . where you been?" Princeton asked.

"Trying to be as successful as you," Max replied.

"Busy?"

"Crazy busy, the customers are blowing out the doors."

Princeton's thought went to that day at Victoria's when she became Max's lifeline.

"Mom really gives you a big part of herself; I know those sketches take up a lot of her time and creativity."

"I know . . . that's why I sent a dozen sterlings to her today, and I'm taking her to dinner tonight."

Princeton felt a twinge that he didn't like. It was somewhat a pang of jealousy. Special moments with Victoria was his. He pushed to dismiss it, feeling ashamed, because Victoria deserved it. She deserved to be wined and dined, and Max deserved to take in all her wisdom.

"Excellent, where are you taking my beautiful mother-in-law?"

"We're meeting at Luna. Her pick."

"Order a bottle of Antiyal 2004 and definitely get her the scallops as an appetizer."

"Are you prepping me for my date? Give me some credit here, I can handle it. Victoria and I have had dinner before."

"Alone?" he asked.

"No! With the rest of the people at the restaurant! What's up with you?"

"Nothing, forget it. You and Piper ready for tomorrow?"

"She's never ready. I'm surprised she's not at your house ripping your closet apart. She probably would be, if she didn't have a big presentation today. I myself am not as fortunate as you. I'm getting my chest waxed tomorrow morning. Other than that I'm ready."

Max was referring to Tallulah waxing Princeton's chest. It started years ago, and since then, no one ever touched his chest again.

"Yeah well, you gotta give her some incentive," Princeton said sarcastically.

Max laughed. "Oh, I see! Are you suggesting that I'm falling short on my sex appeal?"

Princeton laughed and asked, "So was there a reason for this call, or are you just missing me, honey?"

The two of them enjoyed bantering their sarcasm. It went back to their days of coexisting. Max was famous for his divorce plea when they butted heads. Without a doubt, they were each other's best friend, with a long history to prove it.

"Oh yeah, yeah, the reason, wanna do the game Saturday? We'll have to use your tickets because mine are for the winning team."

Each had season tickets, Max for the Sox and Princeton for the Yankees.

"Definitely! We're overdue. Just tell Piper not to be a walking billboard for that pitiful team. That's why we get stared down."

"No, buddy. We get stared down because we're hot!"

"OK, I've had enough of you. See you tomorrow."

He hung up before Max could continue.

He walked over to the desk, watching Zach playing with his new toy. He sat down and looked up at the collection of photos above the desk. He zeroed in on the one of Tallulah blowing him a kiss, and he blew her a kiss. Zach caught it out of the corner of his eye and thought, "Man, I want that. I want to feel that way about someone." Princeton spun the chair around and looked at the stack of photos. Each one was tagged, which meant signatures, titles, and pricing. That was his thing. Each one also needed to be framed, and index cards had to be typed and framed. That was Zach's thing. Displaying them was key and time consuming. He and Zach partnered on that. So as he looked at the stack, he knew he was in for a long day. By tonight, he knew he would be spent. The thought of relaxing in the hot tub, with a massage to follow, gave him the burst of energy to get up, adjust the volume on the stereo. "Too low," he thought and walked over to the day's work.

Zach heard the music heighten, and was so happy Princeton was there. It was always so much better when he was in the studio. He looked forward to their day together.

*   *   *   *   *

As Tallulah scanned the bill, the upbeat voice said, "Hey, chickie, how's my favorite girl?"

"Piper! I miss you . . . come over, so we can destroy my closet, eat junk food, and go on and on about our undying love for Brad and Angelina."

Piper laughed. "Well, unlike you, I have a clock to punch, and today is my big presentation for Porsche. If the boards don't go over well, my short skirt might get the account."

"I'm sure you look incredible, and I'm sure your presentation will be flawless."

"Keep going." Piper was being her witty self.

"I just really miss you . . . lots."

"Well, let's see. We'll be together tomorrow, Thursday's at your house, and Max texted me that we're doing your broken-down team's game on Saturday."

"We are? That's news to me. Don't wear that ridiculous Red Sox cap, it's embarrassing."

"Not as embarrassing as yours! Listen, I got to go. Wish me luck! Better yet, talk to your friend upstairs and put in a good word. I'll call you later."

"Not that you need it, but good luck, and I'll put in a good word. Oh! Piper . . . Piper . . ."

"Yeah," Piper responded, just as she was about to hang up.

"Mom is having dinner with your man tonight . . . just thought you wanted to know."

Piper picked up on the slight sarcasm.

"Great, just great." More sarcasm. "Now I have to sit through the two-hour inquisition with Max."

"Be prepared," Tallulah said.

"You can never be prepared for that. Ciao, bella."

She refilled her cup and dragged herself upstairs to straighten up the aftermath of last night. "OK, first the sheets," she thought as she walked into the bedroom. She stripped the bed and gathered the glasses, silverware, and dish. She was making piles of what needed to go where. After cleaning the petals from the tub, she stopped to throw her hair up and change her shirt. As she took off his tee, she closed her eyes, held it up to her nose, trying to extract his scent. His cologne was always evident on everything he wore. She took a deep breath and smiled. A flash of his face looking down at her, with his body pressed against her, ran though her mind. She heard herself say, "I love you." She threw the tee into the pile of dirty laundry and replaced it with a clean one. Not one of hers . . . one of his. She walked into the weight room and collected the towels and comforter and made a pile on the floor. She started to put the CDs back in their case, when she picked up the red one. "Unbelievable," she thought. Aerosmith's "Dream On" repeated for the entire length of the CD.

Princeton once explained to her that was the one and only song that he could work out to. The song had strength, and when the music climaxed, it would consume him to push harder. He believed it was the sexiest song he ever heard in his life. There was something about it that connected to his soul. The lyrics explained exactly what he believed all his life. He concluded, "If a song has a longevity of thirty-five years, it has to be a masterpiece." She knew that he had an exact copy of the CD in his car, yet it was never played when anyone was with him. She would sometimes hear the loud sounds of Tyler's voice when he was pulling in the driveway. His license plate read DREAMON. The eyes reading it assumed it to be a positive message. However, Tallulah knew different. She often wondered if Max knew Princeton's heartfelt feelings about the song or if he just thought it was his music of choice for working out. He never worked out to anything else—never. She could testify to that because there were times when she would sit on the floor in the doorway of the next room. She would position herself so that he couldn't see her, and she would witness an hour or sometimes more of his body and spirit working his muscles to that song.

Sing with me, Sing for the Year
Sing for the laughter, sing for the tear
Sing with me, if it's just for today
Maybe tomorrow the good Lord will take me away

As the music would start to mount, Princeton looked lost in the lyrics, the rhythm, and himself. He would be singling along . . . powerful, emotional, somewhat painfully searching. As he progressed and his breathing was saved for his reps, he would close his eyes, and you would know he was singing along internally.

It seemed to be his proclamation, and he never grew tired of it, not once! She would sit there watching him, lost in the image of his body. Captivated by his endurance, strength, and sense of resiliency. The entire time the echoes of "Dream On" playing over and over again.

She would think to herself, "That's mine . . . that beautiful man is mine!" and she would lose herself in prayer. Thanking God for him, asking God to keep him safe and healthy. Asking God to walk with him, to touch his heart, to relieve all fears and anxieties, and always, always pleading that they should never be apart. As she placed the CD in its case and stored it on the huge rack, she wondered if he ever knew about her watching his workout. If he did, he never mentioned it, just as the song was never mentioned to anyone.

There were times when Tallulah thought that Princeton should have been a musician. He had perfect understanding of lyrics, and his body naturally found the beat and rhythm. She concluded, it was his *love* of music that made her think that way. She threw the empty water bottles in the trash, got one out of the fridge for herself, and walked into the dressing room. As she passed the guest suite, she thought about tucking Zack in. She was hoping Makenzie would be "the one."

She slid the pocket doors and fingered through Versaces, Dolce & Gabbanas, Hollisters, Diesels, and Armanis. She thought, "You think you have enough jeans, Princeton?" The denim parade never seemed to end. That was the bulk of his closet. The storage units above held massive amounts of sweaters and scarves. Ralph Lauren Black Label, Dolce & Gabbana, Burberry—nothing trendy. Big classic sweaters quietly contemporary, of the best quality. Scarves were his insignia. He thoroughly enjoyed the pairing of scarves and gloves long before it became an esquire statement. Tallulah thought, "Fall is definitely your season, Mr. Princeton." There was a small space for high-ticket designer suits and shirts. Even though he looked amazing in after-five, she also preferred his denim parade. It suited him. She eyed the Ralph Lauren Black Label and took it out. She unzipped the garment bag and placed it on the chaise. She traveled the shirts until her eyes rested on the perfect collar. She checked to make sure it would accommodate cufflinks and laid it next to the suit. "Great combo," she thought, "now let's give you a little European flair." She hit the button, and the carousel of belts turned slowly. She stopped it and thought, "Forgot about this one . . . perfect." The basic black belt had an intricate cutout pattern on the small gunmetal buckle. She held it up to the waist of the slacks, smiled, and placed it on the chaise. Shoes were easy. A. Testoni. Done! Just as she was ready to hang the collection on the large P hook, she remembered her gift. She opened the credenza drawer and lifted her gloves to reveal the box. She opened it, and the beautiful tiny aqua stones that sat in the hexagon sparkled. She placed the box in his shoe.

She slid the doors on her closet and took out the velvet hanger and unzipped the garment bag. As she looked at it, she started to have second thoughts. She was so sure when she bought it. It was exactly how she wanted to look and feel. Fresh, current, and different. She didn't want to be sleek and black. She was tired of all the Stepfords in their after-five uniforms. She suddenly realized, she wasn't second-guessing herself; it was everyone else that she was unsure of. They might not get it; after all, this was Connecticut. "Well, Tallulah, it wouldn't be the first time," she said to herself as she stripped down. She stepped into the bouffant dress, fastened the neck, zipped the back, buckled the belt, and looked in the mirror. She loved the image of what she saw. It was sexy yet very soft. The fabric was sheer buttercup organza, with soft grey muted appliqués. The halter had an uplift that exposed exactly the right amount of cleavage. There was no back. The black patent leather belt sat on her skin in the back because it only zippered to right about her tailbone. The layers of fabric on the bottom were slightly flared so that there was movement as it danced around her thighs. She stepped into her Marc Jacobs black patent peep toes. All five inches of them. She tied a knot in her hair at the nape of her neck so that it covered the clasp, and then lifted enough to reveal her entire back. She found her sheer, crocheted wrist gloves and attached a black stone earring to each one on the ruffle. When she looked into the mirror again, her first thought was "Thank you, Mom. Thank you for allowing me to understand this!" She looked at her gloves. She couldn't explain the way evening gloves made her feel, but Victoria said it was a piece of glamour that never should have went away. Princeton came to know of evening gloves early on. She had white beaded kidskin ones for the winter and sheer appliqués for the summer. They were one of the few things she collected. Other people had Hummels; she had evening gloves. They became a mission every time she and Princeton were in Soho or specialty shops or estate sales. Princeton was intrigued with them. He thought they were one of the sexiest statements a woman could make. As a matter-of-fact, the ones she had on were his find. He scooped them up at one of the boutiques as a customer was eyeing them. That was on one of their city trips.

*   *   *   *   *

They would plan a day trip every month, so that it would combine business and lots of pleasure. They would suck up all the facets of the city that was humanly possible in twenty-four hours. They would hit the bowery in hopes of Tallulah finding the perfect pieces for clients. Then visit ABC so she could get some instant inspiration. She would tour guide him through Little Italy and the village. Then off to Barneys and Fifth Avenue in and out of the finest boutiques and jewelers. Lunch or dinner, or both, at sidewalk bistros, squeeze in a little gallery hopping to view the up and coming artists, and always, always ending at Serendipity and then to their hotel of choice. They always stayed over, they always had lots of packages, and they always had the discussions Princeton initiated, probing Tallulah's memory.

She transported him to a place that he wished he was a part of. As they walked through the streets, Tallulah would point something out and say, "Mom and I would love to go there and people watch." His heart would jump, trying to imagine his Tallulah and this part of her life. He hated not being connected to it. He wanted to be a part of every dot that connected the finished picture. When they first started dating, Princeton asked her to be his eyes and ears of her childhood and tour him around the city. He would lose himself in deep thoughts as he walked. He would think, "My baby walked these streets as a child." He wished he was right next to her, seeing what she was seeing. Hearing Victoria teach and explain. It was foreign to him, yet there was something very comforting about it all. Serendipity became their soul to soul. The first time they went in, Tallulah started reminiscing about how much she loved it there when she was a child. Victoria would take her there to end a day of go-sees, when Tallulah was doing print ads. They would laugh and laugh, and Victoria would declare her love for her wonderful little girl. Sometimes she would bring a friend, and Victoria would make them the princesses of the day. They would each have a magic wand, which they stopped to purchase at Bloomies. They were able to make special wishes and cast magical spells on the patrons at Serendipity. Tallulah remembered that game to be the most wonderful time ever. Victoria would fuel their imaginations with tales of the prince and princess. She would give them special words needed to cast different spells. "Dream, dream, this I beam" was for spells on little girls. "Dragon, dragon, red, red, wagon" was for little boys. "Dove, dove, this is for love" was for couples. That one would always make the girls giggle. Princeton was amazed that she remembered each word so clearly. There was a moment when Tallulah was telling Princeton about her birthday at Rockefeller Center. They were ice skating and having a great time. They had dinner and then off to Serendipity. She started to tell him about the beautiful present her dad handed her, and then she just stopped. Her eyes filled up, she put her head in her hands, and she never finished. Princeton was lost as to know how to comfort her. At the time, that wound was so new, so fresh, that he was in unfamiliar territory. His heart was aching for her. He moved his chair over to her, and with his mouth to her ear, he whispered, "It's OK, baby. It's OK to hurt. I'm here for you; I'll never leave you, never. Your dad sees us, and he knows our hearts. He's so happy for you right now. It's OK to cry. That's your heart telling you it was a tender memory."

After that, it became their special place. Every time they watched *Serendipity* at home, Tallulah would say, "Look, baby, there we are!"

Princeton grew to absolutely love that movie.

*　　*　　*　　*　　*

She turned to view herself at all angles. She examined every move she made to be sure the dress moved with her and not against her. She focused on her legs. Although they were tan, they needed to be glossy. She reminded herself to glaze them. That was a trick Victoria took with her from her modeling days. Tallulah never wore hose; she hated the feel of them. They felt artificial and interfered with the wonderful fabrics touching her skin. Glazing was a process that left your legs looking like glass. You applied lots of cream, and before it dried, you would gently spray a hair-finishing product. She took her last look and was thrilled! As she undressed and was hanging it on the T hook, she was hoping that Princeton would love it. His opinion was far more important than her own.

*　　*　　*　　*　　*

Zach took the photo off the wall and sighed.

"What are we looking for here?" he asked.

Princeton was deep in thought as he looked at the empty space.

"I'm not sure. I can't quite get it right."

They were at this for hours. Everything was moving along smoothly. Zach was displaying a series of photos of children. They weren't close-up portraits; they were candid shots of children in their natural environments. Somewhere playing, some eating, one of the children waiting at the school bus stop in the foreground, with others shadowed behind him. Zach announced, "These are incredible!" Now hours later, they were stuck with the proper placement on the wall. Each time Zach put them up, Princeton would stand back and say, "No, something is missing."

"All right, buddy," Zach said exhausted, "make the call."

Princeton looked at him and smiled. He grabbed his cell, positioned himself far enough to view the empty space, and hit the button. Tallulah's heart skipped a beat as she answered.

"Hey, baby, what you doing?" he asked.

"Missing you! Are you coming home early? I think you need a date with the hot tub. You must be exhausted! Please, please, come home early!"

"Slow down, baby. As soon as I'm done, I'm there. If you weren't so good at selling my work, I wouldn't have to be here now, doing this. I can't wait to be home with you, baby."

Zach couldn't help but listen.

"Amazing," he thought.

"Did they ever tire of each other? Did their love take them through every day wanting each other? How is that possible?" He just stood there, waiting for his direction.

"OK, baby, I need your help. Walk me through this OK?"

Tallulah stopped what she was doing to give her full attention to his request.

"Go," she said.

"We're working with the wall above the coffee bar."

"The entire wall?" she interrupted.

"Yeah, from column to column," he responded. He took in a deep breath, hoping the subject wouldn't affect her.

"We have eight shots of children, natural habit, somewhat of an urban feel. Do we row or scatter? Something is missing, I can't figure it out."

Tallulah was sitting on the floor with her eyes closed and imagined herself walking in and looking at the wall. She focused on the size of the space and thought about what would impact her.

"What age group?" she asked.

"Uh . . . about five through ten."

Princeton looked at Zach, who was patiently waiting as he listened to silence. He thought to himself, "C'mon, baby, save me here as you always do." Tallulah was almost there; she saw it slowly coming together. Princeton grabbed his water as he held the dead phone. Zach mirrored his movement and grabbed his. They "toasted" their bottles and guzzled the Evian. Finally, her voice asked, "Do you still have the shots we took in the city? The ones of Houston Street and Amsterdam Avenue?"

"Yeah, I have a few left. That was a great day!"

"Perfect! Just perfect. One row on the left of the kids, vertical, four down. Same on the right. Leave a lot of space in between the two rows, but hang the verticals tight. In the center, place three of the city shots vertical. One beneath the other, but traveling down as steps. If you still have it, use the one of the boarded-up tenement as the center focus. Voila! Done!"

Princeton immediately became excited with the direction. He could see it. It was powerful.

"Do you know how much I need you?" he asked.

"No, tell me again! Actually, save that thought so you can tell me when your beautiful arms are wrapped around me."

"Love you, baby."

"Love you too," she replied as she hung up.

"OK, Zach," Princeton announced.

"This is going to be great! It's poetry!"

Zach was ready with anticipation; he became accustomed to this process.

"What are we doing?" he asked.

"Well, first, let's get the city shots out."

"Which ones?" he asked.

"I'll get them. You take those down."

The two of them worked diligently to follow Tallulah's precise instructions. Zach hung the last index card, and they both stepped far back to view their project.

"Wow! I mean, wow! That's a masterpiece," Zach exclaimed.

It was perfect; deep and somewhat joyful and sad. Princeton was in awe. Not only because it portrayed exactly what it was supposed to, but because *she* knew that, she knew his work, and she knew his heart.

"Who has it better than me? Just look what my lady can do. God's hand is on our shoulders, you know that, right?"

Zach looked over at Princeton and couldn't help himself by asking, "I might be too personal here, but are you two always in sync? I mean you've been together for years, are there times when you're just not into each other? You know, like normal people? I'm sorry, I shouldn't have asked that, but it's so unbelievable, sometimes it's scary."

"In answer to your question, yes, we're always in sync. No, we're never *not* into each other! We need each other . . . to be each one separately. God made it that way. We were groomed for the expectation of us. Yeah, sometimes we're sick, physically. You know, a cold or flu. But even then we depend on each other to know what the other needs."

"Why do you think you and Tallulah were . . . so to speak . . . chosen?" Zach asked.

"We believe it resulted in years of work and preparation. Long before we were adults. It was being manifested through the life of Victoria and others."

Zack loved to listen to Princeton when he became deep and rooted. Sometimes he didn't understand what Princeton was saying, but he basked in the aura of feeling like he was part of something that was meaningful and above other's understanding.

"Do you think I'll ever have that?" he asked.

"I don't know," Princeton replied.

"But each day you need to get into contact with your soul. Listen to your heart and be open to God's plan."

"You tell me that, but I'm not sure what that means."

"Have you been reading *the* book and the others Tallulah gave you?"

"Yeah . . ."

"Then give it time and be honest with yourself. Not until you surrender will you be ready."

"See, that's what I mean. I don't even understand what you're saying right now."

Princeton smiled and put his arm around Zach's shoulder. He walked him over to the stools, and they sat down. Princeton faced him, and his eyes locked into Zach's.

"Be patient, buddy. Don't look for answers all the time. Sometimes you have to sacrifice some of yourself to find yourself. We were made to be *in* the world, but not *of* the world." Zack sat there listening. "When you give in and get sucked up by the world's never-ending desires to want more, be more, have more, you become everyone else. You start treating people with no regard. Especially woman. They're used as objects for selfish motives. Don't be part of that. Loneliness can sometimes be your friend. Believe me, I know. It's like you're all dressed up with nowhere to go. Stay dressed, don't give up. One day, someone will knock at your door to go to the party."

Zach felt like he was going to cry. He was full of emotion and inspiration.

"You know, I should pay *you* for working here."

"Done! No more paychecks for you!"

Princeton looked up at the wall as he started an internal prayer. Zach wanted to continue the conversation, but turned to see the man walking in and went to greet him.

"Hi, how are you?" Zach asked as he extended his hand.

"I'm Zach."

The man smiled, extended his hand, and said, "I'm good. Larry."

"Can I get you something to drink, Larry? Espresso, cappuccino, water?" Zach asked.

The man's eyes started to canvass the walls.

"I'll have a cappuccino, thank you."

Zach walked over to the bar and started his request. Princeton was still sitting there. Zach thought, "He's definitely praying." He knew his look when he was praying. Zach called across, "Sugar?"

Princeton snapped to attention and watched Zach.

"Yes, two, thank you," the voice responded. Princeton turned to see who Zach was talking to.

Zach brought over the cappuccino and placed it on the table. The man sat and sipped his cappuccino, looking at the huge photo. Zach sat across from him and took in all the details of his suit, shoes, and watch. He was meticulous and expensive.

"First time in?" he asked.

"Yes, I was referred by Victoria Lucia-Bari."

"Oh! Her son-in-law is the artist."

"Yes, I know." He stood up with cup in hand and started to walk the studio. As they approached Princeton, Zach said, "Princeton," and said as he pointed to the man, "Larry."

Princeton smiled as they shook hands.

"Thanks for coming in," Princeton said.

Larry's eyes went to the newly finished wall.

"That's beautiful," he said as he put his cup on the bar.

"Thank you," Princeton responded.

"Are they sold as a group?" Larry asked.

Princeton answered, "Individual or as a series. I've just decided to continue the work as you were walking in. I'll be adding more to the series."

Zach interrupted, "There are no duplicates. Each is an original. When they sell they're replaced with different photos, keeping with the series theme."

"May I?" he asked, pointing for permission to walk behind the bar.

"Of course," Zach said.

As Larry was eyeing the photos, Zach was looking at the pricing, thinking, "This series is mega expensive." He was quickly calculating the cost of all eleven photos. Eight times eight hundred, and three times one thousand equals $9,400. Larry turned and pointed to "Life and Death."

"I didn't see pricing on that one," he said.

Princeton followed his eye and said, "Sorry, Larry, that one's not for sale."

"Too bad, it's really moving."

Zach looked at the photo, and it prompted him to say, "Princeton, Larry was referred by Victoria."

Princeton's face immediately took on a whole new look.

"Oh! You know Victoria?" he asked.

"Not as much as I'd like to, but yes."

Princeton chuckled and started to examine him from top to bottom. His mind started to work. "Maybe one of her clients?" he thought. Before he could speak, Larry looked back up at the photos and said, "I'll take them."

"The entire series?" Zach asked.

"Yes, I couldn't imagine breaking them up."

Zach looked like he swallowed a canary; he was thrilled. For Princeton, it was bittersweet. He was also thrilled with the purchase, but now he felt compelled to replace them with new ones. He only got to enjoy the wall for a few minutes, and he loved what he saw, and now it would be gone. He started to think. He had some other city shots, but none of the kids. He would need to shoot some new ones on Sunday, no Monday, no school on Sunday.

"Would it be OK if we packaged these and delivered them on Tuesday? Or would you prefer to take them with you now?" Princeton asked as his mind was working.

"No, Tuesday is fine. You don't need to deliver them, I'll pick them up," Larry answered.

"OK then. Let me get the paperwork. Do you have a business card?" Zach asked.

Larry took out his wallet and handed him his card. Zach started to walk away. As he eyed the card, the words popped out:

Larry McCabe

Trump Enterprises

"No way!" he thought. "You gotta be kidding me." As he completed the new file, his mind wandered. He was guessing if this series was for business or personal. It would be something if Princeton's work would be at a Trump property. Zach returned, and it seemed Princeton and Larry were enjoying their conversation. Zach handed Larry the printout, which was inside the embossed trifold, and in return, Larry handed Zach his platinum card. As Zach left to swipe the card, he heard Larry ask, "So I'll see you tomorrow night?"

Princeton nodded and said, "Absolutely, we're all looking forward to it."

Zach handed Larry his receipt for his signature and kneeled down behind the bar to retrieve the small black box of Godivas. "Nice touch, Tallulah," he thought as he handed it to Larry. They all shook hands, and Larry thanked them on his way out.

"Unbelievable, huh? His card said Trump Enterprises. Maybe you'll be hanging with the big boys," Zach exclaimed.

"Yeah . . . maybe," Princeton responded as he was preoccupied with the conversation he and Larry just had.

*   *   *   *   *

Piper was a little surprised by the applause. She knew her presentation was good, but she underestimated this reaction. She smiled and said, "Thank you, I'll assume you liked it."

Her boss Steve got up from the table and walked to where she was standing.

"See? That's why she's the best we have. She's our Dream Maker," he announced.

Piper looked at him and said, "Remember you said that, OK?"

The four men sitting at the table laughed. One of the men was the PR person for Porsche. During the entire presentation, he couldn't keep his eyes off her. He was hypnotized by her combination of beauty and intelligence. She was completely different from any woman he knew. Whether it was her air of confidence or her wit, it kept him interested. He was in thought as he watched her. "Beautiful face . . . different . . . great body . . . love the way she moves." He checked her finger . . . no ring. "Excellent," he thought.

"OK, gentlemen, hopefully we'll be talking again," she said as she smiled and left the room.

She walked into the ladies' room, looked in the mirror, and told her reflection.

"Way to go!"

Her immediate thought was to call Max and grab drinks, and then she remembered the plans he had with Victoria. "Just as well, I need a manicure anyway," she thought as she walked to her desk to call him. The voice behind her was close to her ear, saying, "Ms. Woods?"

She turned. "Piper," she said as she took in the scent of his cologne.

"Piper, that was great! The boys are excited."

"And which boy are you?" she asked.

He laughed. "Trevor."

"Well, Trevor, I'm glad you liked it. Just a little something I put together . . . for the past four months!"

"Are you always this amusing?" he asked.

"No, only with important men that determine the security of my career!"

He chuckled. "You're a handful . . . it's very appealing."

"As appealing as the presentation?"

As the words came out of her mouth, she thought, "Piper, are you flirting? Stop that. Keep it business."

Trevor was enjoying the volley of the playful words.

"My people are talking with your people. I'm sure we'll be getting back to you soon."

"Steve handles all that, I'm just the fluff."

"You are definitely more than fluff," he said.

"Well, I hope I did Porsche justice. My sister Tallulah has one. So I myself totally believe in the product."

"Really? Which model?" he asked.

"Cayenne Turbo."

"Excellent choice!"

"Yeah, well, we all can't afford 90k choices now, can we?"

He laughed again and asked, "Well, what ride is *your* choice?"

"Me?" Piper asked as she lowered the bridge of her specs to look above them, "I'm just an old fashion girl."

"Meaning?" Trevor asked.

"Meaning, '69 Corvair," she replied.

"Well, that does it," Trevor thought. "Beautiful and also eccentric."

"Wow! Pretty gutsy," he said. "I like that. And I like you!"

"OK, far enough," she thought as she extended her hand to end the conversation.

He looked at her hand, smiled, and said, "I'll call you tomorrow."

She remained standing there as he joined the others. "He was very tempting," she thought, but not even close to the dynamics of her Max. At that moment, she was sad that she hadn't sealed her deal with Max.

PROMISES

Tallulah tried desperately to focus on the tasks at hand. She finished getting the house in order and was now cleaning up her e mails and appointment schedule. Her mind and body were restless. The feeling of butterflies and anticipation was constant. She thought to herself, "Princeton, Princeton, I miss you, I need you! I need your strong arms wrapped around me. Your eyes soaking up every detail of me. Your beautiful smile lifting my spirit. I need to touch you, to smell you, to inhale your closeness that leaves me with that exaggerated sigh as I exhale. I need you next to me, to feel the safety, that security of our special world that only we share."

Her mind wandered in and out of those feelings and thoughts all day. Now again, unable to concentrate as if she wouldn't be complete until he was breathing the same air, in the same place, she closed her laptop. The "newness" of him was still exactly the same as it were the day they met. She could never get enough of him, never able to push away her longing for him. It was as if she *wasn't* Tallulah in full form until he completed the portrait.

She looked at the clock and hoped he would be home soon. She wanted to pamper him and show her love by giving him everything he needed after his exhausting day. She forced herself to get started in preparation for his arrival. "OK, Tallulah, get with the program," she thought as she started dinner. The rule was whoever was home first would prepare dinner or call for takeout. She made a checklist in her mind, going over the details. "First, an hour or so with the weights, then dinner, lots of candles to replace. Half an hour or so in the hot tub, I'm going to massage every inch of your body."

As she went over her list, she realized she was more excited about tonight than she was about the fund-raiser.

*   *   *   *   *

Princeton pulled into the parking spot, thinking, "Can't wait to get home." He grabbed the box of framed photos and titles from the backseat and walked into Yesterday's Yearnings. It was the only place, after his studio opened, that was allowed to display his work. He and Tallulah decided that Jack would be the only one offered this privilege. It was due to God's hand in Jack's connection to them finding one another. He also was the only person outside their circle that attended their wedding. Jack looked up as the door closed.

"Ah . . . the artist! How are you?"

"I'm great, Jack, and you?" Princeton asked as he put the box on the display case.

"Couldn't be better, and your lady?"

"She's amazing . . . as always."

Jack carefully took the photos out of the box and made an expression of approval as he looked at each one.

"Beautiful, just beautiful! Clients are disappointed when we start to run low."

"Well, leave a spot for a new series I'm working on . . . maybe nine or so."

Princeton walked over to the display case, which housed the "weapons." His eyes immediately rested on the most obvious in the group.

"Looking for a new one for Victoria?" Jack asked.

"Yeah, and that's the one," he said as he pointed to the Zippo with the raised circa pinup girl.

Jack walked over to the case, followed his finger, and said, "Funny, I was going to call you about that one, just got it yesterday."

As he took it out, Princeton walked the shop. His eyes touching on every piece. He rested on the jewelry display case, hoping something would jump up at him. Like himself, Tallulah wasn't a jewelry person. They both wore their wedding bands, which were estate pieces Victoria found. Very stately and elaborate—white gold bands with layers of diamonds and black etching. Although they were a pair, each one was completely different. You really had to study them to see the craftsmanship of the repeated pattern in each. They were very eye catching, and he and Tallulah were crazy about them. Other than that, they each wore a cross, and they enjoyed their watch collection. As Princeton examined the pieces, he looked down to see the name coming across his cell.

"Hey, Dad," he said.

"Hi, Princeton, how's it going?" Derek asked.

"Great! Getting ready to head home."

"How's Tallulah?" Derek asked.

"She's great! Absolutely great!" he exclaimed.

Derek heard the change in his voice. It was joyful with an almost boyish quality.

"Well, she sent your mother some type of crystal vase. Apparently, a collector's piece because she's over the moon about it. She was more excited about that than our trip to Hawaii!"

Princeton laughed and got lost in the glow of his amazing Tallulah.

"You there?" Derek asked.

"Yeah, Dad, I'm glad Mom liked it so much, you know Tallulah, she doesn't miss a beat."

"You're a lucky man."

"Don't I know it, but it's not luck, Dad."

"Whatever it is, you've got it. So you think you could give your mother a call?"

Princeton thought for a moment, trying to recall when they spoke last.

"I spoke to her last week, is everything OK?"

"Everything's fine. I just think she misses you."

"Well, we'll all be together tomorrow night, but yes, I'll call her."

"OK, son, see you tomorrow."

As Princeton turned his attention back to the display case, he felt somewhat guilty. A week would never go by without him talking to Victoria. He spoke to her almost every day. Sometimes it was with a purpose and other times, just because he needed that connection. He made a mental note to be more timely with his calls to his mother. Jack looked over again, saw that Princeton was finished with his call, and walked over.

"Did you see anything you like?" he asked.

"I think so," he replied.

"Let me see that piece there," he said as he pointed to a business card holder.

Jack handed it to him, and Princeton was surprised by its weight. He held it in his hand as he examined the beautiful piece of art. He had never seen anything quite like it. It had an open cut pattern of a design similar to branches of trees. There were a few large stones of amethyst and citrine and many tiny chips that reflected a dark amber color. The entire front was three dimensional, and as he turned in over, the inscription on the back filled him with excitement. They were tiny letters that read Sterling Silver, which explained the weight. However, the deep bold inscription done in a bold font sent a chill through him. "*With God all things are possible* ILS."

"My gosh, Jack, where did you get this?"

Jack was surprised by Princeton's enthusiasm.

"I picked it up at an estate sale in Rhode Island. The family was selling off all the belongings of their great-grandmother, who had passed. I was very surprised when I saw the tremendous amount of items they were willing to part with. I mean the whole gamut—furniture, art, linens, jewelry—everything. Apparently, she was a renowned artist in Europe decades ago. Everything was much too pricey for this market, but I managed to pick up a few pieces, and that's one of them."

Princeton listened and was so excited that God was sending him a message. That's the way he viewed it. All through his life, he tried hard to be in tune with signs, signals, and messages that confirmed God speaking to him. They were either confirmations, directions, or sometimes just a simple "I am with you, Princeton." Victoria told him that the more he kept his heart open to receive, the easier it would be to have it flow through. He looked at the piece in his hand and felt sad for the artist's life that ended with strangers going through her existence.

"Where's the respect to the legacy of this person?" he thought.

"Do you know this woman's name?" Princeton asked.

"Uh . . . I'm not sure. It was mentioned. I'm sure people were referring to it, especially with the art pieces. Sorry, Princeton."

"Do you have a receipt?" he asked.

"No, cash and carry," Jack replied.

"An address?" Princeton probed.

Jack was trying hard to remember. Finally, he said, "I'll tell you what. My wife was with me that day. Let me see if she can remember, and I'll call you."

"Great, thanks, Jack."

"So I assume you want it?"

"Absolutely," Princeton replied.

Jack walked over to the counter and was trying to figure out what to do. He was so happy when Princeton came in, but he always found himself struggling with how to charge him. After all, Princeton's pieces brought in more profit than anything in his shop. Princeton wouldn't take any money upfront from Jack. He would leave his work, and when it sold, Jack would get 75 percent of the sale. That was unheard of, but Princeton wouldn't have it any other way. Jack was indebted to him. Every time he tried to give him the items he wanted to purchase for free, Princeton would fight him on it. There was one time when Jack was standing firm and said, "No matter what you say, there's no charge." Princeton just smiled, went in his pocket, and left a stack of twenties on the counter. In essence, that was far more than the item's worth. So now, Jack was trying to be creative with the pricing.

"What do I owe you, Jack?" Princeton asked.

"Nothing," Jack replied, "I owe you."

Princeton sighed. "Let's not go through this again, Jack."

"OK, let's do this instead. You take one of your charities, or something to do with your church, and make a donation instead of paying me."

Princeton thought about it for a minute and then said, "OK, great! Thanks, Jack."

"My pleasure, now I have to get to work. I need to hang these beautiful photos."

Princeton smiled, took his package, and left.

Jack looked at him as he was walking out the door and thought, "If I had a son, I would want him to be exactly like Princeton." Princeton was anxious to get home. He popped in his red CD and became lost in the music and his thoughts about Tallulah's gift. He decided to have Victoria design a new business card for Tallulah and place it in the holder when he was ready to give it to her.

Sing with me, sing for the year
Sing for the laughter, sing for the tear
Sing with me, if it's just for today
Maybe tomorrow the good Lord will take you away.

As he listened to the verse, his heart swelled, and the familiar feeling of adrenaline racing through him took over his body. "Thank you, Aerosmith," he whispered, "thank you for taking me through so many chapters of my life." As he stopped at the light, he glanced over to the car next to him. A woman was eyeing him and smiling. He smiled and thought, "A few more minutes, and I'll have my baby in my arms."

*   *   *   *   *

Victoria pulled into the parking lot and looked for the FJ Cruiser. She parked alongside of it and checked herself in the mirror. She was looking forward to spending time with Max. As she walked in, she immediately found his blue eyes as he stood up and smiled. The hostess started to speak, and she said, "It's OK, I found my table" and pointed to Max.

Victoria loved the atmosphere at Luna. The food was average, but the décor and ambiance were exceptional. It had an old-world flair, a mixture of beautiful lighting, repetition of excellent art, and European fountains. She walked over, and Max gave her a big hug and kiss. His fragrance was wonderful. Max pulled out the chair for Victoria. Whenever he was in Victoria's company, his gentleman qualities were always exercised. He secretly enjoyed it and wished he was forced to display it more often.

"You look beautiful!" Max exclaimed.

"As do you," Victoria responded.

"No, really, Victoria, you look fantastic."

"Well, that alone, was worth the drive."

Max laughed and pointed to the bottle of wine.

"I took the liberty," he said as he poured two glasses of Antiyal.

"Excellent," Victoria said as she toasted his glass.

"To my future son-in law?" she asked.

"It's funny you said that. I need to talk to you about Piper, but first let's catch up!"

"Before we do that, I want to thank you for the fabulous roses. They were perfect, just perfect."

Max was thrilled that Victoria liked his choice. The conversation was nonstop. In between ordering their dinner, they discussed Victoria's projects and Max's work.

"I could never thank you enough," Max said.

"You do thank me . . . with who you are to Piper, Princeton, and Tallulah."

Max was always taken in by Victoria. She had an effect on him that always made him feel manly and accomplished. As he looked at her, he was embarrassed by his thoughts of wondering what it would be like to have Victoria in his life 24/7.

"You know, Max, I was thinking, you should change your signage and business card to state something about custom work or one of a kind . . . I don't know, something that is prominent to set you apart from other inkers."

Max looked at her as his mind was wandering. She was so beautiful and beyond classy. The way she moved, her posture, and her confidence, pure thoroughbred.

"Max?" Victoria was waiting for an answer.

Max was confused and uncomfortable about his thoughts. He often wondered what it was like for Princeton to be such an important part of Victoria's life.

"I'm sorry . . . what did you say?" he asked.

Victoria repeated herself, and Max listened.

He responded with "Why do you take such an interest in me? My work?"

"Well, that's easy, it's because you're important to me. We tend to put effort into so many meaningless things in our lives. Things that will either break or eventually be obsolete. At the moment, they seem to have meaning . . . until something new replaces them. My family . . . my circle can't be replaced. It's the cliché of quality versus quantity. I'd rather have one of you than ten other insignificant people. I make it a habit to concentrate on the really true blessings God has given me."

"Well," Max said, "you certainly have been blessed."

"Yes, you're right," Victoria replied.

"However, it's been a long journey. If I didn't open my heart and believe, it might have been quite a different scenario. I tried desperately to mature in my faith, hoping it would refine my character. I prayed for spiritual wisdom, to have the ability to see God's perspective, and then know the best course of action to take. That in itself is painful and difficult. You see, the more you understand, the greater the pain. You see more imperfections in yourself and the world around you. The more you observe, the more prominent the meaningless efforts become. So if you're not careful, the trade-off can be that you become disappointed and self-sufficient. When I say self-sufficient, I mean without God's direction. The minute life appears certain, we become complacent . . . comfortable. That's when we need to recognize how important it is to be grateful and prepare ourselves for the realization that in a split second, it can all change."

Max listened and felt a wave of inspiration. Originally, his purpose for dinner with Victoria was to thank her. On his drive to the restaurant, his desire seemed to shift. He felt this need to be nourished. Something inside of him was restless and looking for direction. He wasn't exactly sure what it was, but he knew he felt it.

Victoria looked at Max and saw a sweet vulnerability in his eyes. It was clear that he was needing something; she wasn't sure what it was.

"Max, what is it?" Victoria asked.

Max looked at her as his eyes started to fill up and said, "I don't know."

He moved closer, readjusted his body in his chair, and concentrated on fighting the urge to cry.

"Everything is good. Financially, it's never been better. Piper is such an incredible woman that tests my patience every day! My family, my friends are healthy. So I should be happy, right? I mean, I am happy . . . but something is missing . . . I don't know, I can't explain it."

Max pushed his half-eaten plate to the side and searched Victoria's eyes, looking for an answer to the question that he didn't understand. The waiter came over to check the table, and Max was fixated on Victoria. It was almost an annoyance that he was intruding into their space.

"Should I take these away?" he asked as he pointed to the dishes.

Victoria hardly ate due to her full immersion in the conversation. As she looked at her dish, she had no desire to consume the wonderful salmon.

"What a shame," she thought. "A bottle of wine, coffee, and dessert would have sufficed."

"Yes, thank you," Victoria replied.

"Max?" she asked.

"Yes . . . thank you."

Max looked at the nearly empty bottle of wine.

"Another bottle please."

"Max," Victoria announced, "how about we move to the courtyard and have some fabulous coffee and dessert?"

Victoria adored the courtyard, and with Max's mind-set, a second bottle of wine seemed too dangerous.

Max said, "Great idea." He looked at the waiter and asked, "Is there a spot in the courtyard?"

"I'm sure there is, give me a minute, and I'll set you up."

"I'm going to the ladies' room, don't sneak out on me."

"Not a chance," Max replied.

As Victoria got up, so did Max. Again, he found his manners that rarely made an appearance. Princeton was his constant reminder of the etiquette of courtship. "Where did all those learned lessons go?" he asked himself.

The waiter came back and told Max their table was ready.

"I'll wait for the lady, thank you."

"I'd wait too," the waiter replied.

Max smiled and felt uncomfortable again. There was this unidentifiable feeling tugging at him as he watched Victoria moving toward him. He caught a glimpse of the many eyes following her. Her stature was almost regal. It wasn't a forced, intentional stride. It was fluid and graceful. "How did this woman come to live her days in Connecticut?" Max thought. "She would be better suited in the company of renowned artists, musicians, or maybe philanthropists." When she reached the table, she said, "OK, let's figure out your dilemma."

Max smiled and felt a surge of safety, as if he could just stay in this moment, then everything would be all right.

The waiter led them outside, and immediately, Victoria was taken in by the beauty of the European architecture. The weathered carved stone fountains . . . the slate walkways . . . topiaries . . . tiny white lights cascading from the olive trees . . . bistro tables with intricate wrought iron details. It was her Tuscany vision. She actually closed her eyes for a second to breathe in the essence of its magnificence. In her mind, this was the courtyard of the villa, where she longed to be. The place where she could speak her rarely used first language, develop her ideas, and bask in the texture and complexity of the vineyard's finest. The reality of the role she played in her family's life left her conceding that it was probably just a dream. However, at the moment, she was transported to the place where she knew she belonged.

"You love this, don't you?" Max asked.

"More than you know," Victoria replied.

The combination of the serenity of the courtyard, Victoria's frame of mind, and Max's open heart made for a wonderful collaboration of thoughts, desires, and fruitful conversation.

Victoria was sipping her coffee, and Max was trying to untangle his ball of confusion. As the words came out of his mouth, his face blushed with embarrassment.

"I want you . . . I need you . . . I mean, oh god . . . someone . . ."

Victoria was calm and smiled.

"I know what you mean, but you already have that."

Max was relieved that his outburst was understood, and at the same time, he was trying to understand her statement.

"Do you think I'm the same woman I was twenty-five years ago?" Victoria asked.

She continued, not waiting for a response, "Not by a long shot. Sure, the foundation was there, but the woman you're looking at is the result of years in the making, and it took a tremendous amount of faith, dedication, and pain."

Max was taking in every word.

"You see, you've been blessed. The history you have with Princeton was by no means a coincidence. He, my son, is an anomaly. I haven't quite figured out why he is the way he is, but it's very similar to my story. Going at it, so to speak, alone, was just what God graced him with. The fortitude to understand and follow the direction must have been very lonely and painful for him. But he kept his eye on the prize. So here we have Tallulah and Piper. Tallulah having many more years of direction, yet Piper being brought into our circle at such an early age. Again, not a coincidence. That work in progress is still growing. However, Piper is truly an amazing woman. She has 'it,' she gets it! She's a combination of beauty, wit, and has a heart that's loyal and compassionate. So, in twenty years or so, she may very well be very similar to me!"

Max was going to speak, and Victoria cut him off.

"She chose *you*! All of her dimensions, and she chose you. That's her statement that you're worthy. However, it's a give and take. Do you feed her desires to rise above? Are you her protector? Do you focus on displaying your gentlemanly charm and manners to make her feel thrilled that she 'belongs to you.' If you forget to do that, then all she has to offer lays dormant, and that would be such a shame. If you want more from this life, which it seems you do, then you have to go deep into your faith, deep into your love for your woman, and orchestrate a symphony of your lives intermingled for not only yourselves, but for the whole world to hear. Your restlessness is a signal that it's time to make changes, it's time for a new season. That change is already available to you . . . through Piper. Woven into the human fabric is the desire to learn and understand. How far you take that is what separates greatness from just OK. Max, listen to your heart, not just your mind, and put your love into action. Then one day, years from now, you may be sitting with someone who is asking of you exactly what you're asking of me. Then you will be capable of continuing the lineage of inspiring and directing someone's life to a superior level. Embrace your gifts."

If someone would have shaken Max physically, it probably wouldn't have had the effect that Victoria's words had. They ignited an awakening inside of Max that was both stimulating and peaceful. He sat there lost in thought, trying to connect the fragments of the words just spoken.

Victoria examined his face and decided to continue with her synopsis of Max's search.

"Did you know that we attract what we continuously think about? We also tend to become the expectation of what surrounds us. Your job, so to speak, allows you to surrender yourself to becoming a better man through your artistic signature. As you do that, you will set the tone for what you expect to get and what you're willing to give. You need to constantly be focused on your goal and work hard every day to reach your level of success. Now that's where it becomes complicated. There's success in the result of wealth, prestige, and power. That's the success most people strive toward. However, the greater success is the journey of obedience and faithfulness regardless of opposition and personal cost. Usually, when you follow the latter with a pure heart, the rest falls into place. So you see, you have the tools to achieve that! Don't you see, Max? Piper is your greatest tool! She was groomed to heighten your expectations and desires because within herself, she has the capability to catapult you to a whole new level. Her love for you made that possible. Unfortunately, if she is not being 'fed' with strong, loving expectation, if she's not nurtured to constantly grow as the wonderful woman that she is, then she will slowly retreat into the walls of her existence. She will live her life with her treasure buried. That treasure is for both of you! Remember what I said, she chose you. You sitting here with me, at this exact moment, is also not a coincidence. In a way, I'm blessed to be part of a monumental plateau in your life. God doesn't make mistakes. Everything has its reason. So now that my mouth is dry, I'm going to take a rest so that you can come to terms with what you're going to do."

Victoria stopped and sipped her coffee. She was looking at Max, trying to see if her words had an impact. Max was so taken in that physically he was a mess. He honestly believed that somewhere in Victoria's conversation, he felt aroused. His stomach had butterflies, and he couldn't stop his foot from tapping the floor. He felt as if Victoria sucked the emotion and strength out his body and mind. It was a paradox. His adrenaline was flowing, and at the same time, he was drained.

"Victoria . . . Victoria . . ."

His speech was low and exaggerated.

"I'm a bit of a mess here. Please excuse me, I'll be right back."

Max got up, and to his own surprise, he bent over, and with his mouth to her ear, he said, "There will never be another you".

As he made his way to the men's room, he was in a state of euphoria. His body felt warm. Everything around him seemed distant. He was cocooned in his realization of wanting to have Piper now, this minute. He wanted to explore her body inside and out. He wanted to proclaim his desire to change their relationship, to begin something new and exciting. He was searching for his connection to God, wishing he knew how to start a personal relationship, the one that Victoria states is her grounds for all she thinks and does. He was also recognizing that he and Victoria turned a corner tonight. They had dinners before this, and through the years, they had a nice relationship. This . . . this was different. He felt like he entered her private domain. The connection was deeper than anything before. It was as if he graduated to the next level. He stood looking in the mirror as he splashed water on his face. He couldn't help but think about Princeton. All the conversations that he and Victoria must have had over the years. The enormous love she displayed for him. "Wow," he thought, "lucky man, Princeton. To think, you held out waiting for this. As if Tallulah wasn't enough, which anyone and everyone would agree she is, you get Victoria as part of the package. Amazing, just amazing." As he stepped out of the men's room, the waiter approached him.

"Is there anything else I can get you?" he asked.

"I'll take the check, please. No, wait, please see if the lady would like anything else. I'll take an espresso and the check."

*   *   *   *   *

Tallulah finished lighting the candles and checked herself in the mirror before she put on her boy shorts. Her undergarments were beautiful, sexy, and seemed to illuminate against her tanned skin. Just as she hit Play for Boccelli to fill the rooms, she heard the door slide. She bolted down the stairs and caught a glimpse of Princeton walking in.

"Baby!" she exclaimed.

"He looked up and saw her huge smile as she was running toward him. She jumped up, locked her legs around his waist as he caught her with both arms. She held on to his neck with her face buried in his neck.

"Oh, baby, I've missed you, I've missed you so much."

Just the feel of her body on his, her fragrance, her mouth on his ear, kissing his neck, kissing his face, instantly propelled him into a hot, throbbing rush. He held her tight as she pressed against him, moving herself to find his desire.

"Oh, baby." His voice was already changing; his body was aching. He stepped back to lean against the door to gain stability. Tallulah was still locked to him, feverishly moving, talking in his ear. His hands grabbed her weight from her bottom and moved her in a strong rhythm against himself. He closed his eyes and escaped into the blackness, groaning with every connection to his tightening and release. She was in charge, and he assisted with her desire to stay exactly where they were, without the need to remove a single piece of clothing. "I love you so much." The voice was distant in his black paradise. He wasn't aware of the strength he was using to keep the steady passion. His thoughts were dancing in and out of his deep immersion. "This would be an expected welcome for someone so long gone. A soldier returning after a tour or maybe an extended missionary trip, not for someone who walked out of these walls only this morning." As he gasped his final breath of release, he immediately slid himself down the door, with Tallulah still attached to his sculptured structure. He sat knees bent, with his face buried in her chest. She lifted his face with her hands, and their eyes locked. She looked raw—tiny beads of sweat on her forehead, not an ounce of makeup, and stunningly beautiful. She did that thing with her mouth that Princeton adored. It was a close-mouthed smile, where the ends of her lips would turn up. It was playful and extremely sexy. She exaggerated her gaze, so as to demand that he wouldn't leave her eyes.

"I can never get enough of you, you know that, right?"

She wasn't expecting an answer. She still had his chin in her hand as she said, "You're all I want from this life . . . all I need."

His body was wet, and his heart was sitting in her hands. He managed to speak.

"This life is something I could never have imagined." He kept his stare.

"It was only what? Seven, eight, nine years ago that I dreamed of you. But this? Never this! I don't feel worthy of our life . . . you . . . the prosperity . . . our home . . . I'm afraid I'm going to wake up, and it's all going to be gone. Promise me . . . promise me . . . you will always want me this way . . . that you won't tire of me. Promise me!"

His plea sounded desperate, and his expression was breathtaking. There, the two of them far away from the world, his beautiful face boyish and vulnerable, and the feeling of his hands, which seemed to cover her entire back, caressing her skin seemed to be enough for their lifeline.

"Not that it's necessary, but here goes, Princeton Cooper."

The sound of her saying his name like that startled him.

"I promise that I will always want you . . . just like this. That I will never grow tired of you. Not in this lifetime and definitely not in the next."

She paused to be certain he was satisfied.

"Shouldn't we exchange rings or something?" she said as she started to playfully kiss his mouth.

He responded with laughter, and the feeling of safety overwhelmed him. He was such a confident, successful man, the envy of so many. Yet just the thought of not sharing his life with Tallulah would leave him with feelings of fear and anxiety. Once she confirmed her adoring love for him, he felt secure. She stood up and extended her hands to him. He grabbed them and lifted himself up. The aura of the candles and the dimly lit chandeliers played on his emotion of exactly what he was *just* talking about. Tallulah poured him and herself a glass of wine, toasted his glass with "promises," and took a sip. As Princeton felt the warm red wine running down his throat, Tallulah asked, "Weights or hot tub before dinner?"

"You . . . just you" was his response.

"That's very flattering, but I'm sure you're exhausted and probably starving. I called Sophie and asked her to come on Monday instead of tomorrow. I'm hoping you'll sleep in, and then you can have your weights all to yourself tomorrow, so what's the call?"

Princeton had almost finished his glass of wine and was enjoying the effects. The idea of a leisurely day of sleeping in and working out was very comforting. As he poured himself another glass, he said, "Tub and dinner."

"Excellent! Let's go!"

She took her glass and his hand and led him upstairs. His eyes followed her body traveling the staircase. He looked to the left as he reached the landing and caught a glimpse of his attire hanging on his hook and thought, "My baby doesn't miss a beat."

As Princeton undressed, Tallulah hit the button on the tub. She adjusted the volume for Bocelli's beautiful voice and lit the candles.

Quando sono solo
sogno all'orizzonte
e mancan le parole
si lo so che non c'e luce
in una stanza quando manca il sole

"I wish I could sing this like my mother does," Tallulah thought to herself, wishing now that she would have paid more attention to her mother's first language.

Princeton came up behind her, kissed her neck, and slid into the powerful movement of the water. He leaned back and closed his eyes. Tallulah quickly retrieved his glass of wine as she moved his pile of clothes on the floor with her foot. She placed the glasses on the ledge, removed her clothes, and slid in behind him. **TALLULAH** was staring her in the face. He leaned back against her, stretched his body out, and took in the feel of her face on the back of his neck. Her fingers were gently massaging his head.

"Hey, baby," he said, his voice was low and relaxed.

"Catch up?"

"Sure, let's see. Piper had a presentation, which I'm sure she nailed. Mom's having dinner with Max. We're ready for tomorrow night, and Thursday is all set."

She continued to massage his neck and shoulders.

"I have a meeting with Tom White on Sunday. We'll see how that goes."

"Tom White, huh?" Princeton replied.

"That should be a big one. The direction you gave me on the series today was genius! Actually, it sold immediately. Do you know Larry McCabe?" he asked.

Tallulah thought for a moment.

"No, I don't think so."

"Well, he was referred by Mom, bought the entire series! I decided to expand that series. After seeing it today, I thought it was beautiful. I'm taking Zach to shoot with me . . . maybe Monday."

"Zach?" Tallulah's voice was full of surprise.

"Wow . . . that's a first!"

"We'll see, he has such a desire and drive . . . we'll see. I stopped by Jack's and picked Mom up a Zippo. Oh! Whatever you sent my mother, she's ecstatic about it. I love you for the way you always think about the perfect something for everyone."

Tallulah was resting her arms on his shoulders as her fingertips gently massaged his chest. She felt his weight increase against her chest.

"Baby, do you know where Max took Mom?" she asked.

Silence except for Boccelli.

"Baby?"

She tilted her head to come over to the side to confirm Princeton's sleep. She knew she had to wake him, if only to guide him to bed.

"No big deal," she thought. "If he gets up later, he can eat. If not, food in the fridge." She knew she would have to be quick in the kitchen, in case he searched for her. She didn't want to chance him not sleeping. She tried to maneuver herself out of the tub to grab a towel. She quickly dried herself and released the water.

"Baby? Baby?" she whispered in his ear.

His eyes found her; she held the towel as a matador, waiting for his signal. Princeton stood as she dried him, eyes not quite open, and she led him to bed.

"On your stomach, baby," she ordered as she grabbed the lotion and positioned herself between his legs.

Princeton was somewhere between sleep and pleasure. Her hands were warm and tender. She took the sheet and covered as much of him as possible. She continued to caress his body. In his mind or out loud, he wasn't sure, he kept repeating, "You . . . only you."

Tallulah moved like a cat, trying not to disrupt his deep sleep. She slid to the side of the bed and carefully got up. She wrapped herself in the damp towel, which sent a shiver up her spine and went downstairs. She didn't bother with the candlesnuffer as she quickly moved around the room, blowing out the candles. She picked up his gear, which was lying in the floor by the door, and placed it on the counter. Within minutes, the beautiful sautéed veal medallions were transferred and put in the fridge. She hurried upstairs hoping he would be exactly as she left him. As she slid back into her spot, his arms found her, and he wrapped himself around her. She nestled perfectly into his body form and forced herself to close her eyes.

*　　*　　*　　*　　*

As Victoria pulled into the garage, her mind was still full of the dinner conversation with Max. She concluded that Piper was fortunate to have him. He had great potential. She felt a little drained and was happy to be home. Tomorrow night was big, and she didn't want to be tired. As she entered the house, she realized that she hadn't talked to Princeton today. Still, to this day, she was always surprised at how much she loved him. She threw her bag on the bench and walked past the office to go upstairs. The blinking light caught her attention, and she walked over to the answering machine. "Good grief," she thought. "Must be calls about tomorrow." She listened for a moment to each one, hitting the Advance button rapidly.

"Hi, Mom." Princeton's voice caught her attention, and she let go of the button.

"I didn't want to disturb your dinner; besides, you probably had your cell off anyway. I just wanted you to know I miss you, and I thank God for you. Thank you for bringing the most amazing woman into this world. Well, hope you had a great time with Max. Love you."

She hit Repeat and listened again. "Unbelievable," she thought. "My beautiful Tallulah, how blessed you really are."

As she walked into her bedroom, her mood changed. Most of the time, she thoroughly enjoyed her private space. As others viewed it as lonely, she found it to be refreshing. There were times, far and few between, that she *did* feel lonely. Tonight was one of those times.

Max was in full throttle. His adrenaline was flowing, and he was experiencing a feeling of being high. As he drove, his mind was full of Victoria's conversation. His heart was racing, and he felt as if he was going to explode. There was a sense of strength, control, and urgency that was occupying his body! The newness of his realization about himself excited him. It was as if a green light was blinking in his head. It was the go-ahead to begin his life with a new direction. He wanted so much to reach a new level in his life, and now he felt equipped to do so. He laughed as he thought about this sudden change. He never imagined words to be so powerful. Nothing was different about his life as compared to hours ago. He didn't suddenly hit the lottery, become famous, or change his profession. Yet everything seemed different. He made a vague attempt at prayer.

"Thank you, God, thank you for bringing Victoria to me, thank you for this insight."

He wanted to call Piper, Tallulah, and Princeton. He just wasn't sure what to say. In his whirlwind of emotion, he pulled over and dialed Victoria. As soon as he hit the Send button, he panicked. "Are you crazy, calling her?" he thought.

"Max?" Victoria asked surprised.

"Hi, Victoria, I'm sorry I called you. I'm just a mess right now. I'm excited and not sure what to do. I'm sorry, what do I do with all this?" Max was rambling.

Victoria's speech was deliberately slow and controlled.

"OK . . . OK . . . just relax. It's good that you're excited. You shouldn't do anything right now. Let what you're feeling resonate for a while. Channel your energy into thoughts of what you want to accomplish and how you can achieve that. Think about where Piper fits into your plan, try to pray for direction. Let yourself be open to receive the answers you're looking for."

Victoria was waiting for a response.

"Max?"

Max was listening, lost somewhere between what Victoria was saying and his immediate vision of what his future looked like.

"Max?" Victoria asked again, concerned.

"I'm here, Victoria. It's just so hard right now."

"Just try to relax . . . don't try to explain what you're feeling. Don't share what's inside of you until you even out a bit. My suggestion is that you take your energy right now and use it on those weights that you love so much."

Max took a deep breath, saying, "OK, good idea."

"Victoria?" Max asked.

"Yes?"

"I love you! Good night."

The phone went dead. Victoria was a little stunned. It wasn't what he said; it was the way he said it. She found herself reminiscing years gone by when she too needed direction. She forced herself not to go into that memory bank. She reminded herself to include Max in her prayers.

*   *   *   *   *

As Piper looked in the mirror, she finally decided on the black lace dress. It was hugging her curves precisely right, and the flesh tone underlay was a perfect match to her skin color. She was happy she decided to buy it. Although at the time, the price tag for the Cavalli was outrageously high. Her blush-colored patent pumps were perfect with it. "OK, Piper" she thought. "Let's see if you can get through five hours of those five-inch beauties." She was a little disappointed that Max hadn't called. She knew dinner with Victoria would be lengthy, but somehow she wished he had called. She didn't get to share her news about Porsche with anyone . . . especially Max. It worked out fine, seeing how she needed a manicure and time to put herself together for tomorrow; but somewhere deep down inside, she longed to be doing this in *their* house. There were times, she second-guessed her decision to stay put and not move in with Max. After Tallulah's re-virginizing and the whole momentum that followed, it left her wanting more than just sharing an apartment. She was holding out for the bigger picture. She wanted it to mean something, and secretly she thought old fashion was romantic. Now all this time later, here she stood in her same existence. She loved Max so much but was disappointed that they fell into their average lives. She wanted more—more romance, more commitment, deeper, 'rock your world' type of love. She knew she was capable, but she held out. Max needed to be the orchestrator; otherwise, she would always be leading. Ms. Independent Piper wanted to be taken care of. She wanted her knight to rescue her, from herself. So since the horse hadn't showed up, she continued with her strong, well-equipped persona.

"Max," she thought, "if you don't find me soon, I may get lost in the cracks of life." "Wow," she said out loud, "that's definitely Ma talking. Where would I be today, if not for Ma?"

Her mind couldn't remember life before Victoria and Luke rescued her. It was dark and empty. Maybe she chose to erase it from her memory. Dysfunctional parents, dysfunctional home, life was about surviving, getting through a day without pain, embarrassment, and a routine visit from the police. She looked at herself in the mirror and said, "Great, now you're talking to your mirror!" She took the dress off and carried her cell to the bathroom to take a shower.

BE CAREFUL WHAT
YOU WISH FOR

The feeling of the fingers gently caressing her head and running down her hair made Tallulah stretch her body and slowly open her eyes.

"Good morning, baby." She focused on the voice attached to the beautiful smile.

With one hand, Princeton propped up a pillow and handed her a cup of coffee with the other. This was Tallulah's favorite simple luxury. Being able to have that first cup of coffee without getting out of bed was wonderful. Having Princeton sitting there, so happy to greet her, made it absolutely perfect.

She leaned in, kissed his mouth, and said, "Good morning, beautiful."

The coffee was exactly right, and she closed her eyes as it traveled down her throat. He sat there smiling, taking his imaginary photo of her. The clock read 8:10, and she assumed he started his day a while ago. He rested his head on her stomach as his hand found her back, and his arms cradled her. She rested her cup on his shoulders.

"Did you sleep?" she asked.

"I had the best sleep." Princeton's response was muddled as he buried his face into her skin.

Hearing that, Tallulah was happy and relieved.

"Hey, baby, get dressed and let's go out for breakfast," he announced.

"You hit the weights already?" Tallulah asked surprised.

Princeton thought about his workout. On his way to the weights, he stopped to view the clothing choice on the hooks in the dressing room. He stood before the T hook and lifted the hanger. He turned the dress around and tried to imagine it attached to Tallulah's body. It was definitely beautiful and somewhat odd. He couldn't get the full picture but was sure it would be stunning. He carried it to the chaise, sat down, and ran his fingers along the ruffles as it lay on his lap. He closed his eyes and went into deep conversation with his Almighty Father. His prayer was full of praise and gratitude. He begged for guidance and direction, to be a better man worthy of his blessings. He confessed his inadequacies, asking for forgiveness, promising God's glory to be center stage. His heart was open, and the steady stream between his emotion and his mind left him feeling renewed. He prayed with her dress in his hands, as if the physical connection to the fabric included Tallulah in his conversation. He sighed deeply, and with wet eyes, he placed the dress back on the hook. He eyed his suit and smiled. The last time he wore it, Tallulah made such a fuss about how fantastic he looked that he actually enjoyed the constricted tailoring. He picked up the box in his shoe and slowly opened it. The thought of her taking time to complete his look excited him more than what the actual contents were. "Wow, beautiful! Just beautiful."

He placed one against the cuff of the shirt and knew they were perfect. He stood there, taking in every inch of the room. His eyes moved from corner to corner, examining him and Tallulah's existence. Everything about the room was a chapter in their story of life. His mind captured moments of the time and places connected to the hats and clothing: baseball games, dinners, city excursions, Broadway productions, and the actual development of the room. "What an incredible journey," he thought. As he exited the space, he felt ready to push himself to Aerosmith. Tallulah repeated her question, "Did you and the weights have a successful date?"

He lifted his head, started to laugh, and in between kissing her stomach, he replied, "Yep, all two hours of it. I'm starving! Let's get me fed!"

"OK, give me fifteen and fifteen," Tallulah said.

Princeton knew to leave the room. The first fifteen was prayer, and the second fifteen was to get ready. It amazed him that all she needed to do was brush her teeth, wash her face, throw her hair up, and voila, she was a true natural beauty. She extended her arm to reach the table, where she placed her empty cup. She took his head in her hands and guided his body up so that she could look into his eyes. She did that sexy thing with her mouth as she ran her fingers down his chest, resting them on his hips. His body responded with a deep breath as he closed his eyes for a second. Tallulah understood the signal and repeated what she just did, only a little stronger and deeper. She wanted him . . . she wanted a piece of the magnificent physique she was staring at. Her body was starting to become warm with a fantastic stirring deep inside.

"Oh . . . baby." Princeton's voice was gravely and a little hoarse as he extended his upper body to welcome her touch. He took his hands and firmly outlined her body starting at her shoulders and working his way down. As he traced her structure, she arched herself up, closer to him. His eyes were synchronized with his hands, and as he took her in, his body was restless, starting to move against the restriction of the waistband of his sweats. They were both working their hands to explore each other. They were still at arm's length, and while Tallulah watched him, she found herself moaning as he moaned and moving as he moved. It was exchange of pleasure between gasps. Princeton was moving stronger and against her touch, and as their bodies were pulsating, he could no longer be separated from her connection. His head was reared back, and his words were cut off by moans and deep inhales of breath.

"Oh my god . . . baby . . . baby . . . oh my god . . ."

In one quick swoop, she brought his waistband down, and he pulled her in with tremendous strength. The second their bodies touched, the fusion sent them into a wild, desperate search. Tallulah was moving so steady and hard that she couldn't grab on tight enough. The feel of his damp chest against hers sent her into a deep, euphoric state as she tried to express her feelings into his ear. She was professing her love, stating her pleasure, and asking him to express his. They were so tangled in their heat that their explosion didn't seem enough. As Princeton choked out his enormous pleasure, he immediately started to move quickly again, as if it were only an introduction to his desire for her. They continued to use each other to reach heights of continuous release. She guided him, and he guided her. Together, apart, leading and following. All the time draining each other of every deep movement. The dialogue only enhanced their physical state. Their bodies reacted to the words that they managed to exchange between breaths, gasps, looks, and seeking out the satisfaction of their work in each one's eyes. Their wet bodies were exhausted, and still moving as Tallulah took him to a place so deep that Princeton was begging for her not to stop. He was out of control with verbal requests, not hearing his own words, just captivated by his inner body's strength to thrust and feel so full and warm. She tried to meet his every request because the more he begged, the more he fueled her direction. They both reached their final destination in a moment where their eyes were locked.

Princeton collapsed on to her chest, and they could hear the beats of their hearts loud and steady.

"I could never be this for anyone but you. You make me the woman that I am." Tallulah's voice was deep and raw in his ears.

Princeton lay there, breathing deep, wrapped in her arms. For obvious reasons, his mind started to sing the lyrics to "Home." He stretched his arm to reach the button on the stereo. He looked at the five CDs in place and arrowed to the fourth one, then chose the third song. Chris Daughtry filled the room.

I'm staring out into the night
Trying to hide the pain
I'm going to the place where love
And feeling good don't ever cost a thing.
And the pain you feel's a different kind of pain.

Princeton was singing the lyrics as his head rested on her stomach. His hands were tapping her skin, mirroring the beat. Tallulah loved that Princeton would sing out loud. He really had a wonderful connection to music.

"This song is my conversation with God."

"What? What do you mean?" she asked surprised.

The music continued to play, and Princeton explained.

"Well, I'm telling Jesus that I'm going home, meaning *he's* my home. My safety. I'm not running from my life, just wanting more from it. Ever since I could remember, there was something missing, something that didn't seem right. My parents were great, and to everyone's eye, my life seemed perfect. What made it worse was, my inside didn't match my outside. People assumed I was interested in partying, sex, drugs—it didn't appeal to me. I felt like I was in this constant battle, trying to live this life, yet not be part of the world's demise. So . . . I would retreat deeper into myself, and the only thing that kept me going was my relationship with God. He chose *me* . . . It wasn't like a conversion. There wasn't this one moment of revelation; it was just sort of with me always. I remember being so young and

141

feeling this 'thing' . . . that he was embracing me. That he understood me. So through the years, he became my BFF."

Tallulah interrupted and asked, "What about Max?"

"Max was great," Princeton replied.

"But how could he understand my struggle . . . if I didn't even understand it, not completely?" Princeton continued. "So I'm telling God that he's always been enough for me. It's easy to understand why I loved him, but the part that says 'Your love remains true / I don't know why / You always seem to give me another try', wow! To think that he loves *me* so much . . . is amazing. The part about the places and faces getting old is me telling him I've had enough. I'm ready for more . . . I need more! Then God responds,

'Be careful what you wish for 'cause you just might get it all, and then some you don't want.' That's him telling me, if I give you what you want, meaning you"—he pointed to Tallulah—"that I'd better be ready to know what to do with it."

Tallulah clenched his body, and a tiny tear formed in her eye.

"What about the part about some you don't want?" she asked.

"Oh, that's the price of having you! The fear . . . that if I ever lost you . . . I'd die. I'm sure that Daughtry's intentions of the lyrics are different than my interpretation, but the moment I heard the song, that's what it meant to me."

Tallulah lay there, taking in his words. She heard the song dozens of times, yet now it was completely different.

"How do you do that?" she asked as she held him tighter. She didn't wait for an answer.

"How does your mind process things that become so deep and profound? Sometimes I wish I could be inside your head just for a minute to know what it's like to be you."

Princeton chuckled, turned his head, and rested his chin on her stomach as he looked up at her.

"You're kidding me, right? You're exactly the same! There are times when I'm so blown away by the way you approach things . . . your thoughts. The way you give new meaning to everyday occurrences. Baby, baby, we're exactly the same!"

"Do you have this CD in your car?" she asked.

"Yep."

"What color?"

"Black."

"Do you listen to it a lot?"

"Yep, why?" he asked.

"I just like knowing things like that. This way I can imagine you driving and listening when I'm missing you."

"This song has actually been inspiration for some great photos."

"How come you never told me about this before?"

"Don't know. I guess it was meant to be for right now."

The song had already finished, and Tallulah asked him to play it again.

"Sure, baby, listen to the small break. It's like a symphony is in the background."

He hit Play, and they listened to the song again, each lost in their own thoughts.

I'm staring out into the night,
Trying to hide the pain.
I'm going to the place where love
And feeling good don't ever cost a thing.
And the pain you feel's a different kind of pain.

Tallulah started to fall asleep and forced herself to open her eyes and concentrate on waking up.

"Now . . . I'm really starving!" she exclaimed.

Princeton rolled off of her, kissed her forehead, and read the clock, 10:40.

"If we don't move, it'll be lunch instead of breakfast. I'm giving you fifteen and fifteen."

Tallulah smiled. "After this conversation, it might be thirty and fifteen."

Princeton got up, threw on his sweats, and made his way down to the kitchen. He poured himself a glass of peach fusion and checked his phone. Five missed calls. As he checked the log, each one read Max. He hit the Return button, thinking something may be wrong. "Five calls?" he thought.

"Is this the Prince?" Max's voice asked, sounding joyful.

"Hey, buddy, what's up?" Princeton responded as he felt relieved hearing Max's tone.

"Well, let me see, life is great! Absolutely great! You're great, I'm terrific, Victoria is amazing, Tallulah is stupendous, and I'm going to marry Piper!"

Princeton stared at his juice, taking in Max's words, and felt a rush of excitement as he exclaimed, "What? Are you serious? What happened? Did you propose? This is fantastic! Tell me what's going on! Tell me everything."

Max made an attempt to explain the revelation of last night. He was caught in a momentum of action created by Victoria's words. Princeton listened and completely understood Max's feelings of being inspired. So many times, he was on the receiving end of the words that would lift his spirit, fill his need for hope, and cleanse the open sores of his heart. That sense of direction and recognition was by far one of the most incredible awakenings that he experienced over and over again. As Max was finishing his testimony, Princeton interrupted.

"Did you call Piper?" he asked.

"I didn't speak to her, I left her a long message telling her how much I love her and why . . . I don't think I want to discuss this. I want to be romantic and just propose."

Princeton was caught in a space between listening to Max and remembering his own desire to want to marry Tallulah.

"This is so fantastic, Max! I prayed so many times that you and Piper would find your place in one another."

"Do you think God used Victoria to open my eyes?" Max asked.

Just hearing Max say God out loud in connection to his feelings made Princeton smile.

"Well, it appears so, huh? Listen, Tallulah and I are going to grab some breakfast, why don't you meet us?" Princeton asked.

"You think I should?" Max asked.

"Are you kidding? Tallulah's going to be off the charts with this! Meet us at the Boulevard in half an hour."

"OK, see you in thirty."

Princeton was filled with excitement. He gulped his juice and ran up the stairs, and as he grabbed a pair of jeans, he called out to Tallulah, "Baby, you ready?"

Tallulah was throwing her ponytail through her cap as she called back, "Perfect timing."

"Wait till you hear the news!" Princeton exclaimed.

"What news?" she asked as she stood in the doorway, waiting for Princeton to tie his Diesels.

He brushed past her, stopped, backtracked, grabbed her chin, and kissed her gently with a huge smile, and replied, "You'll see."

She waited for him to brush his teeth and started wondering why Princeton seemed to be so elated.

"Tell me, what is it?" she asked.

"You'll see, let's go!"

*   *   *   *   *

Zach was placing the bird of paradise in the vase and sipping his cappuccino. His eyes were confirming that the arrangement was proportioned correctly. A simple thing like a flower arrangement was a task that he had mastered. It wasn't so long ago that all of this had been foreign to him. The strategic placing of art, the lighting, music, floral arrangements, all contributed to an ambiance of the studio's statement. He found tremendous satisfaction in his ability to understand it and successfully execute the finished product. When he was in the studio, it was as if he was living a different life. His days were filled with culture, expression, and interaction with clients that had reached a level of notability.

His pursuit to be driven to absorb the genre of Princeton's work fed his desire to want to reach a different level within himself. He was training his mind and spirit to embrace the artistic value of every nook and cranny of not only this space, but all that he came in contact with. He wanted to see himself as an artist. His new circle seemed to master that talent. Princeton, Tallulah, Victoria, Max, Piper—they all were artists in different areas. He believed that their success and happiness were connected to their work. He was the new kid on the block, having to go to great lengths to prove his desire wasn't just a fleeting novelty. Seeing an object and wanting to photograph it from the precise angel to get the perfect shadow or exact expression thrilled him. It filled him with a paradox of adrenaline and peace. Some of his attempts were good, but there was so much to learn. He would replay Princeton's words over and over again in his mind.

"Don't get caught up in the mechanics," he would say. "Let your soul do the work. Feel it in your heart and have your eye align with that feeling."

"Easy for you to say," he thought. "You're Princeton! You're the man that creates incredible photos that have depth and beauty. You're borderline celebrity." As his mind embraced that thought, he turned to the sound of the door opening. He was startled to see Makenzie walking in with two garment bags hanging from her fingertips.

"Hi you," she said as she smiled.

"Hi . . . this is a pleasant surprise!" he said as he walked toward her.

She quickly scoped the area to be certain no one was there and then gave him a full tender kiss. His eyes locked in on her face, and he whispered, "You look beautiful . . . as always."

"It's a lucky thing you said that because I'm frantic about tonight."

She stepped back and took in the area, pivoting herself in a circular motion.

"Wow! This is so beautiful! No wonder why you love coming to work."

Zach just stood there, observing her reaction. Her eyes rested on "Life and Death."

"Could it be any bigger?" she asked.

Zach laughed and then became pensive.

He replied with "That's Princeton's lifeline, so to speak, his alpha."

She slowly walked the studio with Zach following behind.

"So that's the couple of the hour?" she asked as she peered at the collage of photos above the desk. No matter where her eye traveled, there was this striking beauty staring at her. She finally was able to put a face with the name. She imagined Tallulah to be pretty, but nothing as captivating as what she was looking at. She had seen a photo of Princeton in one of the local journals. It definitely didn't do him justice. As she continued to look at the photos, the thing that struck her the most was the connection of the looks shared in the photos of them. There was this beautiful, genuine sexiness about them. Not individually but as a pair.

"They're beautiful," Makenzie exclaimed.

"Inside and out," Zach replied.

"So who photographed the ones of them together?" she asked.

"Oh, that's a tripod with an auto set. Princeton said he sets it up whenever he's compelled to catch moments of their life. Eventually, they forget it's there. Probably hours of film. When he develops them, he says it's like Christmas morning, never knowing what you're going to open. There have been times when there were dozens of completely empty shots . . . and then bam! The image of one perfect picture that captures the whole story. I guess Tallulah's used to it by now."

She had heard so much about Princeton and Tallulah. Zach seemed to idolize their relationship. He would speak about their life, explaining their faith, choices, careers, almost the way a proud parent would. She knew they were very important to him, which made her even more nervous about tonight! She would rather be meeting his parents.

"So, beautiful lady, what brings you to my place of retreat?" Before she could respond, he asked, "Would you like a cappuccino?"

"That would be great, thanks."

He walked behind the bar and started to brew her coffee. He was watching her as she moved from photo to photo, apparently reading titles and prices. Makenzie was the first woman that Zach felt in sync with. He had changed so much over the past few years that his attraction to woman had also changed. He no longer was interested in the obvious beautiful woman. Although Makenzie was very attractive, it was her charm, manners, and artistic drive that caught his attention. She was an aspiring fashion designer, which explained her cutting edge choice with her wardrobe. She was slightly eclectic, which was appealing to Zach. Tallulah once told him, "When you find someone that expands your vision, you'll know it."

As much as he didn't want to admit it, much of his initial attraction to Makenzie was that he felt sure she would get the seal of approval from Princeton and Tallulah. He would justify his slight guilt by telling himself that was a good thing. After all, he wanted to be a better man, which needed of course a better woman. Now as he looked at her, still holding the garment bags, he felt a wonderful emotion of "belonging." He wanted them to be a couple, an extension of each other.

He said, "OK, Ms. Micali, step into my private office" as he pointed to the stool.

"One sugar?" he asked.

"That's right," she answered as she sat down, hanging the bags on the frame of the adjacent stool.

He placed his elbows on the bar and held his chin in his hands. He examined her face, following the lines of her jaw up to her eyes. She definitely had makeup on, yet it was subtle enough to appear natural. Her medium skin tone was flawless as if it were airbrushed. Tiny flecks of iridescent colors bounced off her cheeks. Her large brown eyes would alone be ordinary; however, contrasted against the deep burnt sienna hair, they became a wow factor.

As he took it all in, he was convinced that she never would have been attracted to him pre-Princeton. Or maybe it was vice versa, he not to her. She complimented his evolving persona. The aura that she expelled stated class and creativity. She was the first woman he had met that fit into his new lifestyle and circle.

"What's the secret password?" she asked.

Zach looked at her puzzled.

"My coffee?"

"Oh!" He slid the cup to her and smiled.

"I was lost in your face," he said as he blushed.

She smiled and replied, "You always have a way of making me feel special . . . you know . . . different from what I'm used to hearing. I think it's your sincerity."

Zach had heard women say a lot of things about him, but sincerity wasn't among the top ten. He leaned in close to her and said, "I like hearing you say that—sincerity. My feelings for you *are* genuine, I'm just new at this."

"Well, that's very appealing! New means it's different. I don't want to be just another woman on your long list of conquests." She smiled and moved closer toward his face.

"You will never be *just* another woman. You already have more of my heart that I've ever given."

They locked eyes, and Makenzie gently kissed his mouth. She spoke as her lips were ever so slightly still touching his.

"Your heart is safe with me. I fell for you somewhere between the beginning and the end of our first date."

As he took in her words, his heart started to pound, and he began to feel light-headed. He was about to explore her mouth when he caught the reality of where they were. He pulled back and said, "Makenzie, you have this effect on me that's just wonderful. I have to be careful because you're making me feel things that I'm not sure how to deal with. It's very physical, yet it's much more. I really want to be with you . . . only you."

Makenzie let out a deep sigh and smiled.

"I was hoping you were feeling what I was feeling. Since the day I met you . . . I've been yours."

Zach gently ran the back of his hand along her cheek. She closed her eyes for a moment, opened them, and said, "Well, this is more than I bargained for. I came in for a dress choice, and I'm leaving with a beautiful memory."

Zach forced himself out of the moment.

"OK, beautiful lady, let's see what you have," he said as he pointed to the hanger.

Makenzie stood up and unzipped the garment bags. She let each hanger dangle by her index fingers at shoulder level.

"Now remember the accessories and shoes complete the package. I really was looking for your color choice, seeing how you're going to have to look at it all night."

Zach's eyes bounced from one dress to the other. Each one looked simple but beautiful. The fabrics appeared to be expensive. Frankly, he couldn't imagine what either one would look like as a finished product. He just felt like he could trust her to look fantastic and appropriate because of her design talent. Her slender, model-type figure was the perfect foundation for her fashion statements. Up to now, whether she was casual or dressy, she always turned heads. Zach enjoyed the anticipation of what she would be wearing on their next date. Makenzie's voice interrupted his thoughts.

"You don't like them?" she asked.

"No . . . no, it's not that. They're beautiful. I'm just out of my league when it comes to this."

"Nice try, which do you prefer?"

"Hold the pink-and-orange one up against you."

She put the black-and-white one on the stool and did as he asked.

"OK, now the black-and-white."

She looked so sweet and innocent, waiting for his decision. Zach realized he liked having his opinion matter. This also was new for him.

"Sweetie, I'm gonna have to go with the pink-and-orange."

Makenzie seemed ecstatic.

"Thank you, thank you, I was leaning toward that one too! That's my design! I designed this dress, and my friend made it for me off my sketch!"

"Are you kidding?" Zach was amazed. "That's incredible!"

Makenzie seemed to be blushing as she said, "No, it's mine! As a matter-of-fact, quite a few of the pieces you've seen me in are my designs. My friend is so awesome, she just keeps 'whipping' them up for me!"

"Well, Ms. Micali, we better figure out where you're going to showcase your works of art."

Laughing, she replied, "I only wish."

She grabbed the dresses, quickly zipped the bags, and walked behind the bar.

"I'm going to get out of your hair now because I need to be sure that you will love what you're looking at tonight."

Before he could answer, she kissed him, turned, and then turned again to face him.

"I am sooo into you. See you at 6:30."

Zach just stood there, watching her walk out the door as he thought, "She's the one . . . oh my gosh, she's the one?"

*   *   *   *   *

Princeton and Tallulah were discussing the details of tonight's extravaganza as they drove to the Boulevard.

"Baby, remind me not to forget Mom's gift."

"OK, when you were downstairs this morning, I spoke to her for a minute."

"Of course, you did. I don't think one day has gone by since we've been together that you haven't touched base before beginning your day. I think that's one of the things that makes me love the two of you even more."

"You think? It's kind of weird, but it's our thing. I just don't feel ready to face the day without that conversation."

"You don't need to explain, I completely understand."

"You would, wouldn't you? Well anyway, she's actually going to take some time for herself! She's going to the salon to get an overhaul. The one you gave her as the gift certificate, remember?"

"She hasn't used that yet? You're kidding me. Good thing she's a natural beauty."

Princeton looked over to Tallulah, saying, "Just like her daughter."

Tallulah smiled and leaned over and kissed him. Then she got this urge to kiss his cheek, his chin, his forehead. She was laughing and covering his face with kisses. Princeton loved being showered with her affection.

"Should I pull over?" he asked as he was smiling.

"Not if you want to be fed and definitely not if you're willing to get a ticket for indecent exposure!"

"Just as well, I don't want to be late for the surprise," he said as he winked at her.

Max was finishing his juice, patiently waiting to share his news. His eyes looked at the door each time someone walked in. He checked his watch and was hoping they would be walking in any minute. He glanced at the menu for the third time when he saw the dynamic duo out of the corner of his eye. Princeton had his arms wrapped around Tallulah's shoulders as she was saying something to him that obviously was funny because he was laughing. Max took note of Princeton opening the door for her and allowing her to enter first with his hand on her back.

"That's what I'm talking about," he said to himself. "He really takes care of her."

Tallulah stopped, waiting to be seated, when she spotted Max.

"Max!" she exclaimed.

"Baby, Max is here," she turned to see Princeton smiling as she started to walk over.

Max got up and gave her a big hug and kiss. Princeton caught the stare of a guy at another table, checking out Tallulah.

"Hey, buddy." Instead of the usual greeting, Princeton hugged Max and whispered, "This is going to be great."

Tallulah sat down as Princeton pulled out her chair. She was wondering what was going on.

"Was this planned?" she asked.

"Is this part of the surprise?"

"You didn't tell her?" Max asked Princeton.

"Tell me what?" Tallulah asked inquisitively.

"No, and let's order first," Princeton said, "I'm starving."

The waitress came over and asked for the drink order.

"What's your name?" Tallulah asked.

"Sarah."

"Sarah, that's a nice name."

"Thank you."

"OK, Sarah, we're really hungry, so I'm going to give you my order now. Did you order yet, Max?"

"No, I was waiting for you."

Sarah was looking at the table, thinking, "Could there be three people at one table that are sooo attractive?" She took their orders, trying not to be obvious about her attraction to Princeton. "Drop-dead gorgeous," she thought. Tallulah picked up on her body language. When she left to get their drinks, Tallulah leaned over to Princeton, who had his hand on her thigh, and said, "Baby, you're going to give her a heart attack."

"Better not, I need my food!"

They laughed as Max cleared the space in front of him to lean in closer to them, ready to make his presentation! Tallulah was filled with anticipation as she watched Max.

"Well?" she said as she saw Max look at Princeton as they both smiled.

Max cleared his throat with exaggeration and said, "I'm going to change my life."

Princeton was focused on Tallulah to be certain he would not miss her reaction.

"What? What do you mean?"

Tallulah's words were heightened with excitement as she quickly glanced over to Princeton, waiting for Max's response. Sarah appeared with the drinks, and all three quickly sat back as to signal for her to put them down.

"Your food will be over in a minute. I took the liberty of getting you a large cranberry juice, is that OK?" she asked as she placed it in front of Princeton.

"Yeah, that's great, thank you," he said as he was still focused on Tallulah.

"C'mon, Max! You're killing me here. What's going on?"

Princeton laughed. "C'mon, Max, she's going to hyperventilate if you don't get this going."

"OK . . . OK . . . well, I was with your mother last night," he said as he looked at Tallulah.

"Oh well, that explains it," she said as she smiled.

Max continued, "And something happened. Something wonderful, really wonderful! It was probably one of the best times of my life! It was as if your mother knew what I needed and was able to help me understand things that I've been struggling with."

Princeton was listening to Max and nodding yes as he recognized exactly what Max was explaining.

"It's time for me to make some changes in my life. It's time for me to grow up and commit to being the man I want to be."

Tallulah still wasn't certain where this was going.

"Max, that's wonderful! Just for the record, I think you're a very special man already. After all, you were Princeton's choice. He knew he could trust you."

Max beamed as he said, "Thank you, beautiful lady, but now it's time for me to take some steps toward my dreams, my future."

"How long was this dinner date?" Tallulah asked playfully. "You're not enlisting, are you?"

"They wouldn't take him . . . not with all that ink on him," Princeton said as he followed Tallulah's lead of friendly sarcasm.

"No," Max said, "besides I think I've already missed the cutoff."

Tallulah laughed. Just as Max was going to continue, she saw Sarah approaching with her hands filled with dishes.

"Did we order all that?" Tallulah asked as Max and Princeton followed her eye.

"That's just mine," Princeton said.

"Here we go," Sarah said as she placed the dishes in their appropriate spots.

"I'll be back in a second with your toast."

Princeton took his hand off Tallulah's thigh, clasped his hands, and bowed his head to give thanks.

"No, let me," Max said.

Tallulah was stunned. She couldn't ever remember a time when Max initiated grace.

"Oh my god! Max! Did God reveal himself to you? Is that what this is about?"

"In a way . . . I think . . . I'm not sure," Max replied.

He said a simple thank-you prayer, and they began to eat. As Princeton finished swallowing his first bite, he said, "Max, if you don't speed this up, we're going to miss the fund-raiser tonight."

Max directed his focus to Tallulah, and she put her fork down, knowing that Max wanted her full attention.

"I'm going to marry Piper."

Tallulah stared at him as his words seemed to slowly reach their destination.

"What? What?" Tallulah's voice was getting louder.

"Oh my gosh! Oh my gosh, Max! That's wonderful."

She got up, threw her arms around his neck, and said, "Congratulations."

Princeton looked at her and saw the joy and excitement she was feeling.

"Baby, when did you know about this?" she asked as she looked at Princeton.

Princeton was smiling and answered, "A little while ago."

Tallulah returned to her chair, and the parade of question gushed from her mouth.

"Did you propose? When did this happen? How come Piper didn't call me? When's the date? Did you . . ."

Max interrupted, "No, I didn't propose . . . not yet, that's why I need your help. How should I do this?"

As Tallulah started to calm down, her mind was remembering the many conversations she and Piper had the last few years, concerning her and Max's relationship.

"Well," Tallulah answered, "do you want an engagement period? Do you even want to get engaged? You know the traditional on one knee? Is this a surprise for Piper? Or have the two of you discussed it?"

"We haven't discussed it . . . and I think I want to take a chance and propose without discussing it."

"That's pretty brazen, buddy, but very romantic, what do you think, baby?" Princeton asked as he looked at Tallulah.

"Well, I agree, I think the romantic road is the best, but it all depends on the time frame and if there's a ring involved."

"Tallulah, you and Princeton didn't really have an engagement, you just set a date, right?"

Princeton looked at Tallulah, remembering the night they professed their love and made their wedding plans. His heart was starting to beat faster as he answered, "Yep, we moved right into the wedding thing. Tallulah didn't want a ring."

"That was just *my* choice, Max. Every woman is different."

"Tallulah, no one knows Piper better than you. Well, maybe your mother. So what do you think *she* would want?" Max asked looking intense.

Tallulah looked pensive as her thoughts were going a mile a minute.

"OK, OK, let's put this into perspective. The choices are, you propose, no ring, and state your desire to get married within a short time frame. You propose with a ring and have an engagement period, traditional party, etc. Or you can do a ring and still get married quickly."

Max was listening and asked, "Is a ring important to her? I can afford a rock, if that's what she wants."

"Well, first off, with Piper it's the style, not the size that would matter. You know how 'off' she is. Let me think about this for a minute. Your eggs are getting cold."

Max and Princeton were relieved to let Tallulah take the reins as they both started to consume their lukewarm breakfast. Tallulah looked like she was deep in thought as she hardly touched her plate. Princeton glanced over in between bites to see if Tallulah had reached a decision.

"Baby, please eat something," Princeton said as he placed his toasted bagel in her mouth.

She took a bite, scooped up a fork full of eggs, and tried to swallow quickly.

"All right, these are my thoughts."

Both Princeton and Max put their forks down and turned to Tallulah.

"Max, I think you're a wonderful man."

"I like where this is going," Max said smiling.

"And of course you know how much I love Piper, but I think if we overanalyze this, it will become a project, instead of your proclamation of love. Whatever you're feeling now is what you need to embrace. You know? Keep the momentum going . . ."

Max interrupted, "That's something similar to what your mom said."

Princeton chuckled. "Great minds think alike."

"Profess your thoughts and feelings to Piper. Tell her what's in your heart, set the foundation as far . . ."

"Why? Do you think she's not in the same place?" Max asked.

"I don't know. But that doesn't matter. What matters is that you pursue your desire wholeheartedly 110 percent, you know. Be the knight and don't give up until you can begin a new chapter, a new life together."

Max looked happy and somewhat peaceful as he nodded his confirmation of yes to Tallulah's words.

"What I was going to say was, if you want to get a ring, I can help. I can go with you. No wait! Actually, my mom would be the best person for that. She knows a zillion places for beautiful vintage pieces, which Piper would flip for! You know, something to match that car of hers? Which, by the way, can't you convince her to get with the living? I drove it last month, and my heart was in my mouth. The steering and brakes are scary!"

Max and Princeton were laughing.

"Not a chance," Max replied.

"I tried. She loves that dinosaur. She told me that when the snow comes, and she concedes to driving the SUV, she feels like she's giving up a piece of herself, her identity. She said she becomes everyone else. It's a big deal to her."

"Well anyway, do not go to a retail jewelry store. That's not her."

"You think your mom would do that? Because I'm onboard, let's go today!"

"How are we going to contain you, buddy?" Princeton asked.

"Actually, don't answer that. I like you like this. So full of emotion, it's great!"

Tallulah swallowed another fork full of eggs and said, "Today is out. Tonight is huge! Did you forget? I'm going to call her now, and I'm sure she's going to be over the moon. After all, Piper is her 'daughter' too."

Tallulah took her phone out of her bag and got up to walk to the entrance.

"Finish up, boys, this is going to be a crazy day."

Max and Princeton continued to eat and talk as Tallulah stood in the entryway lost in conversation. Princeton glanced over and felt a surge of love for his beautiful woman, so full of expression and laughter. Her excitement was so obvious as he watched her body movements, trying to imagine her words. He thought to himself, "I can't believe that's mine . . . that incredible beautiful woman is mine!"

Max studied him watching her and thought, "That's what I want. I only wish that Piper and I can have that."

Princeton turned back to Max, and Max said, "You know all those years, I didn't *really* get it. You were so sure that there was something missing . . . a piece of you incomplete. I just went along because, well, because you were my best friend, and I didn't want to ruin your dream. These past few years, I always wanted to tell you . . ."

"What?" Princeton asked.

"Well, that you're my hero. I was so envious that you were able to stay on track, you know, with your faith, your celibacy, your dream. And you were right! You always told me to keep my eye on the prize, and I didn't get it. I went ahead and lived my life carelessly. If I could take it all back, if I could start over . . ."

Princeton's heart was touched, and he knew his friend's profession was a longtime coming.

He leaned in toward Max and said, "You always stood by me . . . even when you didn't understand. I knew you thought I was searching for something that didn't exist, but you always stood by me. Even when you gave me a hard time and tried to cover up your loyalty with sarcasm, I knew you were silently rooting for me, and I love you for that. Don't look back and wish you did things differently, just look ahead and do things differently *now*! Keep your eye on the prize, and if you tell anyone that I said I love you, I'll deny it."

Max looked at Princeton and impulsively grabbed his hand, and gave him their infamous handshake from back in the day. He was still flying on the tail end of last's night emotional encounter, and now hearing Princeton's words, it ignited his better understanding of their bond.

"The day we came upon each other at school was the mark of the beginning of so many changes in my life. I guess the direction we took together was meant to be. Now all I am, all I have, my fiancé, my business, my possessions are all somehow linked to *you*! Deep, deep, stuff."

Max stopped to take a moment to control his emotion.

"God watches his flock," Princeton said with a huge smile.

They both looked up as Tallulah stood in front of them.

"What is going on here? Male bonding?"

Tallulah sat down and let out an exaggerated sigh.

"Just as I said, Mom is ecstatic."

"She thinks it's a good idea?" Max asked.

"She is thrilled, and she said she knows exactly where to go for the ring. She said I was there once, but I don't remember. Somewhere on Rhode Island."

"When is this taking place?" Princeton asked.

"She said the three of us can go on Monday. That works for me. I have Tom White tomorrow."

"Tom White?" Max asked, excited.

"Why is everyone soooo impressed with Tom White? I personally think he's boring. Anyway, does Monday work for you, Max?"

"I'll make some changes with my appointments. I'll make it work."

"Well, I feel out of the loop here. While you're diamond hunting, I'll be shooting with Zach."

"Talk about out of the loop. Since when does Zach shoot with you?" Max asked with a tone of surprise and a little envy.

"First time. I think he's ready."

"Well, he's definitely come a long way! Have you guys met Makenzie yet?"

"No," Tallulah said. "The poor thing is making her debut tonight. Let's be kind to her. I wouldn't want to be meeting all of us at one time! Hopefully, she'll still come to dinner on Thursday."

"Pass that on to my future wife. Hey, I like the sound of that. She can be a tough one to crack," Max said.

"That's because she's protective of the people she loves," Tallulah said as she winked at Max.

Sarah appeared and started to clear the dishes. She looked directly at Princeton and asked, "Should I bring fresh coffee?"

"No, thank you, none for me. Baby?"

"Yes, that would be nice. This has been some morning, huh? Max, more coffee?"

"Sure, a quick one. I need to get going. Not only do I need to look rockin' tonight, but I have to be on time. I promised Piper."

"OK, two more coffee?" Sarah confirmed.

"In that case, make it three," Princeton said as he wrapped his arms around Tallulah and rested his head on her shoulder.

Sarah left with her armload of dishes, thinking, "Lucky girl, must be newlyweds."

THE EASTER BUNNY

If you were watching a movie, the footage would be the camera bouncing from scene to scene with quick snap shots of the nine characters getting ready for the big gala event. Each one excited about the promise of great food, magnificent atmosphere, glorious music, wonderful conversation, and the opportunity to have time mixing it up with the "power people." Not only did the formal black tie guarantee a genre that stretched the everyday conversation to new heights of awareness and style, it did it with the end result benefiting a great cause. There was something about $1,500-a-plate gatherings that made people feel worthy and purposeful. The expectation was high, but if you were familiar with Victoria's fund-raisers, you would know you wouldn't be disappointed. Maybe it was her designer savvy or her passion to help the children, but whatever motivated her, the final product was always breathtaking. As if the price tag wasn't high enough, you would have the opportunity to purchase an array of fine collectibles, estate pieces, Princetons, and anything else she felt was eclectic and desirable. The way they were displayed was always an anticipated unveiling. There wouldn't necessarily be a theme, but the overall feeling would dictate a sense of old-world money and impeccable taste.

One time, the centerpieces were a collection of elaborate women's hats. Each hat sat high on white ceramic face stands surrounded by an assortment of feathers and roses. It was stepping back into the millinery era. Whether women were wearing hats or not, each one sold before night's end. The small red dot next to each table card describing the hat insured the four to six hundred dollar pieces were going home with one of the guests. There was also the night when the champagne fountain had buckets of bottles of Perrier-Jouët sitting in ice, arranged in a large circle. Each bottle had a beautiful bracelet draped around its neck. The pieces were one of a kind treasures, and they sparkled in the beautiful dim lighting waiting to get their dot. They averaged four digits, and each one had a home before ten o'clock.

One thing remained the same, and that was the space dedicated to the Princetons. Whether they were sporadically placed throughout the room or grouped on an entire wall, you could be certain that you would have a choice of at least twenty to thirty pieces. Princeton wouldn't take any of the percentage of the proceeds. Every penny went to the benefit. That was a lot of pennies, considering each piece held a tag of three hundred to fifteen hundred dollars. So, in essence, Princeton's night out could easily be a contribution of twenty thousand dollars. He never even mentioned it. He was thrilled that so many people wanted his work, and secretly he enjoyed watching which person would match up with each piece. The overflow of compliments would make him feel accomplished and a little uneasy. There would be times when someone would ask him to sign his autograph on their place card setting, and he would genuinely be surprised. Business would immediately increase within a week or so following each event. Once people saw his work hanging on someone's wall, they found their way to the studio.

Tonight's collection was one of Victoria's most time-consuming projects. She was fortunate enough to find a small vintage boutique that exceeded her expectations for the rings she had in mind. Due to its location on the Cape, she wasn't able to just pop in. She was so impressed by the initial pieces that she did a lot of the purchasing via phone sight unseen. She was using her personal dollars and was certain she would get her initial investment returned with a large profit for the fund-raiser. Her initial purchase was eleven rings. They were all different and all amazingly beautiful pieces of the highest quality. Her goal was fifty, and tonight there were fifty-three rings each displayed on a finger of the most unusual gloves. They were kidskin, butter soft, and had the most distinctive details—elaborate stitching, buttons, and appliqués. You could never find gloves like these at local retailers; they were vintage and screamed Old Hollywood.

Each ring would bring in a donation of $500-$700, and each glove $200. The total dollars generated for the four-hour bash was mind boggling. If you did the math, you would add the cost of the $1,500 plates multiplied by 100 guests, equaling $150,000. The sales of the collection of rings and gloves, approximately $33,000. The Princetons at least $20,000, and the "love offering" envelopes at each table usually brought in an additional $10,000-$20,000! Her total cost for everything—food, music, staff, florals—never topped $25,000. So minus her initial investment, Victoria's kids could look forward to at least $180,000-$200,000 coming their way! That's why she was respected, admired, and deemed the best in charity circles. Although all would confirm her gift of business savvy, it was her depth of her commitment to her kids that made people want to be a part of her projects. Her sincerity and compassion was what people were sucked in by when she marketed her events. That was the part that touched their hearts. There also was the egotistical, superficial part that made them want to attend, so their level of status quo was recognized. Victoria also used that to fulfill her mission.

*   *   *   *   *

As Victoria stood before the full-length mirror, her mind was working overtime. She rechecked the list in her head, covering every last detail of tonight's gala. Her thoughts were being pulled in different directions—the news about Max and Piper, her conversation with Max at Luna, Zach's new girlfriend, the inevitable conversation tonight with Larry McCabe, looking forward to spending time with Rachel and Derek, and of course, the anticipation of tonight's success. She suddenly felt a wave of sadness as she thought about her circle. Her mind was caught in a small ball of nostalgia wishing her sister and the rest of her family were weaved into tonight's celebration. The years played their part in slowly separating their everyday lives. There was a time when Victoria and her sister physically shared every day and every episode of their lives. After all, she nurtured her sister all those years through her adolescence and coming of age. In the early years of her sister's marriage during the birth of her niece and nephew, the family was top priority.

Now twenty years later and geographically challenged, the gatherings were usually reserved for holidays and big family events. The love hadn't changed, each one still reaching out, keeping contact via phone, trying to hold on to their family tree. What did change was the ability to jump in the car and drive over for a quick cup of coffee or grab a movie at a moment's notice. Victoria let out a deep sigh and concentrated on the image in the mirror. Was this the reflection of a woman who had reached a notable level of success? Everything is relevant in comparison. Sure, compared to the life around her in Connecticut, she had arrived. However on a bigger scale, she felt small. If she would have remained in New York . . . traveled that path? "No, Victoria, don't do that!" she thought. "No rearview mirrors, remember?"

She turned from side to side, examining all angles of her Michael Kors. The fit and feel was perfect, and that's what mattered most to her. She would only wear a garment that was comfortable and needed no attention to restriction. When deciding on the perfect dress, it needed to move with her as she bended, twisted, and danced. Once on, she wanted to forget about the dress and concentrate on her massive role. There was no time for smoothing, tugging, or worrying about fabric creasing. She discarded many fabulous choices because they were what she referred to as statue pieces. They looked beautiful so long as you didn't move.

As you viewed this stunning piece from the front angle, the silhouette was long and lean. Black fabric hugged every inch of her extremely tall and thin frame. Flat stomach with protruding hipbones rested beneath a thin layer of black open crocheted lace. The neckline hugged her collarbones. The sleeves were without fabric, only bourdon lace, so that you could see the intricate pattern against the bronze skin of her arms. The lace scalloped right below her wrist, giving the eye the direction to see the impact of the black silhouette against the flesh-tone lace arms, nothing revealing from that angle. However, the back! That was the deal breaker. No back! Complete exposed skin coming to a halt an inch above her tailbone. That was something both she and Tallulah were crazy about. For some reason, exposed back was the ultimate sensual expression for Victoria. She only purchased numbers with permanent uplifts so not to have to ever worry about lingerie straps. This one was cut so precise that no matter how she moved, it remained pasted to her frame. Her only regret was the four-inch Givenchy's, which brought the final package to over six feet of fashion. She didn't mind the height; she just preferred flats. When she wore tuxedos and palazzos, the flats were a bonus. Not tonight. She checked her makeup, which to most would appear minimal, but to her it was a lot. Makeup was a chore to Victoria. "Good skin only needs bronzer and lipstick. Tallulah could carry that off, not at my age," she thought. She ran her fingers through her hair and lifted the crown, making sure it was natural and not starched. She sprayed her back with cool water, took one last look, and said "showtime" out loud as she grabbed her clutch.

*   *   *   *   *

Piper couldn't resist playing the message one more time. As she held her cell to her ear, the tone of Max's voice sent chills up her spine. His words were so sincere and seductive that they made her insides stir. She listened to it four or five times, and each time she felt excited and oddly aroused. The warm feeling covering her had almost become foreign. She had forgotten the rush she would get from Max's demeanor: so rugged, clever, intelligent, and obviously sexy. Hearing his words of love and commitment attached to his deep voice sent her into fantasies of their most private and seductive moments. "Where was this coming from?" she asked herself that question all day long. She didn't return the call because somewhere deep inside, she wanted to freeze this feeling. She wanted to savor every ounce of thrill and wonder. Her knight was coming, and he was going to whisk her off to their new life. She was anticipating the feeling she would get when she opened the door and their eyes would meet. "What *is* that new life, Piper?" she asked herself as she put down the cell and finally slipped on her Marc Jacobs. She wanted Max . . . now. She wanted him to bring her to heights of pleasure that she had suppressed for too long. "Marriage, he didn't say marriage, see? Now you're going to be this clingy, insecure female waiting for the end-all, be-all question, stop it! Screw your head on and your specs and get with the program!" As she completed that thought, she heard the FJ pull in.

*   *   *   *   *

Makenzie couldn't remember ever being this nervous as she applied another coat of twenty-four-hour lip color. "Well, your lips are good to go for five days now," she thought as she pulled on each angled layer to create her trademark edgy hairstyle. Whether it was the color or the sharp pronounced layers reaching her mid back, it was always a point of complimentary discussion. She stepped back to take in the total package and started to panic.

"Too much color, too much makeup?" The dress was a short chemise. It was simple, but the bold pattern of pink-and-orange muted diamonds made it a runway potential. The neckline was what she referred to as her work of art. The fabric was cutout in diamond shapes to mirror the pattern. Her skin peeked out through the large holes as the cutouts wrapped around to the zippered back. As she twisted herself to look at the back of the dress, she eyed her orange patent pumps. She absolutely loved the shoes, hoping they wouldn't put her above Zach's height. She concluded that her fear was she might be too edgy and not classic enough for the "out of her league" bash. "Well, it's going to be a hit or a disaster," she thought. "Either way, this is me! This is me, Zach. I'm not changing for anyone, not even for your circle of royalty." She applied another coat of lip color and waited for the bell to ring.

*   *   *   *   *

Tallulah stood perfectly still in front of the mirror with her eyes closed as she concentrated on Princeton's hand tracing her spine, which stopped at the belt of her dress.

His mouth on her ear, whispering, "You take my breath away."

With her eyes still closed, she drew in a deep breath as she zeroed in on his other hand slightly trembling as it held her waist tightly. Her mother had spent years preparing her for her great love to come, but nothing and no one could have prepared her for this love. The world outside looking in would see the perfect fairy tale existence. What they couldn't see was the tiny microscopic line bordering the pleasure and pain. How could both be equal? How could this love come with so many threshold moments of examining and reexamining the core of this obsessive unity? The extreme pleasure of their connection—physically, sexually, mentally—deeper than the average human understanding. The *need* to breathe each other. The exchange of touch, breath, and saliva. The insatiable desire to be in each other, primal as air and water. The safety and security of their world, only wanting and needing each other, the alpha and the omega of their purpose. The far and few between conversations regarding pure demons, if there was such a thing. A persistent force driving their intense devotion to one another. Their brain transfer of exact thoughts and ideas. Their sublime levels of euphoria and the addiction of wanting to go there over and over again. All that came with the price of pain and fear. Fear of losing each other, pain of having to be separated, if only to be a part of everyday life. Sometimes even *that* was a withdrawal, pain of not being able to wait until their bodies collided, fear of their inability to control their emotions and actions in public. Their love was bigger than they were as people.

The trembling from Princeton's hand transferred to his body as he took in deep breaths with eyes closed, inhaling Tallulah. She felt herself surrender to his wet mouth on her skin as she leaned her back into him. Her legs became unsteady, and her breathing increased with deep intakes of air. She opened her eyes to watch him in the mirror as he stood behind her with his hands firmly gripping her thighs. He was in "that place," moaning, talking, trembling. The image she saw catapulted her to an instant frenzy. The image of him taking her in, the way she affected him, his uncontrollable verbal reference to her belonging to him made her crazy with desire.

"Only you, baby, your taste, your skin, you're mine, come to me." Princeton's voice was low, focused, and in rhythm with each time his mouth released from her skin. Tallulah moaned and started to beg for him.

"Please, baby, please . . . take me with you."

Her words were getting frantic as she tried to hold on, waiting for him to connect to her, even just his mouth on hers would have been enough. Instead, he canvassed her body with his hands, using all his strength to hold them both up, with her weight resting on him. His hands went beneath the organza beauty as she dug the heels of her peep toes into the floor.

"Oh my god!" Tallulah was welcoming his touch as he found her. He moved and directed her to where and how he wanted to orchestrate his symphony of pleasure. His strength was amazing as he lifted her while still exploring her deepest existence. Each time he moved her, he melted his body into hers enveloping her until she couldn't distinguish herself from him. She was floating inside his words. "You're my reason . . . my beginning . . . my end." His demand was strong and sweet. "Give me you . . . all of you!"

Somewhere during their exchange of passion, Tallulah surrendered her deepest secrets as her wet body went limp.

"Baby, I can't move . . . I think I'm going to faint," Tallulah managed to say as she opened her eyes.

"I got you . . . I got you."

Princeton swooped her up and carried her to the chaise. As he seated her, he knelt down in front of her. Always, at that exact moment when he would see her spent, damp with sweat, exhausted from traveling with him, was when he felt totally fused to her. He found her eyes as she lifted them to show her expression of confirmation that he had touched her soul, and she was completely caught in the web of her love for him. He held on to her slightly shaking hands as his words were slow and deliberately accentuated.

"Inside us is a miracle," he said.

Tallulah held on to his hands, while she studied his face. She tried to accept what she was feeling, which was childlike, exposed, naked. He stripped her of her shell, and as always, he reached a place that didn't have a hint of confidence or glamour or sex appeal. He consumed her physically, but it was their spiritual connection that made her succumb to his use of her, to feed his appetite to want them to be transferred to "their place."

Most women would be preoccupied at this moment, worrying about their dress and makeup being ruined just before having to go out. Instead, Tallulah was worried that her words wouldn't be enough.

"Princeton . . . what are we?"

Hearing her words made him feel that familiar slight panic in the core of his chest. Although he looked at her a little puzzled, he completely understood the question. He took a moment to wrap his head around the words he wanted to say.

"We are who we are baby. We're the great American love story."

"I know that . . . but it's more . . . much more than that."

Tallulah paused as she tightened her grasp on his hands.

"You know, I find myself thinking that if I had to leave my family, my genetic heritage, my home, my existence, to be with you, I would! Could everything that I am only be complete through you?"

Princeton was on point to feel panicked. It had been a long time since they had one of these conversations, and every time they did, it resulted in each one loving and wanting one another more, and that resulted in the magnified fear that would surely follow—having to imagine what it would be like if their world were to change.

"My sweet, sweet angel, we were made separately with beautiful gifts that reach their glorious potential through each other. You're my muse, my inspiration, my light. You're the reason I look forward to another day, to begin the cycle of loving you all over again . . . and . . . and . . . to feel what it is to be loved. You're my life! And I'm not ready to die, so we're OK, baby, we're OK."

He took her face in his hands and kissed her mouth gently. He started to rise, grabbing her hand as he said, "Let's go and get ourselves presentable and make Mom proud."

"No wait," Tallulah said as she pulled him back down.

As he knelt down, Tallulah traced his face with her fingers. She locked her eyes into his and said, "My beautiful, beautiful Princeton. I love you with every breath of my life. I'm not ready to die yet either. Do I really make you feel loved? Truly loved . . . the way you deserve to feel? The way you make me feel?"

"Are you kidding me?" Princeton's face became intense as he asked the rhetorical question. His eyes started to fill as he seemed to explore his memory.

"I never imagined someone could make me feel so worthy, so powerful, so completely adored. My inner confidence, my direct response to the world around me is due to you making me feel that I am all you need . . . that you chose me! That you constantly remind me I'm responsible for your joy, your ecstasy, your happiness. You give me all and everything I need day after day. Your devotion to me is my drug. I become bigger and better because of you. Loved? Do you make me feel loved? You make me want to live . . . because of the way you love me."

Satisfied with his answer, Tallulah stroked his hair as he put his wet face into her lap.

*   *   *   *   *

Victoria leaned against the bar, took a sip of wine, and basked in the breath of the room. The pulse and heartbeat was intoxicating to her. Everything was moving in slow motion as she captured the total picture. The reflections of crystal bouncing off the zillion white lights in the dimly lit room; silhouettes of dresses, gowns, and bow ties, clinking glasses; enormous tall floral arrangements of deep purples flagging the perimeters of the space; identical smaller scales of the floral beauties serving as each table's centerpiece; dyed purple rose petals scattered upon the stark white matelassé linens; beautiful hand-painted stemware of purple rosettes defining each seat; champagne fountains releasing the liquid "diamonds" into pools of crystal perfection; dozens of spectacular gloves, owning their treasures on their ring fingers; the Princeton collection forming an abstract design, as each piece rested on a step of the different height white ladders, stretching across an eighteen-foot wall, all that enveloped in the beautiful subtle acoustics of the ten-piece orchestra, it was intoxicating! As the Chilean traveled down her throat, she was pleased with her choice of the Neyen. Her initial pick was the Montes Alpha M. However when comparing the fifty-dollar bottle to the hundred-dollar bottle, the Neyen won with more profit to the kids. Her body relaxed as she let out a satisfied sigh of approval.

"Stunning, just stunning."

Victoria turned to the voice and smiled as she said, "Hi, Larry, were you referring to me or the room?"

"Both! You look beautiful."

"Thank you, flattery will get you everywhere."

"That's the plan," he said as he smiled, while his eyes traveled the outline of her back.

"What will it be, sir?" the bartender asked.

"I'm all set," he answered as he pointed to his glass of Perrier-Jouët.

"Be careful, Larry, flower bottle is infamous for sneaking up on you."

Larry smiled and said, "Well, it's been a very long time since *anything* has sneaked up on me."

"Touché," Victoria said as she toasted his glass.

"How do you manage to orchestrate yet another beautiful event?"

Victoria thought for a moment and responded with "I think it's the driving force behind the train, you know, the kids. Pain is a greater motivator than pleasure, and the past doesn't equal the future."

Larry leaned in closer and said, "Why is it every time I'm with you, I feel just slightly inferior to your deep-seeded wisdom? You make me feel and think things that otherwise wouldn't be important to me. Can we try another evening together . . . please?"

Victoria studied his face and felt disappointed with her apparent nonexistent feelings for Larry.

"Larry, you're a wonderful man, which I'm sure many women would be thrilled to be a part of your world . . . just not this one."

Larry immediately regretted his invitation. "Too soon," he thought.

"My world is not very different from yours. It's just more elaborate on the outside and less purposeful on the inside."

Victoria smiled. "Keep talking like that, and I may just reconsider."

Larry smiled and felt relieved. "I met your son-in-law, quite the man. I haven't seen him."

Victoria looked to the entry, saying, "Speaking of which, there's one of my brood now. Excuse me."

Victoria started to walk toward Piper and Max.

"You two look fabulous!" Victoria exclaimed.

"Ma, wow! Talk about fabulous."

Max pulled Victoria in as he kissed her cheek, while Piper watched them feeling an unusual strong bond between the two.

"Doesn't she look drop-dead gorgeous?" Max asked, pointing to Piper.

Piper felt as if she were blushing. "Very schoolgirl," she thought.

"Absolutely! And, Max, you look fabulous as well."

Max grabbed on to Piper's waist, and she immediately responded to his strong yet gentle hold. She was so taken by his obvious display of claiming her as his. The tray of Perrier appeared before them, and Piper and Max each took one.

Max touched Piper's glass and said, "To us" and then gently kissed her cheek.

Victoria watched and felt satisfied that they were reaching their turning point.

"Ma, everything is sooooo beautiful. The Princetons look amazing."

"Is the man of the hour here yet?" Max asked.

"No, they should be arriving any second."

"Has Makenzie made her appearance?" Piper asked.

"No, and be nice, my little girl. If she's important to Zach, then we need to welcome her. Put yourself in her place."

"Don't worry, Ma, I'm feeling extra nice tonight," she said as she smiled and winked at Max.

Just as Victoria was getting ready to turn, she caught a glimpse of Zach walking in.

"Well, here's your chance," Victoria said to Piper as they turned to follow Victoria's eye. Makenzie thought she knew what to expect as she visualized this night in her mind, but as she and Zach entered the space, she was floored! The artistic value alone left her frozen.

"Hey, buddy," Max said as he hugged Zach.

Piper kissed Zach's cheek, and Zach kissed Victoria's and then started the introductions.

"Everyone, this is Makenzie." They all exchanged smiles as he pointed to each one. "Max . . . Piper . . . and this is Victoria."

Victoria made direct eye contact and said, "So nice to meet you, you look beautiful."

"Your dress is amazing," Piper said as she checked her out from head to toe.

"Thank you, this is uh . . . breathtaking!" Makenzie said as her eyes traveled the room.

Max chuckled and said, "Welcome to our circle."

"I'm going to make the rounds," Victoria said. "You know which table is yours . . . I'll catch up in a minute."

Victoria started the official meet and greet as she weaved through the tables, feeling a little uneasy. Her thoughts were with Princeton and Tallulah. Her daughter was never late—Ms. Punctuality. As she caught a glimpse of her Concorde, she realized it really wasn't late. Everyone else was just a little early.

Zach pulled the chair out for Makenzie as she seated herself. She found the aura of the space to be an instant inspiration for ideas of fabrics and patterns: the dinnerware, crystal, gloves, rings, all of it was very overwhelming. Her eyes traveled with Victoria as she watched her move. Imagine having a mother like that? It was all over the top for her. Max and Piper were so trendy? Artsy? Sort of a contemporary version of Bonnie and Clyde. She examined all the dresses, suits, and accessories that were passing by. "More money in this room than I've ever been a part of." She never thought of Zach as having money. At least not in this magnitude. How could he afford this? Was this what his life was like prior to her? How many women have sat at his side at these events? She tried to escape her thoughts as she sipped on her champagne. She didn't know what she was drinking, but she was sure it was a luxury brand. She felt as if at any moment someone from *E!* or *People* were going to be standing there snapping a photo of the weekend fashonistas for their next publication. You know, when you see photos and read the names below and they're not celebrities, but you know they have arrived!

"Something, huh?" Makenzie turned to Piper's voice, realizing Piper was studying her face as she asked the question.

"Yes, *really* something. Princeton's work looks amazing, his talent is amazing!"

"Speaking of which, it's not like them not to be the first here," Max interjected.

"Well, the wait is over," Piper said, gesturing to the entryway.

Victoria looked up as she was standing before a table, and her heart swelled as she saw the dynamic duo. As a matter-of-fact, many heads turned toward the entryway. Victoria excused herself and started walking to the *Esquire* couple. Makenzie's eyes were locked into the image at the doorway. "Beyond beautiful . . . literally beyond beautiful . . . devastatingly attractive!" She searched her mind for the appropriate description. "How could two people be equally gorgeous, sexy, and charismatic? Opposing genders equally matched?" She scoped Tallulah's dress as it was always a force of habit. "Off the charts, oh my gosh, the gloves!" Makenzie loved bracelet gloves. She just never saw anyone wearing them, aside from magazine shoots.

"Stand in line for his autograph?" Zach announced as the four of them watched the guests' eyes locked on the family portrait.

"I was getting worried," Victoria said as Princeton wrapped his arms around her.

"Sorry, Mom, we had something come up," Tallulah said as she kissed Victoria. Tallulah's eyes went to the collection.

"Perfect, just perfect. Baby, your work is ridiculous!"

Princeton smiled and said, "That's *your* work, I'm just the carrier."

Tallulah squeezed his hand that was resting on her back.

Princeton's eyes took in Victoria, and his heart skipped a beat.

"You're soooo beautiful."

Victoria smiled and then winked as she said, "Compared to you two, everything pales."

She placed her hands on their shoulders and gave them a once over.

"I absolutely love your dress, and you," she said as she looked at Princeton, "words aren't adequate. Your circle is getting restless. Max and Piper are definitely in a zone, and Makenzie is lovely. The drug of choice is Neyen, there are three bottles on your table."

"Are Rachel and Derek here?" Tallulah asked.

"Not yet, they're going to be a little late. They just got in from Maine."

"Maine?" Tallulah asked.

"Yeah, a seminar of sorts. Let's go have fun!"

Before they reached their table, there were seconds of stopping, shaking hands, introductions, and a parade of compliments for the black-and-white collection.

Piper poured two glasses of the red jewel, while Max and Zach were already standing, waiting for their guru. Makenzie watched as Princeton guided Tallulah to the table. Although he seemed to be aware of his surroundings, his attention was directed solely to her. She took a deep breath and hoped for the best. As Piper handed them their glasses, she announced, "Here you go, my lord and my lady."

Tallulah's and Princeton's smiles were so genuine, so pure, Makenzie felt that they were easy and natural to be around. Lots of hugs and kisses, and then Zach introduced them to Makenzie. Tallulah reached over and gently kissed Makenzie's cheek.

"So nice to meet you. Well, Zach, how did you manage to secure such a beauty?" Tallulah asked as she winked at Makenzie.

Makenzie blushed, which Princeton found charming. Princeton extended his hand, and the sparkle from his cuff links caught Makenzie's eye.

"Welcome," Princeton said as his other hand was still attached to Tallulah's back.

Makenzie was nervous that she was obviously staring, but the two of them were difficult to look away from.

"I'm so glad to meet you," Makenzie said. "Zach has told me so much about you."

"Imagine that!" Piper said with her usual wit.

"Behave, young lady, or we may have to get Mom here," Princeton said.

Tallulah immediately responded with "Don't worry, Makenzie, once you get to know my sister, you'll find her irresistible, I promise you."

Makenzie smiled, and immediately decided that Princeton and Tallulah were something special. All the fanfare had merit.

The night progressed into a symphony of conversation, laughter, dancing, eating, drinking, and successful red dots. As Princeton stood before the ladders, he examined his life through his work. Every photo had a memory attached vividly in his mind. Each memory had a piece of Tallulah occupying its space.

"You should be very proud." The voice behind his ear made him turn and say, "Did you ever see this for me, Mom? Did you think I was capable of this?"

Rachel kissed his cheek and said, "Maybe not exactly this, but you were destined for something greater than I understood."

Princeton traced the rim of his glass with his ring finger, mesmerized by the photos.

"All of this is not just me. This is a collaboration of God, Tallulah, and Victoria."

Rachel wondered if Princeton ever knew the extent of pain attached to not being included in his inspiration.

"But it *is* you, Princeton, that's why God gave you this gift. Tallulah and Victoria were the tools that were chosen."

Princeton looked at Rachel and put his arm around her shoulder.

"Mom, you know . . ." Princeton seemed to be struggling to choose his words.

"Sometimes there's not enough of me to be what you need as a son. I'm so consumed with Tallulah . . . and my faith, you know? And work . . . and . . ."

"It's OK. I'm so happy for your happiness. I had you for so many years. My heart would break over and over as you fought your demons, you know? This was your destiny. I understand, and I wouldn't want it any other way."

Tallulah watched the two from across the room. Her heart was full, seeing that snapshot. She only wished she could see it more often. Princeton made his decisions about his life, and Rachel respected them. She often wondered what it was like for Rachel and Derek to watch their son's life from the sidelines. How hard it must be to let go?

"Tallulah? Tallulah? Hello?"

Tallulah looked at Piper, saying, "Sorry, where were we?"

Piper gestured toward Princeton and Rachel and said, "Well, I was just telling Makenzie to take in the moment. It's very rare the Prince isn't at your side. This may be the longest time without his hands somewhere on your body!"

Tallulah leaned into Makenzie and said, "I still love her, in spite of herself."

Makenzie laughed.

"Well, we've covered all of us. Now what about you, mystery Makenzie? Are you and Zach an item?" Piper asked.

"I hope so." Makenzie's response was sweet and sincere. "I'm crazy about him. I just didn't anticipate this! Can he afford this? Oh! I'm sorry, Tallulah, let me get my foot out of my mouth; after all, he works for your husband. What I meant was, this all seems so much!"

"Well, it is!" Piper responded. "So make sure you're having a good time. This night set your Zach back at least four thousand."

Makenzie's mouth fell open.

"Don't worry," Tallulah quickly responded, "Zach is very capable. He didn't use to be, but now he is, and that's great, isn't it?"

"Makenzie, don't you know that the royal family makes things happen?" Piper looked at Tallulah and then said, "Go ahead, tell her about Princeton and Zach's agreement."

Makenzie focused on the stunning beauty, who obviously didn't know the power of her presence. She just seemed so comfortable in her own skin. As she took a sip of wine, Makenzie waited for Tallulah's answer.

"Princeton respects Zach and is appreciative of all his hard work. When Zach came to work for him, there was a fund-raiser about a month out. Princeton wanted to include him and start grooming him for a different direction in his life. He saw tremendous potential in Zach. So . . . he cut a deal with him. He told Zach that he would take care of his end and every fund-raiser after that . . . until Zach was able to hold his own. In Princeton's mind, it's all about the kids."

"Just like Ma," Piper interrupted.

"Princeton told him, once he was financially secure, he expected him to participate in each one. So you see? He can afford this, and that means he's doing well."

Tallulah raised her glass, and the three of them toasted to "the kids."

Piper looked at Makenzie and said, "Only two years ago, imagine? I already told you how Ma and Princeton put Max in a league of his own."

Tallulah continued with "Zach is very special to us, you're fortunate to be with him. Now, Makenzie, what about you? You obviously have a strong fashion sense, you're put together beautifully. I have to say, your hair? Just stunning! Love the dress."

"I'm hot for the shoes!" Piper said with a sly laugh.

"Well, thank you, that's it."

Tallulah and Piper looked at one another. "That's what?" Piper asked.

"That's what I do or at least what I'm trying to do. I designed this," she said as she ran her fingers along the neckline.

"What? You're kidding, right?" Tallulah's enthusiasm was surprising to Makenzie.

"No, really, I did. My friend just works off my sketch and the fabric I choose . . . and voila!"

"Oh my gosh, Makenzie! You need to market your talent! How long did it take you to design that?"

"Uh . . . I don't know . . . a couple of weeks maybe?"

"Have you got a collection together? You know, others that you've done?" Piper asked.

"Yes, lots, but only because I wear them, not with any intention of anyone actually wanting to buy them."

Tallulah was running her eyes up and down the dress.

"Stand up," she commanded.

Makenzie obeyed as she was quickly on her feet.

Tallulah stood up and grabbed Piper's and Makenzie's hands, and started walking toward the bar where Victoria, Derek, Rachel, and the boys were.

Princeton's eyes found Tallulah coming toward him, and he smiled as if he were watching an episode of *Lipstick Jungle* in slow motion. He watched the beautiful tan skin coming closer, pieces of hair bouncing, white fluorescents attached to that broad smile. She was captivating to him—so classy, so sexy, so his! His insides started to stir.

Zach always noticed the change in Princeton when he was connecting to Tallulah. His passion for her became evident in his physical sate. Whatever he had inside his heart and mind, it would transfer to his physicality—the expression on his face, his voice, his posture. It was like watching the immediate effect of a drug, minus the drug.

"Looks like your lady hit a home run," Max said to Zach, gesturing toward the trio approaching them.

Zach smiled and felt a surge of emotion. He knew she would fit; he just knew it.

Tallulah put pressure on their hands and stopped them right before they reached their partners.

"Mom, ladies and gentlemen," Tallulah announced, wanting their full attention.

She took Makenzie's hand, held it above her head, and twirled her in a slow circle.

"May I introduce, the Makenzie." She stopped and whispered in her ear, "What's your last name?"

"Micali," she whispered back.

"Makenzie Macali? I love it!"

She redirected her voice, saying, "May I introduce the preview of the Double M collection!"

Everyone seemed confused by the display of their blank expressions.

"Mom," Tallulah exclaimed as she pointed to the dress, "Makenzie *designed* this. This is her work!"

"Makenzie, that's fabulous!" Victoria said enthusiastically.

As her eyes scanned the dress, she continued with "Definitely a great choice of fabric, and I love the chemise cut. Beautiful work on the neckline, you're a very talented young lady."

Zach thought he was going to have a heart attack. So much attention to his lady made him bask in the glory of his choice for a partner.

Princeton knew the look in Tallulah's eyes when she was on a mission. He smiled and validated her idea with saying, "Your work is beautiful, Makenzie."

Max and everyone nodded their approval. Makenzie kept looking at Zach, hoping he was pleased.

Tallulah continued enthusiastically, "I think Makenzie should find a space and start a small collection and get Double M marketed!"

She looked at Princeton, saying, "Maybe somewhere in your area?"

Makenzie's heart was beating fast, and her thoughts were bouncing off Tallulah's words. She couldn't afford a label maker, let alone a boutique! But for that exact moment, it was total bliss hearing the excitement attached to her dress. Tallulah looked at Valerie, her mother's graphic art designer, who was sitting close enough at the bar to be part of the unveiling.

"Valerie," she asked, "would you buy this dress if you saw it at a boutique?"

Valerie smiled, saying, "Well, I don't have the legs to carry that number off, but if I did, yes! I would definitely buy it."

"See?" She clenched Makenzie's hand and said, "We'll talk about this on Thursday at the dinner party."

Tallulah walked into Princeton's arms, leaning against him, melting into his back. He closed his eyes and took in the scent of her skin from behind her neck. Derek watched in amazement. It was evident that Tallulah was his aphrodisiac. He wondered how that must feel.

"Well, she's definitely in," Piper said to Max, looking at Makenzie.

Max smiled, saying, "Don't worry, sweetie, there's enough love for everyone."

Piper laughed. "Well let's concentrate on *this* love."

Rachel asked Victoria, "Are creative people just drawn to you, or do you take out ads?"

Victoria smiled, saying, "We appeal to the senses of what we're most focused on. Apparently, Zach sent out those signals. The circle feeds itself."

"Mom," Princeton said.

Both Victoria and Rachel turned. He caught Victoria's eye and asked, "Was that Larry McCabe I saw you talking with earlier?"

"Yes, why?"

"I wanted to introduce him to Tallulah."

"Oh, he had to leave, but not before red dotting three of your pieces."

"He bought another three?" Zach asked.

"Sounds like a fan," Tallulah said as she winked at Princeton.

"I hope he ate before he left," Max said "The food is amazing."

Zach asked the bartender to get everyone a drink.

"OK, everyone, we need to toast! What will it be? Tonight's success? Makenzie's future?" He looked at Princeton and Tallulah. "The dream team?"

As the glasses came around, Piper was the one to initiate the decision.

"Let's toast our belief that love conquers all."

She raised her glass, looked into Max's eyes, and said, "To love."

The echoes of "To love" streamed across the bar. Princeton savored the Neyen traveling down his throat, and as he put his glass down, he said, "So Mom, speaking of love, any chance with Larry?"

Piper's eyes widened, and she dramatically lowered her specs.

"Yeah, Ma, any chance?"

Tallulah reached her hand over and touched her mother's hand.

"OK," Victoria replied, "let's not go there"

Max used his new connection to Victoria to be brazen with his next words.

"Why not, Victoria? Why not go there? You seem to go there with all of us, why not you?"

Princeton listened to Max's words and knew that Victoria and Max experienced some deep dialogue to be so bold with his statement.

"Larry is a very nice man," Victoria said as she smiled. She hoped she would be short and sweet about this.

"But he's just an Easter bunny."

Only Tallulah understood Victoria's words. The puzzled expressions from the other eight urged Victoria to continue.

"You know, that perfect, enticing, sweet bunny? Looking so good, tempting you to break it and eat it? But you resist because you know if you do, the inside will be hollow. So you leave it alone because that way you won't be disappointed. Then the bunny's only purpose is to give you the impression that it's something you want, but you know you really don't."

There was silence. Makenzie was so intrigued by Victoria's words, she said, "You should write that down Victoria, maybe publish it, like a quote or something."

Piper laughed. "If Ma wrote down all her thoughts and quotes, the book would be too heavy to carry."

The others nodded and joined in with laughter.

"But sometimes we do eat the Easter bunny, don't we?" Derek asked.

"Yes!" Victoria responded. "Usually with later regret. But let's look at it this way."

The circle moved in closer as if they knew Victoria was going to hold court.

"All day long we're inundated by claims and desires that will change our lives. Whiter teeth . . ." She looked at Tallulah and smiled.

"Wrinkle free skin . . . status autos . . . skinny food . . ." She winked at Piper, acknowledging her advertising savvy.

"All will bring happiness, success, and friends. Where's the advertisement about buying an open heart? faith? how about buying some compassion?"

Princeton was already sucked into Victoria's direction. So many of her thoughts were his own thoughts that he wrestled with through the years. He knew she would nourish him now, and he waited patiently.

"Where's the catalogue guaranteeing a full refund, if you're not completely satisfied with your partner of choice? We spend so much energy seeking the best investments for our talents, treasures, and time. We believe if we settle for less, it would be wasteful and foolish. So . . . why would I settle for less with one of the most important areas of my life, my partner? The person that I would allow into my world, my soul?"

Victoria stopped and intentionally looked at each of the four couples, and then continued, "Your partner is the root of all you are. Everything branches from you and your partner's choices—where you live, what you eat, vacations, entertainment, music, art, and if you seal it, then family, the continuing lifeline, whether biological, adopted, blended, it becomes the product of everything you are and are not. Let's not forget that somewhere in the mix of things, you reveal your dreams, fears, anticipations, and disappointments to the person that holds your heart, your soul . . . in their hands. Imagine having that power?" Victoria stopped and let out a deep sigh.

"So when it comes to partners, I focus on all of that and try to remember that what I've learned is stronger than the quick gratification and eventual regret of eating the Easter bunny. So through the years, we hope to eat less chocolate."

Makenzie's question cut the silence like a knife. She couldn't help but be drawn in, and her thoughts just bounced to her mouth and into the air.

"Is there such a man?" she asked.

Victoria smiled and said, "Yes, right there" as she pointed to Princeton.

For a split second, the response left everyone feeling a little uncomfortable. Princeton's heart beat faster with the public acknowledgment of Victoria's answer. Victoria could read their minds, and she deliberately waited before concluding with . . .

"Him with twenty more years of mileage."

"Ma!" Piper said. "You exhaust my mind! You know that, right?"

Victoria responded, "I certainly hope so."

"Why should now be any different than the last fifteen years?" Tallulah asked as she began to laugh.

Except for Princeton and Tallulah, each one of them seemed lost in thought as Victoria's words resonated with them.

Princeton took Victoria's hand and said, "Time to make me look good."

As he guided her to the dance floor, he was aware of his feelings of respect and admiration for his mentor. As he took her waist, he asked, "Did you really mean that? About me with more mileage?"

"Absolutely, the complexity of our souls, remember?"

As they danced, Princeton glanced at his collection and said, "We left you a gift with the maitre d', there's also a check in there from Jack."

Victoria smiled and said, "You know I hate to admit it, but I was looking forward to my surprise. You see what happens when you start traditions?"

Princeton smiled and then looked pensive before responding with, "Well, the next tradition is selfish, you know?"

"'You asked them to play it?" Victoria asked.

"I couldn't help myself. I told you it was selfish."

"That's OK, I understand, but you never told me what prompted that song. Did Tallulah tell you it was my wedding song?"

"No, I just felt it. Even those words aren't enough for her . . . nothing is enough to describe my love for her."

"I know, well, thanks for the warning, it's either the ladies' room or a box of tissues or both."

As Princeton's hand rested on Victoria's hipbone, he couldn't help but think how similar her and Tallulah's bone structure were. He looked into Victoria's eyes and smiled.

"Hey, beautiful lady, could you make up a new business card for Tallulah? I got her a holder . . . from Jack, and I wanted to have something vintage, you know to match the holder."

"Colors?"

"Uh . . . deep topaz? Maybe with a little garnet, something smokey."

"Sounds fabulous . . . done!"

As the song completed, Victoria leaned into Princeton's ear.

"I'm going to make the rounds and check the dots."

As they separated, Princeton eyed the bar . . . empty. He looked to their table and saw everyone seated as the silver trays of desserts were being passed. He came up behind Tallulah and ran his hand down her back. As her body flexed, she looked up and said, "Hi, baby."

He took his seat, reached under her dress, and placed his hand on her thigh. He took the cup of coffee Tallulah had poured ready to go with the exact amount of milk and leaned into her ear.

"Thank you, baby."

Max had his arm around Piper, and she gently played with his hand.

"So, boys," she announced, "what is it tonight? Gloves or rings?"

"What do you mean?" Makenzie asked.

Zach was caressing her shoulder as he said, "You'll see."

"Makenzie," Piper said, "or is it Double M?"

Everyone smiled.

"You, my dear, will be going home with one of the treasures here tonight."

"Oh no . . . no . . ." She looked at Zach. "That's too much."

"Maybe," Piper said, "but these boys here know the drill. That's one of the best parts of these nights. Not the tangible, just the memory, and of course the money for the kids. See this beauty?" Piper lifted her clutch for Makenzie to view.

"Yeah, it's beautiful," Makenzie said as she eyed the beadwork.

"Fund raiser 2006." She leaned over and kissed Max.

"Thank you, sweetie."

Tallulah watched Makenzie as she was looking into Zach's eyes.

"I really like this girl," she thought as she sipped her coffee.

Max was explaining his one of a kind ink collection to Makenzie when the sounds of the bandleader overpowered his words.

"Princeton would like Tallulah to join him on the dance floor."

Tallulah's heart started to beat faster as she looked at Princeton stand up and pull out her chair. Due to the formal introduction so clearly heard by all, dozens of eyes watched the two walk to the center of the floor.

Rachel leaned over to Derek and said, "They are something, huh?"

Derek nodded recognizing his feelings of awe and envy.

Princeton's hand firmly rested on Tallulah's skin as he pulled her in. Their eyes locked, and the tight connection of their bodies separated them from everything present. Tallulah placed her head on his shoulder so to be able to speak into his ear. To all watching the beauty of their physical presence, and the obvious affection was the reason their eyes remained glued to the silhouette on the dance floor.

Someday, when I'm awfully low
When the world is cold
I will feel the a glow just thinking of you
And the way you look tonight

As the instrumental break took over, Tallulah's emotions were finding their home on Princeton's shoulder. With each release of breath, he pulled her in tighter and tighter. Their movement was slow, synchronized and perfectly matched.

"I want you right now . . . I want you always."

Princeton's words in Tallulah's ear made her hand clench his back. He abruptly released her, twirled her, and pulled her deep into his chest. The separation and then the reuniting of their bodies left them breathing hard.

As the applause reached their ears, they both opened their eyes and returned to the world around them.

Victoria looked in the mirror and pressed the tissue beneath her eye to remove all signs of her breaking heart.

"Damn you, Luke! How could you leave me?"

THE ULTIMATE
EQUALIZER

As Tom White watched Tallulah get into her car, he thought, "Outstanding." He was totally taken by her exceptional beauty. More than that, it was the mix of her poise and panache that sent his senses soaring. Professionally, she was more than capable. It wasn't so much her intelligence (which was obvious); it was her ability to understand his vision—her foresight! He knew he was stepping into dangerous territory because she aroused his deep-covered feelings of desire. As the car disappeared down the driveway, he stood by the window, thinking, "Be careful, Tom, don't go there."

Tallulah glanced at her watch as she approached the highway. She had mixed feelings about the consultation. Her overpowering emotion was excitement and a slight adrenaline rush. She was so anxious to share her synopsis with Princeton, and yet beneath that, there were feelings of uncertainty. This was going to be huge! She hadn't prepared herself to commit to such an extensive project. After all, her initial understanding was, it would consist of a makeover of one room. As she sat in the gilded wing-back chair, reviewing her notes of the walk-through, she smiled and asked, "Which room needs to have a new breath of life?"

Tom's response left her speechless.

"Excuse me?" was the best she could do.

So Tom repeated, "The entire house."

The entire house equaled twelve rooms of accumulated art, political flavor, and endless paraphernalia of memories and accolades.

"Well, Mr. White . . ."

"Tom, please."

"Well, Tom, I'm flattered, however this is a huge undertaking. To redesign a house of this size? Colors, textiles, fixtures, furniture, art, there's after all the structural . . . to connect that all with purpose and aesthetics would take months and months. There are contractors, plumbers, electricians . . . the cost would be astronomical, and the time invested would be staggering. Your life would be wrapped around your house, so to speak. I wasn't prepared . . ."

Tom cut her off. "I've thought long and hard about this. This is what I want, and you're the lady to do it," he said as he pointed to her.

"May I ask you why you didn't solicit my mother's services?" Tallulah asked.

"I've heard wonderful things about your mother's work. She's an icon in the business! However, when I saw the Richards finished product, I just knew you were the one."

"If I were to commit to this, I would be consulting with my mother. She would be doing all the free hand, not because she's my mother, but because she's the best."

"I'm not interested in who is part of your team, that's your call. I'm only interested in you heading up the project."

Tallulah smiled and asked, "Will Mrs. White be available for the initial consultation, assuming I do take the project?"

"No, that won't be necessary," Tom replied with slight hesitation.

She wasn't sure if she was more surprised by the job offer, the absence of his wife, or her impression of Tom White. Everything that she believed he was, he wasn't. Her preconceived notions were a boring vanilla flavor politician. She based that on her previous experience with other politicians. Tom was handsome, warm, witty, and very engaging. Maybe it was because he was younger than the others, or maybe it was due to his contemporary mind-set. Very John-John Kennedy. Whatever it was, Tallulah concluded that working with Tom would be exciting, not boring.

Her mind snapped back to concentrate on stepping on the brake as the parade of cars came to a halt. The guy in the car to her left caught her attention as he was gesturing to his heart, patting his chest. He rolled down his window, lowered his stereo, and called out to her.

"My heart is pounding! Or maybe I'm having a heart attack!"

He was smiling hard and apparently trying to convey his reaction to his glimpse of Tallulah.

"You are drop-dead gorgeous!" he called out to her.

Tallulah smiled and directed her attention to quickly change lanes as she retrieved the call coming through on her cell.

"Hey, baby!" His voice immediately sent a rush through her body.

"Where are you?" Princeton asked.

"Hi, beautiful, I'm on 95." When she called him beautiful, he would make this very specific low sound. He told her once that hearing those words made him melt.

"How'd it go?" he asked.

"It was phenomenal, scary, and very, very surprising," Tallulah said with excitement.

Princeton listened to the tone of her voice and responded with, "Can't wait to hear about this one, you have me in suspense. How far from home? Because I have an incredible dinner waiting your arrival!"

Tallulah took in a deep breath, savoring her feeling of complete love for him.

"How did you manage that? I thought you were going to spend the day with Max?" she asked.

"Well, baby, it has been seven hours, and when you left after church, Max came over, but he came with Piper . . . so that changed our plans."

Tallulah's voice heightened. "Piper? I missed an afternoon with Piper? How's my favorite girl?"

"She's great, actually they're both great. It was awesome to be in the mix of them, knowing about the ring tomorrow."

"I'm disappointed and jealous. Did you guys have a great time without me?"

"You know when I'm with them, it's always good. We talked, did some Chilean, got some of that fantastic white pizza you love from Sparta."

"I missed Sparta?"

"Sorry, baby, but dinner will compensate. Chef Ramsey assisted, and you know how trying she can be in the kitchen."

Tallulah laughed as she imagined Piper working the cutting board, with her specs halfway down her nose, handing out directions.

"Max and I caught some of the game, while your sister ransacked your closet. Pretty big bag she left with!" Princeton said as he chuckled.

Tallulah started to feel anxious, wishing she was home wrapped in his arms. She sighed and said, "At least another hour before I see your beautiful face."

"Keep talking like that, and I'm going to be pacing."

"Hit the weights, baby, and you'll forget I'm gone."

"Never happen! Nothing, I mean, nothing replaces you."

"Love you, see you in a few." Tallulah ended the call before Princeton could respond. She liked leaving him with that sudden anticipation.

She realized the drive home was way too long as she checked the exit. She hit the button on her cell and leaned back.

"Hi, Mom."

*   *   *   *   *

Makenzie was trying to concentrate on the sketch she was working on, but her eyes kept resting on the incredible ring Zach placed on her finger when he kissed her good night. Her preoccupation with last night made it impossible for her to get into the zone of her work. Her mind was constantly registering bits of what she believed was the most glorious night of her life. It was as if she were a character in a movie she had watched and wished that person were her. Now, instead of wishing, she was repeating the footage with herself as the main character. It all seemed surreal.

Everything about herself and her life appeared to be different now. She stepped into a space that two days ago would have been a fantasy. She kept thinking, "This is what it must be like to find a religion or have an epiphany." The heightened awareness of feeling something was different, and directing her every thought left her excited, anxious, and aroused. The snapshots of the beautiful room, the conversations, Victoria's soapbox, her dress debut, and Zach's ability to fit and flow perfectly with that circle left her exhausted. Her mind and body were in overdrive, and she wished Zach was there with her right now, handing her a cappuccino as he looked over her shoulder to watch her sketch. "Oh my god, Makenzie, you're losing your mind!" she thought to herself as she put the sketch pad down. She closed her eyes and thought about the car episode.

Never, never had she been so taken by someone. The ride home was a moment in her life that she was sure she would not forget. That private intimate cocoon of her and Zach transferring thoughts and touch was making her heart beat faster again. "You're gonna have a heart attack, Makenzie! Breathe . . . breathe." She couldn't help herself. There she was again in the passenger seat glancing over to Zach.

"Did you have a good time?" Zach asked. "Because you definitely were the belle of the ball."

"You're kidding, right? Zach, this was without a doubt one of the best nights of my life."

Zach looked over to her and smiled hard.

"I'm glad because this is my life or at least where my life is going." He hesitated for a moment and then said, "And I want you to come with me on the ride."

Zach's words were compelling, and she felt her eyes fill as she took in a deep breath.

"So . . . aren't the Prince and Princess something?" Zach asked as he continued, not waiting for a response.

"I mean Max and Piper are incredible. They're so perfect for one another. They have this 'air' about them that people find so attractive and eclectic, but Princeton and Tallulah? They're waaay out there! So captivating, so beyond what people can understand."

Makenzie interrupted, "Well, with Victoria at the reins, what would you expect? She is by far one of the most insightful women I have ever been in contact with. She draws you in."

Zach smiled. "Absolutely! You're right, but it's not Princeton's and Tallulah's wisdom that captivates. It's their raw, pure, undying love for one another, you know?"

Makenzie nodded as she stared at Zach.

"You know, Princeton believes that if you're attracted to someone in your mind, if your thoughts lust for someone, other than your beloved, then you're cheating! Could you imagine? In your mind! I've been around him for two years, and I'm still stunned by his beliefs. He really has his faith thing all figured out. When you're around him, watch him. If he gets a vibe that a woman is flirting with him, he won't make eye contact! He's always polite, you know? A gentleman, but he won't make eye contact. You would think with his looks and resources that he would get off playing the game, feeding his ego? Just the opposite! He's absolutely 100 percent committed to his love for Tallulah."

"Wow," Makenzie replied, "that's the most romantic thing I've ever heard. No wonder Tallulah is so addicted to him. Who wouldn't be? You know? To have that safety?"

"That appeals to you?" Zach asked as he studied her face for a moment.

"Not only does it appeal, but it's the type of love that I always imagined. I think every woman would say the same."

"Well, it's not only women. I myself want that," Zach said as he stared at the road.

Makenzie placed her hand on the back of Zach's neck and moved in toward him.

"We could have that, Zach. I believe we could have that. With focus and direction . . . and"—Makenzie paused as emotion traveled through her body—"And with love." Makenzie took a deep breath and said, "I love you, Zach, I love you."

Zach abruptly pulled the car over and threw it in park. In a quick motion, he unstrapped his and Makenzie's seat belts and pulled her in. His mouth was strong and wet, canvassing her face as his hands found her flesh. Her immediate response threw him into a deep warm place. Hearing her say she loved him was unexpected. So deep and simple, without expectation of affirmation on his part. Brave and sexy and pure. Makenzie was welcoming his hands and started to move in a fluid erotic way—soft, strong, and graceful.

Zach was savoring the heat he was experiencing. His mind and body were going places that caused him to breathe heavy and search for her ear.

"You love me?" His words lost as his mouth tasted her neck. "That's perfect," he whispered as his hands traced her body and went under the Double M creation. They found her thighs as she took in a deep breath. He stopped as his hands found the perfect resting place. She opened her eyes to see his face aligned with hers. As he spoke, he transferred the words into her mouth, touching her lips with his.

"That's perfect," he repeated.

Makenzie was starting to ache, wanting his hands to continue, yet there was this new strong feeling of also wanting to sustain. She was inspired to want this to be different than past relationships. She wanted the hope of a Princeton and Tallulah package.

Her next words were foreign to him and amazingly seductive.

"Last week, I would have said take me now . . . just like this . . . but now, I'm asking you to stop."

She paused, acknowledging the warmth of her own desire.

"Every fiber of me wants you . . . so . . . please stop . . . we're going to prove our love, you know?"

Zach was so moved by Makenzie's words. She affirmed all he had been wishing for these past few years. As he gently removed his hands, both he and her exhaled simultaneously. If he thought he loved her a moment ago, he was now absolutely sure that she was the one. He started to imagine them taking this journey together, helping one another to resist immediate gratification, holding out for the prize! Maybe purity rings? And as he finished that thought, he did something that he never did before. He did nothing.

$$* \quad * \quad * \quad * \quad *$$

Piper was in a full-blown daydream when the irritated voice made her come back to the line she was standing in.

"Oh sorry," she said to the woman behind her as she moved along.

She expected to have a wonderful time last night because that's the way it always was, but now her daydream was fueled by the sudden change in Max's attention to her. He was always a great guy, but they had reached a place where they were more comfortable than romantic, more assuming than spontaneous. It was in his eyes. She concluded it was the eyes and also the touch. It was different now, new and exciting. She tried to remember if Max ever looked at her like that, and maybe she had forgotten? No! This look . . . this connection was new. She drained her mind trying to figure out what had changed. Was it something she did? Something she said? Did he find out about Trevor's pursuit for her? The floral arrangement? The numerous phone calls?

"No," she thought, "he would have said something."

She analyzed the looks exchanged between Princeton and Max earlier while they were preparing dinner.

"What was that all about?"

As she looked to her right, she caught a glimpse of a woman eyeing someone coming toward her. The woman turned to her friend and said as she giggled, "Now that's a beautiful specimen right there."

Piper followed her eye to see Max approaching. Her heart suddenly remembered that emotion of seeing his impact on women. He crossed in front of the woman.

"Excuse me," he said as he wrapped his arm around Piper.

"No spots, babe, we're parked in the next town."

Piper turned and unexpectedly kissed his mouth. "Find another specimen," she thought.

Max returned the favor with a full wet exchange.

"Do that again, and we're not wasting our time with a movie," Piper said as she smiled.

Max accepted the tease, only this time he ran his mouth across her face to her ear and said, "Let's go."

As they left the line, they were struggling to keep their hands off each other.

*   *   *   *   *

Victoria was fielding calls all day. So many details of the night's day after whirlwind: vendors confirming product retrieval, faxes of the guest list for handwritten thank-yous, guests expressing their approval, and staff excited about the generous gratuities. As always, Victoria was pleased with the outcome of the dollars generated for her kids, and as always, she was left feeling sad and empty. The completion of a project meant the momentum had suddenly stopped. Most people would be relieved, but Victoria was already anxious about starting the next chapter of her being. She sat at the table with a glass of Chilean and thought, "If you had a life, Victoria. If you had someone to share your day with, you probably wouldn't be feeling this."

As she took a sip, she continued, "Rephrase that, Victoria, you do have a life. You are blessed with an abundance of gifts—Princeton, Tallulah . . . What you don't have is a life outside theirs, at least not an intimate one."

As her mind tried to calculate numbers, she felt a surge of accomplishment.

"Definitely over 200,000," she thought.

"That should get someone something, right? Hope for a better life? A belief that dreams can come true? A computer? A pair of socks? If all the successful people would just give a little . . ."

She didn't complete her thought because she felt that familiar empty pit in her stomach and knew if she allowed herself to continue that path of thinking, she would be ruined for the day. She would get so absorbed in life's injustices that she would send herself into a deep depression. Her displacement came in the form of her conversation with Tallulah regarding Tom White. That opportunity would be the cross over for Tallulah. Victoria calculated six to eight months to complete the project. She was only guessing based on the info Tallulah gave her. That would definitely be Tallulah's showcase. Once the word spread and photos for publications of Senator White in his newly remodeled home hit the public eye, Tallulah would be at an entirely different status level. Not to mention the buzz generated from the Princetons that Tallulah would surely incorporate in the finished product. Victoria found herself cross-referencing her life and her daughter's at the same age. How different! Yet some similarities remained consistent. She would do that a lot. When Tallulah was a little girl, Victoria would access her life at a specific point and compare it to her own when she was exactly that age. It was her way of validating and gauging a job well done. Keeping in tune with not repeating the cycle. She would remind herself, "The past doesn't equal the future. Once you find your leverage, your trigger point, and you act on it, you control the path of your destiny. God has the final say on all and everything, but your thoughts, desires, motivation, and action are left to your free will. After all, everything put in our paths are placed there by the Almighty. He waits to see what we will do with it."

Victoria believed the reason some people reached success in their lives while others didn't wasn't due to their circumstances. It was a result of surrounding themselves with the best circle: positive influences that offered support and understanding. The common thread of motivation and belief that all things are possible. Love and faith are the most powerful driving forces that a person can encounter on their journey. The key was to recognize the opportunities and focus on them. Being passionate about changing their state of mind to in turn change the quality of their lives.

That's why she hoped all those beautiful children would feel some love and support through her works. They were too young to make the choices of finding their circles. They were stuck in their challenging circumstances. She hoped they would feel and know that they were not forgotten.

She sighed as her mind raced with her thoughts of reminiscing.

"There is only one equalizer," she whispered.

"And that is death. Death is the ultimate equalizer. We all die—rich, poor, black, white, intelligent, uneducated—our creator's sons and daughters, we all die."

As she returned to her glass of Chilean and the surroundings of the kitchen, she recognized that she had successfully put herself into a somber place. She readjusted her posture, concentrated on her blessings, and slowly forced the positive energy to run through her veins. She began to smile. She would not allow herself to fail by concentrating on the negative. She had too much good in her life, and she was better than that! Mission accomplished. Every time she turned her mood around, she felt victory. She needed to be grateful and believe that God was pleased with her. She wasn't taking any aspect of her life for granted. She was a designer by trade, and what better way to utilize her gift than by designing the path of her life? As she looked at the name of the call coming in on her cell, she smiled.

"Hi, Rachel."

"Hi, Victoria, how are you? You must be exhausted."

"I'm OK, you guys have a good time?"

"It was fantastic, as always! Derek and I were just saying how much we love you and of course Tallulah. We never imagined Princeton's life to be so full, so successful and purposeful."

"Really?" Victoria responded, a little surprised.

"Your son has every ingredient to do extraordinary things! You and Derek deserve a medal of some sort, you know?"

Rachel blushed with hearing Victoria's words.

"I wish we could take complete credit, but we both know Tallulah influences his every move. Talk about medals."

"Ha! So when are we going to get together? It's been too long."

"Exactly!" Rachel chuckled. "That's why we're inviting you to dinner Tuesday night. Can you make it?"

"Of course, I know your schedules are difficult to align. I'll be there. What time?"

"How's six?" Rachel asked.

"Six it is. Are the kids coming?"

"Uh . . . we didn't invite them. Instead we invited one of Derek's friends."

"Oh!" Victoria exclaimed.

"You're doing the matchmaking thing? You know I'm really bad at that. Who is it?" Victoria asked with a bit of excitement.

"If I tell you, then you'll start imagining what he's like; and before long, you'll talk yourself out of coming."

Victoria smiled and said, "You really have come to know me pretty well, huh?"

"I guess. That being said, I'm waiting for the infamous question."

Victoria pretended that she didn't know what Rachel was implying.

"What question?" she asked.

Rachel called out to Derek, "Victoria is playing games!"

"All right . . . all right . . . well? Can I learn anything from him?"

"Bingo! Just wait and see!" Rachel's response was very confident and enthusiastic.

"Now you've piqued my interest. Compared to your last attempt, where are we on a scale of one to ten?"

"My last attempt was sincere. You just intimidated him so much that he wasn't able to show his attributes."

"Attributes? He couldn't complete a sentence!" Victoria exclaimed.

"I say ten." Again Rachel was confident.

Just as Victoria was going to continue bantering, the office phone rang.

"Hold on, Rachel, someone is leaving a message," she said as she walked to the phone.

She didn't recognize the number but waited to hear the message.

"Hello, Victoria, it's Larry. Sorry I had to leave so early last night. I'm sure it was a total success. You . . . you looked wonderful. I'm hoping we could have dinner, maybe Tuesday? Please call me."

Victoria turned her attention to her silent cell.

"Rachel? Tuesday is great . . . see you then."

*   *   *   *   *

As Tallulah pulled into the driveway, her eyes landed on Princeton standing on the loading dock. She still felt that flurry in her stomach when her eyes canvassed him. Hands resting in the front pockets of his perfection jeans, hoodie housing his beautiful structure, hair tasseled and spiked as if he intentionally worked at it, and that face! God, that face! Chiseled, dimpled, seductive mouth, killer smile, and that incredible innocence. It was his pure vulnerability that grabbed you and pulled you in as if he wasn't aware of his effect on people. As he moved toward the car with that broad sexy smile, Tallulah felt as if her breathing changed. Every time she was in his presence, her breathing seemed fuller, more complete; it was in harmony with her heart's reaction.

"Princeton," she thought, "you really are mesmerizing, and to think, you're mine!"

Those thoughts disappeared to make room for the concentration of watching him approach her. He quickly opened her door, leaned in, and gently brushed her cheek with the side of his hand. He was looking at her as if it were the first time he saw her, taking in every detail of her face. Tallulah was caught off guard. On the phone, he was playful and lighthearted. Now he seemed deep and intense. He closed his eyes as he moved closer and inhaled her scent.

"Hey, baby, missed you."

Tallulah wanted to cry. She wanted to release the tremendous sudden emotion he had on her. Either that or scream: scream with happiness or scream with confusion. After all these years, she still couldn't control the direction of her mind when she was in his grasp. It only registered him: his undying love for her, his ability to haunt her dreams. She had yet to speak a word.

"Leave your stuff," he said as he took her hand and led her to the sliding door.

Once inside, he firmly held her shoulders from behind and brushed his face along her neck.

"I was doing OK . . . till about an hour ago. Then it started to happen. I became overwhelmed with anxiety, you know? My needing you becomes . . ."

Tallulah waited for his next words.

Silence.

She glanced over to the beautiful table setting with the many candles burning. She took a deep breath, spun around, and smiled hard.

"Hey, beautiful, I'm starving! What did you and the Ramsey team whip up?"

Princeton knew exactly what she did at that moment. She forced him to focus on her lighthearted question, redirecting his thoughts.

"Well, madame, get into something comfortable." As he eyed her from head to toe, he continued, "Not that you don't look absolutely stunning, I love that on you!"

Tallulah laughed as she twirled around, playfully acknowledging his nod of approval. He scanned the short sweater dress that was hugging her amazing figure, paired with the tights and riding boots. She reeked sexy! He thrilled that she never needed to expose cleavage to be sexy. There was nothing cheap about this thoroughbred. It was her gait, her posture. She was confidently classy and knew exactly how a garment should hang. Her choice in clothing was avant-garde and always quality. His mind caught a glimpse of the first time he saw her standing at the pub where they met.

He said as he directed his attention to her, "I'm sure your sweats are waiting their turn."

Tallulah hurried upstairs to change while Princeton poured the wine, brought one of her favorite dishes to the table, and loaded the "Cure" into the sound system. There were times when they barely finished a glass of wine with dinner, and other times the bottle quickly disappeared.

Now as Princeton drained the last drop into Tallulah's glass, she sighed with satisfaction.

"Hungry, baby?" Princeton asked smiling.

As Tallulah looked at the last tiny piece of salmon on her plate, she replied, "You think? That was sooo delicious!"

"Ha! I learned from the best!"

Tallulah studied Princeton's face as she slowly ran her finger over his hand, tracing each finger.

"Such strong hands," she thought.

"You know," she said, "I could sit here and run down the list of all the reasons why I love you . . . it's endless. There's the reason of why because of who you are . . . as a man, your deep-seeded faith, your intelligence, your creativity, your gentle manner. Then there's the reasons of why because of who you are in connection to me: your unselfish giving, your ability to touch my soul and understand my every thought, your over-the-top masculinity . . ." She seductively winked as she said "masculinity."

Princeton listened to her words as her love song covered him in a blanket of fulfillment. As she continued, he became lost in watching her eyes and mouth move, painting a picture to bury in his memory so he could later retrieve it when he needed to.

"Right now, at this exact moment, if I had to pick one? It would be my love for the way you love me. The way you take care of me. Always, always putting me first. Giving me exactly what I need, at exactly the right time. I look at you, and the physical beauty just floors me! Then with that comes layers and layers of intricate design. So many colors . . ."

Tallulah paused for a moment, and then her voice heightened as she appeared to have made a discovery.

"You know what, baby? I just figured it out! You're a masterpiece! Your God's *Mona Lisa*, his *David*."

Princeton squeezed her hand and said, "You're killing me here, your words are. Baby, what can I say to that?"

He got up and knelt before her. He firmly held on to her hips and looked up into her eyes. She took his head with both hands and moved her fingers deep into his hair. As he bowed his head, she buried her face in it and kissed his forehead.

Without looking, Tallulah knew Princeton was quietly sobbing.

"Those better be tears of joy!"

His wet eyes looked up, and in one smooth move, he stood, lifted her, and carried her to the sectional. He placed her with her upper body resting against the pillows, as he laid on his stomach, opening her thighs with his shoulders, resting his head on her stomach. She loved that position, and he knew it. She would be able to play with his hair and caress his shoulders. She knew that Princeton would be thinking or possibly imagining snapshots of their conversation, having certain words resonate for his later retrieval.

She was right. As Princeton lay there, he replayed her words over and over again. She had given him a cupful of inspiration. His mind started to take on vague images of masterpieces. Old world, Renaissance, he wasn't sure. He started to imagine a collaboration of the great works with his present style. He was trying to marry the two with his lens. "Wow," he thought as his adrenaline started to peak.

"This could be powerful. She really is my muse. My best works come from her."

"Baby?" Tallulah's voice pulled him back.

"We need to talk about the White project."

Two hours later, and they were still talking. The discussion of tomorrow's ring was fun and easy. They walked down memory lane hitting all the high points of Max and Piper's time line of romance. Tallulah was really looking forward to tomorrow's adventure. She was hoping and praying Piper would be ready and receptive to Max's proposal. Princeton, on the other hand, felt secure she would. They firmed up the details for Thursday's dinner party, which led to conversation about Makenzie. Tallulah obviously was very much a fan. Princeton not only enjoyed hearing Tallulah's opinion of her newfound friend, but he was genuinely happy for Zach. He hoped Zach had found what he was searching for. The conversation about Tom White was lengthy.

That was yet another thing Tallulah loved about her prince. He was always attentive, but when he recognized that something was really important to her, he gave it his full attention. He became a sounding board and offered suggestions, advice, and took her through the pros and cons of the potential project. He chameleoned himself into not only her life partner, but also her business partner. The bottom line was Princeton knew this project would be huge. It would be very time consuming and very draining on Tallulah. She would have to immerse herself totally. Not that she didn't do that with every project, but this one was going to take at least a half a year of commitment. She also needed to be ready for the potential work that would follow. Princeton had this intuitive feeling that something big was on the brink of unfolding for Tallulah's career. He didn't share his secret with her, but it was something that would surface within his thoughts for the past few months. When they were discussing the project, Tallulah gave him her calculation of the income that would be generated.

His response simply was "Wow, that much, huh?" His thoughts went to the days of him and Max sharing the apartment. He couldn't believe where he was now. He never imagined not needing the figures Tallulah was throwing out. Five years ago, that would have seemed like all the money in the world to him, and now he was reaching a decision solely based on his desire for her to be happy.

Princeton's selfish motives of wanting her to say no were evident. He didn't want to have to share so much of his beloved with anyone or anything else. On the other hand, he truly wanted whatever Tallulah needed for herself. He found joy in witnessing her creativity. So at all costs, he would completely support her decision. He tried to analyze and dissect her speech, body language, and facial expressions to decide which road he should take in gently pushing her to the direction he believed she wanted. He was a master at knowing Tallulah's needs, sometimes before she did. He needed to be very careful however because he knew she would do whatever pleased him. She wouldn't think twice about not doing something or not going somewhere, if she believed he wasn't for it. She said it was easy for her to accept and act on his opinions because she completely trusted and valued his input. He would never hurt her, and he probably cared more about her success than his own. That was Victoria's affirmation of the power they had over one another. He wanted to be certain that he didn't take advantage of his reigning position.

"Refill, baby?"

"Yeah." He paused and then said, "I think you should go for it, the White project, you know?"

Tallulah looked into Princeton's eyes and saw the sweet, unselfish man she married, so willing to be what she needed, time and time again, giving all of himself to her.

"Really? Well, beautiful, I'm going to sleep on it."

She kissed his cheek and got up to fill his cup. As he sat there on the couch, running his fingers through his hair, he watched her. The image of her long hair falling in front of her face as she tucked it behind her ears, the silhouette of her beautiful figure, washboard stomach slightly exposed, the tiny flow of light illuminating her bronze skin—what a beauty! Talk about a masterpiece! He sighed deeply and turned his attention to the wall facing him. He examined the tremendous cross, which she titled *Reason*. It occupied the entire wall, stretching up to reach the ceiling: so simple, yet so breathtaking. As he stared at the eight-foot wonder, with the hidden recessed lighting framing its glory, he looked at her again and then back to *Reason*. "How can she be that?" As he glanced back over to her, he thought, "And that?" His mind returned to the day that *Reason* impacted his faith and his respect and admiration for his beautiful woman.

It was in the final stages of the warehouse renovation. The constant work of so many contractors, plumbers, and electricians started to subside. Piper and Victoria started to fade out as their continuous input and help had come to a close. Every day was filled with choices, decisions, and anticipation of the final product. Tallulah referred to that phase as the icing. All major work was done, colors found their home on the walls, and furniture and art was waiting to be placed. Princeton had a firm request to showcase one of his photos of Tallulah. He said aside from "Life and Death," it was his favorite. It took a little convincing on his part because Tallulah wasn't sure if she wanted a five-by-five photo of herself overpowering his other works. It was so large. Once he made her understand his heart's attachment to the photo, she conceded.

It was in fact a beautiful reflection of that magical weekend they shared at the Cape. She was a little surprised that he was comfortable displaying such a seductive piece. However, if you looked past the subject, which was Tallulah on her knees, water and waves bouncing off her ripped jeans, head bent back, hair dragging the sand, eyes closed, reaching for the sun's warmth, you saw the incredible quality of the shot.

It wasn't planned, but when Tallulah fell to her knees, it just happened to be magic hour. That exact hour when the sun produces the most flattering light at dusk. The shadow in the sand behind her, with tiny shells and rocks magnified as a result of the filter he used, was genius. Specs of water glistened as they dripped down her wet tee. The flesh on her stomach slightly visible with accumulated drops of water resting on her belly button, as if she was trying to absorb the magnificence of the earth's creation.

He probably took five hundred shots that weekend, but when he exposed that one, his heart raced. He was floored by Tallulah's expression. He literally had to sit down and examine what his eye had the privilege of seeing.

Tallulah had directed the electrician to place recessed lighting in specific places throughout the first floor. She shared her plans with Princeton as to where and why so that the space would be deserving of his brilliance. The one large empty wall that Princeton was now staring at had three lights installed precisely according to Tallulah's measurements. He had no idea what would be showcased on the blind wall; he left all those details to her. After all, aside from Victoria, she was the expert in that area.

He remembered sliding the door, and as his eyes found Tallulah on the floor, he immediately panicked. As he took another step, he saw her surrounded by three massive pieces of wood. With hammer in hand, she was banging the wood with fierce thrusts of energy. Each time she raised the hammer and found her target, she let out a deep exhale as the tears ran down her face. Princeton remained pasted to the floor; he was frozen. She turned herself on her knees to attack each piece as she wept. That image remained permanently burned in his head and heart. He slowly came up behind her and knelt down.

"Baby? You OK?" he asked, not daring to touch her, not wanting to invade her emotion.

She quickly turned, dropped the hammer, and grabbed him with a strength that caught him by surprise. He wrapped his arms around her and gently rocked her as she wept. Her face was buried in his shoulder as she attempted an explanation.

"Oh, baby . . . baby . . . he died for us! For you . . . for me!" She was weeping so hard her words were muffled.

"He felt every nail . . . every pain . . . piercing, ripping his flesh! A man . . . a man . . . just like you . . . having to suffer the ultimate death . . . for us! I'm not worthy . . . we're not worthy! Her voice escalated as she fell limp into his arms. As he cradled her, he made the connection of the purpose for the wood. That moment . . . that exact moment Princeton felt as if she offered a piece of herself as never before. He was sure this magnificent woman was the missing link to his soul.

She worked on that cross for weeks: hammering and distressing every inch as she proclaimed her love for her Savior. The staining took hours of application and reapplication. It was a very close re production of the perceived size and scale of the actual cross that held the world's salvation. When the contractor arrived to attach and hang it, he said that he had goose bumps just touching it. Hanging it was a tedious process because it had to be aligned with the lighting so that only a hint of its reflection was seen. Once done, Tallulah and the contractor stepped back to access if it squared the space.

"I've never seen anything like that," the contractor said as he viewed the piece.

"No? Well, just so you know, that's the reason," Tallulah replied.

"The reason? For what?" he asked.

Tallulah smiled and said, "For you, for me."

He wasn't quite sure what she meant, but that day he felt sure he had contributed to something special. When Princeton got home that night, the chandelier was dimly lit, and *Reason* was in place. He sat there staring for what seemed like forever. He prayed, wept, and begged God to never separate him from his lifeline. Tallulah's work brought about a great catharsis for Princeton that evening.

"Hey?"

Princeton felt the cup touch his hand as he looked up.

"Where'd you go?"

Princeton took the cup and placed it on the table. He pulled her down to lay on top of him as his mouth found hers. Her body responded welcoming his touch as her lips played with his and her hands traced his abs. The combination of his thoughts of their earlier conversation regarding him as her masterpiece and his renewing of *Reason* and her flesh touching his made him immediately ache. A tremendous surge of hot rhythm moved through him, transcending him to a deep place. His body was tightening and releasing as he felt Tallulah's breathing change. He forced himself to abruptly lift her off of him as he searched for the stereo remote and the huge faux fur throw and guided her to the floor.

"This is for you, baby," he managed to say into her ear as he hit Play.

Instantly, they were melting into one another. Her sounds of pleasure escalated him so quickly; he needed to be in his black space.

Whenever I'm alone with you
You make me feel like I am home again
Whenever I'm alone with you
You make me feel like I am whole again

Tallulah loved the deep, erotic, offbeat rhythm, sort of a cappella sound and twang of the guitar attached to the lyrics. She found the words to be simple and brilliant. He was singing in her ear, gasping between words. He was pulling her in, both physically and mentally. His hands covered her back as his body pressed so hard and deep, moving her to verbalize her desire for him. Somewhere in the back of her mind, she knew the track would go on and on because she knew he remixed it to cover the length of the CD.

She adored the way he sang to her. He seemed desperate for her as if he was cleansing his soul, reminding her, and his heart of his unequivocal love for her.

They pleased each other over and over again as they went around the world. Every time they reached satisfaction and exhaustion, they wouldn't let go. Their insatiable need to have eye, body, and spiritual contact drove them to episodes of complete pain and pleasure. She begged for him and him for her. Their connection was wild and simple as they explored the possibilities of how much they could give to one another. The place they were in was beyond physical; it was beyond the understanding of how much they needed to be fused. Did they create this? Or was it the anatomy of their beings? Or was it that they knew how to find each other's soul?

The physical was exactly that—physical. The forces of their bodies were the instruments they used to tell each other their story. When Princeton was covering her with his flesh and muscles, it was the perfect pressure aligned with his movements. That made her feel as if he were painting; she was the canvass, and every stroke had a purpose. It was the story he was telling her with his eyes. They were open windows bringing in sun, rain, and a fierce storm. His words made her body move, melt, and surrender under his smoldering flesh.

She in turn would take the reins and get lost in her ability to bring him places that not only made him moan, gasp, and beg, but he would find a way to surrender himself that allowed her to go so deep into him that he was exposed from the inside out. That was the beauty of their connection. They only knew each other. They both saved themselves to only want to give this to one another. They knew that no one before them had the opportunity to experience what they were capable of giving. There were no past physical victories, no memories of previous encounters. That's what made it sacred!

That was the irony of their lovemaking. It was so hot and steamy because it was innocent, with an undertone of naïve purity. Each one believed God made man and woman as unique puzzle pieces, made to fit perfectly into one another. The gift was meant for husband and wife to cherish the pleasure of their union.

Each time they would watch a movie or pick up a tabloid that focused on promiscuity, they would feel sad and somewhat embarrassed. Princeton would think, "Why can't you just hold out? Why can't you wait for the prize? Why do you have to take something so extraordinary and make it so meaningless?"

Even though Princeton came to her after abstaining for so long, his biggest regret was that his hands touched someone else's flesh. Even though it was easy enough to justify because he was young and lost, he wished to this day that he could take that one piece of his life and permanently erase it. He knew he was forgiven through his prayers, but it was the one thing that he couldn't quite find absolution for.

The only other thing that was worse was the thought of someone else touching Tallulah's body. It made him crazy: upset, angry, and sick to his stomach. He wouldn't allow himself to go there because he hated the feelings it would ignite. He placed that thought deep, deep, in his "don't open memory box."

Finally now, as Princeton's body trembled beneath her, wet and spent, she collapsed into his embrace as his hand found the throw to cover them. She drifted off into a deep sleep.

THE FORGOTTEN LAND

Tallulah was startled by the buzzing sound.

"What the—?" she thought to herself as she opened her eyes and quickly scanned her surroundings. It took a second for her to realize she was in her bed. Her eyes traveled to the buzz. As she reached over to stop the alarm, she felt nervous about not remembering how she got from the floor to her bed. She quickly sat up while she stared at the numbers on the clock. She grabbed the blanket and wrapped herself as her naked body felt cold.

"Nine o'clock? No . . . no . . . can't be!"

She searched her mind for the slightest recall of lost time between falling asleep on Princeton and now. Nothing. How could he have carried her upstairs and she not remember anything? She looked at the empty space next to her and picked up the note.

Baby,
   Good morning.
   Can't imagine my life without you.
   Last night was incredible as always.
   Coffee is set.
   Hope you and Mom give Max a run for his money.
   You'll be on me all day.

She read it twice and then held it to her chest as she sighed. She started to see his face: snapshots of him smiling, his mouth moving toward her, his expression of euphoria with eyes closed, calling for her, his hands strong and beautiful, working her, his glistening biceps, large with veins protruding as she held on. Her insides were stirring, and she wished she was back on the floor.

"Oh, baby! I soo love you, absolutely love you!"

After a few moments of daydreaming, she reluctantly decided to start her day. As she lowered her feet to the floor, they landed on the white robe he placed for her. Stepping into it, she thought, "Unbelievable, just unbelievable, even when you're not here, you know exactly what I need."

She raced downstairs to get her first fix of caffeine, thinking how she had forgotten to tell Princeton that she decided to have a coffee bar installed in their bedroom. She knew she made a mistake when she didn't incorporate it in the initial renovation. She thought about it so many times, but it got lost somewhere. When she thought about Tom White's project, she immediately knew she would be putting one in his bedroom, and that made her remember to follow through with one for them. As she hit the button on the coffee machine, she scribbled a note to call the plumber and contractor. She grabbed her phone, which was still in her bag, and checked her calls: three missed calls from Piper and one from Max. Victoria rarely called first thing; she always waited for Tallulah's call. It was their tradition that she didn't want to change. She knew there wouldn't be a call or message from Princeton. That was their quirky thing: they didn't like to talk on the phone unless it was about a schedule change or assistance with work or a last-minute dinner change. They felt like it took away from their uniqueness, and they never texted. Neither one of them cared for it. They felt that it was impersonal and eliminated the tone and beauty of conversation. It may have had something to do with their creativity or Victoria's conversations about the lack of luster in the texting world; it made everything seem less important, losing feeling and emotion.

She hit the Send button as she swallowed her perfect cup of coffee.

"Hi, honey, I was getting worried."

"Hi, Mom, sorry, we're on for eleven, right?"

"Yeah, Max is on his way, and then we'll swing by for you."

"You spoke to him already?" Tallulah asked surprised.

"You're kidding, right? I've been up for hours."

"Of course, are you excited?" Tallulah asked as her own excitement reached Victoria's ears.

"Beyond excited! It's all I thought about last night. After all, my other girl is getting married, you know"—Victoria paused—"I'm really thrilled for both of them."

"Mom, you think Piper is going to say yes? You know with all her talk about them not being where she wants them to be?"

"Absolutely, no doubt," Victoria answered confidently.

"Funny, Princeton feels the same way."

"I just spoke with your prince. Have I told you that I adore him? Oh, and you're one of the luckiest woman on this planet."

"Yes and yes, and I know it," Tallulah answered with a smile. "Gotta go, or I'll be getting in the car in my robe."

"OK, see you in a few, love you."

"Love you too."

As Tallulah hit the button for Piper, she stared at the throw on the floor. It was the only evidence of last night. Everything had been cleaned up: dishes, glasses, cups, candles—all gone. The huge mosaic centerpiece was returned to its place. She smiled as she knew he left it there intentionally. He "marked" their spot for her to see when she came down.

"Hey, chickie! I miss you."

Tallulah laughed and said, "Hey, sis, miss you too."

"Did you love your dinner last night?"

"It was fantastic, thanks."

"Don't be so grateful, it came with a price. Did you check your closet?" Piper asked with her usual wit.

"No, never made it upstairs!" Tallulah said with a hint of suggestion.

"Of course! Why would I think that you would find time to do anything aside from the love thing you two do 24/7?"

"Jealous?" Tallulah teased.

"Well, maybe last week I would have said yes . . . but now? No!"

Piper's response made Tallulah start to feel excited. She felt like Piper was in perfect timing with today's itinerary.

"Really? C'mon tell me. What's going on? When did this happen?"

"I'm not sure. Max is different. It's his eyes, you know? Or the way he touches me, I don't know. I'm just so sucked in, like we're new. I daydream about him! Could you imagine? I thought that was way back when . . . remember when we use to sit and talk and daydream about the four of us? We were so thrilled that those boys were the perfect match for us. Seems like a lifetime ago."

Tallulah's mind returned to that time when Max was so smitten with Piper. It wasn't her obvious beauty; it was the image she projected: very European and artsy. If Tallulah had to compare her to someone, it would be a female Johnny Depp. Max said he was afraid to ask her out because he would have to fight off all the guys wanting to get next to her. That quickly changed as he enjoyed parading her out and about. He basked in the obvious stares and the remarks regarding her originality. The biggest attraction for Max was when Piper opened her mouth. Hardly anyone could keep up with her wit, intelligence, and knowledge about every and any subject. Max said Piper could hang with the big boys, and even they would be left feeling inadequate. He didn't hide the fact that he took pride in how she intimidated people. The soft side of Piper was only available to the chosen few.

Tallulah had to sit down as she listened to Piper's words. She was serious and full of sincerity. She was comfortable exposing herself to Tallulah. Through the years, she proved her heart was safe in having Tallulah listen to her episodes of pain, tears, uncertainty, and vulnerability. Their relationship blossomed into both needing one another: Piper became the protector, and Tallulah became the safe haven.

Tallulah was filled with joy. For a moment, she tied to trace the change with the time line of when Max had dinner with her mom.

"That's the best news! I'm so excited. Now I really can't wait till Thursday. Can you come over tomorrow?"

"I'll swing by tonight."

"Uh . . . I'm booked tonight," Tallulah said as she scrambled for an excuse "The White thing, you know?"

"Oh! How'd that go? Cover of *Metropolitan Home*?"

Tallulah laughed and said, "Not quite yet."

"All right call me later. Love you, chickie. I'll swing by tomorrow."

"Me too . . . you."

Tallulah let out a loud "Yes!" as she ran upstairs to shower.

*   *   *   *   *

Zach was so anxious as he loaded the gear into the Jeep that he had to exhale because he had butterflies. This would be the first time he would be shooting footage side by side with the Prince. He had assisted him many times and also tried his hand at the lens in private, but he never shot the same subject alongside his mentor.

Princeton had been looking forward to continuing the series of the kids all week, but now his main focus was his preoccupation with the masterpiece project that he visualized in his mind in Tallulah's arms last night. Every time he thought about her referring to him as a masterpiece, he felt a strong surge of satisfaction. To think that she saw him as a masterpiece. Wow, such a strong word. He needed to push that away, so he could give his all today, especially for Zach. He needed to be on point so that Zach could get the best understanding of the mechanics. Princeton believed he couldn't teach someone how to find the point of shot. It was personal and different for everyone. What he could teach was the generalities of the equipment and the depth of field. Hopefully, he could inspire Zach to find his zone, his reference point.

Princeton walked over to the Jeep and threw the remaining cameras into the back and leaned against the door to clean his sunglasses.

"Ready, buddy?" he asked.

"Yeah! I love those," Zach said as he pointed to the sunglasses. "Who are they?"

"Smith," Princeton replied as he lifted them to his face.

"Doesn't Victoria have those?"

"Yep, only about ten pair."

Zach laughed and made a mental note to check out a pair for himself.

"Ok," Princeton said as they got into the Jeep "Quick check . . . changing bag?"

Zach turned to the backseat to find each item as Princeton called out the list.

"Got it."

"Mask?"

"Check."

"Hot shoe?"

"Check."

Princeton turned to scan the back quickly for lenses. As his eyes found each item, he pointed to it.

"OK, fog filter, macro, fisheye, scrim, sky filter, light meter."

He looked over to Zach and said, "We're good, buddy, let's roll."

Zach couldn't help noticing how many flirtatious attempts were made by women as they stopped at traffic lights. The combination of the eye-catching Jeep with its sexy, rugged appeal and Princeton at the wheel with his over-the-top good looks packaged behind his Smith's was an object of enormous attraction.

"You realize that you may be responsible for lots of divorces today, right?" Zach said as he caught the eye of a woman hoping to get Princeton's attention.

Princeton smiled and asked Zach to find the yellow "Wow" CD. Zach flipped through the CDs, searching for Princeton's request.

"Got it!" he said as he looked at the titles, he asked, "Which one is this?"

"That is the one I need right now. You know with the divorce dilemma?"

"What do you mean?"

"Well, you're telling me that these random women want my attention, right?"

"Uh . . . yeah?"

"Well, I need to direct my attention to the right place. Temptation is something you need to look away from: it's cheap and shallow. I wouldn't sabotage what I have for all the women in the world, not that it would be possible anyway. Nothing and no one comes close to my wife. She's a thoroughbred compared to all these ponies."

Princeton had a smirk on his face as he seemed to bask in the thought of his thoroughbred.

Zach attached Princeton's words to a snapshot of Makenzie.

"What do you think about Makenzie?"

"She's great, seems like a real genuine person, love the creative side of her" He laughed as he continued with "Tallulah is a big fan! She has plans for your lady, you know? You better watch out. She's going to reel her in, and then you'll be stuck!"

Zach thrilled in knowing that Tallulah wanted her in their circle; it made him feel like he was right up there with Max and Piper. He truly valued Tallulah's opinion.

"Let me ask you something. What do *you* think about Makenzie?" Princeton asked.

Zach handed Princeton the CD as they maneuvered through traffic.

"I never knew there were so many people on the road at 7:30 in the morning," Zach said as he avoided the question.

"Well?" Princeton asked as he loaded the CD.

For the first time, Zach felt slightly uncomfortable discussing his new romance. Prior to this, he would have easily answered with a "she's hot" or "I'm into her." Now he hesitated, trying to find the right words to describe his feelings.

Princeton glanced over and smiled.

"You're not answering and sitting there with that look on your face is really a major step for you. Not being able to verbalize your deep feelings is fantastic! That's gonna be your private place, you know? For you and your lady."

"I love her." The words just fell out of Zach's mouth.

Princeton's reaction surprised Zach. He was thrilled and excited for Zach's find. His hand clenched Zach's shoulder as his voice heightened, saying, "That's great! Great news, buddy! Tallulah's going to flip. You know with all this love going around, what with Max and Piper . . ."

Zach cut him off, "What? What's with Max and Piper?"

"All good . . . it's all good," Princeton said as he caught himself before letting the cat out of the bag.

He hit track 2 and raised the volume.

Father it appears to me a mystery
Why you still love me
When you see the bad in me
You show me mercy, you show me grace

Zach was watching Princeton as he soaked up the effect of the song on him. The car was vibrating with the lyrics as Princeton sang along, tapping the wheel to the beat with the palm of his hands. He was belting out his praise, totally oblivious to everything around him. If you were watching from the outside, you might conclude he was listening to a rock song or a Top 10. Not Princeton. His passion was attached to the worship track. Zach was moved by Princeton's confidence and joy in expressing the song's impact on him.

Zach found himself lost in the moment he was witnessing. He was sure he wouldn't forget the image of Princeton belting out those lyrics, giving all of him while driving the streets of the city. He recalled Princeton's words referring to the song as "what he needed right now."

Princeton hit stop as the song concluded.

He looked at Zach and said, "Pretty incredible, huh?"

Zach nodded, feeling inspired.

As Princeton ejected the CD, he turned to Zach.

"That's what it's all about, buddy, amazing grace and mercy on my damaged soul. I'd be dead now, if not for that."

Princeton's word hit so hard, him saying he'd be dead; it left Zach confused.

"When you say things like that, I can't make the connection. Not with who you are now. You're Princeton the artist! In some circles, you're a celebrity! You were showcased in magazines for God's sake, which I don't understand why we don't have those articles framed in the studio?"

Princeton answered with "I don't want people to attach me to the articles and then assume I'm good. I want them to look at a photo and be so moved that they have to have it, not because a magazine says so."

Zach was still pushing. "Yeah, I get that, but isn't the fame the result of the accomplishment? The hard work? That's how we gauge everything . . . according to the public's buy-in. We do it with music, clothes, cars—everything. What's the point of working so hard if we're not going to reach the next level of success?"

Princeton really enjoyed when Zach would challenge him. Even though at times Zach seemed to be thin in his philosophies, Princeton knew he had layers of intelligence and depth in him. He had so much potential. After all, he trusted him to oversee his business.

"You're right," Princeton said, "but when you have the good fortune to have a life so full, when you reach a place of surprising satisfaction with not only your craft, but with your love and your faith, it becomes less important to reach the fame. You just do what you do because you're passionate about it. You don't find the success in the dollars; you find it in the realization of your gifts."

Zach chuckled and said, "Yeah, well, that's easy for you to say because you have so much money! I think you've reached the point of being referred to as wealthy. You know, there's this big mystery about you and your life prior to when I met you. You talk about being dead, and all I see is this super successful, drop-dead good-looking guy, who has a stunning wife and all the bells and whistles to go along with it. You know Max told me stories about you being pursued for modeling. He said not just at school, but serious offers. Why didn't you do that? You know, be every woman's fantasy? Plastered on billboards and magazine covers!"

Princeton laughed and said, "It didn't interest me. I would never take my shirt off for a camera. I was saving that for Tallulah."

"But you didn't know her yet, right? I'm confused."

"I always knew her," Princeton said as he grabbed a bottle of water off the backseat. He emptied half the contents and then continued, "When I said I would be dead? It's because I was walking the end of a tightrope, and then I was saved, mostly from myself. If that emptiness would have continued"—Princeton paused as if he were back in that place—"I don't think I would have made it. My searching became obsessive, you know? I needed so desperately to have this void in my heart . . . physically filled. Something wasn't right. I wasn't right. I didn't know at the time I was being groomed for the door he was going to open. I just barely held on."

Princeton turned the mood because he didn't want to get caught up in remembering the pain.

"See these?" he said as he lifted his shirt exposing his six pack.

"You kill me with those," Zach said, staring at the perfection of the defined muscles.

"I work out a lot," Zach said. "But those? Those are crazy!"

"My point exactly. You work out to gain bulk and definition, right?"

"Yeah, doesn't everyone?"

"Probably, but when I started pushing the metal, I had no intention of dramatically changing my body. I was young and needed something to get lost in . . . something to release my energy and pain. Once I started, it became like a medication for me, you know? Every time I felt like I was going to explode, I pushed that all into the bench. It was ridiculous! I could have gone 24/7. I developed this love for what it did for me mentally, not physically. It was my safe place, no temptation of backsliding as I waited. The results were just a bonus. I can easily do three, four hours now because I still have fears and anxiety, and I still love my safe place. Sometimes you have to wait, find something to take you through the dark times."

Zach asked with amazement, "You do three hours? No wonder why you're so ripped. How many times a week?"

"Depends. Four, five, sometimes seven."

"When do you sleep?" Zach asked sarcastically.

"Ah! That's another story for another time," Princeton said as he parked the Jeep.

"I just shared a lot of myself with you. Let's refocus here. OK, we're doing mostly infinity shots, so we're not invading anyone's space. But if we want solos and close-ups, we have to introduce ourselves, give our cards, and get permission, especially where children are involved. So we're going to be using a lot of change outs."

Princeton's spot of choice was a city school bus stop that offered multicultural dynamics. The demographics were perfect for his hopes of capturing urban living.

"After this, we're going inner city. That's a different approach. We're basically shooting the tenements, but if a subject is present, we'll offer them money to sit for us."

"Money?" Zach asked, surprised.

"Open the glove compartment," Princeton instructed as he put on his Yankee cap.

Zach looked at the large roll of rubber-banded twenties.

"That's the easy part," Princeton said as he looked at Zach's expression.

"The challenge at the tenements is to leave with your broken heart intact."

*   *   *   *   *

Max rode the wave of anticipation all morning. He was full of excitement as he drove to secure his future. The ride to Rhode Island was one of the best mornings Max ever had. Victoria was sitting passenger, making him laugh with throwing out bits of food for thought, and Tallulah was resting her head on his shoulder, bobbing back and forth as she pushed herself up to be between the two of them when something excited her or when she needed to join in for the moment of laughter. They listened to Max's tracks of his favorite music, emptied their venti Starbucks, ate their scones, and took strolls down memory lane, hitting on the early days of him and Piper's relationship. There was talk of some things that Max had completely forgotten. The biggest kick for Max was the periodic reference to him as "my brother-in-law" from Tallulah and "my son-in-law" from Victoria. He always knew that Piper was theirs; through the years of hearing "my sister" or "my daughter," it just became natural. However now was the first time he was referred to as theirs.

Max had very few opportunities to share time with Piper's parents. She somewhat wrote them off. Anytime she would talk about her life, it always included Victoria, Luke, and Tallulah. Max knew the deal with Piper's life and what she went through in her early years, but she hardly ever felt the need to talk about it and didn't seem interested in reconciling with the pair that brought her so much pain. She found peace in accepting that it was what it was. She would occasionally touch base with them, but they weren't a part of her life. Max hurt for that empty space in Piper, but he also thanked God for Victoria. Piper was a result of her living with them, aside from biological circumstances; the Lucia-Baris were her family. As Max sighed, he asked the question that had been nagging at him all week. He lowered the volume and looked at Victoria and Tallulah and asked, "Assuming Piper says yes, where are her parents going to fit into this?"

There was silence for a moment, and then Tallulah offered an answer.

"Well, first of all," she said as she moved up to be closer to Max, "she's definitely going to say yes!"

"You think?" Max asked skeptical.

"Oh no, I don't think, I know."

"Really?" Max asked with new excitement.

"Yeah, done deal!" Tallulah confirmed with a wink.

As she sat back, her voice became more monotone; lackluster was a good description.

"I don't know about her parents. Whatever Piper thinks is appropriate is all right with us." She leaned up and rested her hand on Victoria's shoulder. "Right, Mom?"

Victoria glanced at Tallulah and then Max and said, "Absolutely, it's Piper's call. Whatever she wants is where we'll put our support. The main focus is that she is going to be married to this fabulous talented man." She touched Max's shoulder as she referred to him.

Max smiled hard, and Tallulah playfully razzed him about now being in competition with Princeton.

Victoria immediately came to the point of protection for Princeton and said, "Not to take anything away from you, Max, but Princeton has a hold on my heart that can't be waivered."

Max smiled and said, "Believe me, I know that, everyone that knows you, knows that!"

*   *   *   *   *

Princeton and Zach were sipping their Starbucks, standing in the forgotten land. Zach was hurting as he took in life's demise.

Princeton looked over to him and said, "Anytime you want to gain perspective, just spend a day here."

Zach was feeling ashamed about his earlier conversation. He felt guilty about his perception of life. He was amazed at how "at home" Princeton seemed to be in these surroundings. He chameleoned himself to seem as if he belonged there. You forgot what he looked like or what he was wearing; he had an air about him, which wasn't condescending to the people he came in contact with. Zach was shocked that some of them knew Princeton. He shook hands, talked, looked into their eyes. He actually touched them, sometimes placing his hand on their shoulders, sometimes discreetly putting money in their pockets. It all seemed very Robin Hood to Zach.

He thought to himself, "How many times has the Prince been here?"

There weren't that many shots of inner city in the studio. Zach was trying to acclimate with the swing of being at the bus stop and now here. Those hours were productive, upbeat, and lighthearted. Zach felt like he did really well. At first, it was intimidating to have Princeton right next to him, directing, commanding, watching him. Then he slowly became more comfortable. Princeton eventually left him to his work as he became absorbed in his own zone. When he became confused or needed assistance with the proper piece of equipment, Princeton was gracious and never appeared to lose patience. Zach kept thinking about what his photos would look like as Princeton developed them alongside with his.

Zach got a kick out of people staring at them, as if they were photographers for a major magazine or an advertising firm. The biggest kick was when a man approached Princeton and recognized him, explaining he was a big fan and had his piece "Surrender" in his home. Princeton stopped and gave him his full attention. He described how much he loved shooting that piece, and when they finished exchanging conversation, the man asked him to autograph his messenger bag. Princeton blushed and took his laundry marker and boldly covered the front of his bag. The man thrilled and thanked him as Princeton shook his hand.

Zach now thought, "Autographs one moment, and now stuffing money into torn, dirty pockets? Unbelievable!"

If he thought he admired and respected Princeton before, now he was sure that he was his hero. He concluded that if he were a chick, he would be in love with him.

They had yet to take a shot. Princeton seemed to be easing his way into their existence, as if he were asking permission to enter their world.

Zach leaned against the car and waited patiently as Princeton was kneeling down, engaged in a conversation with an elderly man who was sitting on the ground leaned up against the building with a newspaper and coffee in hand.

As he looked to the side, he saw a woman approaching him.

"You from DSS?" she asked.

"Uh . . . no," he answered as he searched his memory for the meaning of the DSS initials.

"When they coming? That little girl needs to go to some foster home, you know? They never come!"

"What little girl?" Zach asked.

"Who you?" the woman asked as she peered into Zach's eyes.

"I'm Zach, nice to meet you," he said as he extended his hand.

She looked at his hand and repeated, "Who you?"

"I'm here with Princeton," he said, hoping it would relieve the tension as he pointed to him across the street.

The woman followed his finger and got excited when her eyes found Princeton.

"You with the man? Well, why you didn't say so! He feed my family last week. I been looking for his car. This his car, right?" she asked as she hurried over to Princeton, not waiting for Zach to answer.

Zach watched as the woman hugged Princeton affectionately. He couldn't get past the picture of the three of them talking, smiling, laughing as if they were friends hanging out, catching up on their small talk. Then his eyes rested on the backdrop of the decrepit building, and he got a rush, a tremendous rush. He searched for his camera and fumbled with uncovering the lens and positioning himself as he started to snap frame after frame. He was finding brilliant moments in the contradiction of the story.

When he was satisfied, which came as a high that dissipated, he put the camera back in the car and leaned up against its door, remaining where he was instructed to do so. He watched as Princeton discreetly put something into their hands before he made his way back to the car.

"How we doing?" Zach asked, feeling inspired and exhausted.

"We're good, let's unload," Princeton said as he appeared to be in deep thought.

"Can I ask you something?" Zach said, building courage.

"Sure, shoot."

"How often do you come here?"

Princeton didn't look up and replied, "I don't know, it depends. Victoria and I come here at her request, and there are times I come with Tallulah and other times by myself."

"Victoria?" Zach thought with complete surprise. He couldn't register Victoria here. Yeah, she was all about saving the world, but here? Zach realized that after two years of thinking he knew all about Princeton's world, there were so many eye openers today, which left him feeling as if he had only touched the surface of the mentor he longed to mirror.

His thoughts returned to the day he stood before Princeton in the studio and was so blown away by him. He was determined to land the job and was confident that he was more than qualified holding his resume in his hand. He first eyed Princeton and Tallulah at a mutual friend's birthday bash at a local nightclub. Zach was totally drawn to them and kept inquiring about them. He watched them and studied their every move. His friend from work told him to take a good look because they rarely came out to these things. Apparently, Tallulah did some work for the birthday boy and felt it was the appropriate thing to do. Zach remembered the conversation with his friend as he filled him in on the details.

"That is a success story right there," he said as he pointed to them.

"Listen, you hate your job, right?" Zach reluctantly nodded a yes.

"Well, let me introduce you because I know for a fact he's looking for someone to assist at his studio. A couple of guys applied, but I think it's still up for grabs."

Zach was surprised at Princeton and Tallulah's easy gracious manner. He was intrigued with their connection to one another and how warm and welcoming they were with their conversation with him. He had recently been struggling with the crossroad in his life of wanting to make a big change with his job and with his entire lifestyle. It was his desperation that made him boldly inquire about the position he had just heard about.

Princeton simply said, "Stop by the studio, we'll talk" as he handed him his card.

Zach diligently researched everything he could find out about Princeton and his work before the day he stood before him. He didn't know at the time that day would be a monumental turning point in his life. He started work the following Monday.

"Zach, buddy, you OK?"

Zach looked up and smiled. "Yeah, I'm great! Sorry, what are we doing?"

*   *   *   *   *

As Max was about to reach his final decision, he couldn't believe how many beautiful rings he had looked at. Every ring was vintage, high quality, and surprisingly inexpensive compared to what he was prepared to spend. He kept thinking why hadn't he come to places like this instead of the cookie-cutter retail stores? This shop was high specialty, and Victoria obviously had a history with the owner John. She told Max she trusted him, and they needn't worry about the quality.

Now with Tallulah standing there with her arm in his, she said with anticipation, "Which one, Max? They're both sooo beautiful."

"You pick, which one will Piper love?"

Tallulah laughed. "Both, but if I had to pick one? It would be that," she said as she pointed to the three-plus karat emerald cut diamond sitting in its raised white gold intricate band that housed tiny emerald chips.

"OK, that's it!" Max said relieved.

Tallulah turned to Victoria who was sitting in an ornate slipper chair having conversation with John. She called out to them full of excitement, "We're set here. He decided. Come look!"

Victoria eyed the ring and said, "Fabulous choice, Max!"

John smiled and said, "Let me clean it and get the ownership papers."

Tallulah smiled and teased Max with "You think it belonged to royalty?"

"You get papers?" Max asked, surprised.

"Of course," Tallulah answered. "That's part of the mystique. Piper's gonna flip!"

As Max wrote the check, he couldn't help but think, "Eight grand. That's nothing. That's what Victoria's collection brings in, in a week. His and Princeton's Cartiers were each more than that."

Max looked at Victoria as he thought about his collection and that it was only this morning when she got into the car, and handed him a folder with so many new designs. He leaned over and kissed her. "Thank you, Victoria, thank you for everything."

"My pleasure," she said as she smiled. "You're worth it."

On the drive home, Tallulah asked Max to hand her the box. As she sat there admiring the ring, she said, "What a beauty! This little guy here has drained me. What time is it?"

"Almost four," Victoria replied as she checked her watch.

Max hit the button on his cell, waiting impatiently for Princeton to pick up.

"Hey! How's it going? How are my ladies?"

"It's done! Your ladies are really something!" he said as he glanced at Victoria and Tallulah.

"Where are you?" Max asked.

Tallulah was focused on listening to the broken conversation.

"We're leaving the city," Princeton answered.

"How'd Zach do?" Max asked.

Princeton glanced over to Zach and smiled, knowing he could hear his words.

"He did great, very productive day. I'm going to have to feed him. He's losing all that spray tan." Princeton winked at Zach, referring to his bronze skin. "I think his blood sugar is low."

Zach intentionally spoke loud, so Max could hear.

"I'm exhausted, starving, and I'm hitting the labor board tomorrow!"

Max laughed hearing Zach's words. Tallulah tried to imagine the words attached to Max's reaction. Princeton's heart was beating faster as he imagined Tallulah sitting in the car.

"Hey!" Max exclaimed as he looked over to the dynamic duo, "let's all meet for dinner."

He checked to see if his idea was welcomed and continued when Victoria smiled and nodded, and Tallulah said excitedly, "They're done? This is perfect. Let's celebrate."

Princeton heard Tallulah's voice and started to get that pang of anticipation.

"How far are you guys?" Princeton asked as he looked at Zach, hoping they were close.

"We'll hit the city in thirty, maybe forty. Stay there, what's the call? Max asked as he waited for dining suggestions from Princeton.

"Your call, it's your day. I'm assuming we've officially broken up?" Princeton said, starting their usual banter.

"Why? Because I didn't buy you a ring?"

They both laughed as Max searched his memory for a good choice.

"How's Temptations?" Max asked.

Tallulah and Victoria both expressed their approval with facial gestures of euphoria.

Princeton continued to play with Max, saying, "Oh! We're hanging out with the big boys? Hope you didn't deplete your funds. The ring may be less than dinner."

Zach pieced the conversation together and was thrilled with Princeton's response. He laughed out loud as he thought, "Yeah sure, depleted funds? Not with these guys."

"Where are we going?" Zach asked.

"Temptations," Princeton responded.

"Yeah, Temptations, that's what I said," Max answered.

"No, not you, I was talking to Zach."

"OK, set us up. We'll be there in thirty." Max laughed as he whispered, "Just so you know, she's wearing the cat suit."

Princeton ended the call, already lost in his thoughts of imagining Tallulah in his favorite look. The Spyder Winterskyn two-piece suit was marketed for skiing, but Tallulah found a way to transition it into her everyday wardrobe. She had three different variations. This one was a black second skin with zippers and thumbholes, so her hands were covered to the knuckle. It screamed athletic; she made it scream sexy. She would pair it with Uggs, DC fur, or Oscar boots. Her hair would usually be in a tight ponytail or tasseled high with her Burton ear band covering her forehead. It was perfect for subzero, but she didn't care. Early fall was close enough. Princeton just loved the way she looked in that; Zippered to the neck, and she managed to create a sensual sensation. Between the two of them, they had at least twenty pieces of Spyders, including two performance suits. Max came to affectionately refer to it as the cat suit, associating it with Catwoman and the never-ending stares, which led Max to once openly ask a guy, "What? What are you looking at? You think you're Batman?" Tallulah, Princeton, and Piper broke out with a roar of laughter, and after that it just stuck.

It was one of those times Max couldn't resist with getting irritated with what he called disrespectful. He said, "It's one thing if she's here by herself, but c'mon, she's with the Prince, her hands are pasted to him."

Piper challenged him, saying, "What do you expect? Look at her! She's every guy's fantasy."

Princeton appreciated Max's loyalty to him, but he wouldn't allow himself to go there; it would be too dangerous. If he got caught up in every guy's stare, he would constantly be in turmoil and fall prey to the green-eyed monster. Tallulah always reinforced her love for him intentionally when they were out, so he never allowed himself to waste their time together worrying about the men around them.

However, body contact was something that enveloped him in rage. There was an episode that resulted in Princeton lifting a guy off the ground while his one hand was attached to his throat as he plastered him against the wall. When he saw the guy rest his hand on Tallulah's butt and he heard her gasp, he lost it. He believed he could have sucked the life out of him right there against the orange wall. It took two men to pull him off and two weeks of prayer to come to terms with his rage. Fortunately, that was the only incident that tested Princeton's self-control.

Now as he drove he smiled, thinking soon he would have his cat in his arms.

*   *   *   *   *

The drive to the restaurant was lacking in conversation. Both Zach and Princeton were satisfied with conversing with their inner thoughts. Princeton was occupied with last night's mind tease of his masterpiece collection. His eyes were scouting buildings and architectural details, hoping something would pop out and talk to him. Weaved into the stone and concrete were images of Tallulah reaching the heights of his effect on her. Just thinking about her face, her body, remembering the words she saved for him only him made him wish he were alone in the car; Zach was a distraction to his daydream.

Zach was thinking about Makenzie, Princeton's testimony, and today's footage. He broke the silence with asking, "Are you going to develop after dinner?"

Princeton reluctantly pulled himself away from Tallulah's mouth on his shoulders and looked at Zach as he smiled and said, "Yeah, you know the drill."

Zach was hoping for a yes, knowing that tomorrow he would be able to view his work and see if there was an indication of a promising career.

As they parked the car, Princeton checked the clock. "We're good, buddy, just enough time to set up."

Zach learned that setting up was a ritual the circle practiced when someone arrived before the rest of the group. Instructions were given as to what wine should be opened and ready to be poured, what soft drinks should be on the table, and always a cup of coffee with a sidecar of ice readily available for Victoria.

Princeton grabbed his messenger bag, checked to make sure his toothbrush and toothpaste were there, took out his Unforgettable and sprayed his neck, ran his fingers through his hair, and checked the smoothness of his face. He then opened the side compartment and took out his electric razor.

"You have your shampoo?" Zach asked with playful sarcasm.

"Would you want tiny needles running across your face?"

"Point taken."

As they approached the door, the hostess and server looked, and immediately exchanged a look with one another.

"Oh my god!" she exclaimed "Please seat that eye candy in my section . . . please."

"Slow down, cowboy, he's soo taken, but I'll seat them with you because the tip will secure your car payment."

"Money too? Who is he?"

Before the hostess could answer, the door was opening, and she was frantically trying to check herself in the mirror.

"Good evening," she said as she made eye contact.

Zach smiled and just knew what they were thinking as he looked at the server fetching for Princeton's attention.

"Good evening" was returned from Zach and Princeton.

"Two?" the hostess asked.

"Five please," Princeton responded as he glanced away.

"Right this way."

"Could we please have the round table in the back?" Princeton asked, forcing them to change their direction.

"Certainly," the hostess said, thinking, "Too bad, that's James's station.

As they approached the table, Princeton inquired if James was on tonight.

"Yes, I'll send him right over."

"Thank you," Princeton said as he eyed the seating, deciding who would sit where.

She started to place the menus when Princeton said, "No menus, thank you."

"James?" the voice called out in the kitchen.

"Yeah, over here," James responded as he tasted the bruschetta in his mouth.

"It's your lucky day. The photographer is here."

James dropped the bread and passed her quickly, saying, "Put some fresh coffee on."

Princeton extended his hand as he stood by the table.

"Good to see you," James said as he shook it.

Princeton pointed to Zach, saying, "You remember Zach?"

Zach shook his hand, thinking he had only been there once, no way he'd remember him.

"Yeah, your coworker, right?"

"That's why Tallulah says you're the best!" Princeton said with a big smile.

"Will your better half be joining us?" James asked, appreciating the compliment.

"Absolutely, with Victoria and Max."

"Excellent!" James said enthusiastically.

"OK," Princeton said, anxious to freshen up. "Wine glasses all around. You can pour me and Zach from a bottle of Purple Angel. Keep another one opened and ready to go. Coffee with a sidecar of ice, two ice teas, nonsweetened, two Diet Cokes, and two bottles of Pellegrino. Start us off with four or five appetizers, your choice." Princeton winked.

James took so much pride in knowing that Princeton trusted him to have the authority to decide what their palettes would experience. It would be a safe decision because almost everything on the menu was to their liking. Princeton enjoyed being able to "family style" his choices without it being a project. The chef always accommodated his requests.

"Let's do reds and pinks," Princeton announced.

James understood that to be a combination of big thick prime steaks and salmons.

"Don't forget Max is coming, so throw on some really big pieces of beef."

James chuckled and said, "Will do."

"The sides are your choice," Princeton continued, "but make sure there's broccoli rabe and asparagus. Thanks, buddy."

James disappeared, and Princeton directed Zach where he and Tallulah would be sitting and then rushed to the men's room.

Zach sat, watching James return within minutes placing the wine, as another server placed the bottles of Pellegrino and distributed the soft drinks to empty seats. He noticed one or two servers observing the attention being given to the table. He couldn't help but feel accomplished like he had arrived, and yet there was this unpleasant feeling tugging at his heart as he remembered only hours ago he was standing in the forgotten land.

"How does he do it?" he thought. "How does he balance and justify the polar opposites of today? It would be better if he didn't put himself in that place so he wouldn't have to see it. Wouldn't have to remind himself that people lived like that, but no, not Princeton. He would rather deal with the pain than to pretend it didn't exist." Those thoughts were still weighing on his mind as he looked up and saw Tallulah entering the entryway. Simultaneously, Princeton became visible out of the corner of his eye. He watched his face illuminate as he found her quickly walking toward him. She found his embrace as he wrapped his arms around her, dropping his bag to the floor.

"Hey, baby." His words were in her ear as he deeply inhaled.

"Hi, beautiful," she said as she pulled back to view his face before placing her mouth on his.

Still attached, he guided her to the table, pulled out the chair, and waited as she bent over and kissed Zach hello. Zach stood up as Max and Victoria made their way over. Princeton pulled out Victoria's chair and kissed her, adding some complimentary words, and then bear hugged Max. Zach pecked Victoria's cheek and did the boy thing with his handshake to Max.

They settled in as the red jewel was distributed into their glasses. Princeton's hand found Tallulah's thigh, and she wrapped her arm around his shoulder as she adjusted herself to move closer to his face.

"Well?" Princeton said as he looked at Max. "Do you have it with you?"

"Have what?" Max said jokingly.

"C'mon, Max!" Tallulah said impatiently excited.

Max pulled the box out of his pocket and passed it to Princeton.

Zach was eyeing the box being passed.

Princeton opened it, and the big piece of ice sparkled.

"Wow . . . beautiful . . . just beautiful!" he said as he looked at Max. He winked at Victoria and said, "Piper's going to be over the moon. Nice job, Mom."

He passed it to Zach, who stared at the rock and then said, "I had no idea! This is great. Congratulations!"

The ring went back to Tallulah, who smiled as she left the beauty exposed sitting in her bread dish so she could admire it.

Princeton raised his glass as the others joined in to toast "To Max!"

"I wish Piper were here," Tallulah said. "I feel like we're being deceitful."

"Don't worry, honey," Victoria said, "we'll have another opportunity to toast both of them, believe me, but right now, it's all about Max!"

The exchange of conversation about the day's events was endless. Tallulah imitated Max's expressions, while Zach touched on their incredible day as they all tried to connect the dots of their separation. The dishes came and went, with remarks of satisfaction about the fabulous food. Max did in fact devour a huge steak as Victoria and Tallulah polished off the majority of the broccoli rabe. At one point, there were at least six large platters circulating the table, with everyone in agreement that if they ate anymore, they would explode. In between bites and conversation, Princeton and Tallulah exchanged whispers and affectionate glances.

"You guys did just see each other this morning, right?" Max asked with exasperation.

"Not exactly," she answered as she moved to Princeton's ear.

"I lost time, baby, when did you carry me up?" Before Princeton could answer, she asked, "Did you sleep?"

Princeton's mind went to him placing her in bed, tracing her body gently with his hand. He adjusted himself in his seat as he felt the warmth travel his body.

"It was late. If we continue to talk about this, I'm going to have you right here."

Tallulah closed her eyes for a second and adjusted herself beneath his hand.

She recognized that he didn't answer about sleeping and forced herself to direct her attention to the table.

"So, Max," she announced, "when are you going to propose?"

Max answered immediately, indicating he had already made his decision, "Your house . . . Thursday."

"What? Oh my gosh!" Tallulah's expression of surprise matched Princeton's and Victoria's.

"This changes everything. When were you going to tell us?" she asked, already making a list in her head of additional things needed to accommodate the celebration.

Max seemed pensive as he answered with "I just decided on the drive here, it seemed like the best time what with everyone going to be there, you know?"

"Well, I think that's a great idea," Victoria added.

She looked at Princeton and Tallulah smiling. "You better stock up on flower bottle."

Zach interrupted and said, "Makenzie and I will take care of that, OK?"

"Thanks, buddy, OK great," Princeton said as he looked at Tallulah, knowing her mind was going a mile a minute. "Don't worry, baby, we'll make this really special for your sister."

Tallulah gave him a big kiss and said, "I'm sooo excited!"

Max leaned toward Victoria, and his body displayed an intimacy that caught Princeton's attention.

"Will you bring something from Bella's?" he asked as his eyes were locked on hers. "You know how much Piper loves those deadly desserts."

Victoria laughed and said, "Actually, I wasn't coming for dinner, but I was going to stop by with dessert anyway. I'll just turn it up a notch."

"No, Mom," Princeton said, "you have to be there for dinner. Piper will need you there from beginning to end."

Victoria sighed and said, "This week is just so full. It's like I'm on vacation what with today, and then tomorrow, and then Thursday at your house."

"What's tomorrow?" Tallulah asked.

Victoria smiled seductively, looked at Princeton, and said, "I'm having dinner with your parents." She paused and then dramatically added, "And a mystery guest."

"Oh my gosh, a date? A date? That's fabulous!" Tallulah said as she was apparently thrilled.

"We'll see," Victoria said as she sipped her coffee.

Princeton's mixed emotions were obvious on his face. He was excited Victoria was having dinner with his parents and that they were in a close enough relationship to set up a blind date. The uneasiness came when he recognized again his weak communication with them.

"What's wrong?" Max asked.

Princeton exited his thoughts, looked at Max, and said smiling, "Wrong? No, nothing's wrong. Everything is perfect, just perfect."

As James cashed out their check, he looked at the signature on the credit card slip and thought, "That's got to be worth something," then he looked at the tip and was shocked. Princeton always took care of him, but this was over the top. "I could just go home now and not work all week," he thought to himself as he returned to the table and emphasized his appreciation to Princeton.

"Great job, James, thanks, we'll see you soon."

James added humor with "Tomorrow is good" as he poured Victoria a fresh cup of coffee.

"You going back to develop?" Max asked, knowing the drill.

"Yep," Princeton said as he looked at Tallulah confirming she was OK with it.

"I'm sure they will be beautiful, baby," she said and then looked at Zach and said, "Debut time, huh?"

Zach looked nervous as he nodded his head.

"Hey," Max said looking at Princeton, "thanks for the new shots," referring to the pack of the collection series Victoria gave him this morning.

"My pleasure . . . comes with a price. Make sure you get my ladies home safe, OK?"

He clenched Tallulah's hand, brought it to his lips, and kissed it.

"Take notes," Victoria said to Max playfully as she gestured toward Princeton's show of affection.

"I've been taking notes for years," Max replied as he stared at the Romeo and Juliette duo.

"I've come to the conclusion that's not something you learn," he said as he winked at Victoria.

After some procrastination and long good-byes, they separated to go to their cars, but not before Princeton and Tallulah spent a few minutes wrapped in each other's arms, glued to the pavement.

James peered out the window and said to the server next to him as he pointed to the romantic image, "That's my benchmark."

"Yeah? Good luck with that!"

CRASHING

Zach helped Princeton unload the gear, all the while wishing he could stay to see the results of their day. He was so nervous thinking that tomorrow he would have to face the reality of his future potential behind the lens.

"This is killing me," he said as he grabbed a bottle of Evian. "It's going to be the longest night of my life."

"Try not to worry so much," Princeton said as he stood before "Life and Death." "It's a learning curve. Don't set your expectations too high, and you won't be disappointed. We're not looking for perfection here. We're looking for a point of direction for you to focus on. Remember that our greatest rejections sometimes bring our greatest directions."

Zach smiled as he said, "Write that down for me!" and then looked at his watch and said, "Well, either way, it was a spectacular day! Long but spectacular!"

Princeton nodded, acknowledging the thirteen hours that escaped them.

"How long did you know about Max's proposal?" Zach asked as he thought about the beautiful ring.

"We found out Saturday. This was a long time coming, you know?"

"Why do you think now?" Zach asked, thinking about Makenzie. Before Princeton could answer, he added, "They've been together forever. You and Tallulah sealed it almost immediately."

Princeton smiled and waited a moment before answering. He seemed to be collecting his thoughts.

"I guess now is their time. Both people have to want exactly the same things at the same time, or it won't work. It becomes a struggle, and then each person analyzes and reanalyzes every aspect of their relationship. There's so much emphasis on waiting—waiting for the completion of something, waiting for enough money, waiting for the right job, waiting for all the stars to be aligned, you know? With us, it was what we knew we both wanted. We were exactly in the same place." Princeton looked up at Zach and said, "It's just great that it did happen for Max and Piper. Most times, the opportunity goes missed. That's why so many people live in the should-have could-have."

Princeton examined Zach's face, feeling that he might be inquisitive because of his feelings for Makenzie.

"My belief is that there is no universal time line. For some, it works very early in the relationship, other's later." Princeton placed his hand on his heart and said, "You feel it right there, so deep, so pronounced, you don't have a choice, you know? It directs your decision. Love is an emotion that needs to be cherished . . . nourished. Once you start dissecting it, ripping it apart, you have all these little pieces that are hard to glue back together. Your feelings for Makenzie are your feelings. No one aside from God can really know what you're feeling. No one can tell you what's right or wrong. That's why it's so glorious and personal. It's all you."

Zach smiled and appreciated Princeton's words. He needed some confirmation for his new, slightly confusing waves of emotion.

"I'm gonna head out, or you'll be here all night."

Princeton hugged him and said, "Good work today, see you tomorrow."

*   *   *   *   *

Tallulah's thoughts were capturing bits of conversation from dinner as she hurried to change her clothes in hopes of having a long conversation with Piper. There seemed to be so many possibilities generating in the circle—Piper and Max, Zach's photo debut, his apparent feelings for Makenzie, Mom's date, Makenzie's designing talent, the Tom White project. She was tempted to announce her decision at dinner but held back, not wanting to take the spotlight. She knew the conversation would shift to her and the politician and didn't want to take anything away from Max's moment.

The minute her body felt the soft comfortable sweats against her skin, she felt liberated as she glanced at the cat suit on the floor. She positioned herself on the bed, looking forward to some girl time as she hit Send on her cell.

"Hey, chickie."

"Hi!" Tallulah said, smiling to Piper's infamous reference to her.

"Listen," Piper said, "I'm on the other line with Max, I'll call you right back, OK?"

"Oh . . . OK."

Tallulah sat for a moment and then had an urge to want to talk to Makenzie about some ideas that were popping up in her head since the fund-raiser. She dialed Zach, anxious to get some answers.

"Tallulah?" Zach asked a little surprised. "Hi! Great dinner, huh? And a wedding coming . . ."

Tallulah smiled and said, "Appears to be so . . . I can't wait." She paused for a moment and then said, "I was wondering if you could give me Makenzie's number? I have some ideas I wanted to pass by her . . . for her future couture extravaganza."

Zach loved Tallulah's use of her vocabulary. She always made simple sentences sound important and romantic. He felt an immediate rush of excitement. Tallulah asking for Makenzie's number? That was a first. All the girls Zach had been with were sort of an extension of him. They were welcomed, but Tallulah never developed a relationship with them, let alone want to converse about creative projects.

"Sure, of course, she thinks you're the design goddess."

"And you don't?" Tallulah asked, laughing.

Zach laughed and gave her Makenzie's number.

"Thanks, see you Thursday. Zach?"

"Yeah?"

"I'm sure your photos are going to be fantastic!"

"From your mouth to God's ears."

"What is it with that expression?" Tallulah asked. "Do all Italians learn that at birth? My family use to say that all the time, and then afterward, they immediately crossed themselves. Did you just do the sign of the cross?"

Zach's loud laughter led Tallulah to conclude he did.

"OK, I'm going to call your lady. Love you."

"Tallulah?" Zach hoped she was still on the line.

"Yeah?"

"Thank you, love you too." Zach stared at the phone and knew something was going to emerge for Makenzie with Tallulah at the reins.

"Thank you, God," Zach said as he looked up to the black sky.

Tallulah was making her way downstairs to get a caffeine fix, thinking, "Can't wait to install that bar" as she saw Piper's name coming across her phone.

"Hi! How's Max?" she asked with a sly smile.

"I'm not sure. The guy posing as Max for the last week is beyond fabulous!" Piper said with a girlish laugh.

"What do you mean?" Tallulah asked as she scooped the Starbucks.

"This guy . . . this guy that just hung up with me? Is Max, only a thousand times better. He's so into me . . . into us . . . it's a little scary! If I didn't know better, I'd say he reached a turning point, but that's probably just me, wanting to be with him on a different level, you know?"

Before Tallulah could answer, Piper continued, "You think I'm stupid? You know, waiting so long? For something that is obviously not going to happen. It's been four years! Four years of watching you and Princeton and always hoping we would be there. Did I tell you about Trevor?"

"Trevor? Trevor? Who the heck is Trevor?"

"Don't get all twisted. He's the PR guy for Porsche, who by the way is relentless in pursuing me for a date."

Silence.

"Chickie?"

Tallulah hit the button on the coffee maker and sat down trying to disguise her nervousness.

"First of all, you're not stupid. You love Max, and Max loves you, right? You were just waiting for the prize, instead of settling, right?"

"Yeah, but when you're waiting so long for someone to be where you are, it makes you think that maybe . . . maybe it's not meant to be."

"Well, you're not exactly an easy-read. You with all your 'I can take care of myself' attitude. It's OK to need him. Actually, it's wonderful to need him. That's why it was meant for you to be with him. You were the tool for him to reach his grandiose."

"Well, I don't want to be a hammer. I want to be his . . . his . . . I don't know."

"See? See what I mean? Hammer? I get it—tool, hammer. You're such a beautiful, funny, complex woman. You think it's easy for him?"

"Compliment accepted."

Tallulah was searching for affirmation that Thursday was going to be a success and not a disaster.

"This Trevor guy, he's your test. We all get tested at the most crucial times in our lives."

"Why is it crucial now?"

Tallulah ignored the question.

"Yeah, at first, its enticing, but the layers of your years with Max should be enough to sustain you. You're attracted to this guy wanting you, right?"

"Yeah, I guess."

"Well, what happens when you stop playing cat and mouse? When the novelty of the new attraction is gone? Do you think he could be a Max? Do you think he could feed you mentally? Do you think he could ever begin to understand who you are or where you came from? Can he be strong enough within himself to not be intimidated by your superior beauty and brainpower? And still be able to calm your fears?"

"Well . . . we'll never find out, will we? Why do you always do that?"

"Do what?"

"Why do you make everything I'm feeling and thinking seem silly and superficial? Yeah, you're right, he can never be Max, but what good is having Max if he doesn't give me what I need? I retract that, if he doesn't give me what I want?"

"What do you want?" Tallulah asked sharply, starting to get upset.

"Why are you getting upset?" Piper asked, confused.

"I'm not getting upset!" Tallulah said, again irritated.

"Oh no? Then what is that?"

Tallulah took a deep breath.

"OK, I'm a little upset. I can't stand the thought of you entertaining the idea of another man. It's mentally cheating. What *do* you want?"

"Do I really have to answer that? You know me since we bought training bras together. You know what I want. I want to be with Max . . . under one roof as husband and wife."

Tallulah felt an immediate wave of relief.

"Good things come to those who wait."

Piper sighed, diffusing the edge of tension.

"How long, Tallulah? How long do we wait?"

"According to the architect's timetable."

"I knew you would eventually bring the big guns into the conversation. The architect?"

"Yeah, the architect of the universe, it's all according to his plan. Stay focused. Believe in your love. You did say Max has been different, right?"

Piper hesitantly responded with a "yeah."

"OK, that's a sign. Stay focused."

Piper pushed harder. "What happened to the knight on the horse? What happened to not having to think? Not having to stay focused? Having whirlwind emotions take over?"

"Whether you realize it or not, we all have to stay focused. There's too much ugly . . . too much dark that can take hold of us. We all have to focus on God's good . . . on purpose. Your knight already came. He took you through so many painful chapters, remember?"

Piper's mind quickly traced her time line with Max. All the private moments, when he was her knight, knowing what to say, how to say it, making her feel worthy and beautiful and accomplished. Her heart was embracing the surfacing of those memories.

Piper's eyes filled as she answered, "Yeah, I remember."

"Good!" Tallulah said with conviction in hopes of ending the conversation pertaining to Max. "You know, underneath your shield, you're one of the most loving, caring, loyal woman I know. That's why I love you so much."

Piper switched gears with "Tell me about Tom White."

Tallulah had forgotten that she used Tom to cover her tracks for not meeting Piper.

"We'll talk Thursday."

"What's for dinner?" Piper asked enthusiastically.

"That's a surprise, but I did want to talk to you about Makenzie."

"We're adopting her?" Piper asked playfully irritated.

Tallulah laughed and said, "Well, sort of. I was referring to Double M."

"You're really locked into this, aren't you?" Piper asked, surprised.

"Well," Tallulah said, "I was thinking about the possibilities. Small boutique . . . couture. I think we should all get behind this, maybe offer financial help, and partner with the potential growth."

Piper interrupted, "Look, you may be the interior guru, but what do we know about starting a clothing line?"

"Nothing!" Tallulah exclaimed "But we know design. You're an advertising genius. Zach could network snow. Mom has all the right real estate connections. Princeton could photograph dirt and make it look amazing. Max has all the experience of growing a business and an extraordinary hand, see? We're an empire. I think we could really pull this off."

"We don't even know if she has people to produce the product! This is complicated."

"Maybe, but my gut tells me it's something I need to pursue."

Piper thought for a second. "This is serious. By doing this, you're bringing Makenzie in. Is this for Zach or the obvious talent, or do you really like this girl?"

"All of the above."

"Are you going to prospect Ma for money?" Piper asked, already knowing the answer.

"Absolutely . . . but . . . er . . . we're all going to invest!" Tallulah said and then held her breath.

"What? Great, there goes my season's wardrobe! Did you talk to the Prince?"

"Not yet. You're the first."

"Well, in that case, I feel honored. You sure about this?"

"Yeah, I'm going to call her now, and then we'll all touch base on Thursday, OK?"

"It's your dog and pony, whatever you want," Piper concluded, thinking if Tallulah felt this strong, she was in; after all, she once was that girl.

"Love you, sis, stay focused!"

As Tallulah ended the call, she thought, "Thursday can't come soon enough."

*   *   *   *   *

Zach was hoping he was making the right decision going to Makenzie's unannounced. It could be a great surprise or maybe not. He wanted to see her; he wanted to share his day with her. He was falling fast.

"Better call first," he finally decided as he grabbed his phone off the dash. Just as he was going to hit the button, her name came across the screen.

"Hi, sweetie!" he said excited. "I was just going to call you."

"Hi . . . er . . . do you think we could grab a coffee?" Makenzie asked hesitantly.

"Oh my god! Talk about perfect timing. I was just driving over to you. I could be there in ten. Everything OK?"

"Not really."

"What's wrong?" Zach asked, concerned.

"I'm just . . . a . . ." Makenzie stopped as she sniffled.

"Are you crying? What's wrong?" Zach felt a pit in his stomach.

"I'm just a little overwhelmed," Makenzie said as she tried to compose herself, wiping her tear. I'm sorry . . . I didn't even ask you about your day."

"That can take all night," Zach said with a slight laugh, hoping to calm her down. "Be ready in ten, we'll grab some incredible cappuccinos at Tomasso's."

"You're the best! I'm so glad I have you. Ciao."

"You definitely have me," Zach thought as he hung up. He was guessing that Makenzie spoke with Tallulah. "Maybe not? Maybe something else."

He glanced at the clock as he accelerated to her house. "This day never seems to end, one thing after another. Geez, fourteen hours since I started, and it's still going."

Princeton's words were speaking in his ear as he quickly checked the smoothness of his face. He popped a couple of mints and checked his appearance in the mirror.

As he turned the corner, he saw the image of her pacing curbside. "What the—?" He accelerated and abruptly stopped as he moved quickly to get out of the car.

"Hey . . . hey . . . what's wrong?" he asked as he cradled her in his arms. She threw herself to him, resting her head on his shoulder, enjoying the strong sense of safety.

"I'm sorry," she said, still clinging to his embrace.

"I'm just nervous, overwhelmed." She pulled her face away from him, wiped her eyes, and stared into his.

Zach held on and tried to read her emotions. He was totally caught up in the moment.

"What are you nervous about?"

Makenzie took a deep breath and exhaled as she kept contact with his eyes. Her hands gently cradled his face as she spoke with a loving innocence.

"I'm so happy to be with you."

Zach smiled when he heard her words and felt his heart swell as she continued to study his face, as if she were memorizing every line on it.

"That's good, right?" he managed to ask, slightly confused.

"It's wonderful! But your life . . . your world . . . is so different from mine. I feel out of place, sort of like I don't belong." Zach started to interrupt.

"Let me finish. Up until now, I really liked me! I knew who me was. But now . . . now I'm not sure. I had dreams, you know?"

Zach nodded.

"Dreams about my future, my talent. Dreams about the perfect guy that would come and find me and understand me and appreciate me. Your world makes it a little too real."

Zach wanted to pick her up and whisk her away, calm her fears. He wanted to love her and make love to her, kiss her beautiful face . . . body. He was being swept with so much emotion, he felt like he was having a panic attack.

"Oh, sweetie." His heart was racing.

"It's so real," Makenzie continued, "that now I feel inadequate. It's as if my dreams made me bigger. Better than I actually am. And now I feel like I need to be something, someone different. The last couple of days, I've been totally occupied with thoughts of Saturday night, you . . . your circle." She stopped to look at her ring. "So accomplished, so complex, you're sooo beautiful, you know that, right?"

Zach was absolutely lost for words. He was locked into the expression she had on her face when she said he was beautiful.

"My world seems to be turned upside down, and that's only after one night with your friends. Tallulah called me, and the conversation should have made me jump up and down, but instead I was overwhelmed." Makenzie sighed as she released her tension. "I'm just not sure I can be the woman to compliment your life."

Zach loved that she said that. She was concerned for him and wasn't putting herself first. He knew what he was feeling must be love. He never felt anything remotely similar to this. For the first time, Zach felt the power to be responsible to deeply change someone's feelings. He needed to convince this woman that she was worthy. She was looking to him to get her answers. She needed him and wasn't ashamed to let him know it.

"Makenzie, I love you, I love you because of the woman that you are. You make me feel things about myself that I've never experienced. My world may be different from yours, but up until now, it wasn't complete . . . not really. Not only do you fit, you make it more than it is. I love you! I need you."

As Zach's thoughts and words were resonating, he buried his face in her neck, welcoming her scent, as she stroked his hair.

"You love me?" she asked with a childlike inquisitiveness.

"I absolutely love you!" Zach said as he inhaled her. "You are the perfect compliment to my life." He lifted his face to find her eyes and kissed her mouth as he grabbed on tighter. Makenzie's face was weary, drained, and beautiful—beautiful because it was so pure, so real.

"God must be trying to talk to me," Zach said gently, "because I never imagined finding someone so beautiful, so perfect for me."

As Makenzie kissed his mouth, she felt totally connected to his words, his emotion, and his ability to reassure her. Zach didn't want to move. He didn't want to separate himself from the warmth of his realization.

"Couldn't we just stay here?"

Makenzie laughed and said, "No, I want to be closer to you."

*   *   *   *   *

Princeton tried to massage the ache in his left shoulder. He felt tired and drained, and yet the possibility of some beautiful photo emerging from the liquid kept him focused and in tune with his escalating adrenaline. So far, he liked some of the shots of the kids. One in particular jumped out at him—this little boy waiting patiently with his backpack slightly falling off his shoulder. In his eyes were a story of apprehension and uncertainty. Princeton welcomed the feelings of that little life, waiting, doing only what he knew. Princeton's imagination led him to ask, "What is your life going to be like? Are you going to find happiness? Maybe get married? Have a family? Be a plumber? Doctor? Make a medical discovery. The cycle of life . . . so uncertain. Don't give up, little guy, never give up! Maybe someone will save you, or you'll do the saving. God's plan is truly a mystery."

As he conversed with his thoughts and the little set of eyes, he looked to the right and became startled.

"What do we have here?" he thought.

His intensity grew as he watched the image developing before his eyes. It took a second for him to realize he was looking at himself. The image made his heart race. He was kneeling next to Lloyd who was sitting on the ground, leaning against the building with his coffee and paper. Harriet was standing behind him, and the focus of the frame was the precise lines of the decrepit building, with the three of them as an elusive afterthought.

"Oh my god!"

Princeton's skin crawled as the sharpness of the black found its place. He raced to continue the roll. His mind and heart were in overdrive.

"Zach! Zach! What have you done here, buddy. What have you done?"

He continued to wait for the next Christmas present as each photo introduced itself. He was struck with awe. The photos were genius! Bigger than life. They had depth; tragedy and hope revealed perfectly! He kept scanning each one, all sixteen of them; Sharp where it needed to be. Sharp . . . hazy . . . pronounced . . . detailed . . . crisp . . . sad . . . joy . . .

"Beautiful Pain. That's it! Beautiful Pain."

The story was captivating. Something similar to what you would see in *Time* magazine in the fifties or sixties. He couldn't decide which was the best because they were all beautiful. He looked at himself in the photos and for the first time viewed his life through someone else's eyes—the artist's artist. He was so moved as he touched the paper that tears filled his eyes and rolled down his cheeks. He felt inspired and broken at the same time. His feelings of hope and joy collided with despair and inequity.

"Zach, Zach, you've touched my soul. No, you grabbed it and ripped it open."

Princeton sat with his head in his hands weeping. Oddly, he seemed to enjoy the torment; he welcomed it as a cleansing. He was walking a tightrope of light and dark, pure and wicked, something so real, so gifted. He allowed himself to feel the hurt and followed the rise of the slow penetration of hope and justice. After what seemed to be a long time, he stood up exhausted from the talk with his Maker.

"Zach, you have no idea, no idea," he thought as he shut the door behind him. He had almost forgotten where he was. As he looked up, he saw a couple standing outside pointing to "Life and Death" and peering at the shadows of the works on the walls. When their eyes acknowledged his presence, they smiled. Princeton returned the smile, feeling slightly uncomfortable. He thought, "I wonder how many eyes travel these walls when I'm not here." He wanted the couple to leave, not wanting to encourage conversation so he could lock up. He felt a strong urge to be home and in his angel's arms.

As he waited at the red light, he felt restless and impatient. He tapped his palms on the steering wheel to Aerosmith and checked the clock again. This day was physically and emotionally draining. He felt so small in life's circle. He was so taken by Zach's photos that he surrendered to such deep emotions, that he now felt panic and anxiety. So many blessings in his life, he believed he was undeserving. He traced his lifeline and felt that he could never be thankful enough. He could never have earned this. He dove into scripture, reminding himself it's not earned. How merciful his Almighty Father was to walk with him, carry him. He felt physically sick.

When the light changed, he pulled over and started to breathe deep breaths. He searched for a bottle of water and gulped as he tried to control the beginning of a full-blown panic attack. He leaned his head back against the headrest, closed his eyes, and fought the palpitations in his chest.

"Breathe, Princeton, breathe." He heard his words echoing in his ears. "Breathe.

Deep in, slow out. Deep in, slow out. Deep in, slow out."

As the lightness in his head subsided, he whispered, "Thank you, God" as he felt his breathing return to a regulated rhythm.

"Please, baby, please be up. Please be up when I get home."

He threw the Jeep into drive and continued praying.

*   *   *   *   *

Tallulah hit Pause on the remote to grab some tissues and wipe her eyes. She had watched Shane West comfort Mandy Moore a hundred times, and yet each time, they pulled at her heartstrings so much that she relied on her tissues.

"What a blessing," she thought, "Landon, you're every girl's dream, and Jamie! God equipped you with supersonic courage. I adore both of you." She took in a deep breath as she decided that *A Walk to Remember* was so much more than a movie for her. It was one hundred and two minutes of all her beliefs, dreams, and inspiration rolled into one. She decided not to hit Play and went into the bathroom to wash her face and brush her teeth. She quickly spit out the toothpaste as she heard the door slide. She raced down the stairs to the dimly lit fragranced space where her eyes found her love as she traveled toward him. His face transformed as he smiled broadly, yet she caught a glimpse of that familiar horror, that broken place that occupied the soul of her beautiful half. She moved into the space of his arms and kissed his face, his eyes, his mouth.

"Baby? Baby, it's OK, it's OK."

Princeton's body seemed to go limp. He exchanged his terror with her comfort and conceded.

Tallulah's eyes searched him as she asked, "Why so torn, my beautiful man?"

Princeton couldn't answer. The thought of explaining his feelings and fears was too much for him, too exhausting to be able to find the words. He held her close and wished he could just be asleep at this very moment. Right there, without moving, asleep without any conscious thoughts.

"C'mon, baby." Tallulah walked alongside of him as he draped his arm on her shoulder, traveling the steps to the bedroom.

Not a word was exchanged as he took off his shoes and left a pile of clothes on the floor. He glanced at the still shot on the TV. He smiled for Jamie and Landon, and in a way, it made him feel even more upset. Tallulah followed his eyes, hit the Off button, and dimmed the lights. Princeton got into bed, and Tallulah guided him on his stomach. She caressed his back and neck and gently massaged his body. He turned over and placed her alongside of himself as she found her place with her back against his chest. He pulled her so close, she felt as if she was an extension of him. His muscular torso enveloped her as he closed his eyes and buried his head in her neck.

"So drained, my prince" was Tallulah's last thought.

*   *   *   *   *

Piper sat studying Max's body. He seemed to occupy the entire width of the couch. His shoulders stretched so far, so muscular. As she watched him sleep on his stomach with his arms wrapped around the pillow, he appeared to be a similar image you would find flipping through the pages of a magazine. Her mind always connected with the PR value. It was her "advertising blood" as Max would put it.

"What would you be selling, Max?" Piper asked herself as her eyes rested on his biceps. His muscle definition was apparent, even as he was totally relaxed. She examined each tattoo—so many! It always surprised her when she looked at them. She was never a big ink fan, yet his were perfectly placed and of the best quality. She found them to be sexy and very artistic. She especially was fond of the running time line. That was Victoria's "baby." Max said the day she walked into the shop to get inked, he was so nervous he wasn't sure if he could do it. Aside from feeling indebted to her, he knew he was working on a subject that had an extraordinary hand and felt like he owed it to her to do exceptional work. After all, if she were able to ink her own body, she would probably do a better job than him. He remembered teasing her about using her talents to become an inker. He actually offered her the opportunity to work alongside himself. He said she just laughed and showed him the sketch of the font of the small numbers she wanted running down the extreme right side of her back covering shoulder to waist. Her request was for the vertical line to be very narrow. As Max viewed her back as she lay on the table, he was almost afraid to touch her skin—kind of sacred territory. As he worked, he questioned her about the choice of the ten numbers. Victoria explained it as her life's time line. The ten numbers were actually the five birth dates of what she referred to as her legacy. The first was her mother's, then herself, then Luke's, then Tallulah's, and finally Princeton's. Max loved the idea of it. He was curious as to why she neglected her father's birth date, but didn't dare ask. The finished product was perfect. Victoria loved it, and that was all that mattered. Max felt honored, having placed a permanent marker on the Queen's back. In Victoria fashion, she never mentioned it to anyone; and for some understood reason, neither did Max. The first time Tallulah saw it, she flipped! Once the word got out, everyone wanted to see it. Princeton was especially curious, questioning Max about all the details. Max decided he wanted—no, he said he needed a timeline. Of course, his numbers were larger and the font was different, but the story was the same.

Piper studied her birth date just below his. She remembered feeling elated when she saw her numbers on his back. When she questioned why they stopped halfway as opposed to Victoria's reaching her waist, he said he needed to leave room for his kids' birth dates. Piper remembered reiterating "kids"?

"Absolutely," Max replied with a sly smile.

Her eyes traveled from head to toe. She loved how Max's jeans were always a perfect fit; worn, slightly loose, yet always showing the definition of his physique. That was a Princeton thing. He and Max were so into the perfect fit, the perfect feel, the perfect image. After all, they had many years together to master it. It didn't matter what trend was traveling the market. If it didn't look good, it stayed on the racks. Now with greater resources, they had more opportunity to find the most appealing ones.

"Maybe a jeans ad?" Piper thought. "No, fragrance."

His skin looked so inviting; you could close your eyes and actually imagine a scent attached to it.

"Maybe something connected to sleep? No, he's far too sensual. Something intimate?" She played her game as she studied him and started to drift into his amazing crystal blue eyes staring at her. His large hands held her waist, almost being able to meet at her back. He always teased her that with a little more work, his hands could completely wrap her waist. "More work?" Piper thought. This was more work than she bargained for. She and Tallulah didn't work out, not in the true sense of the word. However, they offered themselves to the thin gods, knowing when not to indulge, genuinely thrilled with good-eating habits, and of course, the occasional once-a-week exercise regimen. Tallulah's philosophy was eat whatever you want, just not for two consecutive days. Actually, that was owned by Victoria. Growing up under the Italian umbrella, she and Tallulah always had good home-cooked meals. Victoria found a balance; she wasn't giving in to the plastic microwave cardboard food.

She went back to his eyes. They would suck you in. For Piper, it wasn't the obvious unusual color; it was the way he used them. He had this way of looking to the side with intensity, always paired with his lips sort of puckered with a downward smile. It just did it for her every time! Those were the little intimate parts of Max that captured her heart. Maybe it was because he was so masculine, muscular, edgy, rugged? Everyone got to see that. Piper got more. She got the gentle, sweet, vulnerable Max. That was her reserved space with him. Max proved to be the first guy that "got" her. He understood her and was able to squeeze in between that door that always appeared to be locked. She found it liberating that there was someone else other than Tallulah and Victoria that she made sense to.

She closed her eyes, and as she sipped her coffee, she prayed. Piper's prayers were very unconventional, just like her. They were more similar to a conversation you may have with a friend or loved one. She came to believe that God truly knew her heart, so no matter what formality she used, he would already know the bottom line. She didn't wear him on her sleeve, and she rarely had discussions about the man who saved her life. She did see him as a man. Of course, he was God the Almighty; but whenever she connected to him, she embraced his time here on earth as a man. His time of pain, confusion, temptation, and loneliness were feelings she could relate to. She didn't learn that in church. Victoria was able to paint a picture for her when she was a young girl, angry about the cards dealt to her. Eventually, her anger was replaced with understanding and a tiny bit of compassion that slowly grew to help her feel pity and absolution for the parents that left her feeling unimportant and afraid.

"Help me to be better. Help me to open my heart. Thank you for having time for me. Amen. Oh! By the way, thank you for giving Max and me the strength to not be intimate. It makes me feel special. Frustrated but special. Amen."

With that thought, she put her cup down and reexamined Max. She gently traced his shoulders with her fingertips barely touching his skin. She felt a wave of emotion as her nose started to tingle. "Don't cry now, Piper," she thought. "When you start crying, it's a long draining thing. Please don't cry."

Max shifted his body slightly as he exhaled with a small smile. He whispered with a sexy sound, "Oooh, feels good. I love you" as he turned his head and buried it in the pillow. Piper squeezed her body into the tiny space between his and the leather. He turned to his side to accommodate her body as she nestled in on her side, wrapping her leg across his frame, and closed her eyes. "So tired, my love" was her last thought.

*　　*　　*　　*　　*

Zach was playing with Makenzie's hair as she leaned her back against his chest. She fit perfectly resting between his legs as he lay on the couch propped up by the multitude of eclectic pillows. He peered over her shoulder to enjoy the sight of the tiny amount of skin exposed between her belt and the trim of her shirt.

"It's so crazy, huh?" Makenzie asked as she adjusted her head closer to Zach's shoulders.

"What? What's so crazy?"

"Tallulah's concept of developing my line. It's so exciting, yet I know it will never happen. I'm just thrilled to have this moment of imagining the possibilities."

"Hey!" Zach said with a strong undertone as he turned her chin to face him.

"Don't say it'll never happen. Don't say that. It most certainly can happen. Tallulah has some great ideas, and I'm sure our circle will get behind it."

"Why? Why would they get behind it?"

"Well, first, it makes good business sense. Then there's the desire for your success. That's the way my friends are. They know you're important to me, and they know you have a talent, and they want to help you, help me. That's part of our bond. We all try to generate and circulate our ambition to support one another."

"You keep saying 'they.' What makes you think they're all behind this or if they even know?"

"If they don't already know, I'm sure Tallulah will bring them up to speed."

"Just like that, huh?"

Zach laughed and said, "Yep, just like that. Our circle is small, but it's genuine and powerful."

"Lot's going on in that circle of yours. It's great news about Max and Piper. She really intimidates me!"

"Oh! You'll get passed that. She's a real sweetheart. She just had a tough time. Her early years were horrible."

"Really? I never would have figured," Makenzie said pensively.

"Yeah, but as she puts it, she got back a lot more than she lost. You know Victoria and Luke took her in?"

"Who's Luke?"

"Tallulah's dad. They took her in completely. I mean clothes, vacations, school, driver's ed, car—everything!"

"Really? Wow!" Makenzie felt her heart swell. "The gods were smiling, huh?" Before Zach could answer, Makenzie continued with "Like you, huh? Do you believe in destiny?"

Zach smiled and said, "Absolutely, more so now than I did before Princeton."

Makenzie interjected with "BP?"

Zach laughed and continued, "We have a free will, you know? But the plan's been laid out. That's what Princeton made me understand. Our free will is set in place to make choices. If you have faith, then hopefully it guides you to make good choices."

"What about today? Did you know that one day you would be shooting alongside Princeton?"

Zach thought a moment and replied, "Know? No, I didn't know, but I hoped for it. After all, he's brilliant!"

"Well, I don't know anything about photography, but I'm sure if Princeton thought you were ready, there must be a reason, right?"

Zach smiled. "I guess," Zach hesitated as he seemed to be drifting into his thoughts.

"It's like with you now. You don't think it's possible to have what Tallulah is talking about. Two years ago, I was in the same place, feeling like I was on the verge of having something life changing happen to me." Zach became very serious as he made eye contact with Makenzie.

"My life did change . . . in so many ways. Sometimes I believe that Princeton is an angel. No, Princeton, Tallulah, and Victoria—all angels sent here to change lives, you know? Maybe ethereal beings?"

Makenzie waited for Zach to continue as she was intrigued with his explanation, "Look at me here with you. Another part of my life changing, changing for the better. It's as if there's this big portrait to be painted, tiny strokes multiplying into the beautiful final result. Me, Piper, Max, you—all colors, all connected."

Zach stopped, realizing he was going into deep thoughts and philosophies that Makenzie may not get.

"Sorry, corny, huh?"

"Corny? Don't you dare apologize for having depth and a promise of hope. Yeah, you're great to look at, very handsome," she said that as she touched his jawline. "And a rocking body to go with that face, and you can put the package together because you know fashion and you know what women find attractive."

Zach playfully said, "Keep going."

"But it's the couple of seconds of what you just said that makes me feel like I found the someone for me. Depth trumps all the tangibles every time. You've already changed my life. There's a domino effect here, huh?"

Zach squeezed her hand, closed his eyes, and said, "And they will lie where they fall."

Makenzie closed her eyes and thought, "So exhausted, my love."

*　　*　　*　　*　　*

Tallulah opened her eyes and viewed the empty space next to her. She threw off the covers and was relieved that she didn't need to search for clothing as she got out of bed moving toward the sounds of Aerosmith. Her head was racing with prayer, not communicative dialogue; it was random scripture and verse. In the deep crevices of her mind, she was having conversation separate from her prayers. She wished she could touch the place of Princeton's torment. She would ask it to go away; she would beg that he be freed from his unending battle within himself. She would bargain for the end of his terror, exchange herself for his freedom.

She stopped just short of the door and soaked up the image of all those well-defined muscles expanding and contracting as the barbell rhythmically did its rise and fall. Princeton's body was working hard, but his face seemed a contradiction to the excessive energy being used. Although he was clearly pushing his limits, his face seemed serene, almost calm, eyes closed, somewhat peaceful. Whatever filled his mind separated him from his physical being.

As Tallulah watched, she thought, "What is it about that song? How can a song do that?"

Whenever she probed, the response would always be the same. He didn't know. He only knew that he felt safe and relied on it to keep himself from drowning in his fears.

Tallulah took a deep breath, grabbed a towel, and slowly approached her lifeline. Standing over him, her body accepted the rush of complete love and anxiety for the man that sent chills through her body.

As Princeton opened his eyes, the instant connection to hers brought that beautiful boyish smile to his lips. His voice was soft as he put the barbell in its resting place.

"Hey, baby."

"Hi yourself," Tallulah said playfully as she fought the feeling of pain in the pit of her stomach.

As Princeton sat up, she sat across from him, straddling the bench mirroring his body as their knees touched. He never took his eyes off her as she draped the towel around his neck.

"Bad dream or Mr. Universe?"

Princeton gently tucked her hair behind her ears as he took in every inch of her face. His eyes traveled from her forehead to her eyes, then nose, cheeks, mouth. It was very deep and deliberate. Tallulah was totally engaged in his awe of her. Her heart beat faster, and she seemed uncertain as to what his answer would be.

"If I could explain it to you, I would. A dream is something you remember when you wake up. You know, bits and pieces or sometimes more than that."

Princeton continued to run his fingers through her hair as he smiled his signature smile.

"This is different; it's not exactly a dream because sometimes I feel the effects while I'm awake, working, driving, talking. You remember when it was more often? Then it sort of subsided. Not as often, not as intense. But recently, it's been stronger and different." Princeton paused took a breath and seemed to stare into space trying to find the words he needed.

"It's as if it's all reaching a climax . . . just before the crash."

Tallulah placed her hands on his knees and moved in closer, searching his eyes. She felt panicked as she disguised her emotion and asked, "What do you mean the climax? The crash?"

"I don't know, baby, maybe like the great story being told . . . before the end. Since I first laid eyes on you, our first conversation, our first kiss, I knew you were my gift. All those years, I always had an insecurity that nothing is permanent, nothing is forever, but we all know that. Some couples are together for decades, right?"

Princeton paused as he took her hands in his.

"It's as if he's talking to me or maybe me to him as if I'm taking stock of my life, my journey . . . up to this point. It's a video of how I started, and all the frames are flashing across my mind in preparation for the conclusion. Things seem to be moving, peaking. Max and Piper's engagement, Tom White, the . . . what was it? Double M line"—Princeton winked before he continued—"Zach's new love, and oh my gosh! the photos he took today were genius! They left me exhausted from emotion. The first photos ever . . . of myself! The collection is going to be his signature. I've entitled it Beautiful Pain, sort of like my life."

Tallulah started to mouth an answer, but Princeton squeezed her hands and gently said, "Sshh."

He continued his thoughts, "Max has reached total success in his business. Every piece of this is a collaboration of each of us feeding off one another to reach the next level. When you professed your love for me yesterday, which only you would use my name and masterpiece in the same sentence"—Princeton took a deep breath of pleasure—"you inspired me to do a new collection, which I know will be by far my best work. We all mix and mesh our gifts and talents to grow this . . . this . . . Most recently, the feelings I have . . . are as if we're getting ready to cross the Rubicon. I wish I could explain it better. I've tried to dismiss it, with justification that I'm just worried or insecure, good things don't last forever, but it's much more spiritual . . . a haunting. Remember the song 'Home'? It's as if it's time for me to pay dues or accept that my time is up."

Princeton's eyes started to fill as he moved in closer to Tallulah's face and whispered, "I'm going to lose you."

Tallulah felt sick to her stomach and was genuinely frightened. She reached for every ounce of fortitude to take her beloved's face in her hands and firmly demand his attention.

"My beautiful prince, you will never lose me, never! Do you understand? We can analyze this until we're exhausted. Prophecy of doom. Cassandra sitting on your shoulder, frightened due to not feeling worthy of our abundance, thoughts of losing me because of the amazing almost unnatural way we love each other. We've gotten through this before. As far as the lives in our circle, it's always been like that. That's the beauty of who we all are to one another. We always depended on our love for one another and our love for our creator to see us through, and this time is no different. We have peaks and valleys. This will subside again."

Tallulah took his mouth and placed it on hers and exhaled a breath into it, and he exchanged his with hers. Almost in a whisper, she said, "Maybe our story is climaxing, but this is only the beginning."

BEAUTIFUL PAIN

Zach examined every inch of the studio as he waited impatiently for Princeton. He went over the checklist in his head as he adjusted the volume on the stereo: beverage cooler full, espresso packed, bird of paradise, frames and borders set for new work, thank-yous waiting for signatures, mail sorted. He moved to the mirror and viewed his reflection. He should look tired and worn considering his exhausting day yesterday and lack of sleep due to his short slumber party on Makenzie's couch.

Instead, he was full of energy, probably nervous energy waiting for the unveiling of yesterday's work. He had a hard time concentrating on the tasks at hand. From the moment he jumped into the shower, his mind was continually racing with possibilities. The dialogue in his head was full of questions and answers. Would his debut be so bad that Princeton would hesitate moving him along to the next step? Knowing Princeton, he might continue to work with him just because of his gracious manner. No, not when it comes to his love of photography. He'd be straightforward. What if he just doesn't have it? What if there's no natural talent?

As he moved behind the bar to make himself an espresso, he looked at the clock and thought, "C'mon, Princeton, where are you? You're killing me."

*　　*　　*　　*　　*

Tallulah stood over Princeton's peaceful sleeping body. When he was sleeping on his stomach with his arms wrapped around the pillow, his upper body appeared to be huge. The tattoo **TALLULAH** seemed to stretch across half the bed as if it were signage for his territory. She felt thrilled and honored to occupy so much of his skin. She placed the two cups of coffee on the table and stood there taking in this simple luxury. It was a rare occasion when she would be able to bring coffee to him. It was always him handing the perfect java to her. That was one of the little things that made them who they were to one another.

Tallulah stood motionless as her eyes focused on every detail of his profile. Her mind registered flash backs of his face as he spoke to her last night. She successfully brought him out of his terror to a place of productive, fruitful conversation. They discussed the menu for Thursday night; she shared her ideas regarding the White project and her newfound mission to get Makenzie's line developed. Princeton had strong input and was clear about what areas he thought were feasible and made suggestions about how they should proceed. She looked at him in amazement; he didn't question her desire or analyze her reasons. He just immediately was onboard. His support was so evident. Princeton always believed in Tallulah's business savvy, and in doing so, he made her feel important, worthy, and very accomplished. He would tease her and say, "Most people have one B or the other, referring to brains and beauty. But not my baby. She got the double dose."

She was so grateful that Princeton's burden seemed to be lifted as he charmed her with his humor, wit, and intense conversation regarding Zach's work. She was so taken by his expression as he described the photos. The passion that occupied his eyes; his body movement, the tone of his voice . . . was captivating. She thought, "I don't think I know anyone that loves their craft as much as him."

Tallulah was so curious about Zach's showcase, she begged him to show her the photos that had such an impact on him.

"Can't do, baby. First of all, they're at the studio. Second, Zach's eyes should view them first—respect to the artist. Third, I think I'll showcase them Thursday night at the original dinner party, now turned monumental extravaganza." He winked at her and said, "Maybe we can work something out? And you can get a sneak peak tomorrow?"

She laughed as she threw herself on top of him and seductively asked, "What did you have in mind?"

As she saw his eyelashes moving, she took another sip and placed her cup on the table next to his. She sat on the bed and gently kissed the skin that occupied her signature.

"Oooh . . . don't stop."

As she continued to kiss his skin, she whispered in his ear.

"Good morning, beautiful."

Princeton slowly turned with an incredible sexy look of satisfaction on his face.

"Good morning, baby."

Tallulah handed him his cup as she toasted his with hers.

"Cheers."

He sat up, took a gulp, and said, "Wow, really good."

"It'll be better when we brew it a few feet away," she said, reminding him of the future coffee bar. "I love that I woke before you"

"Oh yeah? Well, don't worry, you take care of me in ways that people can only dream of."

Princeton handed her his cup, stretched his body, and said, "Come here, baby" as he extended his open arms to her.

Tallulah placed herself into his welcoming reach and smiled as her tiny body disappeared beneath his frame. She listened to his heartbeat as her head rested on his chest. Princeton was staring at the ceiling, lost in the image of Tallulah's tattoo, wet with sweat as his mouth moved across her skin. "*Vision of Love?*" he thought as he continued with his internal dialogue. "You are so much more than I could have ever envisioned."

Tallulah lifted her head and glanced at the clock.

"Hey, baby, you taking the day off?"

Princeton hesitated and then said, "No, I need to get with Zach. He's probably pacing right now. Why? You need help with prep for the extravaganza?"

Tallulah laughed and said, "No, I'm all set."

She lifted her face to his and kissed his mouth. "I'll throw together a quick breakfast while you shower." She gave him a sly smile and then said, "See ya" as she got out of bed.

Princeton watched her body move as she left the room. He spent time in prayer and then sighed as he searched for his phone to call Victoria.

*   *   *   *   *

"Is this the new up and coming designer?"

Makenzie laughed and said, "From your mouth to God's ears."

"Did you cross yourself when you just said that?" Zach asked playfully.

"Oh my gosh! Yeah, so you know all about us Italians, huh?"

"You're the only Italian I'm interested in."

"Flattery will get you everywhere! I'm calling to see how the photos went?"

"Couldn't tell you. Princeton's not here yet. The waiting is killing me."

"I'm sure it's going to be great. I miss you."

"Me too . . . you. Want to have dinner tonight?"

"You're spoiling me, and I'm afraid I might get used to this. I'll tell you what. I'll accept your fabulous invitation because I have a lot of work to do with Claudia today. She's going to cut some fabric, but the next dinner is compliments of yours truly. I'm skilled in the kitchen, did you know that?"

Zach laughed and said, "And she cooks too! Another attribute of the beautiful Double M."

"You really bought into that Double M, huh?"

"Absolutely! Tallulah knows her game."

"OK, well, I'll talk to you later."

"How's seven?" Zach said quickly, not wanting to end the call.

"Seven's perfect, oh, and I love you."

Zach took in a deep breath. He adored the way she was so comfortable saying that.

"I love you too."

Makenzie hung up and kissed the phone as she twirled around the room.

*   *   *   *   *

As Princeton drove to the studio, he was grateful that his mind was filled with anticipation of his conversation with Zach. It replaced his deep-seeded fears with joy and excitement. He had already come up with a plan for displaying Zach's brilliant collection and was anxious to see Zach's reaction to his scenario. Although he already had breakfast with Tallulah, he was determined to get Zach's favorite croissants. So now as he stood in the long line impatiently waiting, he reminded himself that it was worth the wait; they were feather light and melted in your mouth, and whether you chose praline, almond, nutella, or cheese, you would conclude that they were by far the best croissants your palette ever entertained.

"Good morning, Mr. Princeton."

"Good morning, Belle, busy as ever I see."

"Which is good, no?"

"Yes, very good!"

Princeton enjoyed Belle's broken English and her total foreign package. She secreted French flavor with every move and with her poor pronunciation of every word. Her netted hair seemed to be a prop, too rare in this modern world. She was a one-woman show—proprietor, baker, and front house Gestapo. Although she had ten-plus employees, they seemed to disappear into the hectic stage when she was present.

"You see how beautiful you are?"

Princeton flashed a huge smile as she pointed to his work on the adjacent wall.

"You beautiful on face, but that . . . that is magnifique!"

Princeton felt himself blushing as he looked at "Life as a House."

"Excuse me?"

Princeton turned to the voice from behind.

"Is that you?"

"Er . . . yes."

"Stunning! I've been admiring that every time I come in here. You're Princeton?"

Princeton nodded as he examined the beautiful face attached to the voice. It was regal, just as poised as her posture.

"Well, this is certainly a good day. Not only the best pastries, but a talented artist in my reach. Yes! This is a good day."

"Thank you."

"Mr. Princeton, you decide?"

Princeton turned and said, "Yes, sorry, Belle. I'll take three separate half dozen, assorted."

"Aah, very hungry today?"

Princeton smiled and turned to continue his conversation with the woman admirer.

"Well, ma'am, you know I'm Princeton, and you are?"

"Ma'am . . . I like that. Most people would think it's a title attached to being old, which of course I am . . . older than dirt."

Princeton chuckled.

"But I like it. Very respectful. I'm Isabella La Salle, pleased to meet you."

As Princeton gently shook her hand, he felt that her name suited her perfectly. He adored that she used her surname.

"I just located here . . . about a month ago. Still finding my way around. Very congested here."

"Oh! Well, this is the heart of the town, very citylike. It's not like this everywhere. Are you familiar with Connecticut?"

"Yes, really didn't have a choice though. My son has a house here, so here I am. I didn't come far, Rhode Island."

"Well, welcome, Isabella!" Princeton searched his pockets for a business card and came up with zero.

Disappointed, he said, "I thought I had a card. My studio is just a few blocks from here."

He grabbed a piece of paper off the counter advertising the multitude of flavors and wrote the address on it.

"Please stop by. I would love for you to see the collections. Also grab a cappuccino?"

"Well, thank you, I may just do that."

Princeton wanted to kiss her hand, just as the gentleman did back in the day; she made you want to do that.

Belle handed him the boxes. He counted out the cash and said, "Thanks, Belle. Hope to see you soon, Isabella."

She returned a smile and nodded yes.

Princeton placed a box on the backseat and the other two on the passenger seat. He smiled as he hit Send on his cell.

"Princeton? How's it going? Are you close?"

"Two minutes away. Put on two cappuccinos and fasten your seat belt!"

"Huh?" Zach waited for a response; instead he listened to silence.

"What the—? What does that mean?"

He packed the espressos as his mind indulged in various scenarios, hoping his wait would soon be over. He thought "time stood still" must have been coined with this moment in mind. He began frothing the milk when the sound of the door opening made his heart beat faster. As he turned, the image of Princeton flashing his signature smile, walking toward him with the boxes in hand made him conclude, "Must be bad. Ease the blow with croissants."

Princeton tossed him the boxes.

"One is for you to take home."

Zach disguised his nervousness and said, "Great! Thanks."

"Cappuccinos ready?"

"Just about."

Princeton laughed and said, "Well, grab a seat, you shouldn't be standing for this. I'll be right back."

Zach fumbled with the string on the box and placed the two cups on the tile. Princeton returned with the manila envelope and sat on the stool.

"Come sit down."

Zach obeyed his command, trying to analyze Princeton's expression. Princeton said, "Cheers" as he tapped his cup, took a sip, and leaned against the back of the stool as he eyed Zach. Zach glanced at the envelope and then at Princeton.

"Well? C'mon, I can take it."

"No, Zach, you may not be able to take this."

Zach's heart sank as his expression clearly indicated so.

"Zach? No, no, buddy. These"—Princeton pointed to the envelope—"You . . . genius! Absolute Genius!"

Zach stared into Princeton's eyes and said, "What? What do you mean?"

Princeton grabbed him by the shoulders and squeezed as he said, "The best I've ever seen! They brought tears to my eyes. I was an emotional wreck!"

"Really? Really? Are you playing with me?"

"Not a chance. They are genius."

Princeton started to pull the photos out one by one and lay them on the counter. Each time he pulled one out, he shook his head and said, "Unbelievable, huh?"

Zach stared at each result of his impromptu moment. His eyes canvassed the beauties bouncing from one to another. The sharpness, the shading . . . it all seemed surreal. Seeing Princeton as one of the subjects just floored him. Princeton continued to point out attributes of each one, remarking on the precision, depth, and quality associated with each story being told. Zach heard most of what he said; some were a blur. He just couldn't get past the admiration the Prince had for his work. All he could muster was . . .

"Wow! I did these?"

"Beautiful Pain!"

"Huh?"

"That's what I think they should be titled—Beautiful Pain. Do you like that?"

"Yeah, you're titling them?"

"Of course, how else can we showcase your collection?"

Zach stared at Princeton.

"Zach? Buddy?"

"You're going to showcase them?" Zach's voice elevated. "Here? Here at the studio?"

"Of course!" Princeton laughed. "We'll dedicate a separate space for you . . . maybe over there as you walk in?"

Zach felt his eyes filling and wasn't sure if he could speak.

"We'll keep the matting the same, cohesive, and change out the frame color so it's easy to distinguish and give a sense of ownership . . . maybe burgundy? What do you think? Tallulah thought a different color frame would be the way to go."

"Tallulah?" Zach cleared his throat. "Tallulah saw these?"

"No, although she's dying to see them. Artist first, but I told her that they were genius! How about unveiling Thursday night at the house?"

Zach conceded, and his emotions won as he felt the tears run down his face simultaneously as he gently ran his fingers across the photos. Princeton threw his arm around his shoulder, bent his face into his, and in a low voice said, "That's what a photo should do. It should make you feel."

Princeton sat back, sipped his cappuccino, and thoroughly enjoyed watching Zach in his moment.

"You're going to make a good dollar with those. You realize it's the only work with me as a subject?"

Zach looked over to him and said, "You OK with that?"

"Not sure, but at least I'm in good company." His wink was paired with a beautiful smile as he was referring to Lloyd and Harriet. "So how much are you attaching to those beauties?"

"I don't know . . ."

"You better not let one go for less than seven."

"You decide . . . seven really?"

"Me? I say a grand each!"

Zach laughed and said, "Yeah right, I don't know it's different."

"Why? Because they're yours? Feels funny, right? I remember the first time I had to put a price on mine. Believe me, buddy, they are worth every penny." Princeton laughed and said, "Well, now you can help Double M."

Zach looked at Princeton a little perplexed and said, "You want me to keep the money from these?"

Of course, they're yours."

"Oh no! Absolutely not! If it weren't for you, there would be no those."

"Maybe, but there are, and they're yours. I think I should pick up some additional equipment for you. Probably need to get you some additional cameras too."

Zach looked concerned, hearing Princeton's plan.

"What if it's a fluke? Maybe beginner's luck. What if I can't repeat something like this?"

"Aahh"—Princeton smiled—"the pressure . . . the pressure to be better than the previous. It happens sometimes. You know there are peaks and valleys. That's part of the territory."

"Not with you," Zach exclaimed.

"Oh yes, my friend, with me. Do you realize how many photos I've taken over the last decade? A gazillion! Yet I don't see a gazillion here, do you?"

"There could be. You're just such a perfectionist."

"And you will be too. Don't worry, you're not a one trick pony. You trust me?"

"More than you will ever know."

"Good! Because I believe you have the gift, natural talent. Funny, huh? That night at the party? And here we are. God is good! God is so good!"

They both sat lost in their thoughts of how they arrived at this moment.

Princeton broke the silence.

"Oh! There's a chance that a beautiful, regal lady named Isabella may stop by. If she does and I'm not here, will you call me?"

"Sure." Zach seemed pensive as he spoke. "Beautiful? That's not like you."

"If it makes you feel better, she's beautiful for a woman that could be our grandmother."

Zach chuckled feeling embarrassed that he questioned Princeton's description.

"OK, let's get this show started. We have a lot to do today. The photos of the kids need to be replaced. The new ones are really good—not as good as yours—but good."

Zach was enjoying every moment of Princeton's compliments. He may have been overdoing it, but Zach knew it was his way of letting him know that this was a big deal. As Zach reviewed his photos, he concluded that they were great, but to his eye, they couldn't compare to the Prince's masterpieces.

*   *   *   *   *

Tallulah was inputting the schematics of Tom's kitchen into her laptop. With all the new software available for designers, it made the process less talent oriented and more computer directed. She reached for the call coming in, grateful for the break.

"Hi, Mom."

"Hi, honey, how's it going?"

"Great, trying to get the White project underway."

"Oh! That's going to be a handful. Listen, I can't help feeling awkward about Rachel and Derek not being included in Thursday's dinner; after all, they have such a history with Max."

"No, don't worry. We felt the same way, but this started out to be a dinner for us to welcome Makenzie. It just grew into this big thing. I spoke with Rachel . . ."

"Oh! She knows?" Victoria interrupted.

"Yeah, Princeton shared the news. Anyway, I explained what was going on. I did invite them, but Rachel is working third shift, and I'm sure there's going to be an official something, right? Max's parents, whatever."

"I would think so. Well, I'm glad you invited them. I don't want to feel uncomfortable tonight."

"What's going on with that?" Tallulah asked, realizing she had forgotten about the blind date.

Victoria sighed and said, "I don't know, but I'm happy to get to spend some time with them. We don't see them that often."

"Tell me about it. They really like their work, and it's so difficult with their schedules. There are so many times I think we could do a better job of making time."

"Well then, try to make time. I'll fill you in on the disastrous blind date thing."

"Don't be so negative! Maybe it'll be great."

"We'll see. Gotta go. Love you."

"Me too . . . you."

Victoria couldn't help but be curious about the mystery man. She had moments of anticipation and excitement and moments of feeling like this was too much work. Meeting someone for the first time always included that awkward period of getting to know someone—questions, answers, profiling—just too much work. Even if she convinced herself that she would just have fun, it always turned out to be uncomfortable or disappointing. She would tell herself that it was far better to meet someone at the grocery store—no anticipation, just spontaneous conversation.

Now all her thoughts were confirmed as she tried to decide what to wear. Usually, she would be confident with her athletic wear, jeans, or casual dress, but meeting someone for the first time?

"See? Too much work," she thought as she decided on her Lulu athletic suit. She loved the way she felt in it, and that was going to have to be good enough. She checked herself in the mirror and was pleased with the fit as it left no room for error; if you had to suck in your stomach, Lulu wasn't forgiving. Every inch of your figure was out there for the world to see. Overall, Victoria was confident with her casual attire and minimal makeup.

She grabbed the wine that sat in its beautifully crafted box and adjusted the ribbon on the bird of paradise. She learned early on to always present the hostess with a gesture of gratitude; it was an Italian thing. "Never go empty-handed" rang in her ears since she was old enough to accept dinner invitations. Her mother also instructed her to be careful when bringing desserts as the meal may not accommodate specific tastes. With Rachel and Derek, it was easy. She and Tallulah had their hand in much of their home design, and Victoria knew Rachel's choices with wine and floral arrangements. Tallulah had searched for a perfect vase to house bird of paradise as it became one of their favorites. The traditional bouquets became a thing of the past once they saw the display at Princeton's studio.

As she drove, she was trying not to be excited, convincing herself that the drive home would be the same as all the others, filled with disappointment and internal dialogue ending in "I told you so."

Pulling in to the driveway, she checked for the car her mystery man was driving. Her eyes scanned the Land Rover as she chuckled and thought, "Well, that's a plus." Victoria stopped driving cars decades ago. SUVs were the obvious choice when she needed to transport pieces for work. Functionality was the reason, but through the years, she became a huge fan of the wheeled wonders.

She took a deep breath, cradled the goodies, and started up the walk. Before she reached the door, Rachel was standing open arms with a big sly smile. Within seconds, she hugged her, gave a kiss, took the bird of paradise, all the while rambling her thank yous and expressing her excitement.

"This is going to be great! We have scored big this time."

"You are so adorable right now, that if it doesn't work out, this alone was worth it."

"You nervous?" Rachel asked, smiling.

"Not sure, but you look like you swallowed a canary."

Laughing, Rachel winked and said, "You'll see."

Calling out to the kitchen as they entered, Rachel announced, "She's here!"

As they turned the corner, Victoria's eyes caught Derek with wine in hand, looking a little uncertain as she connected with Larry's smile. Victoria felt a surge of surprise and confusion as she returned the smile.

"Larry? Larry! Well, this is certainly a surprise!"

Larry picked up the glass of wine from the table, moved quickly toward her, placed it in her hand, toasted it "cheers," and kissed her cheek.

"OK, glad that's done," Derek said, sounding relieved as he hugged Victoria.

"I didn't even know you knew each other?" Victoria said, still trying to absorb the situation.

Rachel found her glass raised it and said, "Well, that makes for great dinner conversation."

"It smells delicious. Needless to say, this is going to be very interesting," Victoria said with a relaxed smile.

As Victoria sat sipping her coffee, she was intently searching for reasons why Larry couldn't possibly fit into her life. To her surprise, she found herself waiting, as if any moment she would say, "Aha, see?" But her "I told you so" still hadn't come. Larry displayed impeccable manners, obvious attraction with tasteful flirtations, and was very comfortable wearing it on his sleeve. His conversations were intelligent, witty, and downright charming. He orchestrated his presence with ease and fluidity and seemed very pleased in his own skin.

Why hadn't she seen this Larry before? Maybe she didn't have the opportunity to see him outside his professional amour? Maybe his high executive position allowed her to judge the book by its cover? Maybe . . ."

"Victoria?"

"Yeah?" was the best she could come up with as she struggled to find the conversation that she obviously missed, lost in her internal dialogue.

"Want to take a cigarette break?"

She looked at Larry and smiled. "Oh! So you know about my dirty addiction?"

Larry laughed and said, "I smoke occasionally."

"How does someone smoke occasionally? I never understood that." As the words fell out of her mouth, she was almost annoyed as it made her think of Luke who also was an occasional smoker. She usually thought about Luke in her private moments. Now he had crept into her date. "Great timing," she thought as she pushed her sadness to the side. She grabbed her bag and headed for the deck.

Larry took the Zippo from her hand, helped himself to the long white cigarette, and lit hers first. As he exhaled, he smiled and said, "Great dinner and great company. That tennis injury was a blessing in disguise, huh?"

Victoria was intrigued hearing how Larry went to Derek for physical therapy and making the connection to Princeton, seeing his work in the lobby and connecting the last name, sent him on a mission to get himself a dinner date with Victoria. He was hoping for an eventual double date at a restaurant, but Derek took such a liking to him that he spontaneously asked him to their house as they crossed paths at the fund-raiser. Rachel's duty was to get Victoria to accept. She was thrilled that Derek was so fond of his new patient and thought it a sign that Victoria knew him and that Larry disclosed his recent purchases of their son's work. "Meant to be" was Rachel's answer as she agreed to get Victoria to participate in their master plan.

"You sure you didn't plan that too?" Victoria asked Larry after hearing the details of the events leading up to this encounter.

"Wish I could take credit for that, but no, it was exactly that—an accident. Guess it was meant to be, huh?"

Victoria leaned on the ledge and looked out to the beautifully manicured backyard. She smiled with satisfaction as her eyes rested on the cottage garden. It had matured so beautifully. She and Rachel had put so much love and effort into what Rachel referred to as her sanctuary. She was tempted to go and sit down on the Napoleon Gray marble bench, close her eyes, breathe in the fragrance, feel the soft breeze, and smoke her cigarette. Although she felt curiously attracted to Larry, she still searched for all the reasons why she didn't have time for this.

"You know, I'm really flattered by your pursuit. But I'm still trying to figure out why you're so determined."

Larry chuckled and said, "I'm attracted to your championship genes!"

Victoria turned to him as he leaned in. For a split second, she thought he was going to kiss her. Her heart raced; his face was so close, such an attractive face.

"Championship genes? That's a first, never heard that one before."

He smiled, and she moved in closer.

"Never judge a book by its cover. I'm not all that. You do know I have obsessive behaviors?"

"We all do."

"No, I mean obsessive behaviors—the need to have everyone and everything in my circle nourished? Fulfilled? My judgmental views on people not caring, not giving enough? My unending reminders of the importance of being a gentleman, a lady, always pushing to have my loved ones reach their full potential."

Victoria was hoping Larry would say something; he just continued to smoke and watch her lips as she spoke.

"My spiritual beliefs could put someone over the edge, and oh! let's not forget that I'm a neat freak. My junk drawer is alphabetized. And of course there's my addiction to coffee and cigarettes. See? And if you let me, I could find another hundred things about myself that would have someone heading for the door. Quite a package, huh?"

Larry produced this sexy, boyish smile and simply said, "We'll work on the cigarette thing."

When his mouth touched hers, she was unprepared for the rush of heat that was exchanged in that one second of his kiss. He had successfully reduced her to a girl being caught in a moment of bliss. Not the powerful woman she earned the title to, just a girl feeling captivated.

She couldn't even remember the last time someone kissed her like that. Had she ever been kissed like that? Her mind scrambled to remember life after Luke. Five years and she couldn't remember one kiss comparable to this? She was taken by surprise, and the feeling of butterflies in her stomach was unnerving.

Larry produced the ashtray, signaling that their moment had ended. As he guided her through the door with his hand on the small of her back, her senses were awakened by his pleasing scent. Dolce & Gabbana? She wasn't sure, but it definitely was delicious.

"You guys ready for some sweet indulgence?" Rachel asked as she searched both of them, hoping for an indication that they enjoyed their time together.

"Come help me," Rachel commanded to Victoria as she darted for the kitchen, like an impatient schoolgirl.

"Well?"

"Well what?" Victoria asked as she pretended to not understand the question.

"You know what! Isn't he great?"

Victoria placed the lemon squares on the tray, thinking that this was too surreal—boys in the other room doing the man thing, girls chattering romance . . . very high school.

"Definitely hits a high note with his charm."

Rachel smiled, "Charm is good, right?"

Victoria was so appreciative of Rachel's desire to want to have her hand in something that she believed Victoria needed. She hugged her and said, "You're a good friend."

Rachel kissed her cheek and tried to identify the feeling that was attached to that kiss. She felt a small pain for the complete woman that had a piece of emptiness in her.

"Well, I think you and Mr. Charm are a good fit."

"We'll see," Victoria said as she secretly agreed with Rachel's conclusion.

THE LAST SUPPER

Princeton and Tallulah were in full throttle preparing for the extravaganza. The house was carrying the rhythm of all the wonderful notes that would create the symphony of this anticipated gathering. There was a pulse of energy and warmth that propelled them to totally embrace the moment. Although all their work since the early morning was geared toward their guests celebration, this was their time together, orchestrating every detail that was *their* celebration, their cocoon of glorious syncopation that covered them in an intimacy of love and satisfaction.

The entire first floor was carefully transformed into a space that resembled the finest dining ambiance available. When Princeton and Tallulah had a dinner party, the menu was always carefully created; however, the design of the space was equally important. The two of them would feed off one another, visualizing the impact of candles, florals, linens, and dinnerware. Even though Tallulah mastered the vision, Princeton's input was always on point. His suggestions helped Tallulah to expand her horizons as she embraced his ideas. The two collaborated on colors, theme, and visual impact.

They seemed to easily designate their roles prior to the main event. Sophie did a thorough clean on Wednesday, following instructions left for her regarding specific details. Princeton was hitting the black top, picking up various ordered menu choices. Their huge order of two sides of beef tenderloin and filet mignon cuts were waiting at the butcher. "Melt in your mouth" was Princeton's request. Last-catch-of-the-day scallops guaranteed to be the freshest, and salmon steaks cut to specific size were waiting for Princeton's arrival as he hit one location after another checking off his list. The produce and Salumeria requests were scattered throughout Connecticut's version of Little Italy.

Tallulah hit her favorite spot, enjoying every moment of selecting fabulous florals. Charles was thrilled when she walked in. He knew his talent would be tested as it always was when he worked with Victoria, Princeton, and Tallulah. Whether it was a small order or an over-the-top one, he knew it would be classy and expensive. They were three of his top clients, and their referrals helped to catapult his business to star status. Victoria's fund-raisers alone kept him in the style he had grown accustomed to.

Each time he delivered the truckload of magnificent centerpieces that had his business card artistically tucked into a petal, he knew the calls would come. Princeton was on an auto delivery, always Bird of Paradise and seasonal change of other arrangements. They earned his white-glove treatment and not just because of the obvious; he was completely taken by the dynamic family. He admired their unaffected quality—so much beauty, talent, and resources—and yet they were genuinely a pleasure to work with.

The first time Victoria walked in with a Starbuck in hand for Charles, he was floored. It was such a simple thing, yet she remembered from their previous conversation his comment about being an espresso man. She went to the trouble of bringing sugar, sweetener, and cream on the side because she wasn't sure how he liked it. As time passed, it became routine, obviously passing the word to Tallulah and Princeton because they would do the same. That's the way that family was—they made you feel important and personally connected. Charles was impressed with Tallulah's choices and couldn't wait to use his creativity to bring it to life. One thing was certain—whatever was happening at their house Thursday evening was huge!

Each time they had a dinner party, it always included party favors, which Tallulah referred to as "Of the Moments." They ran the gamut of Princetons to specialty glassware. Usually, Tallulah ran with that task; however, this time she suggested that Princeton find something to communicate Piper and Max's engagement. He initially decided his collection of *I Do* would be appropriate. He had over a dozen photos he had not yet displayed, waiting for the right moment. However, now with the Zach's new collection, he felt that unveiling his masterpieces for the first time on the date of the official engagement would combine two milestones at the same time.

"See?" Tallulah said. "You're a genius! Let's downsize them and place them at each setting."

"Perfect!" Princeton agreed.

"Don't forget to have him sign them after the unveiling," Tallulah reminded as he checked off his list.

The purchase of candles and place card settings fell in Tallulah's lap. After much thought, she decided to go with two large candelabras, which each held a dozen tapers. They were one of Tallulah's favorite dining room pieces, which were rarely used due to the stately formal nature of their presence; with candles included the thirty-six inches of silver statement with dimensional rosettes and leaves, were breathtaking. They were enough to light the entire area without need for their chandeliers. Tallulah was careful to always use unscented candles when dining, so as not to interfere with the aroma of the meal.

Once everything was purchased and under their roof, the rest was easy. They genuinely enjoyed the preparation and cooking time together. It was private and intimate. Somewhere between the fabulous arugula salad and sautéed portobellos, they melted into each other's existence. That was the beauty of Princeton and Tallulah! They could never seem to get enough of each other, and they were focused on being who they needed to be for one another before they could spread their wings to be what everyone else needed.

*   *   *   *   *

The biggest surprise was Victoria's phone call.

"Hey, Mom," Tallulah said hesitantly, "the dessert thing has become a little more complicated."

"Explain," Victoria said with sarcastic lightness.

"Well, we have Max and Piper, so we're thinking big signature cake."

"Yes, I know, already ordered."

"Well, we're also celebrating the possible Double M business venture, and Princeton is going to showcase Zach's collection . . ."

"Great! Any chance the president is coming?"

Tallulah laughed and said, "Not that I know of."

"Let me think, even though this is becoming 'the knock at the door,' I don't think we should have more than one cake. Max and Piper should supersede. I'll just step up the additional desserts."

"Yeah, you're right, one cake. You know you have been saying that for years."

"What?"

"The knock at the door. I know what it means, but what *exactly* does it mean?"

Victoria laughed and said, "Well, there are times that no matter how prepared you think you are, there's always the possibility of a knock at the door. Now, you can open it, and Ed McMahon can be standing there with the star search contract, and other times it's best not to turn the knob; it may be a disappointment, not what we were prepared for."

"This is the Ed McMahon one, right?"

"Ha! Absolutely."

"Baby!" Tallulah called to Princeton. "We're in the 'knock at the door' mode."

Princeton looked at Tallulah and chuckled. He thoroughly enjoyed their private lingo. Victoria was infamous for attaching phrases to moments.

"Are we turning the knob or not?" Princeton called back to her.

Victoria heard Princeton's question in the background and said, "Don't answer yet. I have a question."

"Shoot."

"Can you accommodate one extra . . . for dinner?"

Tallulah was puzzled but immediately answered, "One? Of course, we could accommodate another ten if we had to."

Before Tallulah finished her sentence, Victoria accepted her invitation.

"Good! I'll be bringing someone."

"OK . . . wait! Wait . . . you mean a date?"

Tallulah's voice heightened, and as Princeton looked over, she gestured to him to come to the phone.

"I guess you could say that," Victoria chuckled.

"Oh my gosh, Mom! Who is it? Who is it?"

Tallulah was obviously excited as she tried to mouth her words to Princeton, as he came closer watching her start to do the happy dance.

"What's going on?" Princeton asked as he laughed watching Tallulah's quirky body movements.

"Mom is bringing a date! A real bona fide date!"

Princeton's expression was clearly disbelief; Victoria had never brought a date to their dinner parties.

"Hello? Hello." Victoria patiently waited as she listened to Tallulah's slight hysteria.

"Who is it? You never bring anyone here! Who is it?"

Princeton gestured to Tallulah to hand him the phone.

"Mom? She's temporarily out of commission."

"Hello, my son, are you all set for tonight?"

"Mom, are you really bringing a date?" Princeton was filled with anticipation, waiting for Victoria's response.

"Well . . . that was the plan. Now I'm not so sure. My daughter may have a heart attack, and then we'll all starve!"

Princeton's serious tone grabbed Victoria's attention.

"That's great, Mom. Who is it? Who are you bringing?"

Tallulah was standing next to Princeton, impatiently waiting for the answer as she tried to put her ear to the phone.

"Just set another place, and we'll see you at six. Love you."

"Mom?"

Princeton stared at the phone, acknowledging the silence.

"Well? Who is it?" Tallulah asked with a huge smile.

Princeton smiled as he lifted her up and sat her on the counter.

"Don't know, baby, but whoever it is, he must have made a big impression. Mom doesn't just bring someone to family gatherings, especially one as special as Max and Piper's engagement."

Tallulah's face lit up as she exclaimed, "I got it! I got it!"

"You do? Who?"

"I don't know who, but I bet your mom and dad knows. It's probably the mystery man from last night! Let's call them."

Princeton tossed around the request for a couple of seconds and then decided. "No, baby, that's sort of going where we're not invited. We'll just wait till tonight."

Tallulah's expression of disappointment was obvious, but she nodded yes as her mind tried to imagine who would be walking through her door tonight.

*　　*　　*　　*　　*

Max dropped the visor and lifted the mirror to take one last look. He was filled with anticipation all day, knowing tonight would be a milestone in his and Piper's life. He continually played out the proposal and hopeful answer in his mind, all the while confident he chose the right place for the big question. Aside from the beauty and tremendous attraction Piper had for the dressing room, he believed that Princeton and Tallulah's home was symbolic for their journey together. It was the life that they hoped to have, not the obvious, but the love and devotion that lived in those walls and the long history of Tallulah's impact on Piper's life. It was the house that built her. If there had to be two people present, he knew she would chose Victoria and Tallulah to be part of the memory she would surely share through the years when reminiscing her marriage proposal.

Piper checked the clock and went into full high gear. She was running late and was grateful she had previewed her ensemble in her mind while driving home. She had been waiting for the right time to wear the dramatic vintage sheath dress. Although she had been a part of dozens of dinner parties at Princeton and Tallulah's, this one seemed monumental. Tallulah filled her in on Ma's mystery date. That was big! And the commencing of Double M and Zach's first collection—so many firsts! She just couldn't pinpoint why Max was so into it. But then again there were many things about Max that surprised her recently.

She heard the knock and the door opening as she applied her lipstick.

"Sweetie?"

Max heard her call out, "I'll be right there."

As she turned the corner, Max focused on wanting to remember this moment. He had the advantage of knowing the significance of retaining as many details as possible.

"Wow! You look incredible."

"Wow yourself. Is there something I'm missing here? You look amazing!"

Max smiled, pulled her in, and inhaled her signature scent. His nerves were starting to get the best of him as he tried not to show unexplained excitement. Piper closed her eyes as she took in his soft words in her ear.

"You're beautiful inside and out. I'm a lucky man."

Piper moved her head back slightly, looked into the blue crystals, and wasn't certain why Max looked completely lost in his love for her.

*　　*　　*　　*　　*

Makenzie felt obligated to wear one of her creations due to all the hoopla regarding her newfound designer talent. It was almost as if she dare not wear anything but her own collection. The dress was a throwback to the sixties. She was partial to cutouts and used that technique as much as possible. Although this one was casual, it still had the same effect. The cutout X pattern, which revealed the midriff, had a shear underlay so that the skin wasn't actually exposed. The bronze-colored fortrel fabric, casual in its own right, transitioned into a wow factor with the turquoise beaded cutouts.

She was feeling the pressure to please, knowing all eyes would be traveling her work. She grabbed the crochet sweater that she adored and made a mental note to look into possibilities of adding that feature to her line. As she thought it, she realized she had already referred to "her line." That thought terrified her. She was hoping she wasn't setting herself up for a huge disappointment.

She secretly envisioned the dinner party all day long; this was unfamiliar territory for her. The idea that people actually lived like this was a lot for her to take in. There was an air, a classy, wealthy, "this is the way we live" attitude that made her nervous and excited at the same time. Who knew when she met Zach that he came with all the bells and whistles?

Zach was a whirlpool of emotion; so many thoughts were circling his brain that he actually had a headache. He chased the two Tylenol with a bottle of water and took a deep breath. There was so much riding on tonight's gathering. The idea of him unveiling a collection was surreal. He just wasn't prepared for something this big. He didn't get into the details with Makenzie; he wanted her to be surprised. At the same time, he had thoughts of her future bouncing through his head; not only was she the perfect partner for him, he was also trying to wrap his head around the idea of her career being connected to his circle. In between those thoughts, he visualized Max's proposal and the chain of events to follow leading to their wedding. That in turn gave way to thinking about his future with Makenzie.

"OK," he thought, "slow down, or your head is going to explode!"

He put on his watch as he stood in the living room, and even that became a question as he eyed the space. His trendy bachelor haven filled with the most current electronics didn't seem as important as it used to be. He must have turned a corner where his statement of possessions weren't necessary to fulfill his desires.

"Wow," he thought, "this is what inner happiness must feel like. Maybe it's maturing, or maybe Joel Osteen has tugged at my heart."

He had been reading *Become a Better You.* Victoria, Tallulah, and Princeton were big fans. He made a mental note to pick one up for Makenzie as he carried the flower bottles to the car.

*   *   *   *   *

Princeton's eyes were canvassing the details of the beautiful space that surrounded him. The abundance of the different size and shapes of lit candles created a cathedral mood. The dining table in all its glory was breathtaking. His eyes rested on the dramatic extremely tall floral arrangements that flanked the foot of *Reason*, and he smiled. He made a mental note to include those angles in his photography for the evening's event. Tallulah requested that he take shots for the future album to commemorate the engagement. Although he had tripods set for candid shots, she wanted his eye on this moment. He recognized the importance for her because she rarely wanted him snapping while he was part of the moment. How had he come to this place? This life he was living? His mind volleyed the logical with the spiritual, and as always, he believed that God was his maestro. He felt a physical wave of emotion wash over him. He became familiar with this feeling that he referred to as spiritual dialogue. His mind and heart was filled with gratitude, and the penetration of emotion was what he believed to be God responding to him. He allowed himself to be still as he surrendered all he had through balance of his soul, clearing his mind. His only thoughts were praise for his king. When he felt it was complete, he allowed thoughts to travel through his mind again at his command. It was an imaginary switch that he could turn on and off.

He was back in the space as he took in Zach's collection wrapped in tulle with purple ribbon, placed at each seat. Soon many eyes would be privileged to absorb their beauty. He sighed as he poured two glasses of Purple Angel, waiting for Tallulah to come down. He could bet on her wearing black slacks; it was a dinner party tradition. Victoria taught her to be glamorous and comfortable when hosting. "Concentrate on your guests" was her instruction. "Be able to bend and move about freely without worrying about what you're wearing." An ornate tank usually completed the look.

As he lifted his eyes to the sound from the steps, he felt his breathing change as he took in her presence. He was still amazed by her poise and graceful manner. She truly was a thoroughbred in all aspects of the word. "Stunning" was what came to mind. Her skin shimmered against the flecks of light bouncing off the gems bordering the neckline of the very fitted tank. There was a tiny bit of skin exposed between that and the low-rise black cigarette pants. The tuxedo flat completed the look that was reminiscent of the late fifties. It was her face that beckoned you to stare—that flawless aristocratic face that was the perfect combination of class and sensuality. Her high tight ponytail that wisped her waist complimented her bone structure to make her appear regal. As always minimal makeup, heavy lashes, and pronounced lips were enough to have you catch your breath.

"Oh, baby! You are too much! Just too much!"

Princeton barely completed his statement when that broad sexy smile of hers was close enough for their lips to almost touch.

"You're beautiful. Just beautiful."

"So are you!" Tallulah said with a slight laugh.

"This is a big night. Soooo big!"

She lifted her glass to his, toasted "cheers," savored the wine traveling down her throat, and then announced, "Let the games begin" as she tied her apron.

"Anything you think we forgot?"

Princeton smiled and said, "No, baby, we're ready, just have to time the actual dinner depending on Max's proposal."

"You think they'll get here first?"

Before Princeton could answer, they both turned to the sound of the sliding door.

When Makenzie stepped past the door, her mouth literally fell open.

"You're kidding me, right?" she whispered in Zach's ear.

He winked and said, "Welcome to the Coopers' world."

Her eyes feverishly scanned as much as she could take in without appearing obvious.

"Zach! Makenzie!"

They both looked at the beautiful smile of the woman who looked like she should be on the catwalk, except the apron was a dead giveaway.

Princeton approached them with a smile that could only compete with his other half. He hugged Zach, grabbed the case of celebration, and kissed Makenzie's cheek. Tallulah just behind him leaned in and kissed them.

"Welcome. Makenzie, that dress is fabulous! Yours?"

Zach laughed as Makenzie blushed.

"Yes. Your home is . . . unbelievable."

"Wait till you see the sacred dressing room. Zach will have to pry you out of there," Princeton said as he opened the case and placed four bottles in the cooler alongside the other four, next to the bowl of strawberries.

Zach and Makenzie decided on wine, thinking it fit to wait for the engagement announcement to uncork the bubbly. Princeton toasted "Beautiful Pain" as he tapped Zach's and Makenzie's glass. It was apparent by Makenzie's expression that she didn't have a clue. Just as Zach leaned into her ear, the sliding door diverted their attention.

"Piper!" Tallulah's enthusiastic welcome was full of emotion as she raced over to kiss her.

Max's smile was a little too obvious, so Princeton immediately walked over and joined the greeting.

"Hey, chickie, you miss me?"

"Ha! You look stunning. Come get a drink."

Makenzie and Zach managed a greeting as Tallulah poured their drinks, and all voices were going at once. Piper commented on Makenzie's drop-dead dress, which kept the girls occupied with discussing their fashion desires, while Zach and Princeton shared some conversation with Max.

"What's with all the bubbly?" Piper asked as she eyed the flower bottles in the cooler.

"Oh," Tallulah said as she shot a look to Princeton.

"The Prince is unveiling a new collection."

Zach looked at her as Princeton smiled hard. Makenzie looked at Zach, a little puzzled. Piper looked at Tallulah inquisitively, and Max watched Piper's reaction. It was a domino effect of hidden secrets.

As they settled in, Tallulah checked the clock, impatiently waiting for Victoria and the mystery man's arrival. Her mind was in constant motion as she refilled the scallop tray, opened more wine, and drizzled the bruschetta with basil oil. "Who is this mystery man? When and where is Max going to propose? Zach might be the next big thing." She scanned the room as the boys were in conversation, and Piper was making her way to Makenzie, who was eyeing the dining table.

Piper assumed she was surprised by the twelve-seating beauty. In her usual witty manner, she announced, "They're waiting for the other six apostles."

"Piper!" Tallulah called out as she shook her head in disapproval.

"Take it easy. Deep down inside, I'm with you, you know that."

Max walked over, placed a fresh glass in her hand, and leaned in close.

"You love to get her going, don't you?"

Piper smiled and said, "The day that stops, then you'll need to worry. After all, we've had fifteen years of practice."

Makenzie smiled and walked over to the cross. As she stood before it, Piper came up from behind and said, "It almost makes you want to genuflect, huh?"

Makenzie's expression was clear that she didn't know what "genuflect" meant.

"You know, bend on one knee in worship? Bow?"

"Oh yes, can I ask you something?" Makenzie said as she kept her eyes on the wooden wonder.

"Did Princeton and Tallulah have their faith when they met? Or did they come to it together? Or did . . ."

Piper answered before she could finish, knowing where her questions were going.

"Tallulah had the seed planted when she was a baby, but probably around the age of ten or so, she had a conversion. By the time we were twelve, we started to put an enormous amount of thought into the whole dynamics of what that meant in our lives."

Makenzie listened as Piper's soft words matched her facial expression. The memory that she seemed to connect to her conversation left her unguarded with a beautiful sense of vulnerability. This was a side of her Makenzie had not seen.

"The Prince, as far as we know, was about the same age. He had a different scenario going on, almost a spiritual warfare? Not with the dark side, just a constant battle of wanting to understand more. He was much more driven. No, not driven, more like searching. He had tremendous powerful feelings about his relationship with God. Don't forget he didn't have Ma to guide and interpret what he was feeling. It must have been a difficult journey. Max says that when they were in their early twenties, he was already in a full-blown spiritual walk. He says he always admired his belief in his faith and how he didn't stray. He also said there was a deep-seeded pain of searching for a missing link, so to speak."

"What about you?" Makenzie asked.

"Me?" Piper paused.

"Aside from Victoria, Luke, and Tallulah, God is what has gotten me through every chapter of my life. After all, why wouldn't you want to grab on with both hands, when God offers increasing happiness? He's a progressive God, wanting us to reach new heights in our careers and personal relationships."

Makenzie interrupted, "I didn't know you were religious."

Piper smiled and said, "The word 'religious' doesn't appeal to me. It paints a picture of things I don't relate to. Ma use to say, 'It's not going to church and the rituals that make you a Christian. It's the evidence of God's work in your life shining through, for others to see. It's about love, about love in action, and always questioning, would God be pleased with my actions, my thoughts, my decisions?"

As Piper's words were resonating, Makenzie lifted her eyes to the sound of the sliding door as did every other eye in the room.

Tallulah couldn't help but to look directly past her mother, eager to rest her eyes on the good-looking man standing behind her.

"Hmm, great-looking guy," Tallulah thought. "Don't know him."

The surprise came when Princeton smiled and announced, "Larry?" and immediately starting walking toward him. Zach joined the greeting, obviously also knowing the mystery man. Princeton kissed Victoria and stood in a prolonged hug as he whispered his thoughts of missing her and then welcomed Larry as he and Zach relieved his duty of carrying the large pastry boxes.

Piper, Max, and Makenzie joined Tallulah as they waited introductions, similar to the royal assembly line. Zach felt honored that he had one up on the circle. As Victoria was kissed and hugged by her kids, the introductions were left to Princeton.

"Everyone, this is Larry McCabe." It followed with individual introductions. Princeton placed his hand gently on the small of Tallulah's back and ushered her toward their guest.

"This," Princeton said with deliberate emphasis, "is my beautiful wife, also a.k.a. Victoria's daughter, Tallulah."

As their eyes met, their smiles broadened, feeling an intense understood camaraderie. Tallulah was amazed at his air of confidence. It wasn't arrogance, just refined confidence. His manner displayed unspoken words, which translated to "I know how to take care of Victoria."

"Welcome, Larry! We are so excited to have you share this moment."

"Well, Tallulah, aside from your obvious beauty, it's evident that you're Victoria's daughter."

Tallulah seemed to blush, and just as she turned to introduce Piper, Larry said, "So, you're child number two? The double B threat?"

Piper laughed and said, "Great to know you have all the correct facts!"

As Larry engaged with Max and Makenzie, Piper roped Victoria and Tallulah into a side conversation.

"So, Ma, where have you been hiding the George Clooney clone?"

"Right alongside all the other things I hide from you!"

They laughed as Tallulah watched Victoria watch Larry. She had an expression on her face that Tallulah hadn't seen in a very long time.

"Mom, I think you're gushing!"

"Really? Is it obvious?"

Victoria looked away and helped Princeton shelve the desserts. Zach attended to drinks as Max and Larry continued their conversation. Tallulah crept up behind Zach and whispered, "So who is he?"

"Not sure, big money, involved with Trump."

"Really?"

"Yeah, bought the kids collection last week."

"The entire collection?"

"Yeah, but your mom and him go back, I think, he was at the fund-raiser."

At that moment, Tallulah recalled Princeton asking her if she knew a Larry McCabe.

"So what the heck is going on here?" Piper announced. "The dessert box is huge! Exactly when did this turn into the royal reception?"

"I told you," Tallulah answered with an exhausted sigh, "we're celebrating a multitude of new beginnings."

Exactly on point, as if Max knew Tallulah couldn't occupy Piper much longer, he winked at Tallulah as he walked over to Piper and said, "Come upstairs, there's something new in the dressing room."

"Really?" She raised her eyebrow at Tallulah and said, "Chickie, you better not have made major changes without consulting me."

Once up the stairs and out of view, the six of them gathered at the counter like a group of schoolkids.

"Finally!" Tallulah whispered. "I'm so excited and exhausted at the same time!"

"Well, don't count on this being quick," Princeton said. "I think Max is going the full nine yards on this one."

"And that's how it should be," Larry said with a gentle smile.

"OK, baby, let's get the bubbly ready for the descent."

Makenzie disappeared toward the office. Tallulah wanted to engage in conversation with Larry but felt compelled to follow her. She turned to the group and said, "If they come down, get me immediately. Oh, baby, please be ready with the footage."

Tallulah found Makenzie standing in the office, viewing the dedicated library space.

"Do you like to read?"

"Absolutely," Makenzie answered as she turned to face Tallulah.

"I just don't seem to do as much reading as I used to."

"Ahh, we're all guilty of that. I think with all the technology, there's too much information available at a click. I think it's fabulous and sad at the same time. For me, it's the feel of the book in my hands, you know? The smell of the new beginning as you turn the pages. I love holding a book in my hands and imagining the authors journey of the pen to paper and seducing the reader to be theirs. It's a creative gift that I truly respect and envy."

Makenzie loved listening to Tallulah's play on words. She sucked you in with her beautiful descriptions.

"I think you could probably be a great writer."

"Ha! Thanks but Piper is the one that is brilliant."

"You are very intelligent!"

"Well, thank you, but I said *brilliant*. Academically, she's a force to be reckoned with."

She paused a she ran her fingers along the spine of *Atlas Shrugged*.

"You know, my mother used to push and encourage us to be able to offer worldly conversations. She put a lot of importance on not only the arts, but politics and world influences."

Makenzie clung to each word trying to imagine the duo's early life. Tallulah took a sip of her wine and seemed to disappear in a happy moment. She chuckled before continuing with, "Piper and I would play this game. We would pick a word from the dictionary and have to use it over and over again in our daily conversations. That would go on for a full week until we picked the next. Ha! Vocab was big on my mother's to-do list. But Piper? She was not only determined to want to be smart, she was a sponge, you know? History, science, math, she consistently aced them. Eventually, she developed a reputation at school. Everyone called her brain candy. Well, mostly the boys! You know smart and easy on the eyes?"

Makenzie made a mental note to pick a new word each week. Tallulah continued, "College was unfulfilling."

"Why?" Makenzie asked with surprised curiosity.

"Well, I had this creative bug tugging at my heart, you know? So I wasn't totally committed. Piper, on the other hand, had a choice of the Ivys! Could you imagine? I thought for sure she was material for pre-med or splitting the atom." Tallulah stopped, caught in a moment again, and then sighed.

"She ultimately decided to major in business locally, which to this day I believe broke my mother's heart. Piper didn't want us to be separated. She would say everything she needed to learn about life was right under our roof. Don't tell her I said so, but secretly, I didn't want her to move away either. Selfish, huh? Such a strong statement, her staying. She really is love in action."

"I don't see it as selfish, you wanting her to stay. You had something special, and you didn't want it to end."

Makenzie looked at Tallulah with slight embarrassment and said, "I never had a relationship like that. I was a 'little off.' I didn't really have many friends. I couldn't seem to find a common thread."

Tallulah sat on the loveseat and patted her hand on the cushion to direct Makenzie to sit next to her. As Makenzie sat, Tallulah moved in close, as if she were ready to reveal a secret.

"Well, you know what I believe?" Tallulah asked softly.

Makenzie shook her head, gesturing a no.

"I believe that most people that have a gift of creativity have trouble mainstreaming. Their passion separates them. They are very internal, and it leaves them feeling like misfits. Some creative people thrive on that feeling, so at times, it's a paradox. It's not something they can control; it's just who they are. When God gives a gift, there are consequences, you know? So you not having many friends might have been your time to understand what you had inside and develop your craft without distractions."

Makenzie was captivated by Tallulah's kind words that spoke to her heart. She decided at that moment that she wanted to grow her friendship with this amazing woman forever.

"You, my friend, are going to be a fabulous designer." As she touched her chest, she said, "I feel it in my heart. You know what? After dinner, we're going to talk about your future. I have some ideas I've been tossing around in my head."

Tallulah got up to return to her guests as Makenzie sat unable to move, caught up in her immediate daydream of Tallulah's words referring to her as a designer.

Playfully, Tallulah said, "But not before you get me one of those," pointing to her dress as she walked out of the room.

Makenzie savored the moment of exactly where she was sitting, trying to take a mental snapshot of all the details of the room, because she believed this moment would remain in her head as a milestone.

As Tallulah walked into the space, her eyes rested on *Reason*, and she felt her heart swell as her eyes filled.

"Magnificent! Just like you" was the whisper in her ear from behind.

"No, Mom, *he's* magnificent. We're just ordinary, trying to be more like him."

*   *   *   *   *

Piper was searching Max's eyes, trying to anticipate what was coming next. They sat on the chaise as Max requested, and as Piper waited for the surprise in the room, Max seemed to be lost for words as he lovingly examined every detail of her face, gently kissing each area of his attraction. With his mouth on her ear, he whispered, "You do know you have helped me to be a better man? Every part of our journey, I have learned from you. I have always respected and admired you for the woman that you are. Unfortunately . . ."

He pulled away and faced her.

"You are always ahead of me . . . in every aspect. You are always better, smarter, insightful, confident, I guess I was frightened that I wouldn't . . . couldn't . . . be enough for you."

Piper's heart started to race as she felt a slight panic. She found his eyes as hers started to fill and said, "Max, you wouldn't dare break up with me! Not here? Not now? You wouldn't dare!"

"What? No! No! Sweetie . . ."

Max dropped to his knee, cupped her hands, and looked up with a tender vulnerability. Piper's mind raced as her tears rolled.

"Max? Max? What . . ."

"Piper Woods, would you please spend the rest of your life with me . . . as my wife?"

As he quickly retrieved the box from his pocket and opened it presenting it to her, Piper was caught in a whirlwind of emotion.

"Oh my god! Max?"

"Will you marry me?"

Piper looked at the amazing ring and then into the blue crystals of Max's anxious eyes as she nodded a yes, trying to gain her composure.

She muttered, "Yes, I will absolutely marry you."

Max deliberately took his time taking the ring out of the box while trying to keep eye contact. Piper was floored as she stared at the beauty traveling up her finger. She immediately found joy in the recognition that it was vintage.

"Max, this is the most incredible ring I have ever seen! It's huge . . . the style is so very me!"

Max smiled and seemed to exhale a sigh of relief in knowing that it was the perfect choice.

"Can't take full credit. Victoria and Tallulah were in charge."

Still on his knee, he leaned into her mouth and kissed her passionately. She returned the favor, all the while feeling completely shocked that this moment was actually happening.

*   *   *   *   *

Larry enjoyed conversation with Makenzie and Zach, diving into details of their newfound prospective businesses. Victoria expressed her delight in Zach's future potential and was anxious to see his collection. Princeton explained that it was a true unveiling as they had not seen the work, including Tallulah.

"What do you think is happening up there?" Tallulah asked with obvious concern.

"I'm sure it's all good," Victoria said with confidence, and on that note, the five followed her lead to retrieve the flower bottles, unwrap the foil, set up the glasses, drop a strawberry in each one, and position themselves at the foot of the staircase. Princeton had his hands occupied with his camera, and as Larry watched, he thought the moment to be very real and tender. The six pair of eyes focused upward, hoping to see a foot or face appear. Zach looked at Princeton and asked, "Would it be rude to text Max? See what's going on?"

"No texting right now, buddy, we just have to wait."

Tallulah glanced at Larry's hand resting on Victoria's hipbone as he stood close behind her. She felt a quick surge of satisfaction as she enjoyed seeing her mother in a couple moment.

When the first glimpse of Piper's shoe appeared on the step, the eyes froze as the body started to descend. When Piper acknowledged the audience, she stopped, smiled, and then let out a shriek as she extended her ring finger for the beauty to be make its debut. Princeton was confident that he captured the moment as his eye and heart found its mark. Tallulah mirrored her shriek as they applauded, waiting to exchange their kisses, hugs, and congratulations. Within seconds, the corks were flying as Tallulah officially toasted the future

Mrs. Cafaro. Makenzie was mesmerized with the ring, thinking it was absolutely magnificent as she admired the brilliance of it flashing with each movement. Larry commented that he was in the wrong line of work, suggesting tattoo artists must bring in big cash; and as everyone laughed, Tallulah cried, and Princeton captured the magic.

"OK, Max," Princeton said as he put his camera down.

"We're all thrilled . . . and all starved! So let's get this dinner started."

Everyone took their assigned seats as Princeton and Tallulah attended to the heating and preparation of food. Tallulah wrapped her arms around Princeton's neck and softly declared her love for him. The eyes at the table couldn't help but catch their moment, and each one had an internal dialogue about the amazing Princeton and Tallulah. There was plenty of conversation to go around as the dishes made their way to the table—little coy remarks about the unveiling, Piper's finger stretching across upon "let me see that again," Victoria questioning Makenzie's choice on her chosen fabric, pieces of information regarding the ring purchase as Max gave a detailed picture of the extraordinary day, and Larry offering insight into his business at the NY level.

Princeton gently tapped his glass for attention.

"Ladies and gentlemen," he said.

Zach just knew this was going to be his moment, and he inhaled deeply.

"Please open your Of the Moments and feast your eyes on Zach's collection . . . Beautiful Pain!"

As the fingers untied the ribbons and the images bounced out, the expressions were so powerful. Princeton thought it poetic as he snapped shots of the unveiling of the shots. The comments of approval, surprise, and flattery left Zach speechless and actually blushing.

"Magnificent stuff, huh?" Princeton announced as he retired his camera. "Just be careful, they're not framed yet, waiting the talent's signature. No fingerprints, OK?"

"Oh my god, Zach! These are incredible!" Tallulah exclaimed as she came up behind and gave him a hug. "This is a first, seeing Princeton." Makenzie was in awe of her man's work and felt a sense of pride as she was fixated on the photos being passed into her hands.

Piper leaned over to Zach and whispered, "If I walked into a studio tomorrow, I would buy these in a heartbeat! I don't think I've ever seen Princeton in a work?" She then kissed his cheek.

Zach was patiently waiting for Victoria's critique.

As his eyes found hers, she smiled with approval and said, "Zach, God has blessed you with a wonderful gift that will bring moments of happiness to so many. Lloyd and Harriet look amazing."

Victoria's eyes filled as she stared at Princeton kneeling, and she thought, "So fitting, the Prince on the pavement, looking as if he's home. That's why they're so beautiful."

Larry nodded and said, "They're beautiful."

"Ma, is that Lloyd? Our Lloyd?"

"I don't know who Lloyd is," Max interrupted, "but I can tell you . . . this is art! Way to go, Zach!"

Makenzie grabbed hers, held it to her chest, closed her eyes, and said, "Dear God, thank you."

Everyone was moved by her simple act of affection and innocence, not realizing she was heard.

Zach found Princeton's eyes as he stood up, raised his glass to him, and stood silent as he felt the wetness rolling down his cheek.

Princeton raised his glass, smiled, and replied, "Understood."

As Princeton took Tallulah's hand to his right and Victoria's to his left, the table united their hands for Princeton's dinner grace. As he closed his eyes and bowed his head, the thick, beautiful silence awaited his gratitude.

Heavenly Father,

We come before you in the name of Jesus.

Thank you for this table graced with abundance of food, family, friends, and love. Thank you for the miracle of my wife, the result of your great works, for the constant consistent love you shower on me through my mother Victoria. Bless the new beginnings here tonight, dear Lord. Let each new journey be a reflection of our gratitude and thanks as Piper and Max begin their chapter together, as Zach walks his destination, as Makenzie is embraced, as Larry is welcomed.

Father, stretch our visions. Don't let the world determine our limitations. Help us to pursue new goals pushing us toward higher mountains, work in us to become better—better in heart and spirit, better in our desire to want to thank you for your ultimate sacrifice, better in our love in action, always giving you the glory. *With you,* our best days are not behind us but in front of us. Relieve our fears. Wash over us with your shield of protection and safety. Undo yourself in our lives.

Amen.

THE COMPLEXITY OF
THEIR SOULS

Princeton looked in the mirror, put on his Yankee cap, and grabbed his keys. He came down the stairs and saw Tallulah at the kitchen counter looking at three display boards with satisfaction written on her face.

"Ready, baby?" he asked.

She threw her long ponytail through the hole of her identical cap, looked up at him, traveled her eye from his head down to his feet, and said, "Ready. Do you know that you're beautiful?"

He smiled a huge smile, came over to her lifted her chin, so she looked up at him and said, "Let's not go to the movies and stay home."

"Tempting, very tempting, but Piper and Max are probably already in line."

He gave it some thought and conceded. After all, this was his third attempt to stay at home.

"I guess you're right," he said. He knew they had to leave this minute; otherwise, he would be having her on the kitchen floor. She jumped on his back, and he carried her to the car, all the while she whispered her love for him in his ear. He opened her door, she got in, and he closed it once she was seated. He got in, turned the key, and hit the Power button to remove the disc. Tallulah fumbled through the discs and decided on "The Fray." She loved the feel of the Jeep. Not the mechanics of the car, but the residue of Princeton all over it. Cameras thrown on the backseat, the photo of him and her hanging on the mirror, the packs of gum, the empty bottles of water, and the four pairs of sunglasses attached to the grabbers on both visors. It had his DNA all over it. It was custom and had all the bells and whistles—the overhead bar lighting, the advanced sound system, and especially the hand-painted work. However, it was still a modest purchase. He could afford a vehicle twice the cost. She thought he was coming home with a Hummer. She remembered that his reasoning left her loving him all the more, if that were possible. He said that the Jeep suited him. They were a good match.

Then he said, "Instead of a more expensive vehicle, let's just increase our tithes to the church."

Lost in that thought, she rested her left hand on his neck and looked over at him. He returned the look and said, "Baby, it's a good thing we have friends that we like, or we would be shut-ins".

She laughed and thought he was so right. He looked at the compartment next to the stick shift and realized he left his phone at home.

She followed his eye and said, "Forgot your phone?"

He nodded a yes.

"Do you want to turn around?" she asked.

"No, baby, it's OK you have yours. We're only going to the movies; besides, I wouldn't bring it in anyway."

Tallulah checked her watch. It was only ten exits on the highway. They would make it in time. "The Fray" was playing, and both were lost in thought. Neither one of them needed conversation as they traveled the highway.

Step one, you say we need to talk.
He walks, you say sit down it's just a talk.
He smiles politely back at you,
You stare politely right on through.

Princeton was reliving his last episode of intimacy with Tallulah. His mind was catching fragments of precise snapshots of moments of complete euphoria. His body was responding to his thoughts as he began to feel a rush of warm pressure traveling through his veins. He readjusted himself in his seat as he glanced over to Tallulah. "God," he thought, "I need you right now, baby! Right now."

He recognized the ache he was feeling. It was what he referred to as bittersweet. He loved the aspect of being seduced by his thoughts of her. His body reacting slowly with that wonderful warm sensation and then the reality of the resistance of not being able to go further. *That* seduced him even more. If he could just stay in that exact moment! There was nothing more sensual or intoxicating than that feeling. "You do it for me, baby, you know that?" he asked as he looked at Tallulah.

She immediately knew what he meant as she looked over at him. His face and body were restless—sooo sexy. She just knew he was in "a moment." She seductively smiled and closed her eyes. Although she was tempted to reach over and accommodate his yearning, she instead continued to complete her own thoughts. No use in getting themselves to a place that would leave them both wanting more. She forced herself to focus on Piper and Max's wedding. There was so much for her to do in such a short period of time. As she started her list in her mind, she decided pen and paper were necessary. After all, penning the list was part of the joy of the project.

Tallulah bent down to grab her bag on the floor at her feet. Princeton turned to her, thinking she might need help with something. When she looked up, she screamed, **"OH MY GOD!"**

Princeton tuned to the windshield. The tractor trailer was out of control, screeching, burning rubber, swerving lane to lane. He tried to get out of its way. There was nowhere to go. As it jackknifed, the huge square box came racing toward them. He heard himself scream, **"TALLULAH!"** but never made eye contact.

It felt like the Jeep was being compacted as the hood came up and started to disappear, folding itself into the dash. The crash was thunderous! There were cracking and breaking sounds as glass was shattering. They were spinning, rolling, moving, being dragged as forces pulled them against the dash and the doors. Upside down, right side up, upside down. Over and over again, the repetitions of the roller-coaster ride. It suddenly stopped.

Only seconds had passed, but it felt like hours. Princeton opened his eyes. He couldn't understand exactly where he was. There was a sharp pain in his chest, and his head was wet and felt heavy. He adjusted his eyes and focused on the gas pedal on the ceiling. "Upside down," he thought. He tried to look over to find Tallulah. There was an empty seat and no door. He passed out.

All lanes were shut down. There were six police cars, four ambulances, and two fire engines, all intermingled, each doing a specific job. Each one working intensively to secure the outcome of the disaster. Flares were burning, and traffic was backed up for miles. The call came through on the radio.

"This is Life Star 432, acknowledge." The ambulance attendant picked up the radio. "Go ahead, 432."

"Arriving in ten minutes, what's the call?"

"Multiple MVA; two deceased, we're taking them with us, three with minor injuries. You have one extrication and one thrown fifty feet," he replied.

"Condition?"

"Both critical, have the trauma team at St. Jude's standing by."

"10-4."

*   *   *   *   *

The flight nurse and respiratory therapist on the helicopter were diligently working to insure the aggressive intake of IV fluids. There was excessive blood loss. They were well trained for their daily viewing of life's disasters . . . but this? This was bad.

As they worked in silence, their eyes would meet each other's, and their internal thoughts were conversing through their expression. One of them was placing the saline gauze gently on top of the female's exposed intestines, while looking at the torn body turned inside out. The road rash, which covered most of her, seemed insignificant compared to the huge cavity of disarray. As he stared at her insides in his hands, he whispered, "I think I'm going to be sick."

"No, you're not," John replied. "This is what we do!"

John's words were strong as he successfully disguised his own exact feelings. Looking at the male's chest, he thought, "Sweet Jesus, how can our bodies crack open like that?"

The stick shift was impaled in his chest wall. It was lodged deep, and the sight of this car part occupying the space of his heart and lungs was traumatic. He had seen a lot of life's tragedies, always believing that the last one was the worst. However, this one was by far the most compelling. It was as if the two bodies were no longer theirs. They were torn, cracked, and exposed for the world to see. As he looked at the combination of open wounds and glass embedded in their skin, their lifeless existence seemed to be a gift. He was glad they were unresponsive. As he and Tom continued the longest fifteen-minute ride of their lives, he imagined the pain the families would have to deal with and thanked God that his own family was safe.

Upon arrival, they worked quickly and efficiently. The bodies were covered with sheets up to the neck area. Both sets of hands were keeping the IVs in sync with the travel of the stretchers to the dedicated elevator. As Tom hit the button, he was relieved. In a matter of minutes, the trauma team would accept their shattered package, and he could imagine that they will be just fine, instead of viewing the reality of these unrecognizable bodies.

The team of scrubs were on point. Nurses, respiratory therapist, emergency physician, surgeon, all waiting to utilize their specific gift. The exchange was quick. As they removed the sheets, Dr. Harroll canvassed the bodies and felt a wave of anxiety. One of the nurses muttered, "What the—?" as she stopped herself in midsentence to regain her composure.

The room had the door shut, but sounds were heard by all. So many voices talking, commands given, lots of movement. Both stretchers were side by side. There were machines monitoring each one. IVs, tubes, crash carts filled with every saving device ready to be used. The blood was everywhere. Dr. Harroll was trying to attend to the immediate, obvious importance. As he examined the stick shift, his mind was making mental notes. "Aorta . . . heart . . . lungs . . . thoracotomy . . ." He quickly looked over to the exposed intestines. "Possible tears . . . laceration . . . or contusion to the liver. Need to run the bowel."

"Get Dr. Gennero and Dr. Thompson here, stat," he commanded. "Page the chief and Dr. Murphy. Everyone keep working. Anderson, we need two ORs available. Move it!"

So many hands touching, probing, pushing. Dr. Harroll was loud and firm as he announced, "Let's get the vitals holding, get the blood work to the lab, and infuse both with O negative until we get the transfusions. Come on, people, work with me here."

He looked over to the female and said, "Johnson, severe risk of infection there."

Johnson nodded.

Gennero quickly walked in with Thompson following behind. Within seconds, they absorbed the situation and positioned themselves to use their necessary skills.

Her hair was falling on his face . . .
She threw off her heels and derby laughing . . .
"The complexity of our souls match."
"May I please speak with Tallulah?"
"This is she."
"I now pronounce you husband and wife."
"Baby, you saved me from myself."
"Be careful what you wish for."
She placed the photo on the table . . .
"How did you know I was the one?"

Sing with me, sing for the years
Sing for the laughter, sing for the tears . . .
Sing with me, if just for today
Maybe tomorrow the good lord will take you away . . .

The beeps were loud. Johnson looked up.
"We're coding here. He's crashing!"
The team of scrubs rallied around the drifting life. Gennero found his spot and immediately started CPR.

She was frozen. The bar was applauding . . .
"Who's the artist?"
"A local, comes in, and drops off."
She put in the purple CD . . .

He turned and lowered his shirt . . . "It's beautiful!"

"God knew our hearts"

"Life and Death, isn't it obvious?"

She looked in the mirror, she was nervous . . .

"Oh, that's the price of having you."

"Hey, baby."

You treated me kind, sweet Destiny
Carried me through desperation, to the one that was waiting for me
It took so long, still I believed . . .

"She's crashing!" Harroll called out.

Thompson started CPR.

"He's back!" Gennero announced as he exhaled and felt a flood of relief.

"C'mon, lady, c'mon," Thompson's thoughts pleaded as he pressed firm and steady.

"Anything?" he asked, not looking up.

"No, we're losing her."

"Please, lady, please . . . not on my watch . . . please," he begged as he attempted another series of steady pressing.

"Fight damn it! Fight!"

Harroll looked up; relieved he announced, "She's back."

The dual steady heart beeps made everyone stop and look at each other. The tension was stifling. The room resembled a scene from any and all primetime ER dramas. Prep pads soaked with blood from the transfers, needles, ripped-open packages of paraphernalia, red footprints covering the floor, and every person in the room had Princeton and Tallulah on their scrubs.

One of the nurses was concentrating on steadying her shaking hand as the doctors' eyes bounced from monitor to monitor, watching the temporary visuals of safety.

"Have the families been contacted?" Harroll asked.

One of the voices reported, "Someone is on the way."

*   *   *   *   *

Victoria looked at the name and picked up the phone.

"Hi, honey."

The voice was unfamiliar.

"Is this the parent of Tallulah Cooper?"

Her heart started pounding as she tried to control her breathing. She listened and heard herself ask, "What car?"

"A Jeep" was the answer.

She sat there a second, begging out loud.

"Dear God . . . please . . . dear God, let it not be bad!"

She immediately dialed Rachel, made it short and to the point, and hung up. They didn't give her any info, just that there was an accident, and she was needed at St. Jude's. She threw on her sweats and sneakers, grabbed her keys and bag, and left. The whole ride she prayed and recited Isaiah 40:29-31.

"He gives power to those who are tired and worn out; he offers strength to the weak. Even youths will become exhausted, and young men will give up. But those who wait on the LORD will find new strength. They will fly high on wings like eagles. They will run and not grow weary. They will walk and not faint."

Victoria had it memorized, needing to rely on it so many times before. Now as she heard herself saying the words, she knew she was entering a dark place. She knew this was a "knock at the door," and she didn't dare turn the knob. Her stomach was turning as she pleaded to herself, "Please, dear God, please . . ."

She waited for the automatic doors to open and ran in. She nearly collided into the front desk.

"I'm here about my daughter, Tallulah Cooper."

The nurse looked up and said, "Cooper?"

"Yes, a car accident?"

The nurse was scanning the computer.

"OK, have a seat. The doctor will come down as soon as he's available."

"Where are they? Are they in one of these rooms?"

Victoria's voice was strained as she asked the question walking past her toward the ER rooms. The nurse bolted after her. Victoria's eyes were searching the area.

"Miss, please, your daughter isn't here. She's in OR, as soon . . ."

"OR? I want to talk to someone *now*!" Victoria demanded.

"All right, let's go back to the desk, and I'll get someone."

The nurse was on the phone exchanging information, while Victoria leaned on the desk playing with the strap on her bag.

"Victoria!" the echo of her name startled her.

She looked up as Rachel and Derek were rushing toward her.

"Where are they?" Derek asked.

"I'm not sure where Princeton is. Tallulah's in OR."

"Oh my god," Rachel replied.

"This nurse here"—Victoria pointing—"has been trying to get someone to come and talk to me."

Derek approached the desk and said, "I'm Princeton Cooper's father. I want to speak to someone now."

"A doctor will be down shortly. We really don't have any information yet. I can tell you that Princeton Cooper is also in OR. I'm sorry . . . please try to settle down. There's coffee down the hall in the cafeteria."

The three of them looked at one another, and their silence was overpowered by the tension in their eyes. Victoria was sitting, holding the grayish-colored liquid, taking sips. Derek had his arm around

Rachel as she held Victoria's left hand. They were all lost in thought, watching the hands on the clock.

Victoria was silently reciting "God's strength can overpower the despair of pain."

"Have you called anyone, Victoria?" Rachel asked.

"No, I didn't want people running around here, just us, till we know what's what."

*   *   *   *   *

Piper looked at Max worried.

"Something is wrong! Something is really wrong. Tallulah is never late. She would have called. We've been here more than an hour!"

Max was thinking the exact thoughts, but didn't want to add to her worry. She looked frightened.

"Well, maybe they pulled over to take some shots. You know the way Princeton is."

"In the dark? I left messages on both their phones, they should have called."

"Did you call Victoria?" Max asked.

"No, I don't want her to freak; besides, she would have called me if she knew anything."

Max put his arm around her, and she wrapped her arms around his waist as she started to cry.

"OK, sweetie, take it easy. Let's go home and wait till we hear from them."

As they left the theater, Max's heart was pounding, and his intuition told him something was seriously wrong. He silently attempted to pray.

*   *   *   *   *

Each OR was ready with the surgical team in place. Dr. Harroll was preparing himself both mentally and physically for the work that his skilled hands so desperately needed. He would be performing a thoracotomy. As he opened the chest, it would be evident as to what procedures would be necessary to correct the possible damage of the heart, lungs, aorta, ribs, sternum, and esophagus. They also needed to be ready for any surprises that lay beneath.

Dr. Murphy was in charge of the evisceration. The extent of the work needed would be dictated by the possible damage done to the gall bladder, liver, spleen, pancreas, kidneys, ovaries, and bladder.

Dr. Thompson walked over to Dr. Harroll as they were ready to scrub in and said, "We're still waiting on the blood."

"Did you call the blood bank?" he asked.

"Yes, some holdup with rare antibodies?"

The lab techs were simultaneously cross-matching the bloods. There was a rare antibody pattern in each one. The process was taking longer than usual, and just as the phone rang, the tech found the results he was looking for.

"Lab here."

"This is Dr. Harroll. Need the blood for OR3 and OR5 stat! What's the holdup?"

"We apologize, sir. They were both rare due to the antibodies, but it's completed now. It's on the way."

"Great, get here ASAP."

"Will do."

He and Dr. Murphy were standing outside the ORs, waiting for the transfusions.

The tech appeared with the precious cargo and explained the discovery.

"So," Dr. Harroll asked, "both the same blood type?"

"Yes, sir, they're brother and sister."

"Excellent! All right, Kevin," he said as he looked at Dr. Murphy, "let's not leave this family without both their kids."

"Deal."

They smiled and went into their designated rooms.

Dr. Harroll's team worked as a well-oiled machine. As the scalpel cut the skin, the retractors and rib spreaders were standing by. Even though Dr. Harroll had did this more times than he could remember, the initial feeling was always the same. It was the anticipation of not knowing what work would be necessary that humbled him. He secretly believed that no matter how great his skill level was, God always had the final say. As he closed his eyes for a second, the team acknowledged the ritual of his silent prayer. The six sets of eyes examined Dr. Harroll as he went into the chest cavity. He manually explored the internal organs for extent of injury.

"Jesus," he thought.

The team focused on their ability to listen, follow instructions, and assist with the complicated procedure.

Dr. Murphy's team was a mirror image of OR3. Everyone was ready for the procedure of running the bowel, searching for tears, and discovering what major organs had been injured.

*   *   *   *   *

As much as Victoria tried to convince herself not to feel it, she just knew it was bad. Sitting, standing, walking, thinking, time seemed to stand still. The three of them trying to pass the time with small conversation, flipping through magazines, and drinking coffee and water. Rachel held off using the ladies' room, for fear that she wouldn't be there when the doctor arrived. They discussed if they should call Piper and Max. Each time Victoria's vote was no.

"Jesus!" Derek exclaimed "It's been hours! You would think someone would come and talk to us.

"Until they're out of OR, there's nothing to report," Rachel answered.

"It can't be good, if it's taking this long," Victoria added.

"Well, the procedure might be complicated, but it can still be successful," Rachel said, trying to be reassuring.

Victoria had visions of what Princeton and Tallulah experienced at impact. She was hoping neither one of them saw the other in distress or crying for help. She closed her eyes and traced her daughter's life. So many years in the making . . . Her mind found snapshots of little moments that she had forgotten or buried to make room for recent ones. She caught a glimpse of Tallulah digging into her sundae at Serendipity. Her beautiful, inquisitive eyes, with that joyful smile, made Victoria's heart swell. What a blessed life she was given because of her daughter. It seemed like Tallulah took over the space of the kaleidoscope of Victoria's life. Where before she had empty promises, failures, pain, and embarrassments, she now had joy, victories, peace, and love. Tallulah was her greatest accomplishment! She was just starting to think about Luke, grateful that he didn't have to feel this, when she opened her eyes.

She caught an image of a doctor walking toward them and jumped up.

"Hello, I'm Dr. Murphy," he said as he extended his hand.

Victoria shook it, looked in his eyes, and said, "I'm Victoria, Tallulah's mother. This is Princeton's mother and father. Rachel and Derek."

The doctor stared at them without speaking. His mind was trying to register the introduction.

He thought to himself, "Father? Remarried? She didn't say Tallulah's and Princeton's mom?"

He decided he wasn't touching this one right now, not with the height of all this emotion. He made a decision to dance around it until Harroll came down.

"How are they? What's going on?" Derek asked.

"Dr. Harroll will be down shortly. He was the surgeon in charge. He'll be able to answer all your questions. I'm going to tell him you're here."

"Thank you," Rachel responded.

The elevator doors opened, and Dr. Murphy walked through the double doors. He looked up at the nurse and asked, "Where's Harroll?"

"Stripping down," she replied.

As he walked into the room, he saw Harroll replacing the bloody scrub with a new one.

Harroll looked up and said, "Don't want to panic the family."

"Steve, that was some amazing work we did in there, right?" Murphy asked.

"Sure was, Kevin."

Murphy came over and sat on the bench.

"We have a situation," he announced.

"What?" Harroll asked as he turned his attention to Kevin.

"I'm not quite sure . . . I'm trying to figure it out."

He explained the conversation and ended with "I'm *sure* they indicated they weren't aware of the relation. I didn't give them the recovery info, I told them you'd be down."

"OK, no big deal. People do and say crazy things at times like this."

"Yeah, I guess you're right," he replied with uncertainty as he watched Harroll leave the room.

He stepped off the elevator, turned the corner, and saw the three of them sitting motionless. He approached them, took a deep breath, and stood before them. They all stood up looking weary and anxious.

"I'm Dr. Harroll."

Victoria shook his hand and said, "Thank God. Where are my daughter and son-in-law?"

"How is our son?" Rachel asked.

Harroll looked at them, his eyes moving from one to the other. He thought to himself, "What the—? How can?"

Victoria pointed to Rachel and said, "She's a nurse."

He was trying to think quickly and appear to be calm.

"The surgery went well," he announced.

"Both surgeries?" Derek interrupted.

"Yes, I will answer all your questions; however, I would like to go to a private area to discuss this. Wait here a moment."

He walked over to the desk, and the nurse looked up.

"I want you to page Dr. Murphy and Dr. Thompson to your extension. Tell them to meet me in room 141 and tell them to bring the charts on the Coopers. Also tell them ASAP!"

He turned and saw they were looking at him. He motioned for them to follow him, and as he led them down the hall, he heard the words on the PA system, "Dr. Murphy . . . Dr. Thompson . . . extension 210."

He ushered them into the conference room, which had a large table and eight chairs.

"Please be seated," he said.

Victoria immediately felt alarmed.

"Conference rooms are not good," she thought.

He began slowly. "Your children are doing well, considering the multitude of injuries."

Rachel's heart sank.

"As soon as my colleagues get here with the charts, we'll go over each case."

Rachel seemed uneasy. "Get here with the charts?" she thought. "What's that all about?"

"Just tell us about the surgeries," she said impatiently.

The door opened, and Dr. Harroll got up and briskly walked to them.

"Outside," he said in a low voice and shut the door behind them.

Derek asked, "Rachel, what is going on?"

"I'm not sure . . . this is not the usual protocol."

Victoria finally said what she had been thinking all night.

"This is not good . . . something's wrong."

330

Thompson was holding the charts, and he and Murphy were puzzled as to why they were standing outside the room.

"We have a situation," Harroll said.

Murphy immediately thought about their recent conversation. Thompson was surprised by Harroll's uneasiness. He was one of the best surgeons the hospital had.

"What kind of situation?" Thompson asked.

"Well, we have the mother of the woman, who happens to be the mother-in-law of the man, with the man's mother and father inside."

Thompson thought for a minute and then exclaimed, "Husband and wife?"

"That's right," Harroll replied.

"How's that possible?" Thompson asked, looking perplexed.

"I don't know, but I can tell you one thing, those people in there don't know their children are brother and sister."

"Are you sure?" Thompson asked "This is nuts!"

"Oh, I'm sure. Let's concentrate on all the medical first, and maybe we can unravel this mess. Let's take this nice and slow."

The three of them entered the room, and as Harroll introduced them, they took their seats. Murphy couldn't help but look at each one of them as he thought to himself, "Just when you think you've seen it all!"

Dr. Harroll started to explain the scenario of the last six hours. He looked at Rachel and Derek and said, "Your son's chest wall was impaled by the stick shift. He suffered some muscle damage, a few broken ribs, a collapsed lung, and a tear of the pulmonary vessel."

"Oh my god!" Derek cried out.

Rachel and Victoria sat perfectly still. Rachel's mind was predetermining Dr. Harroll's next words.

"We were successful with repairing the tear and removing the shift."

Victoria interrupted, "You mean the shift was literally in his chest?"

"Yes," Dr. Harroll answered, "however as I said, the procedure was very successful."

"What's the prognosis?" Rachel muttered.

"We have to be careful for risk of infection and the blood's clotting factor. He'll be in ICU on a ventilator, with a chest tube, possibly three or four days. He'll then go to a step-down room and after that a room on the hospital floor."

"How long before he's awake?" Derek asked.

"One or two days," Harroll responded.

"How long do you anticipate the hospital stay?" Rachel asked as she wiped her eyes.

"Hard to say. A week . . . maybe ten days."

Victoria's eyes were filling with tears. "What does this mean for the limitations my son-in-law will have? He loves to work out with free weights, you know? Is he going to fully recover?"

"Well, he won't be working out for a while, but he should fully recover. I don't see any reason why he couldn't eventually resume his normal activities. He will, however, have a scar below his pectoral . . . and possibly some deformity, which later could be corrected."

The three of them were lost in their thoughts of absorbing the conversation when Derek broke the silence.

"How long before he's awake?"

"One or two days," Harroll responded, knowing that he already answered that.

Each was painting a picture in their minds of what to expect when they reached Princeton's bedside.

Victoria's mind snapped back to attention as she quietly asked, "What about my daughter?"

Dr. Harroll looked at Kevin and said, "Dr. Murphy was in charge of that procedure."

Dr. Murphy waited a moment to be sure he had everyone's attention and then began to explain, "There was a tear in the small intestine, which we were able to repair, some contusions to the liver . . ."

"Contusions?" Victoria interrupted.

"Bruising. Fortunately, major organs were not damaged."

Dr. Murphy liked to keep it short, not being graphic with details. If a family asked, he would oblige with the info. If not, no need for them to visualize their loved one with an open cavity and organs exposed. He quickly continued, hoping to cut off additional questions.

"She will follow the same pattern of recovery—ventilator, ICU, except it should be a shorter period of time. She may be awake by tomorrow, assuming there are no complications. She'll be on a hospital floor for maybe five or six days. There will be a scar; however, the recovery should be 100 percent. Also, she has some road rash."

Victoria started to interrupt, but Dr. Murphy assumed the question and continued, "Those are cuts and scrapes of the skin. Nothing serious. It will clear up without scarring."

Dr. Harroll was pleased with Kevin's approach to not wanting to be detail oriented with the surgery procedure. If Rachel knew the extent of the procedure, she wasn't sharing her knowledge. He thought that was very compassionate and was impressed with her obvious consideration to Victoria.

The room was quiet for a few minutes. Victoria broke the silence as she said, "Well, all in all, we are very blessed with the outcome of this disaster. I can't thank you enough for saving the lives of our children. God has definitely done a good work in giving you a gift of skillful hands. Let me ask you something. Do you have the details of the accident?"

Dr. Thompson responded, "No, you can get a full police report. Actually, there will be some questions and paperwork probably needed. You know, for insurance purposes. Information was left here for you to contact the officers on site."

"There is er . . . something else we need to discuss," Dr. Harroll said as he put the papers in front of him on the table.

Dr. Murphy and Dr. Thompson glanced at each other and then focused on the papers.

"We found that"—Dr. Harroll was looking down at the report—"Princeton and Tallulah both have rare blood types due to their antibodies."

"Both of them?" Rachel asked.

"Yes," Dr. Harroll answered.

"That's odd," Rachel thought as she shifted in her chair.

"Well, actually"—Dr. Harroll cleared his throat—"they have the *same* blood type."

Dr. Harroll was waiting for a response, hoping Rachel would begin the conversation that he was not prepared to have.

"How is that possible?" Rachel asked.

The silence was disturbing. It was somewhat unexpected and definitely uncomfortable.

"Doctor?" Derek asked meekly.

Dr. Harroll deliberately spoke slowly and softly, "It's possible with relatives. Brothers and sisters."

Victoria quickly answered, "Well, that's not possible. These are Princeton's parents"—as she motioned to Rachel and Derek—"and I'm Tallulah's mother, so there must be a mistake. When can we see them?"

Dr. Harroll was steady in his manner and speech and said, "There is no mistake."

Victoria felt herself losing patience. She was weary and stressed, and the conversation was bordering ridiculous. She looked up at Dr. Murphy who was fixated on Rachel and Derek. As her eyes followed his stare, she saw Derek leaning into Rachel's ear as they appeared to be having a serious conversation; Rachel looked nervous. As Derek spoke in her ear, she continuously shook her head back and forth to clearly state her answer was no. Victoria didn't know what was going on, but she was sure she had enough of this.

"Look, Dr. Harroll, Dr. Murphy, I appreciate all your effort . . . more than you know. I understand you have your reports, and they're full of important data, but again, there must be a mistake." She turned to Rachel and Derek and sarcastically said, "Anytime you want to help out here . . . will be just fine."

Rachel and Derek sat there perfectly still.

Victoria's frustration was apparent. "Rachel? Derek? Are you with us here? You do realize that this is absurd!"

Neither one of them said a word.

"OK, I've had enough!" Victoria exclaimed as she grabbed her bag and stood up, indicating she was leaving the room.

She looked at the doctors and said, "Thank you for all your hard work. Tallulah and Princeton were blessed to have you. I'm going to . . ."

Derek interrupted as he stood up and quietly said, "Victoria, please sit down."

There was something about the look in Derek's eyes that made Victoria obey his request. She was trying to analyze his face. He seemed sad—no, more a look of defeat. He sat back down and held Rachel's hands. She was looking down and seemed to be avoiding eye contact. Anticipation was filling the room as everyone waited for Derek to speak.

Victoria was sure she heard his words, yet she felt herself being pulled into limbo. She was somewhere between the two extremes of this moment and an imaginary vision of Derek and Rachel thirty-two years ago.

"What did you just say?" Victoria asked.

Derek repeated his confession.

"Princeton . . . was adopted."

The words hung in the air. As Victoria looked at them, her heart hurt for their pain. They looked so ashamed. There was a tenderness about Rachel that touched Victoria's soul. She was careful not to confirm their preconceived notion of her reaction. She spoke softly and asked, "Does Princeton know? Does Tallulah know?"

Rachel looked up, and her eyes were like that of a child seeking approval. The tears were running down her face as she looked at Victoria and answered, "No. We decided there may not be a need to ever tell Princeton. It was a closed adoption, and he was only a few weeks old. Derek and I talked about it and talked about it until we exhausted ourselves with every what-if. And then we came to the conclusion that until something happened that would determine otherwise, we would keep with our plan. The years just kept going by, and then one day, we stopped talking about it."

Victoria got up and walked over to Rachel. She extended her arms, and Rachel came into her grasp. Victoria was holding her tight as she spoke loud enough to be heard over Rachel's sobbing.

"Why are you crying? You didn't do anything wrong! You adopted a son and raised him to be an exceptional man! You should be proud of your accomplishment. If you chose not to tell him, well, that was your choice. Up until now, if you and Derek felt it was the right thing to do, then it was. God's plan is bigger than ours. Princeton was . . . no, is blessed to have such a wonderful mother and father."

Derek stood up and huddled with the two of them. Rachel was repeating, "Thank you, Victoria, I love you. Thank you, thank you."

As Dr. Murphy looked at the families' obvious display of respect and affection, he felt relieved. As he was taking in the Hallmark moment, he mind snapped to attention as he thought, "OK, this is great, but where is the missing piece to the puzzle?"

Dr. Harroll's mind was racing with processing this information and trying to reach a conclusion. No matter how he tossed it, there were only two possibilities.

He thought to himself, "Today was by far one of the most unique, exhausting days he ever had at St. Jude's."

The ball of emotion started to subside as Victoria sat down caressing Rachel's back, supplying the tissues.

"Well," she announced, "this is just another chapter in the written pages of our life."

"Very profound," Dr. Harroll thought.

She looked at the three doctors, who were watching her. Her eyes caught the hint of compassion in Dr. Harroll's face. His eyes were searching hers, questioning, waiting. She was puzzled and slightly confused. The reality of the moment hit her hard.

All the emotion spent on Rachel and Derek immediately dissipated. She couldn't quite understand what he wanted.

The rush of realization started to travel through her body. It was as if a switch was turned on, and the question in his eyes became crystal clear.

All of a sudden, she was in a quiet private panic! Her heart was beating fast, palpitating. She was racing through her thoughts, "Think, Victoria, think!"

It had been so long ago, she locked it away so deep that now she was struggling to bring it back. "C'mon, Victoria . . . 1974 . . . graduation . . . 1975 . . . Revlon. The music started to play . . . she looked at him onstage playing the piano ballad in F minor. Girls screaming, she herself mesmerized every time he looked at her and felt that tingle knowing he was hers . . .

Sing with me, Sing for the year
Sing for the laughter, sing for the tear
Sing with me, if it's just for today
Maybe tomorrow the good Lord will take you away

No one could do Tyler like him. Jesus! Concentrate . . . concentrate. That's the way it always was decades ago. She would try to remember, and the picture and sounds of Aerosmith's "Dream On" would take over her mind. Now trying so hard to remember. There he was again, forcing her to listen to it, looking so beautiful as he played to a packed house on the verge of his superstardom.

"Damn it . . . 1974 . . . graduation . . . 1975 . . . Revlon . . . '76 . . . '86 . . . '96 . . . 2006 . . . 2008 . . . Oh my god! Oh my god! Dear Jesus . . . No! No! No! Can't be. Please, dear God, it can't be!" She felt unsteady, her stomach was turning, she held on to the table with both hands, stood up, looked at Rachel, and started to scream . . .

"WHERE DID YOU ADOPT HIM? WHERE? WHERE? ANSWER ME! HOW OLD WAS HE?"

Dr. Harroll pleaded, "Please calm down . . . please."

Rachel looked at Victoria, confused and still so upset about the news she just made public. She was already sobbing, and now with Victoria screaming at her, she was weeping and squeezing Derek's hands. She looked at Victoria, and in between deep breaths, she repeated, "I told you he was a newborn, a few weeks old. What difference does it make? Why are you interrogating me?"

She couldn't seem to steady her breathing. She felt like she was being attacked and already felt humiliated for keeping their dark secret. Derek was trying to console her, but he too was crying, full of emotion. It was at that moment that Dr. Thompson looked at Dr. Harroll as he quietly mumbled, "Mother of God." He stood up, walked over to Victoria, turned her body to face him holding on to her shoulders, and gently asked, "Did you have a son that you gave up for adoption?"

Thompson and Murphy sat frozen. Derek jumped up, his voice trembling, **"You had a son? A son? You gave up your son for adoption?"** His face was flushed, and his hands were shaking.

Rachel screamed, **"Victoria!"**

Her body went limp as Dr. Harroll placed her in the chair. She put her head into her hands and started rocking back and forth. Her voice was low and monotone.

"I didn't know . . . I didn't know if it was a boy."

She took her head out of her hands and looked at Rachel and Derek, and then the doctors.

"I didn't want to know . . . that was my request. That way, I couldn't ever imagine a picture in my mind. I thought that through very carefully when I signed the closed adoption. Things were very different thirty-two years ago."

There wasn't a sound in the room. Total empty void space. All those minds trying to process this tornado of information.

Victoria looked at Dr. Harroll and said, "I'm going to be . . ." Before she could say "sick," she threw her head to the side of the chair, and her body jerked as she threw up.

Harroll whispered to Thompson, "Let's get some sedatives and water in here and get someone to clean that up."

Rachel's mind was tracing her life with her son. So many things seemed so clear now. It was almost a sense of relief. All those times wondering about his bloodline, playing that game of linking him to famous renowned individuals. Imagining his creative gifts attached to some painter, writer, philosopher, priest.

Derek was the first to speak. "What kind of world do we live in? That you don't even have to get a blood test to get married? We had to get one."

"So did I," Victoria muttered.

Princeton's voice was ringing in her ears . . . fragments of years of conversations.

"Why do you think God made it that we can't have children?"

"Hi, Mom."

"Hello, my son."

"The complexity of our souls match."

"She saved me from myself. There was always something missing."

"You know you're my sage, right?"

"I knew instantly you were the one."

There was a knock at the door, and a nurse appeared with some water bottles and a pack of pills. She looked around the room and thought, "Poor family, probably a death."

"Thank you," Dr. Harroll said as he took the pills and water.

"Anything else?" she asked.

"No, we're all set," Thompson replied.

She gave a compassionate nod and closed the door behind her.

Dr. Harroll walked over to the three of them and said, "These are mild sedatives; please take one so you can calm down."

Victoria asked sarcastically, "Why? Was the last family that went through this calm? I don't want a sedative. I want a reason why they should live. They would be better off dead."

Rachel looked at her and in a strong voice said, "Don't say that! Don't ever say that!"

"Don't say that? Don't say that?" Victoria's voice escalated. "This is Princeton and Tallulah we're talking about here. The great American love story! The two people who live for one another. Their souls connected. Their purest joy and reason to live is because of each other. Do you realize? Can you even imagine what this is going to do to them? Don't you see, they can't be together anymore! They'll be forever broken—damaged goods! Their minds, hearts, and souls are not going to be able to recover. So let me ask you. If you were them, would you rather be dead with your last memory of your life as you know it? Or would you rather be alive . . . with this?"

Dr. Harroll interrupted, "There are professionals that probably should be contacted to help them through this. I can recommend a few that are the best in the field. However, now we have a long recovery period ahead, and we need to deal with the medical issues first."

Victoria was firm when she said, "I don't want either of them to know any of this until they are totally out of danger. Not a word! Do you understand? When we can all agree that it's the right time, we'll figure out how we are going to do this."

She took a gulp of water, looked at Rachel and Derek, and said, "Agreed?"

Before they could answer, Dr. Harroll announced, "I think that's the best way to handle it, we don't need any other complications right now."

"I need to use the ladies' room," Victoria said as she stood up, walked out, and searched for the sign. She pushed the door, walked in, and checked the stalls to see if they were empty. She stood against the wall as her body slowly slid down to the floor until she was sitting with knees bent, head in hand. In her mind, she kept repeating, "My son . . . my son." She was full of a whirlwind of her quotes and beliefs. Little bits of information she fed to Princeton, which now had a new meaning.

"The branches of the family tree from our genetic and related paths. We cling to that for our sense of heritage, identity, and our destiny."

When she shared that that with him, she never imagined the substance of that belief in the context of her life at this moment!

She bowed her head and began her internal prayer.

"Heavenly Father, I come to you in the name of Jesus. Please, dear God, forgive me for this request. Dear Jesus, please take them, take my children into your kingdom, Lord."

Her eyes were fountains of tears.

"Lord you know their hearts, please take them."

She started the twenty-third Psalm:

> The LORD is my shepherd;
> I have everything I need.
> He lets me rest in green meadows;
> he leads me beside peaceful streams.
> He renews my strength.
> He guides me along right paths,
> bringing honor to his name.

Even when I walk through the dark valley of death,
I will not be afraid, for you are close beside me.
Your rod and your staff protect and comfort me.
You prepare . . .

"Miss . . . miss, are you all right?"

She looked at the feet, traveled her eyes up, and saw the elderly woman standing before her. She took a tissue from her bag and wiped her eyes. She forced herself to stand and slightly smiled with a sadness that filled their space.

"No . . . I'm not all right."

The woman felt her pain and answered with "There are so many doctors here! Let's find you one. I'm sure they can help you."

Victoria found the aged, weathered eyes and said, "That's not possible."

EMPTY NOT ANGRY

Tallulah sat waiting in the small reception area. As her eyes canvassed the room, her mind concluded with "Hideously outdated." She thought to herself, "You would think someone that charges this much money would invest in a makeover."

She was fixated on the peach floral wallpaper. She forced herself to concentrate on every line, every curve, every stem, every bud. She traveled deeper into the green border surrounding the flowers. Was it sage or turquoise?

"More sage," she thought.

"Yes, typical sage and peach. very nineties."

The furniture was a collection of off-the-rack professional grouping. Two console tables were the resting place for magazines that held very little interest. Generic publications of some family stuff.

"Come on, Tallulah. Concentrate!"

She forced herself to concentrate so that her mind had little room to think about anything other than what she was looking at.

This game she was playing had become her only source of survival. Her stomach started to turn, and that familiar feeling of anxiety was taking root. She took a deep breath, and as she exhaled, she started to feel clammy. It was beginning to wash over her head and hands. Her heart was starting to palpitate.

She found a repeat pattern on the upholstery of the chair and zeroed in. The tiny triangles were variations of the same colors. Some triangles were vibrant, and some were faded. The faded ones created an outline of the many bodies that sat in the chair waiting. The seat cushions were slightly indented.

"No more bounce in those," she thought.

The lighting matched the space. It was dismal and sparse.

"Such a tired and weathered existence. Kind of matches you, huh, Tallulah?"

As she finished that thought, she searched her bag for the small water bottle and quickly gulped half the contents.

"Breathe, come on . . ."

She was feeling light-headed, and her stomach and chest were on that familiar ride.

"Deep inhale, slow exhale. Deep inhale, slow exhale."

As she raised the bottle to her lips, she caught a glimpse of her unsteady hand, which started to tingle.

She frantically searched the room, hoping for an intervention. Her eyes landed on the poorly framed picture. She immediately glanced away, knowing anything related to art and photos would eventually leave her hugging a toilet. She checked her wrist, only to find an empty space, which normally was the resting place for her watch. The heels of her feet started to tap the carpet as her knees and thighs bounced with every tap.

"No . . . no . . . please," she whispered as she tried to regain her composure.

She was starting to panic. She knew that the process of trying to slow down her rapid breathing would leave her exhausted and frightened.

She stood up, hoping she could walk it off. As she took a few steps to the console, tiny circles started to bounce in front of her eyes. As she closed them, she felt her heart start to find its regular beats.

"Thank you, Jesus."

She emptied the remaining contents of her bottle in one steady gulp.

"Tallulah?" The voice calling her name seemed far away.

"Tallulah?"

She opened her eyes and turned to the body attached to the voice. "Hi, Kate."

"Sorry to keep you waiting. I had a situation."

"A situation?" Tallulah thought.

"You have *no* idea what a situation is."

"Let's go inside," Kate said as she pointed to the room beyond the door.

Tallulah walked past her, focused on her path, never making eye contact.

Kate was perplexed as she thought to her herself, "This can't be the same woman from that night at the fund-raiser."

Her beauty was still vaguely apparent, but there was a different aura about her. Kate followed her in, closed the door, and positioned herself in her chair. She pointed to the choice of two chairs as Tallulah sat; she waited for her to acknowledge the beginning of the session.

As she examined Tallulah's slightly bent posture, she couldn't help but to focus on her eyes. They were lifeless, empty caves holding a glazed stare. This woman appeared fragile. No air of confidence like the woman she remembered. It was as if all life had been sucked out of her. There didn't appear to be even a tiny residue of joy or happiness inside the shell she was looking at. She was also much thinner than the woman in the beautiful floral dress.

"Funny," she thought, "when I saw Victoria's daughter that night, I was so taken by her obvious beauty and manner. She and her husband stole the show. Now . . . now this gaunt, lifeless woman is sitting here. Life sucks!"

A slight smile formed on Tallulah's face, and Kate took that as a signal to begin.

"I'm glad you're here," Kate said.

"How are you?" she asked.

"How am I?" Tallulah thought. "You must be kidding me! That's the best opening statement you have? How am I?"

Tallulah immediately felt that coming there was a mistake. "I can't do this," she thought as she asked, "What do you mean?"

"Well, how are you doing?" Kate replied.

"How do you think I'm doing?" Tallulah responded, appearing slightly irritated.

"OK, look, I know you've been through a lot. I'm trying to understand where you are right now. I'm . . ."

Tallulah cut her off, "You know nothing about what I've been through. Your imagination and all your diplomas couldn't possibly prepare you to understand what I've been through—what I'm *still* going through. So let's make something clear right now. Don't talk to me as if you understand . . . because you don't."

Tallulah's words were precise, cold, and cutting. Kate would have been more comfortable if there were some anger or volume attached to the words. Instead, they traveled the air quietly and even toned. She knew if she didn't redeem herself instantly, she would lose her.

"You're right . . . I'm sorry. Sometimes we say things . . . words . . . without really thinking about the depth or impact they have."

Kate took the show of Tallulah's face softening as an acceptance of her apology.

"What I should have asked is . . . tell me about what you're feeling."

"Feeling? Well, let me see. Feeling?" There was a sarcastic tone behind Tallulah's words.

"I feel like I stepped out of myself, and I am watching someone else's life. Some miserable broken life . . . that's how I feel."

Tallulah sat up, repositioning herself in the chair. Her eyes were locked into Kate's, as if she were preparing herself to take the blows of the next volley of words.

There were no words. Kate sat there leaning back in the chair, twirling her pen between her fingers, waiting for Tallulah to continue.

"Don't you see? I woke up one day, and my life wasn't my own. Everything that I lived for . . . loved . . . changed. It was gone—everything that had substance, value. *Who* I was . . . was gone."

"Everything?" Kate asked. "What do you mean when you say 'everything'?"

"Everything! Princet . . ." She stopped.

Kate watched her face dramatically change. There was so much emotion when she tried to say his name. It was as if the wall came down, and this tender character emerged.

Tallulah slowly stood up, crossed her arms, and walked over to the bookcase. With her back to Kate, she asked, "Do you know what it's like to love someone?"

"Yes," Kate replied.

Tallulah thought her yes was flat and too quick.

"I'm not talking about the love for a parent or a child. I'm talking about romantic love."

"Yes, I do," Kate reiterated.

Tallulah turned to face her.

"Good! Now take that thought and magnify it a thousand times! Take every greeting card you've ever read, every media snapshot of the promise of the idyllic relationship, every novel describing love that you've ever read—everything and anything that the world professes to be the best, the biggest, the greatest love—and magnify *that* a thousand times."

Kate was listening and thought, "Definitely deep seeded."

"Have you created the picture in your mind?" Tallulah asked.

Kate nodded indicating a yes.

"Well, that's what I was fortunate enough to have . . . and now it's all gone."

Tallulah walked back to her chair and took her empty water bottle out of her bag.

"Do you have any water?" she asked.

"Er . . . no . . . I'm sorry, I don't."

"With all the money you earn, you don't stock water for your pathetic clients? And by the way, this office needs an overhaul."

Kate thought, "Good, some anger . . . some emotion."

"I'll give the water thing some thought, and maybe we can talk about the overhaul later on."

Tallulah thought, "OK, now you're pacifying me?"

"I'm going to fill my bottle with the tap in the ladies' room. You do have one of those, don't you?"

Kate smiled and said, "It's the door to the right in the reception area."

"Reception area?" Tallulah thought. "Not much of a reception in that room."

As Tallulah walked out, Kate tried to collect her thoughts.

When Kate agreed to work with Tallulah, it was because of her loyalty to Victoria. This family could easily afford a more prominent professional, but Victoria was certain that Kate was the best choice. Now as she scrambled for the direction she needed to take, she was feeling overwhelmed. Her mind raced through Gestalt, Rogerian, rational emotive, NLP—all the therapies. This may very well be out of her league. She quickly jotted a note to call Dr. Ponte for his expertise. Her thoughts started to paint a picture of Tallulah's words describing the love she and Princeton shared. Although she didn't know them together as a couple, she did catch a glimpse of the relationship that everyone seemed to envy that night at the fund-raiser.

Now she felt slightly embarrassed, remembering her eyes locked into the scene of Princeton's hand on Tallulah's back as they were introduced. There was "something" about them that was obvious to everyone in the room. When she watched them dance, her thoughts were "They're in their own world. Very passionate, very sexy." She felt cheated as she thought about her own relationship. She imagined what it was like to have someone that looked like Princeton, so in awe of his magnificent wife.

She understood going into this project that the basis of the tragedy was the anomaly of the relationship shared. It served to magnify the critical situation a thousand times. That, mixed with the deep-rooted faith and medical oppositions, made it a case that was so delicate that no one wanted to touch it. Victoria tugged at her heart, begging for her daughter's obvious need for help. Kate believed that Victoria was in need of professional help, but she wasn't having it.

She stated, "When my children are safe and healthy, then I will be fine. Until then, it's all about them."

Kate knew Victoria's neuro association of being the giver was in full swing.

She looked around the office, trying to occupy her mind, until Tallulah returned.

"She's right," she thought, "definitely need some water or coffee."

Tallulah looked at her image in the mirror as she twisted the cap on her water bottle.

"Why are you here?" she thought.

"Nothing and no one, aside from God, can fix this."

She contemplated exiting the reception room and going straight to her car, instead of returning to the wasted time with Kate.

"No, Tallulah, follow it through, if only for Mom, follow it through."

She remembered the scene from *All That Jazz* when Scheider looked at his image in the mirror and said, "Showtime."

She mimicked his gesture and out loud said, "Showtime!"

When she walked back into the room, Kate was exactly how she had left her—sitting in her chair, twirling her pen.

Kate glanced over to the clock on her desk, trying not to be obvious.

"This is going to be a long one," she thought.

Tallulah sat in the designated chair again, waiting for Act II to begin.

Kate looked at Tallulah, hoping for her attention, and asked, "Tell me what your days have been like."

"My days? Let me see . . ."

Silence.

Tallulah was running footage through her mind, trying to fight back the tears that had become a constant companion in her daily life.

"Each day, I wake up . . . that in itself is painful."

"Why?" Kate asked.

"Because then I realize I have to do it all over again."

"What?"

"Live."

Tallulah's response was so monotone that it was slightly alarming to Kate.

Tallulah leaned back and continued as if part of her were talking to another person. Her eyes were focused on the ceiling.

"Living is a struggle . . . everything about life disturbs me. The sound of traffic, people's voices, birds, TV, radio—all the sounds of the living are a reminder that life is going on. It's an annoyance, a distraction. I resent that life is going on. People are working, making plans, taking vacations, getting married, getting divorced. Game shows are still on TV, music is still playing on the radio. It's all still going on . . ."

She stopped and let out an exaggerated sigh.

"It takes so much effort for me . . . just to get out of bed and brush my teeth. Have to keep these pearly whites, you know?"

Tallulah sat up and found Kate's eyes. She squinted a bit, slightly pensive, keeping contact.

"My greatest accomplishment in a day is not throwing up more than three times."

"You're throwing up every day?"

350

"Yep."

"Why do you think that's happening?" After Kate asked the question, she wished she had asked to record the session. She didn't want to take notes—too intimidating—and now she was sure she needed to replay this dialogue. "Stupid," she thought.

"Which answer would make you happy?" Tallulah asked. "Because I have a few theories."

Kate heard the sarcasm creeping back into their space.

"No answer would make me *happy*, but tell me about your theories."

"Well, the first is the one that's the safest, the one that people would be comfortable with. Let's say it's because of my accident, you know, seeing how there was so much damage done to my intestines, that area of my body? Maybe I need more time . . . to fully recover. Maybe my body needs to adjust to the intake of food?"

"Well, are you eating?"

"Sometimes."

"Did the doctors say there would be problems with eating? An adjustment period?"

"No."

Kate waited.

Tallulah took a gulp of water and continued.

"Maybe it's just the inability to keep food down because of the constant anxiety. My body and mind are always caught in a horrible wave of physical pain."

She took a deep breath and stood up. She seemed to be getting restless and started to search for a focal point. She found the floral arrangement and thought, "Artificial flowers? You got to be kidding me."

As she touched the tired bouquet, she started to feel a tremendous pang of sadness.

Kate was watching her and trying to determine her silence.

"Tallulah?"

Tallulah turned to find the voice. Kate thought whatever she was thinking or feeling must be painful by the transformation of her face. So sad . . . so stripped.

Kate was taken in by the obvious vulnerability. She felt sorry for her.

"Have you had any contact with . . ."

Before the question could be completed, Tallulah bounced into her next explanation.

"I'm probably throwing up because subconsciously I'm punishing myself."

Kate saw the lifeless eyes filling with tears. Softly, she asked, "Why do you think you're punishing yourself?"

Tallulah was staring at the floor, turning her wedding band with her thumb. It was almost rhythmic, a full turn, and then she would roll her thumb across the diamonds. Then again . . .

"Tallulah?"

"Yeah?" she answered without looking up.

"Why do you think you're punishing yourself?"

"Because . . . I'm . . . I'm ashamed." Her voice started to crack.

"Ashamed?"

"I'm sooo ashamed." Tallulah's chest was rising and falling as she took deep breaths.

"After knowing now . . . that Princet . . ."

She tied to form the word again.

"That he . . . is my . . ."

Her mind said it, but her mouth refused to say it out loud.

"Knowing this, and I still want him! I want his mind . . . his body . . . his soul!"

She picked her head up and continued, "I want his touch, his laughter, his beautiful face looking at me. I want him singing."

The tears were rolling, and her voice started to escalate.

"I want all of him, every minute of every day! We vowed we would never be apart . . . without each other, we're nothing! Dead . . .

just dead! We should have died! It would have been better than living like this . . . knowing what we know . . . without each other. Every day . . . every day, there's not a second that goes by that I don't want him . . . not a second."

As she said her last word, in one quick move, she was on her knees, holding her head in her hands, weeping uncontrollably.

Kate rushed to her, gently placing her hand on her shoulder.

"Tallulah . . . please . . . come sit in the chair here."

Tallulah was losing control of her breathing as her sobbing made her body jerk back and forth.

"Please, Tallulah."

Kate was now kneeling in front of her, holding her hands, trying to make eye contact. She tilted her head way down to find Tallulah's eyes. She locked her eyes with hers, and for a second, she was actually frightened when she saw the extreme pain on her face mixed with the empty, lifeless mirrors of her soul. What made it more eerie was Tallulah's instant recovery as she sat herself up in the chair and wiped her eyes.

Kate, still on her knees, thought, "Jesus, this is serious."

"So you see," Tallulah continued as Kate got up and sat in the chair next to her.

"Maybe I'm trying to do away with myself . . . because I can't live like this . . . and I can't take my own life. So I'm caught between the devil and the deep blue sea. My mother has an expression she uses for the most extreme situations . . . Damaged goods."

Tallulah looked over at Kate as she placed her hand over the cross on her neck.

"I'm damaged goods . . . caught between the reality of my life and my devotion to God."

"Are you angry with your mother?"

Kate wasn't going to go there with this, at least not today, but the circumstances dictated differently.

"No . . . empty . . . not angry."

"Are you sure?" Kate asked softly.

"Yes, I'm sure. How could I be angry with my mother for a decision she made thirty-two years ago? At the time, she felt it was the right choice. She could never have imagined . . . this would be the outcome. Actually, I don't think anyone could have imagined this. My heart breaks for her."

Tallulah faced Kate.

"She's stuck in the middle . . . so much pain and confusion. It's worse for her because she sees both of us, every episode of pain and terror, separated . . . yet joined together . . . ironically by her. She's the common thread for everything we are . . . everything we do. She takes it all in, unable to share the information with either of us, because of our fragile lives."

Kate listened, trying to lock every word into her memory bank. She was feeling exhausted, and this was only a sneak preview of what this family was going through day after day.

Tallulah took a few gulps of water, repositioned herself in her chair, and seemed as if she was making an earnest effort to calm herself.

"Sometimes I think I made the wrong decision, you know? Not staying at the house."

"Was it mutual?" Kate asked.

"Sort of. I didn't think I could take the pain of seeing my past life . . . so many memories . . . so many reminders. I thought moving in with my mother would be safer. Better chance of surviving. Princ . . . he wanted to stay there . . . he insisted."

"Try saying his name out loud."

"I say it a thousand times a day . . . it's all my mind registers."

Kate firmly repeated, "Try saying it out loud."

Silence.

"Has there been any contact?"

"Well, right after the accident, it was a whirlwind. The few in our circle . . . were devastated. My mother . . . devastated. Everyone walking on eggs—talking, not talking, trying to offer support and make sense of this. No one can be prepared for this."

Tallulah shifted her eyes into what appeared to be a daydream, accompanied with a tiny smile.

"We were going to continue our lives as if nothing happened, as if we didn't know."

She was lost in that moment, and then gradually her face saddened.

"Then we realized we couldn't. Even if no one knew, we knew. That roller-coaster ride left us both sick—not eating, not sleeping, tremendous confliction of body and mind, taking meds, sort of a limbo state, walking dead. Particularly more for him . . . because his injuries were more severe than mine. His body and heart were broken . . . literally . . . but the worse pain was his soul was disappearing little by little every day. So we decided the only way to recover physically was to separate and wait for divine intervention."

"Divine intervention?" Kate thought.

"So . . . no . . . no contact the last two months."

Kate was about to talk when Tallulah interjected, "Oh yeah, the CD."

"The CD?"

"Yeah!" Tallulah's face actually took on a smile.

"We use to communicate through music, you know? Make CDs for each other, our anchors. He sent over a blue CD . . . one song . . . but that's all I needed . . . and now whenever I play it, I feel like everything's going to be all right. Three minutes of sanity, you know?"

"You said divine intervention. Are you angry with God?"

Tallulah sat up as if the question appeared to make her snap to attention. Her eyebrows crunched toward one another with an expression of being puzzled. That along with the sharp glare of her eyes made Kate assume she touched a sore spot.

"First of all, I told you, I'm empty, not angry. Apparently, you didn't hear me the first time."

Tallulah was firm as she continued, "*You dare* to ask me if I'm angry with God? With God? God is what gets me through every miserable minute of every miserable day. My faith is my strength . . . my source of courage. If I lose my trust in God, then I've lost everything, I mean, *everything*. Without God, there is no hope. Without hope, well, you know what happens when there is no hope. My God has never forsaken me yet, and I believe he never will. What if my mother lost her trust in God? All those years of her life struggling, overcoming extreme obstacles . . . that was possible because of her faith. Where would she be today if she had chosen a different path?"

Tallulah wasn't waiting for answers.

"I know that sounds contradictory because of what's going on now, most people must think where is your God now? But my mother's darkest hours were overcome because of her faith, because of her trust. God builds our character to face the journey to come. We can't forget all the joy. My mother had so much joy . . . as have I. That never would have been possible, if she didn't go deep and align her will with her spiritual devotion. I don't know why this has happened to us . . . I wish I did . . . but I believe my God will carry me through my darkest time . . . and he will put the answers in my and Princeton's heart. Yes! Divine intervention!"

As Tallulah finished with strength and conviction, Kate acknowledged that she said his name in completion . . . for the first time . . . out loud.

"Don't dare be arrogant enough to think that any of us have a right to question God."

Kate wanted to clarify her question, but Tallulah was holding court.

"Look, Kate, I'm going to make this easy for you."

Kate knew she crossed her line. Tallulah took on an air of cold, hard confidence. She was protecting her love and her faith and was determined to claim her ground. She stood up to continue her proclamation.

"You want to banter words, theories, and intelligence . . . with me? Don't! Because you'll lose. I may be broken." Tallulah looked down at her body, as if she were connecting the words to the physicality of herself.

"The open sores of my heart may be bleeding, but . . . I'm still Tallulah! Somewhere deep inside . . . are the fragments of who I am . . . the woman that has earned a love beyond comprehension. The woman I will be again! Don't let this shell fool you."

Tallulah walked closer to Kate and made sure she had her full attention as she leaned in uncomfortably close. The roles had reversed, and Tallulah was dictating the essence of command.

"If you can answer one question for me, then I will continue to come to your dreary, dismal space you call an office."

Tallulah's sarcasm was loud and clear. Her tenacious aura left Kate feeling inadequate.

"Damn it," Kate thought, "this is exactly what is not supposed to happen."

"You don't even have to answer it today. I'll let you think about it until our next appointment. One question, that's it, just one question. You see, I don't need you for direction. My mother has more insight in her pinkie than you do in your entire body."

Her smirk was perfectly matched to her cutting words.

"I don't need you for conversation because fortunately I have a circle of friends that are committed to supporting me through this . . . if I choose to let them. I don't need you for medication . . . I can get that through any medical doctor due to the circumstances."

Tallulah stopped and intentionally took her time, gulping the warm water from her bottle. Her heart was racing, and she needed to steady her slightly shaking hand.

Kate sat frozen, waiting for the question that Tallulah believed would credit her with the possibility of continuing to treat her.

"Tell me, Kate, how do you mourn your own death?"

Kate took in the words and waited for Tallulah to elaborate. Tallulah didn't expect a response and wanted to be sure Kate understood her question.

"How do you mourn your death . . . while you're still alive? When someone passes, there are formalities and rituals that follow. Those formalities get you from A to B. You know, condolence cards, flowers, service. You know what I'm talking about, right, Kate? Let's not forget the psycho mumbo of denial, grievance, acceptance—all of that is for a reason so that life can eventually continue, right? Well, what do you do if you're still alive, living this life? If everything that constitutes your breathing—joy, purpose, desire, logic, reason—is suddenly gone, yet your physical being is still here. What do you do? There are no rituals, no services, no time frame of grievance . . . so how and when does life go on when you're not a part of the living and you're not physically dead? Don't think for a minute I'm being dramatic to get my point across. If I could let you inside of me to sincerely feel my emptiness, my broken spirit and soul, I would. I'm walking dead, Kate, and that's the most severe form of a wasted life. Not crossed over . . . and not here. The only reminder of this life I'm living is the pain . . . the terror . . . the physical sickness . . . and knowing that the love that sustained my being was ripped out of me. This deformed cavity in my abdomen? Is sort of poetic . . . in a deranged way . . . just like his heart being literally torn. So, Kate, as I wait for divine intervention, you can figure out the answer to my question. Until then, I will go to bed and wake up each morning trying to survive the next twenty-four."

Tallulah walked closer to Kate and put her hand on hers.

"Kate, I really do want you to help me . . . but you're not equipped . . . call me."

Tallulah picked up her bag and walked out never turning back to Kate.

Kate sat there with an uneasy feeling of extreme anxiety and in her mind started to replay the words exchanged in that session as tears ran down her face.

Tallulah walked to her car focusing on her license plate. She got in and turned the key. As she looked in the mirror, the reflection seemed foreign. "Who is this woman?" She reached over and looked at the blue CD. Bringing it to her lips, she gently kissed it and held it to her chest. After a few minutes, she popped it in, put the car in drive, and whispered, "I love you with every breath of my life" and hit Play.

I can't believe it's over, I watched the whole thing fall
And I never saw the writing that was on the wall
If I only knew,the days were slipping past
That the good things never last, that you were crying

BOOK 2
DREAM ON

BOOK 3
DIVINE INTERVENTION